THE FIRST AGENT

Agent Eli Brandt sat in the rear seat of the Mercedes, the man now openly holding the gun on him; the folder with Leiman's fingerprints lay between them. He couldn't see the face of the driver, who appeared to know where to go without any instructions. It was beginning to rain as they swung right past Marble Arch and into Bayswater Road, the windshield a watery kaleidoscope of blurred city lights. If this man wanted the Leiman file, then he had it, and Brandt couldn't understand what further use he had of him.

"I don't think I can help you any further," he said.

"Probably not," said the man.

"Then why all the cloak-and-dagger nonsense? Where are you taking me?"

"On the longest journey of your life, Brandt. . . ."

THE
TARANTULA
HAWK

Arthur Mather

BANTAM BOOKS
NEW YORK · TORONTO · LONDON · SYDNEY · AUCKLAND

THE TARANTULA HAWK
A Bantam Book / October 1989

ISBN 0-553-28017-1

Published simultaneously in the United States and Canada

Bantam Books are published by Bantam Books, a division of Bantam
Doubleday Dell Publishing Group, Inc. Its trademark, consisting of
the words "Bantam Books" and the portrayal of a rooster, is
Registered in U.S. Patent and Trademark Office and in other
countries. Marca Registrada. Bantam Books, 666 Fifth Avenue, New
York, New York 10103.

PRINTED IN THE UNITED STATES OF AMERICA

O   0 9 8 7 6 5 4 3 2 1

"There's one of those Tarantula Hawks, Matt," said the boy, pointing to the ground in front of him.

It was a red-bodied insect, about the size of an overgrown locust, black wings sheathed back along its body, probing at a small hole in the ground.

"Tarantula Hawk?" queried Hegarty.

"Yeah; bet there's a bloody whopper of a tarantula down in that hole."

"She's after the spider."

"She's after the spider all right. She'll get down in that hole, and sting him so he becomes paralyzed, and he'll stay that way for a long time. Then she'll lay her eggs on him and just leave, and when all the little Tarantula Hawks hatch out they'll feed on the spider. Poor bugger gets eaten alive."

"Sounds kinda tough on the spider."

"I s'pose. Grandad says some people are like that; get right inside you without you knowing, then just eat you away."

"You could be right," said Hegarty slowly.

He was sure it was only coincidence, the boy wouldn't make a conscious analogy between him and the murderous life-style of an insect. But it prickled him with unease to recognize the similarity. Christ, it was ridiculous to feel like that, Kisek was Leiman, someone had to play Tarantula Hawk, and if a few innocent people got eaten along the way, then that was the price that had to be paid.

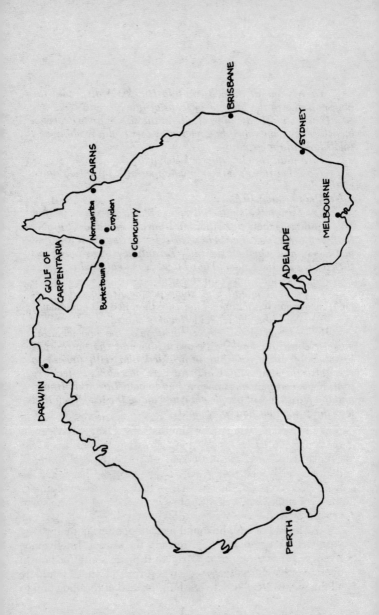

Chapter 1

New York. June 10.

Matt Hegarty positioned himself to the side of the Algonquin Hotel entrance, absently watching the night time flow of people along Forty-fourth Street. It was a warm night, the heat of the day still being transmitted from the sidewalk. He glanced at his watch; Andre Reine was late. Andre had been the one to suggest the Algonquin; he liked to eat well, and it was a good place to talk. And ten o'clock was probably the best time, when most of the early crowd had gone.

"Want a girl, handsome?" breathed a young black girl with the braided hair, as she sauntered past. She paused, with an enticing smile, but he grinned and shook his head. She shrugged, and moved along.

He ran his fingers slowly down the side of his face. Handsome? It was false modesty not to acknowledge that at thirty-five many women saw him that way. Okay, his nose was too long, the jut of his jaw too aggressive, yet he knew the angular face gave an impression of strength. His mother's darkness had been passed on, to give him the black hair he wore close-cropped, the brown eyes that absorbed everything, the easy smile that invited confidences. The fact that he stood around six-foot-three was an added bonus.

As he did of late, he found himself pondering on his long years as an agent of the Mossad, the Israel Intelligence Agency. He was American born, so it made sense for him to operate out of the States, yet he was surprised Andre would fly all the way to New York to see him, instead of recalling him to

1

Tel Aviv for briefing. But then Andre never did anything without good reason. Apparently something big was up. Of course he was sure it had to do with the Wiesenthal Institute report, there was obviously some involvement planned for him. He shrugged. Well, he needed something. The Zurecki business had left him frayed out, he suspected even weary of the way he was living his life. Oh, he was sure he still believed fervently enough, but he craved some vigorous shot to restore what he hoped was only a temporarily jaded appetite.

"I'm sorry I'm late, Matt," a slightly accented voice murmured apologetically at his side.

He turned, startled to find Reine suddenly beside him. "Andre; I didn't see you arrive." He grinned warmly.

They quickly shook hands, then Reine gestured to the hotel. "Let's go in shall we, Matt," he urged throatily.

Hegarty nodded, and motioned Reine in ahead of him. Every time they met, Andre seemed more visibly aged. He was almost as tall as Hegarty, but stooped, with sharp gaunt features, his face a portrait of a stoicism that had successfully endured the worst fate could inflict. Spare gray hair, and an equally gray mustache concealing a thin mouth that allowed scant display of emotion. In his unpretentious gray suit he looked like a banker on the verge of retirement. Certainly he was due to retire in a few months, but he was anything but a banker. Long ago, Reine had perfected the safety of seeming ordinariness, of anonymity, and the reward had been a long life in a dangerous profession. He hadn't said as much, but a quick flinty glance signified his disapproval of Hegarty's colored shirt and casual beige jacket.

They walked through the hush of the carpeted lobby, and were shown courteously to the unobtrusive corner table Matt had reserved. The surroundings had a richness, a nostalgic warmth, that made it seem like a haven from a brash modern New York. There was a faint buzz of conversation, but most of the dinner patrons had gone. They settled down, and both ordered steak.

Hegarty knew he would have to wait, impatience was useless, it was Andre's way. So he enjoyed the meal, while he listened to Andre ramble on of his never-ending passion for Egyptology, of dreaded retirement, of his wife's delight that he

would soon be all hers and they could move from the bustle of
Tel Aviv to the quiet of the country. Mournfully he wondered
how in God's name he would cope with such changed circumstances. But with the steak consumed, he patted delicately at
his mouth with his napkin, gave a small belch of satisfaction,
then hunched forward, his demeanor suddenly changed.
Hegarty knew it was time.

"You've read the Wiesenthal report?" he questioned
abruptly.

Hegarty was ready for him. "Of course; thoroughly."

"You agree with the conclusions?"

"Yes. I think there's little doubt that the cattle rancher
living in Australia, who calls himself Kisek is the Nazi war
criminal Horst Leiman."

"Good. We believe so too." Andre paused, toying with his
napkin. "You have no doubts at all?"

Hegarty knew Reine well enough to know he would
appreciate complete honesty. "The conclusion was certainly
damning enough; he has to be our man, but the evidence is
still only circumstantial. It would be difficult to prove identity
beyond all doubt in a courtroom."

Reine leaned back. His smile was without warmth, like
pale sunlight filtering through frosted glass. "Ah yes," he
murmured. "I knew you would see that, Matt."

"Then you agree I'm right?"

"Unfortunately, yes; one must be realistic. A smart lawyer
could create real problems for us. It's happened before, as you
know."

There was a contemplative pause.

"But I understand you're going ahead and mounting an
operation in spite of that problem?" asked Hegarty.

"We've no alternative. As the report rightly pointed out,
there's always the chance, however slight, that now the lid's
been lifted someone could get wind of what's been going on
and warn Kisek. We couldn't possibly risk having the man
vanish again after all these years." He sighed, nervously
folding and unfolding his napkin. The waiter silently brought
coffee, and they waited until he had gone. "The operation's
already mounted," continued Reine.

Hegarty showed surprise. "You've moved fast. Favett's really putting a fire under headquarters since he took over."

"It was my decision," Reine stated coldly. "Favett agreed speed was essential."

Hegarty sugared his coffee, stirring it repeatedly. Raising department politics was a mistake; even nearing retirement Reine still resented a younger superior.

"We want you to go to Australia," stated Reine bluntly.

Again Hegarty showed surprise. "You want me to bring this Kisek out?"

"Perhaps. More than that."

"You want me to keep him under surveillance?"

"More even than that."

Hegarty looked puzzled. "I'm not following you, Andre."

Reine crouched across the table. "Matt we have to have something to prove identity beyond all doubt—something that will be unassailable in any court, defy any defense lawyer. I want you to go to Australia and get close to this Kisek; get in his pocket if you can, get work on his ranch in this Gulf Country where he lives. You have all the qualifications, more than anyone else we have."

"Qualifications?"

"That year you took off three years ago. The break you desperately needed after Lebanon, to recharge yourself. When you went off working on cattle ranches here and in South America. You remember."

Hegarty nodded slowly. Christ, was that only three years ago? Perhaps that's what he needed again now, tough, mind-healing physical exertion to renew his faith.

"Yes, of course I remember."

"You learned about cattle."

"Sure. But for Chrissake, how do I know for sure he'd hire me? It'd be one hell of a gamble."

"Yes, but we believe a worthwhile gamble. We have very little choice. And there are ways to reduce the gamble."

"Ways?"

"Milhesco will explain."

"Milhesco?"

"He's been on an intelligence survey in Australia where

Kisek lives. He has all the information you'll require. Photographs, history, local details."

Hegarty's grin expressed wonderment. "Christ, you guys have been really moving."

"Grubin will be backing you."

"Jules Grubin." He had a flash of the bearded, swashbuckling Jules, like a pirate from another age. But cunning. And ruthless.

"We've worked together before," he said.

"I know. And of course you have other qualifications."

"Such as?"

"Milhesco will explain when he briefs you."

"You don't want to elaborate?"

"Milhesco's the one who's been in Australia, not I."

Hegarty slowly sipped his coffee to gain a pause in the conversation. It was all going too fast, and he wanted to absorb everything Reine was saying. Andre didn't like to repeat himself, but it all seemed loose as hell at the moment.

"You don't think Kisek could be identified by his victims?"

"Milhesco has seen him. It's been a long time, evidently he's changed beyond recognition."

"Then this . . . something I'm to look for, something that will hold up in court—do you have any idea what it might be?"

"No, you'll be on your own. But there has to be something there, perhaps a memento from the past the man couldn't bear to part with—a photograph, some letter or document that would give unshakable proof of identity.

"I've seen you work. If it's there, you'll find it."

"Thanks for the confidence. If he hires me, and it's a big if."

"That's the gamble." Reine hesitated. "And Eli Brandt might be able to help us."

"Brandt's working on this too?"

"I have to go to London to see him. He claims in two weeks he'll have a set of Leiman's fingerprints coming to him from Berlin."

Hegarty nearly spilled his coffee. "Jesus Christ, fingerprints! That would really clinch it that Kisek is Leiman. Have they been verified?"

"Brandt sent us a form of verification."

"You don't sound too convinced."

Reine fell silent, eyes half closed. A passing waiter paused inquiringly, but both men shook their heads in unison. Two well-dressed women cast lingering glances at Hegarty as they drifted by, but he ignored them.

"You know Brandt's reputation, Matt," murmured Reine.

"I know he's had one hell of a lot of bad luck."

"You could call it that; or he's made stupid decisions. I like Eli. I've found myself having to defend him many times, but . . ." He bit his lip in uncertainty. "I just can't have faith in his judgment any more."

"It would be fantastic if the fingerprints are on the level."

"I agree. But I'll have to double-check the verification."

"That means I'll have to get Kisek's fingerprints for comparison?"

"Yes, if Brandt hasn't made another . . . misjudgment. But we can't afford to chance waiting around for Brandt."

Hegarty sat back in his chair, hands clasped thoughtfully under his chin. "No, I guess not," he said. He reflected a moment. "It's one hell of a difficult assignment you've given me to pull off, Andre."

"You can do it," Reine said confidently. "We're counting on you, Matt."

"What if we're wrong?"

"Wrong?"

"What if Kisek isn't Leiman?"

"You read the report. How can you have any doubts?"

"There has to be a chance, I guess. Sure the report's convincing, but we both agree it's still circumstantial."

"Put it out of your mind, Matt. We're not wrong."

Hegarty dropped it. When Reine was sold on a premise it was useless to argue.

"But what if I don't get anything on Kisek?" he persisted.

"There's no point in being negative," answered Reine crisply.

"I'm not, just realistic."

Reine frowned, brushed irritably at his mustache, then shrugged. "Then we'll probably take him out anyway, and chance conviction, I suppose. That'll be Favett's decision. Don't let's consider that for the moment."

"Has anyone considered extradition?" Hegarty asked tentatively.

Reine threw up his hands and uttered a snort of derision. "Ah, how could you ask such a thing, Matt? Let it be stuck in the Australian courts for God knows how long, while some smart lawyer argues a case of mistaken identity? Never."

"If we take him out, the Australian government isn't going to like it."

"Then let them dislike it. Once we have him they can't do a damn thing about it."

Hegarty didn't take it any further. Maybe Milhesco would clarify it, but it still seemed goddamn loose. He was going to have to feel his way into it like a blind man.

Reine glanced at his watch. "I can't afford much more time, Matt. Do you have any other questions?"

"I guess I'd better leave it to Milhesco. When's he coming in to brief me?"

"He'll be here tomorrow. He'll explain it, but first you have to go to Texas."

Hegarty failed to stifle a frustrated laugh. There were curve balls coming at him from every direction. "Texas! For Chrissake why?"

He saw the words forming on Reine's lips, and he raised his hands to forestall him. "I know, I know—Milhesco will explain."

For the first time Reine permitted himself a smile of near-warmth. "Yes," he said, "Milhesco will explain."

June 24. The Salimeno Ranch, South Texas, out of Laredo.

Bobo Walters didn't quite fit the image of the Marlboro Man, lean and tough as worn leather, out riding the range in all sort of weather, tending the cattle, mothering the calves. He'd started out a short, skinny kid, but somewhere along the way a love of good food got the better of him, and he blew up all over: girth to his waistline, beef to his limbs, jowls to his chin, puffy excess around his eyes. His wife had been riding on top for a long time now. "I love you, honey, but there's no goddamn sense in your smotherin' me," she claimed. That was okay by him.

The ranch owners called him "Barrel" when they were sure he was out of earshot; it didn't seem proper to rile a man who ran the best helicopter herding and roundup outfit in Texas. If you wanted someone who could make a chopper square dance around the sky without knocking your cattle about, then Bobo Walters was your man.

He was an affable, jovial man in his late forties, who loved a joke, when all his chins would jiggle like an old turkey gobbler. He was chuckling now, leaning on his truck, watching the helicopter working the cattle in the distance.

He took off his broad-brimmed cowboy hat and mopped his brow. It was hot! The sun was glaring out of a brilliant blue sky, and every time the helicopter changed direction it threw glittering sparks of sunlight, as if the blades were charged with electricity. If it weren't for the sunglasses he was wearing the reflections would have forced him to look away.

Goddamn, he'd never seen a man master the skill of helicopter herding in just a few weeks like this guy Hegarty. Sure, he might already have a helicopter pilot's license, but that didn't necessarily mean a man could pick up the know-how of controlling a cattle herd. No siree. Bobo figured he was a mean hand at making a chopper kick up its heels, the best, and he'd taught it all to this fella Hegarty, but man oh man, he sure enough had the feeling it was getting close to the student going one better than his teacher.

Bobo mused on the strange request that had come from Sternham, the New York dealer who supplied his helicopters. He'd been negotiating for a new Bell, when out of the blue Sternham said he'd got a friend who wanted to learn all about handling cattle with a helicopter. "Bobo," he'd said, "it's important to this guy, and he knows how to fly a helicopter anyway. I'll tell you: I figure I can do a very special deal on this Bell for you, if you'll take this guy on for a few weeks. Teach him all you know—and you're the best." What could he say? No? Business was business? Besides, this guy Hegarty was offering good bucks for the tuition. "Okay Sternham, but no promises," he'd cautioned. "Herding takes more than just being able to fly a helicopter, yes siree. You got to have the touch. Some guys wouldn't learn in a lifetime. Just ain't got the touch, and never will."

"Give it a try anyway, Bobo; I'd really appreciate it. This is one very bright guy I'm talking about."

It was against his better judgment, but he did it. Sternham had him over a barrel in a way. Well, Sternham had sure been right about one thing, Hegarty was bright all right. Quiet, likable, but tight-mouthed. It only took a short time of shooting the breeze to know he wasn't going to get any answers to questions, so Bobo held down his curiosity and just concentrated on teaching the guy all he knew.

It was really something to watch him now, bringing the cattle along like a mother hen guarding her chicks, knowing how to use the wind direction so he didn't get himself caught in any downwind turns. Not too high or too low, but just right, and positioning himself just slightly behind the mob. And not trying to be a smartass, knocking the all-fired shit out of the cattle by buzzing over them like he was some hot-shot jet pilot, but knowing how to turn the cattle with the noise of the Bell 47. The man had a goddamn natural touch. Christ, he wouldn't be letting him work stock with a valued client like the Salimenos if he didn't think so.

The cowhands took over the mob, then the helicopter banked away and headed toward him. The only regret he had was that this was Hegarty's last day. He really liked the guy, even if he was secretive as all hell, and Bobo would have paid big bucks to have him working for his outfit.

He waited as the helicopter settled close, lighting up a king-size cigar that protruded aggressively from his mouth like a rocket, the smoke making dark clouds against the blue sky. He rummaged around in the cooler box and took out two cans of Budweiser as Hegarty strode toward him.

From the beginning it had struck him Hegarty looked more like a cowhand than an easterner: boots, dusty jeans, checked shirt, lean as a young colt, except for that way of looking at you as a warning not to get too close. He'd never figured the accent. Could have been Boston, New York, Los Angeles, or all three rolled into one. If he wasn't a womanizer then he sure as hell ought to try it. Bobo figured a lot of women would have one hell of an urge to get themselves under this guy. He'd never asked, but he figured he was around thirty-five.

Hegarty came to a halt, wiped the sweat from his face with a bright-colored handkerchief, and gave the self-satisfied grin of a man who knows he's done a good job.

"Well, how'd it look, Bobo?" he asked.

Bobo gave an answering grin, and tossed him a can of beer. "Goddamn, you know you don't have to ask, Matt. Fuck me, just beautiful, beautiful. I figured we'd just celebrate with a beer. You sure enough turned out to be one hell of a cattle pilot, and that's the truth."

"I consider that real praise coming from the best there is."

"It's no praise, boy. I'll tell you, Matt, after watching you out there I'm starting to feel mebbe like I *used* to be the best."

"Forget it. You're still the best, Bobo."

They cracked open their cans in unison, and drank deep, relishing the coldness. Bobo finally lowered his can and wiped a pudgy hand across his face.

"You wouldn't be figuring on working around these parts in competition with old Bobo, would you now Matt?" he asked guardedly.

Hegarty laughed it aside. "That's the last thing on my mind, Bobo."

Bobo took another swig. He knew from past experience it was useless to try and push his curiosity any further; that blank look would come into Hegarty's face, and he would only get evasive answers. Surely it was only natural he'd like to know what Hegarty figured on doing with the cattle-handling skill he'd taught him.

"Well I'll tell you now, Matt, if you're ever down these parts and you're lookin' for a job helicopter herding, then you make sure it's Bobo you come and see. Hell, I'd hire you that fast, and pay top money. Yes siree. Top men are hard to come by, and you're tops, Matt." He waved the cigar in the air, trailing smoke signals like a form of entreaty.

Hegarty swirled his can and caught the faint sound of slopping beer; he nodded thoughtfully.

"Thanks, I appreciate the offer. I'm grateful for all you've taught me, I really am. Sternham told me I was going to be taught by the best, and I know now he was right. I'll tell you

Bobo, if I ever do want to take it up as a job, then you'll be the first person I'll head for. You can count on it."

"Atta boy, Matt, that's what I was hoping you'd say."

Hegarty raised his can to signify a toast. "Here's to you, Bobo. I enjoyed every minute of it, it's been great. Thanks for everything."

Bobo responded with his own can. "My pleasure, Matt, and don't you be forgetting the helicopter pilot is the boss on the roundup—you call the shots. And playing teacher's been fun for me, too. I enjoyed myself." He hesitated, then made one last try. "I just hope what you've learned turns out to be mighty useful to you, wherever you'll be doin' it."

"It sure as hell will, Bobo," replied Hegarty.

It still didn't tell him anything. He lifted the can and drank again, trying to drown the questions still tumbling around in his mind. The hell with it, the guy's paid his money, and he guessed what he wanted to do about it was his business, even if learning helicopter herding without doing any helicopter herding didn't make a lot of goddamn sense.

June 25. London.

When one has chosen to live in a world of shadows, the occasional shafts of light seem more brilliant, even blinding in their rarity, mused Brandt. The last few days in London had affected him like that, even though irritation had been his first reaction at being forced to wait for Reine. He sighed. He assumed Reine would have come running at the thought of having Leiman's actual fingerprints, but maybe after this they would have to learn to trust his judgment.

He had used the time well, taking the opportunity to renew acquaintance with the great city. He had found himself acting like any tourist, strolling down the manicured Mall to Buckingham Palace, eavesdropping on a conducted tour of St. Paul's Cathedral and Westminster Abbey, poring over the treasures in the galleries, gawking through the Tower of London. The Empire might have gone, but the residue still fascinated.

It was a pleasant interlude from being constantly on guard in an occupation where sudden death so often preempted retirement. But then he'd been lucky, slavishingly imitating Andre Reine, and like him sure that his appearance had much to account for his ability to survive, with his rounded short stature clothed in a conservative dark suit, and forgettable chubby features topped by total baldness. He didn't mind looking like a colorless middle-aged clerk filling out time for the inevitable gold watch, for he was sure it gave him an edge. The vain young peacocks might strive to emulate James Bond, but he would outlive them all. And how the same young peacocks would envy this moment of his greatest triumph, would come to realize that old Brandt still had something to offer. Although nothing would ever erase the bitterness of being so often overlooked for promotion within the organization, when he was such a long-serving officer. God, he had had ambitions like everyone else, even if the organization had never taken them seriously. Having to bow and scrape to someone like Favett, who wasn't even born when Brandt had first joined the Mossad. It had never been said to his face, but the caustic sneers had come back to him from other sources: Old Brandt got it wrong again; the man cries wolf too often, he bases too much on false expectations that lead to negative results. But he'd had bad luck. It wasn't his fault some unknown assassin had got to Hebron before delivery in Syria. Or that for a year he'd passed on disinformation fed to him by a supposedly reliable source in Yemen. They were the bad breaks of the business.

It had cost him a year of diligent digging in Berlin to get the fingerprints, but it had been worth it to bring off the coup of his career, silence his detractors for all time. And he had verification. My God, how marvelous—verification to throw in the face of Favett and his kind. But he'd only sent along part of the verification to headquarters, like a morsel of irresistible bait, the prime piece he'd held back as the *pièce de résistance*, but it had been enough for them to send Andre Reine to confer with him in London. Of course under normal circumstances he would have returned to headquarters himself with the Leiman fingerprint file, but that would have wasted valuable time, and it was delicious to have them running after him for once. Sweet, sweet justice. Perhaps now, even at this late stage, would come deserved promotion.

He sighed contentedly, even the polluted balmy June evening air seemed fragrant, and he quickened his step along Oxford Street past Selfridge's, dodging the streams of shoppers. The Leiman fingerprints might be vital to the operation in Australia, but scarcely of interest to anyone else; even so, habit had made him follow his usual precaution of putting another copy in the hotel safe for Reine.

Not that he had anything against Reine. He liked Andre, a man of great influence in the organization, and not one of the sneerers. Experience had made Andre tolerant of the misfortunes that sometimes resulted in the failure of others. Brandt had always tried so hard to model himself on Andre, an acknowledged master of his trade, and who now had only a few months to go to much-deserved retirement. He should be so fortunate. Although from what he'd heard Andre regarded his approaching retirement with all the joy of a man being led to the gallows. Reine always relished being at the center of things, and Brandt knew he would find the Leiman fingerprints an irresistible challenge. He shrugged. All that mattered was that the fingerprints prove or disprove once and for all whether they were right about the man calling himself Kisek in Australia. God, after an investigation lasting five years, it would be traumatic to be proved wrong. Not with an operation already mounted, and Jules Grubin in Australia. The next question to be decided was how the fingerprint file was to be delivered to Grubin. Perhaps Andre would approve of Brandt taking it himself; a trip to Australia would be a fitting reward for all his work.

The thought prodded him with a feeling of sudden urgency, and he began to hurry, slipping past the buses turning into Portland Street, then quickly into the Cumberland Hotel. There was an abrupt realization that he was allowing himself to be lulled into a rather stupid aura of self-congratulation, with all the old doubts rushing into the vacuum. Maybe he'd been tempting fate to leave the file in his room, while he went out for a leisurely dinner. Certainly he'd covered himself with the copy in the safe, but he knew he'd been like a child with a new toy, wanting to have it close, to hold it, feel it, gloat over the joy of possession. He tried to shrug his sudden anxiety aside—after all who in London knew him, or cared?—but he found himself scurrying through the lobby and fretting impatiently while the elevator took him with what seemed maddening slowness to the third floor.

As soon as he entered his room he knew he'd been right about the dangers of relaxation, because he'd just made a primary mistake: Never enter a room and close the door without first switching on the light. The man standing amid the shambles of his room was a total stranger. Tall, slim, with a military bearing, clad in a casual leather jacket; maybe in his early forties; tanned handsome features, with strange emotionless brown eyes that somehow made Brandt more afraid than the pistol leveled at his stomach.

It all looked very professional, drawers gaping wide, clothes strewn about the floor, the mattress thrown back from the bed. He felt the color drain from his face when he saw the folder containing the Leiman fingerprint file on the chair beside the man. Surely that would have no interest for a thief? But instinct told him this man was more than a petty thief. Did such people carry around a .38? And the man seemed to have been waiting for him. Thank God for the other copy in the hotel safe. He knew better than to react with calculated coolness, it would only betray his professional background; much better, and safer, to respond in his outward character. He grasped at his throat as if fear had strangled his voice.

"Don't shoot," he gasped. "Please—don't shoot." His eyes flickered fearfully about the disarray. "You won't find anything of much value here—I've very little cash." He gestured to the gun. "You can just leave—I'm not stupid enough to argue with anything like that."

For a moment the man said nothing, then he allowed a thin, humorless smile to cross his lips. "A man in your profession who lives into his fifties could never be called stupid, Brandt."

It was an American accent, the soft menacing drawl a measure of his total control of the situation. Brandt cautiously studied the man's face.

"You know me? I don't know you."

"It's of no importance," he said curtly. He pointed to the folder. "That's all that matters to me."

Brandt drew a deep breath to keep his voice steady.

There was the usual coldness in his hands to warn that here was great danger, as he suspected; much more than a thief ransacking his room, even if he couldn't identify the threat. But how could anyone outside the organization know about the Leiman file, and what use would it be to them anyhow?

"That can't possibly be of any use to you," he muttered.

"On the contrary, it can be of great use to me."

"Then I think you've been badly misinformed. They're only papers relating to my . . . my security business, and no value to anyone else." He offered a placatory gesture. "Look, I'm not going to yell for help, or anything like that. Why don't you just leave? Really, I'll give you a good chance to get clear before I do anything. I'm expecting a business associate to knock on the door any moment, and . . ."

"Bullshit," the man cut him off harshly. He considered a moment, then he thrust the .38 into his pocket. Brandt could see the bulge of the muzzle still pointed threateningly in his direction. "My information is more accurate than you can possibly imagine, Brandt," he added coldly. "You of all people should know the rules. If you play the game, sometimes you win, sometimes you lose. It's as simple as that. Especially someone like you, with a track record of being a loser anyway."

Brandt's mind whirled. How could the man know so much? What use could he conceivably have for the Leiman file? Unless this was a trick? The organization testing him out? No, Andre would never allow that.

"I haven't the faintest idea what you're talking about," he tried to bluster.

The men merely shrugged, and nodded brusquely to the door. "No matter. You and I are going for a drive now, Brandt. I have a car downstairs. But first it's very important for you to understand that if you try to run for it, make any attempt to escape at all, then I'll shoot you in the back. Do you understand?"

"Look this is ridiculous, I . . . ," Brandt began, but the man picked up the folder, stepped quickly to him, and shoved him forcefully toward the door. "Outside," he ordered sharply. "And just walk a few steps in front of me. Keep locked in your fucking head you mean nothing to me, Brandt, nothing at all. If you force me to put a bullet in your back, then I will, and be

gone before anyone realizes what's happened." He pushed
him again. "Understand?"

Brandt gave a numb shake of his head and began moving.
He recognized the dispassionate ruthlessness of a fellow
professional. It would be crazy to risk a dash for freedom; far
better to play along and wait his chance. Even astute people
could be fooled into believing he was as harmless as he looked.
Maybe it would give him a chance to find out who this man
really was, what his interest was in the Leiman file.

He sat in the rear seat of the Mercedes, the man now
openly holding the gun on him; the folder lay between them.
He couldn't see the face of the driver, who appeared to know
where to go without any instructions. It was beginning to rain
as they swung right past Marble Arch and into Bayswater
Road, the windshield a watery kaleidoscope of blurred city
lights. If this man wanted the Leiman file, then he had it, and
Brandt couldn't understand what further use he had of him.

"I don't think I can help you any further," he said.

"Probably not," said the man shortly.

"Then why all this cloak and dagger nonsense? Where are
you taking me?"

"On the longest journey of your life, Brandt."

The cold finality of the words swept over him like an icy
chill. He turned and stared out the window, trying to control
his fear. Was it possible that on this dreary night his attempt to
emulate Reine's long life would fail?

Chapter 2

June 30. The Queensland Gulf Country, North Australia.

Hegarty knew the Gulf Country wet season didn't begin until around October, so he anticipated no problems about riding the Kawasaki all the way from Cairns, on the east coast of Australia, to the town of Normanton at the base of the Gulf of Carpentaria. But en route at the town of Croydon they warned him of an unseasonal deluge that had turned the roads to mud, which could make it difficult for him to get through. So he had no option but to load the motorcycle and himself on the tiny red-colored motor train called the Gulflander, and travel the remaining ninety miles by rail. The train only ran once a week, so it was lucky he happened to be there on the day it left. He didn't even consider leaving the Kawasaki behind; he'd given a lot of thought to deciding it was the best means of transport to get around the Gulf Country, and he certainly needed it to get from Normanton, where Reine and Milhesco had said he'd find his target, the Nazi Kisek.

The train journey was a hair-raising ride. Milhesco's brief back in New York had been concise enough, and in the short time available he'd read everything he could lay his hands on to familiarize himself with this part of Australia. But the swaying, bucking motion of the train made it difficult to concentrate on the passing landscape. He was sure there were times when the wheels actually lost contact with the rails. The way the flat countryside stretched endlessly to the horizon reminded him in a way of the great prairies of the American far midwest, but here the colors were predominately red earth, and the vegetation mostly an ocean of golden grass, scattered

with spindly, brackish green trees. The addition of enervating
heat gave it all a feeling of unforgiving harshness.

"They call 'er Leapin' Lena," cackled the elderly man
opposite.

Hegarty grinned politely. It was hard to guess the old
man's age; his unshaven face was lined and leathery, in
harmony with the toughness of the country, but the pouched,
crinkled eyes had an ageless twinkle. He was dressed in a
faded blue shirt, much-worn brown dungarees, heavy boots,
and a battered wide-brimmed hat that seemed fixed to his
head with the permanence of hair. He stuck out a gnarled,
brown-spotted hand, carpeted with white hair.

"Name's Cutmore," he wheezed. "Everyone 'round Normanton calls me Snowy."

Hegarty shook the offered hand. "Pleased to meet you,
Snowy," he said. "I'm Matt Hegarty. What do you mean,
Leaping Lena?"

"That's what we call the Gulflander. It's like the old girl
bounces from one blasted sleeper to the next."

"It sure seems that way at times," laughed Hegarty,
bracing himself as the train jostled clumsily into another
curve.

"Sounds to me like you're a Yank, Matt?"

"You're right, Snowy."

"Met a few Yanks in New Guinea durin' the war." He
shrugged his bony shoulders. "Found 'em like the rest of
us—some good 'uns, some bad 'uns. Whereabout in America
are you from?"

"I'm from around Texas."

"Yeah, I've heard of Texas. Cattle country too, eh? Like
'round here."

"That's right."

Snowy gestured to the passing countryside. "This here's
what's known as the Gulf savanna grasslands. You'll see plenty
of cattle 'round these parts. Mostly shorthorns, though there's
Brahmans and Santa Gertrudis comin' into the area. They
reckon gettin' Brahmans and shorthorns together improves the
herd no end." He paused and his eyes roved over Hegarty for
a moment, starting at the heavy boots and running up over the
jeans, checked shirt, tanned face, dark hair. He nodded, then

gave a grunt of satisfaction. "You look like one of those Gary Cooper sorta young blokes, Matt," he concluded. "You been what you Yanks call a cowboy?"

"I've worked with cattle, so I guess so," replied Hegarty.

"We call 'em a ringer out here."

"Ringer?"

"Yeah—stockman—the ones who work the cattle." He paused again. "You're one hell of a bloody long way from home."

Hegarty shrugged and gestured to the backpack at his feet. "I like to move around, Snowy, see the world. No wife, no kids, so I figure I've got nothing holding me to one place."

"Well I'll tell you, Matt, you won't see nothin' like the Gulf Country. Lucky you got here before October when the wet season starts. Gawd, the whole bloody country turns into a blasted lake. Rained here for forty bloody days and nights back in 'seventy-four. Never seen anything like it. Had to evacuate everyone at Normanton."

"Normanton's where I'm headed."

Snowy's face crinkled in a spidery grin. "Jeez, I hope so, mate—Leapin' Lena ain't goin' no place else."

He chuckled, then paused to light up an ancient pipe, and puffed acrid smoke to the wood-paneled ceiling. Hegarty thought of challenging him with a cigar, but decided against it for now.

"Thought someone like you might've flown into Normanton, Matt," he murmured.

"I decided to ride a motorcycle across from Cairns," explained Hegarty. "I figured it was the best way to see the country. I got as far as Croydon, but they told me I might have trouble traveling the road because of the rain." He shrugged. "So I loaded myself and the bike on to Leaping Lena, and here I am."

Snowy gave a snort of derision. "Panic merchants I'd reckon. That rain was a bit of a turn up, but Christ, the country's dry as a bloody bone; it'll all soak away in a coupla hours." He motioned with the pipe to the sweat on Hegarty's brow. "An' it can be bloody hot 'round here if you're not used to it. Not so much now, but Christ during the wet you can sweat like a pig."

"I can take it. It's goddamn hot in Texas too."

"You just passin' through, Matt, or reckonin' on workin' 'round the Gulf Country awhile?"

"Well, I was hoping to get some work. Getting around the world's fine, but you need to put some money in your pocket now and then. Someone at Croydon told me there might be some work at a ranch called Cathedral Rock."

"Cathedral Rock Station. We call 'em station, not ranch. That's old Dorf Kisek's place."

"Yes, that was the name I heard about."

Snowy sucked at his pipe with a sound like loosening phlegm. "Mebbe," he said doubtfully. "Queer old bird, Kisek. German y'know. Came out here as an immigrant after the war and started himself off by roundin' up wild steers." He shook his head. "Jeez, it paid off for him though. He's laughin' now, with money in the bank, an' I reckon he's runnin' about twenty-four thousand head out at Cathedral Rock. In the beginnin', what with him being German y'know, and the war and all, no one wanted to know him for a while. That's all over now, but we still see next to nothin' of the old bugger. Keeps to himself like a bloody hermit; doesn't come into Normanton, and Jesus, he certainly doesn't welcome anyone goin' out to Cathedral Rock to see him. Gawd no."

"You hear anything about him looking for ringers?"

Snowy frowned. "Well, I hear he's doin' some musterin'—roundup work," he explained, noting Matt's expression—"but old Dorf doesn't take too much to hirin' strangers—matter of fact to hirin' anybody. Jeez, I can't even remember the last time I saw the old coot. Works Cathedral Rock with his two daughters, and a few blacks. I've seen the daughters now and then." He shook his head, and grinned. "Christ, I wish I was a young fella again when I see 'em—coupla real good lookers. The way Dorf's raised 'em they can handle cattle like blokes; I hear better than some."

"Someone told me he's got a helicopter out there?"

Snowy threw back his head, and a derisive cackle burst from his mouth. "Shit yeah, you heard right. Old Dorf's folly they call it. I hear it sits out there like some bloody expensive ornament. They say the silly old bastard bought it for musterin', but he won't hire anyone to fly the bloody thing. I heard one of his daughters was supposed to learn to fly it, but I reckon that hasn't happened yet, or is likely to." He shook his head. "Crazy. They say him not hirin' anyone has got to do with this thing about refusin' to have strangers around his place, but I reckon the old bugger's got to have a screw loose somewhere." He sucked reflectively at his pipe for a moment, shrewd eyes on Hegarty. "Can you fly one of those things, Matt?"

Hegarty shrugged. "Sure. I was helicopter herding— mustering—in Texas."

There was a sudden feeling of the train lurching into an airborne takeoff, and both men clung to their seats until the wheels bit again with a screech of metal.

"Leapin' Lena sure knows how to leap," guffawed Snowy. "Christ, has it ever leaped right off the track?"

"Not that I ever heard of." Snowy chuckled and settled back in his seat. "Listen, Matt, if you've done some helicopter musterin', that might be one way you could persuade Kisek to take you on. Silly old bugger, he could cut his musterin' time by two-thirds if he used the bloody machine. I mean I used to be a ringer m'self before I retired, an' I know." He shrugged. "Course there's other places you could try, but they generally hire helicopter outfits to do their musterin', an' don't go and buy a bloody machine like Dorf. That's crazy."

"Well, I'll sure give it a try," said Hegarty.

"You got nothin' to lose," agreed Snowy, but there was no conviction in his voice. He concentrated on his pipe again for a time, the fizzing sound of burning tobacco audible even above the clackety-clack of the train.

"You don't sound too hopeful," said Hegarty, after a moment.

"Yeah, I guess not. I mean I know old Dorf's reputation. I've heard of blokes goin' out there lookin' for work, and gettin' practically thrown off the place." Then he grinned and attempted to inject some reassurance into his voice. "Listen Matt, you bein' a helicopter musterin' pilot could make all the difference. I mean, comin' from Texas sounds pretty impressive. He could take a fancy to your Yank accent." His grin widened and he gave a lewd wink. "Or better still, maybe one of the daughters will."

"I was told Cathedral Rock is over towards Burketown," said Hegarty.

"That's right. You go through Normanton and out on the Cloncurry road. You turn off to the west about five miles outa town. It's pretty rough, but okay at this time of year. Kisek's place is right on the road, 'bout fifty miles or so out. He's got himself quite a house out there so I hear, not that anyone ever gets to see inside the bloody thing—including me." He leaned to Hegarty, his face twisted into a lecherous leer. "An' I hear his girls are pretty bloody man-hungry. Good-lookin' fella like you'll need to watch himself, or they'll have you hog-tied an' their brandin' iron on your bare ass before you know what's hit you. Yeah mate, right on your bare ass!" He broke into high-pitched sniggers that were choked off by a spasm of coughing, but the merriment persisted in his watery eyes.

Hegarty grinned. "I don't hog-tie easily," he said.

"Don' go makin' your mind up until you see the girls, mate," spluttered Snowy.

Hegarty laughed it aside, and decided for a cigar after all. The foul smell of Snowy's pipe needed some sort of counter-attack.

It was valuable running into a local character like Snowy. So far everything he'd said about Kisek and the Gulf area confirmed what Milhesco had told him during the briefing in New York. Like a salesman itemizing an account, the portly Milhesco had ticked off the three qualifications that had made Reine consider Hegarty ideal for the assignment: a trained helicopter pilot; the experience he'd gained with cattle during his year off; women. Matt grinned at the memory of the third category. Sure, he liked women, and generally they liked him—and hopefully he could make it work for him with Kisek's daughters, but he doubted he warranted the Casanova reputation Milhesco had implied. The celibate way he'd been living lately would qualify him for the priesthood. The red-headed television producer in Los Angeles had been a year ago. Kisek's daughters he'd play as it came, but it was obvious he was going to have one hell of a problem getting Kisek to hire him. Judging from Snowy's remarks, Kisek's character was even more intractable than Milhesco had led him to believe. It made getting a job at Cathedral Rock sound god-

damn impossible. At least Milhesco was proved right about
one thing: the helicopter angle seemed like the only real
chance he might have; but it was still a gamble. So much was
riding on Kisek hiring him. Not that the operation would be
stifled if he couldn't get taken on, they'd just have to explore
other alternatives; but it would make it that much more
difficult. There had to be a way, they were all counting on him.
And of course there was Jules Grubin; it was essential Matt
locate the Mossad agent as quickly as possible.

He was relieved when the train finally rattled into
Normanton. After the Kisek conversation, Snowy had gone on
interminably about the various places he'd worked around the
Gulf Country, until Hegarty had lost track of the old man's
words. But the chance meeting had been useful, if only for
confirmation, and he warmly shook Snowy's hand before the
old man went ambling down to the other end of the train in
search of a parcel.

The Normanton railway station consisted of a giant two-
sided, open-ended structure of iron sheeting and girders, with
a great curved roof forming a canopy over the train. It was like
arriving at some way station to the past, with posters along the
walls from another age. "Matchless Pears Soap." "Nicholsons
for the best Pianos." "Dewars Whisky. England's Finest." The
main station building was attached to this arrival area, surrounded by a typically wide sun-protecting veranda, like so
many other houses Hegarty had seen since leaving Cairns. But
the station had a sense of grandeur that was surprising for such
a remote, small country town.

He unloaded the Kawasaki and strapped on his backpack.
The railroad tracks ran out through the brown landscape like
fingers pointing to where savanna met brilliant blue sky in one
long, unbroken horizon. There was an intensity about the light
that forced him to squint. The only sound was the whisper of
the wind teasing the grass, while here and there small eddies
of red dust swirled into the air, as if attempting to escape the
heat. As Snowy had said, whatever rain had fallen the countryside had absorbed like a sponge. A red dirt road let to the
main part of the town, a cluster of buildings shimmering in the
sun.

"Good luck to you, Matt," called Snowy.

He seemed smaller when standing, but gnarled like a tree hardened by a harsh climate. "You stayin' on in Normanton, or goin' straight out to Kisek's place?"

"I figure I may as well move right along, Snowy. No sense in wasting time."

"Okay, suit yerself. Just thought you might like a beer first, wash some of Leapin' Lena's dust down." He thumb-gestured toward the town. "Interestin' old place, Normanton. Only got a population of around eleven hundred but it's the capital of the Gulf Country; goes right back to the 1880's, when three trains a week wuz runnin' miners to the big gold strike at Croydon. Jeez, there wuz eleven thousand livin' here then."

Hegarty nodded. At least that explained the grandiose railway station. He straddled the Kawasaki, and again shook Snowy's hand. "Maybe we'll have that beer later on," he smiled. "I guess if I don't get a job at Cathedral Rock I'll have to come back to Normanton anyway."

"Just make bloody sure you get to smile at Kisek's girls," said the old man, grinning. "Never know—it might do wonders for yer chances."

Hegarty kicked the motor into life. The sudden roar punctured the silence, startling everyone at the station, and he quickly eased the throttle back. "I'll remember that Snowy," he laughed.

"Bloody oath you should. I reckon you'll do all right, Matt," encouraged Snowy, with more feeling than conviction. "But just in case, I'll be watching out for ya 'round at the National Hotel; you can't miss it, a big two-story place." He wagged a warning finger at Hegarty. "An' don't go swimmin' in the river; if the crocs don't get you, the sharks will."

It was two o'clock as Hegarty rode slowly away from Snowy and the station and into Normanton, restraining his speed as if he felt the need to match the unhurried atmosphere. Even the way people strolled the streets indicated a leisured approach to life. Again he had the feeling of traversing a time warp. The gas lamp from a past age standing in the middle of the main street, the imposing structure of the Shire Hall, with its ornate Victorian iron-latticed balcony, the large National Hotel Snowy had referred to, the curved board front of a huge building calling itself the Burns Philp Company, all looked like structures on the back lot for a western movie. They spoke of a time when the town bustled with more life than today.

People in wide-brimmed hats, and clothes that reminded him of Texas, watched with curious eyes as he passed. A good percentage of the town seemed to be black. A dust-coated truck with its load of frightened, uncomprehending cattle, was parked at the side like a predatory mechanical monster from another world. A bus disgorged tourists in bright-colored city garb who languidly assembled outside an establishment called the Stop Shop. He wondered if he'd come to regret passing up Snowy's offer of a cold beer, but he carried Reine's sense of urgency with him like a prod at his back, and no doubt Jules Grubin would be trying to work to a tight schedule, with everything set and ready to go. He hoped the timetable was running smoothly, that Jules had arrived as planned and was safely established in the location Milhesco had found for him. Timing was essential, if they were right about Kisek, and he didn't even want to consider the possibility they might be wrong. Not after five years' work.

He followed the sign pointing to Cloncurry, picking up speed, and rapidly left Normanton behind. Five miles out he turned west on the road to Burketown, again noting how accurately Milhesco's directions tallied with those given him by Snowy Cutmore. He trailed a long tail of gray dust, traveling a landscape that seemed devoid of humankind. The golden grass was speckled with green, probably from the recent rain, and the quivering horizon floated like a mirage. Startled birds winged high above his racketing intrusion. Occasional straggling cattle watched his coming with torpid disinterest, then at the last moment kicked up their heels and fled in snorting fright. He had read of the great Australian emptiness, a void that bred a tough, resourceful people to cope with the loneliness and isolation; he was going to have to be tough and resourceful, too. The two daughters sounded interesting, able to handle the cattle and country like men; they might make a nice change from some of the phony sophisticates he'd been involved with in the past. He grinned at the memory of Snowy's mock warning. Maybe he'd let them put a brand on his ass, if that's what it took to get Kisek to hire him.

He went on for another hour, ignoring the gradual deterioration of the road, until he failed to spot a deep pothole, and hit it going too fast. The motorcycle momentarily became airborne, and as it scrunched back to earth he wrestled frantically for control, sliding, skidding wildly, cutting deep scars in the black earth, spraying dirt like a snowplow before he finally managed to bring it to a shuddering halt. He just sat there for a moment, trying to recover breath, then he stood clear and let the bike drop to the road, mopping at his brow and cursing his inattention. Grubin and Reine would not have been amused if his role in the operation had come to an abrupt end in this isolated part of the world. The sudden loss of cooling speed made him aware of the heat, but goddamn it, there was no point in racing to Kisek's place if it meant wrecking anything as crucial as the bike. He picked it up and examined it carefully; apart from a few scratches there seemed little damage. Stupid sonofabitch—he'd had more luck than he deserved. He tentatively kicked down on the starter, and the motor responded immediately, but he moved off with more caution this time, maneuvering around the holes and ridges. Then he noticed, off to his right, a group of green trees standing like an oasis in the brown countryside. They had to mean water, and perhaps a chance to wash off the dust before he arrived at Cathedral Rock. He cut warily off the road, gingerly steered the bike across the uneven ground, and threaded through the trees until he spied the water. He stopped just short of the edge and switched off the motor. It was a lagoon, a long strip of cool water about two hundred yards wide, winding in a long curve for perhaps a quarter of a mile, the lush vegetation surrounding it like a crush of dependent children. Tree reflections painted the surface green to match the foliage, except out in the center, where the sun caught the water in a dazzling corona. Water lilies spotted the area, bobbing in the gentle breeze, forming a backdrop for a variety of birds skimming the surface. It was peace, utter tranquility, with only the occasional call of birds and the soft buzz of insects. He dismounted, propped the bike against a tree, and stood awhile, just savoring the ambience. It made

Reine and Grubin seem eons away, even strangely irrelevant. Which was crazy. He hadn't come this far to have his resolve melted by a few seconds of reflective quietitude. Yet in a strange way what he saw here, the mood, the feeling, encapsulated the sense of disconnection he'd felt over the last few months. He had an unexplained impulse just to sit down and let the world go past for a time. He irritably shook it aside, considered taking a swim, then decided against it on the basis of time. He knelt in the soft earth of the bank, and stirred the water with his hands, relishing the coldness, and crouched low to wash it over his face. Then he caught the plaintive whinny of a horse, and glanced up quickly to his right in surprise as a saddled roan pony trotted out from the trees, reins hanging loose and with no sign of a rider. It didn't see him as it paused a moment, shook its head, snorted several times, then went to the edge of the lagoon and began to drink.

Hegarty straightened up and peered about the trees, but there was no one, no sound except the slurping of the horse drinking. He swabbed the water from his face, studying the animal. It was small but very beautiful, the sheen of its coat like highly polished timber. He raised himself up carefully, anxious not to startle the horse, and then saw the crocodile: out toward the center of the lagoon, ugly snout and eyes just visible above the surface, moving with scarcely a ripple, yet obviously targeted on the unsuspecting pony. He had a feeling for horses; he didn't want to see one as handsome as this finish up in a crocodile's belly. He opened his mouth to shout a warning, then just as quickly closed it again. It looked young, maybe only a two-year-old, probably skittish as all hell, and a shouted warning might just send it blundering forward into the water. He'd heard crocs could move with lightning speed when lined up on a meal. He reached swiftly into his backpack, pulled out the .45 Colt, and with his left hand steadying his right wrist, aimed for the repulsive head. He knew the old Colt could put a bullet through thick timber, so it wouldn't have any trouble penetrating a crocodile's dense hide. It was close now, and the pony still hadn't seen it, then the head slipped beneath the surface just as he fired. The sudden gunshot shattered the serenity of the lagoon, masses of birds fled the surrounding trees, shrieking in unison. The crocodile reared up out of the water in agony, its fearsome snout gaping with ferocious teeth, claws pawing at the air like a begging dog, long tail threshing at the surface with a crazed thwacking sound, boiling the water white, then red with blood. It began to roll, showing the long brown green back of serrated scales, then the pale underbelly, over and over. At the shot, the horse had jerked its head up, reared with a whinny of terror, stumbled into the shallows with its forefeet, and frantically sprayed water as it struggled to back up onto solid ground. Then it finally broke loose, snorting in fear, kicked up its heels, wheeled about, and galloped panic-stricken back through the trees, throwing a cloud of dirt, leaves, and twigs in its wake. The crocodile shuddered along the length of its body, then was still, floating belly up and drifting gently until it was snagged in a patch of water lilies.

Hegarty slipped the Colt into the backpack as the drumming of the horse's hooves gradually faded and there was silence again. He wondered where the hell the rider was. And what about himself, for Chrissake? He must have been out of his goddamn mind to consider going for a swim. He'd thought the crocodiles were only in the rivers, not in the lagoons. That was one hell of a stupid mistake he wouldn't want to make again.

He became aware of a new sound, much softer than the beat of a horse's hooves, but still the tat-tat of running feet. Then he saw a figure sprinting through the trees toward him, too indistinct through the foliage for details. It broke out into the open only a short distance away, and he realized it was a young boy, perhaps twelve or thirteen, breathing hard: a sapling-thin body clad in jeans and a black tank top, with a crop of fair hair in striking contrast to skin browned the color of toast. The boy came to an abrupt halt when he spotted him, poised in frozen motion as if prepared to bolt, shoulders heaving, wide blue eyes darting from Hegarty to the dead crocodile, then back again. He was maybe closer to twelve, pug nose, generous mouth, frank, enquiring eyes, the imprint already forming of a good-looking man.

Hegarty offered a disarming smile, and a warm gesture of greeting. "Hi there," he said. He nodded toward the trees. "Was that your pony?"

The boy returned a wary smile, and relaxed a little, tongue licking anxiously back and forth over his lips.

"Yeah, mister, that was my pony." His voice was light, not yet broken. He jerked his thumb toward the dead crocodile. "Did you kill the croc? Was that the shot I heard?"

Hegarty nodded, maintaining the friendly smile. "You're sure right, young fella. I figured a dead croc was one hell of a lot better than a dead horse. Your pony was drinking at the edge over there, and the croc had him all lined up for a meal; I figure he might have got him too, if I hadn't got the croc first."

The boy peered uncertainly toward Hegarty, then to the backpack. "What did you shoot it with?"

Hegarty motioned to the backpack. "I've just put the gun away." He stooped, and pulled out the Colt again, and held it out toward the boy. "See, there it is."

The boy shook his head in wonder. "Jeez, I haven't seen a gun like that before. It must pack a real wallop to finish off a croc."

He certainly had the accent Hegarty had come to associate with Australians, but there was something oddly precise about the way he spoke. Matched with the confident way he held himself, it indicated a maturity beyond his years.

Hegarty pushed the gun back out of sight. "Yes it does, a real wallop. Lucky for your horse it does," he commented.

The boy scowled, thrust his hands into his pockets, and kicked at the ground. "It's not like Schon to run off like that, jeez no." He gestured to the brown countryside outside the green trees. "I was looking at a couple of dead cattle back there because I thought they belonged to my Grandad, and the next thing I know Schon had bolted." He shrugged. "Might've been a snake, y'know. I know Schon's scared of them. He got frightened by a taipan a coupla months ago; not that I blame him mind you, jeez no, those buggers would kill anything." He suddenly grinned, with a flash of white teeth, and offered an awkward gesture of gratitude. "Gee, thanks anyway, mister, I sure would hate to lose Schon like that. The crocs are real buggers. They grab cattle like that sometimes; just lie under the water off the bank, then grab 'em by the snout when they come for a drink, and pull them in and drown 'em." He shook his head. "Real buggers."

Hegarty nodded. "I damn near went for a swim. I didn't figure there'd be any crocodiles in the lagoon."

The boy made a wry expression. "Oh there's a few. We had a big wet here last summer—jeez did it rain. All the gullies between here and the Norman River flooded out, and I reckon some of the crocs came down with the flood. Now the water's soaked away, and the crocs are stuck in the lagoon." He gave a gloomy shake of his head. "Grandad's been talking about trying to shoot them out, before they take any of his cattle." He paused, and turned anxious eyes to the trees. "I s'pose Schon's okay?" he said tentatively.

"You want to go looking for your pony? We can go on my cycle."

"How'd he seem?"

"Well he got one hell of a scare, but he seemed okay."

The boy hesitated, then shrugged. "He won't go far, not Schon, not without me." He turned to the trees, and cupped his hands to his mouth. "Schon . . . Schon," he called in a high-pitched voice. "Here boy, here boy. C'mon, Schon." He put his hands down, and waited, listening, head cocked to one side.

"We can still go looking on my cycle," Hegarty offered again.

The boy's mouth set in a stubborn line. "No, Schon'll hear; he'll come back, I bet." He glanced back to Hegarty. "But thanks anyway, mister."

It seemed a matter of pride that the pony would respond to the boy's command, so Hegarty didn't push it any further.

The boy studied him with a challenging curiosity. "I haven't seen you around here before."

"Name's Hegarty, Matt Hegarty." He held out a hand and the boy took it with a firm shake. His thin frame was deceptive, there was a wiry strength in the grip. "My friends call me Matt—so you can too," added Hegarty.

"Okay, I'd like that. I'm Frank, Frank Hunter, and every-one calls me Pony." He grinned engagingly. "And you can call me Pony, because you saved Schon."

"Pony?"

"Yeah, because I love horses—because I specially love Schon." He frowned, suddenly anxious again, and once more scanned through the trees. "Even if he did run off on me."

"Right, Pony it is," agreed Hegarty. "And I love horses too."

"Mum tells me Grandad had me on a horse before I could even walk." He paused, as if assessing Hegarty again. "You sound sort of . . . different. American. Like those blokes I see on television."

Hegarty grinned. The universal village created by television. "Well you're right, Pony; I am American."

"What are you doing out here in the Gulf Country?"

"Oh just traveling around. Seeing the world as they say. Australia seemed like an interesting place to see, specially up around these parts."

They both turned to the faint jingle of harness, accompanied by the soft beat of hooves, and saw the horse glinting in the sun as it cautiously trod the brown grass, head held high, plaintively whinnying.

"There's Schon, there's Schon," cried Pony triumphantly. "See. I told you he'd come back to me, Matt; I told you." He again cupped his hands to his mouth. "Here Schon, here boy, come on, Schon."

The horse shook its head, snorting a greeting as if asking forgiveness, and Pony sprinted to meet it as it began to trot toward him. They came together like long-parted lovers, the boy running his hands caressingly over the horse's neck and head, while Schon nuzzled at his face. Then Pony took hold of the reins, and led the horse back to Hegarty. It appeared outwardly calm, but Hegarty saw it was sweating around the hindquarters, and it shied nervously at first, until Pony quickly settled it down with soothing words and hands.

"Easy, Schon, easy boy," he murmured. "This is Matt. He's a good friend; maybe after me the best friend you've got today, otherwise you'd be inside that old bugger croc's belly floating over there."

"That's a fine-looking horse you've got there, Pony," Hegarty said admiringly. "He looks around two years old."

"Coupla months more. I raised him from a foal y'know," replied Pony proudly. "Even slept with him when he was real young, and he's the best friend I've got." He fondly patted the horse's neck. "Just so long as he knows I'm the boss."

"I like to see something between a man and his horse."

"You know about horses?"

"Some."

"And about cattle?"

"You could say that. Matter of fact I'm on my way looking for a job doing just that."

"You've worked as a ringer?"

"Sure. All over."

Pony stroked at the horse's neck again, his expression doubtful. "Then I reckon you've got to be heading for Cathedral Rock Station?" he questioned hesitantly.

"Hey, you're right, Pony. I heard there was a muster going on there, and there could be work for someone like me."

"Grandad doesn't hire many people," said the boy.

Hegarty tried to keep the surprise from his face. Grandad? This was Kisek's grandson? Christ, there'd been nothing in Milhesco's brief about Kisek having a grandson, but he had the feeling Lady Luck had just planted a big juicy kiss on his cheek.

"Your grandfather's Dorf Kisek, who owns Cathedral Rock Station, Pony?"

"That's right."

"Well, I hope he can give me a job."

Pony's expression turned defensive. "I reckon we don't need any help. My Mum and aunt are pretty good with cattle—I mean real good."

Pony's mother was obviously one of Kisek's daughters. "That's what I've heard," said Hegarty. "It must be great having a mother like that. You must be pretty proud of her. But I also heard there's a lot of roundup—of mustering to be done." He pointed to the sky. "I figure I might be able to save your mother and aunt a lot of time by doing some mustering from up there."

Pony stared at the pointing finger with a puzzled expression. "Up there?"

"Sure, from the air; by helicopter."

Pony's eyes widened. "Say, you're a helicopter pilot? You can do helicopter mustering, Matt?"

"I sure can. I heard your Grandfather's got a helicopter at Cathedral Rock that isn't doing too much work."

Pony fidgeted with Schon's reins and ducked his head in an embarrassed frown. "Yeah . . . well, we don't use it much I s'pose; I reckon Grandad prefers horses."

"Pity if the helicopter's just sitting there not being used. You can muster a lot faster with a helicopter."

"Mum was supposed to learn to fly it, but—well, I reckon she's been too busy to get around to it."

"What about your father?"

Pony shrugged. "I haven't got any father; he drowned— a long time ago."

"I'm sorry."

"Doesn't matter. It was when I was very young; I don't remember him anyhow."

"Well maybe if I got the time I could give your mother a few lessons."

"Say, that'd be great, Mum'd love that," Pony exclaimed, with a sudden flare of enthusiasm. It died away just as abruptly. "But like I said, Grandad doesn't hire many people." He hesitated. "Matter of fact, none at all," he admitted.

"Maybe he'll make an exception in my case, because I can helicopter muster, and he's got a helicopter there all ready to go. And besides, I've had lots of experience, working all over the place."

"Traveling like you said?"

"Sure, all over. Argentina, Brazil, Texas—where I was working cattle. And anywhere else that seemed interesting; Canada, England, France, Germany."

It brought the sparkle back to Pony's face. "Gee Matt, I reckon that'd be just terrific. I want to do that one day. I mean I love living here, but I'd love to see other places too."

"Then you should; it'd do you no end of good. But maybe me traveling around'll persuade your grandfather to hire me. And I figure you and I could have ourselves a great time flying around Cathedral Rock, Pony."

Pony was enthralled. "Wow, that'd really be something. You'd take me up with you, Matt, honest? You really would?"

"Sure, why not. I figure we'd make a good team."

This was the sort of unexpected lucky break he could only

have dreamed of, and he was determined to milk it for all it
was worth. It was a stroke of good fortune that the boy was
already indebted to him for saving the horse, and if he could
manipulate the kid into somehow influencing Kisek, then his
chances of being hired would improve enormously. But he was
wary of letting overeagerness push it too hard, and he tried to
let Pony set the pace.

The boy had fallen contemplatively silent, gazing across
the lagoon to where birds had alighted on the dead crocodile,
tentatively pecking at the exposed belly, while others hovered
expectantly overhead.

"Flying around in a helicopter would be really something," Pony finally breathed, the longing words coming out
like pent-up air.

"You might even fly it yourself one day," Hegarty
shrewdly encouraged.

"Jeez, you really think so, Matt?"

"Sure, why not? When you're older, of course; but you
could watch me, see how it's done. You'd be sort of preparing
yourself. What make of helicopter is it?"

"It's a Bell, a real beauty, Matt. Jeez, I've never even seen
it fly, y'know. I was at school when it came." He appeared
suddenly too excited to stand still, jigging around Schon until
the horse threw its head back in protest. "Jeez. Jeez. Wait'll I
tell the kids at school."

Hegarty held up a warning hand. "Hey, hey, hold it right
there, Pony, hold it boy; I'm not working for your grandfather
yet—and from all you tell me, I'm a long way from it."

It immediately dampened the boy's enthusiasm. "Yeah,
you're right, Matt," he muttered. He scowled, and morosely
kicked some loose twigs into the water. "Grandad can be
pretty tough," he added.

Hegarty let it sit. He figured it was important that any
suggestion of help should come from Pony. "Well I might get
lucky," he said casually. "But it seems kind of like it was meant,
you and me meeting here like this, Pony; me saving Schon like
that. You seem a pretty bright kid to me; flying together would
have been fun."

Pony silently stroked at Schon's nose for a moment.

"Maybe . . . maybe I could talk to Grandad about you," he offered hesitantly.

"Would you do that for me?"

"I don't see why not. Yeah, why not?" he said more boldly. "Grandad and I get on pretty well; and I reckon me speaking to him about you would mean something—a lot, I reckon, specially with you being a helicopter mustering pilot."

Hegarty grinned, and slapped the boy on the shoulder. "That'd be great, Pony; I'd really appreciate it."

"And I reckon I could tell him how you saved Schon. That'd mean something."

"It was just lucky I happened to be here."

"Yeah, but you still saved him, Matt," insisted Pony.

Hegarty gently patted the horse's neck. He was in, instinct told him he was in. "From what I can see Schon was sure worth saving. Good friends are too hard to come by to risk losing one. I like his name too, even if I don't know what it means."

"Grandad gave it to him. It's German, and it means beautiful."

"Then he's well named."

"Grandad came from Germany, oh, long, long ago. There was a big war over there, and he just wanted to get away when it was over, so he came out to Australia."

"And now he's a big cattleman, eh?"

"I reckon so."

He turned abruptly to the horse, as if coming to a decision, put his foot in the stirrup, and swung easily into the saddle. Then he grinned down at Hegarty and pointed to the bike.

"That's a Kawasaki, isn't it?"

"That's right."

"I know about them; a bloke in Normanton's got one. At first I thought you was him when I saw you headed toward the lagoon. You think you can make it go slow enough to ride along with me?" He gestured to the east. "The Cathedral Rock homestead is only a coupla miles away."

"I think I can do that, Pony."

The boy tugged on the reins, and backed Schon away. "Just let me get a little bit away, so Schon doesn't take fright when you start it up. And I'll talk to Grandad, just like I said, Matt. Bet he'll take you on—I'll just bet he does." He wheeled the horse away and waved to Matt as he broke into a trot. "I reckon I like you, Matt," he called back. "You and me are going to be friends. You'll see; after Schon you'll be my best friend."

Hegarty merely grinned and waved back, then went across to the bike. He straddled the seat, pumped the kick-starter, and the motor burbled into throaty life. He gently eased open the throttle and weaved slowly in Schon's tracks. Milhesco should have known about the boy, it wasn't like him to miss out on a detail like that; but it would be invaluable if Pony were the means of Kisek hiring him. There was a refreshing likability about the kid that was hard to resist, and he'd have to watch that if he got the job; it could be awkward, even dangerous, if he let the boy get too close. But he'd be crazy not to use the boy as a way of manipulating Kisek.

It was difficult to match the pace of the motorcycle to the horse, especially as Pony felt the need to demonstrate his skill with Schon, suddenly dashing off to round up a stray steer, or pirouetting the horse around one of the six-foot-high cone-shaped ant hills to show off some fancy footwork while the boy proudly shouted for attention. At times Hegarty was forced to stop, straddling the bike while he watched, restraining his impatience as he made appropriate gestures of admiration. Not that his response was completely contrived; the boy was an excellent horseman.

So the sun was low to the horizon when they finally breasted a rocky outcrop, and the collection of buildings that was Cathedral Rock Station lay ahead. Even from a distance it was apparent to Hegarty that the main house was Kisek's proclamation to the world of his success as a cattleman. The effect was dramatized by the setting of the house, a towering background of weathered, rust-colored rock, with the highest reach tapering to a needle point in the shape of a soaring church spire that dominated the surrounding flat landscape. And the closer he got the more impressive it all became, which was a contradiction if Snowy Cutmore's observation of no one ever being invited to the place was correct. But then maybe that was the behavior pattern he should expect from a man with a hellish secret to hide.

A wide dirt road led to the house, winding like a snake around a pattern of ant hills. The house was long, low, and glistening white, surrounded on all sides by the usual wide, sun-protecting veranda, and set amid a profusion of green trees. There was a scattering of smaller outbuildings, and circular water storage tanks, with their attendant skeletal structure of windmills, the fan blades on top like giant tropical blooms, turning listlessly in the light breeze. To the right, separated from the buildings, was a horse corral, and beyond that several people working cattle in a fretwork of stockyards. Pony reined in beside him, and pointed to the spire of rock.

"See that, Matt?" he said. "That's why Grandad called this place Cathedral Rock. He said it reminded him of a big church back in the town where he was born in Germany."

"What town was that?" asked Hegarty casually.

"I don't know; he's never told me." He stood up in the stirrups, and waved to a figure standing in front of the house. "There he is, that's Grandad now."

He urged Schon into a gallop, leaving Hegarty to wend slowly after him through a swirl of gritty dust. He took his time, deliberately holding back to allow Pony plenty of time to lay some groundwork with Kisek.

When he reached the house Schon was already tethered to a railing, with Pony talking animatedly to a man he presumed was Kisek. He eased the bike into the shade of a tree and waited there a moment. So this was Kisek. Milhesco was right: if Kisek was Leiman, then he bore no resemblance to the old photographs he'd been shown; time and age had wrought changes that made recognition impossible. He was a big man, which at least tallied with the description, around Hegarty's own height of a few inches over six feet, and with presence, someone you would immediately notice in a crowded room. Perhaps close to seventy, with the girth and coloring of the legendary Santa Claus: white beard, thick white hair, ruddy complexion of a man constantly exposed to the sun; but there was nothing benign about the intense, deepset eyes beneath the shaggy white brows. There was a sense of great strength in his bulk, like a trained wrestler, the brown muscular arms thickly grassed with white hair. He wore a red checked shirt, blue dungarees daubed with dust, and heavy stock boots. He held a wide-brimmed stockman's hat in one craggy hand, raising small puffs of dust as he beat it against the side of his leg.

Hegarty leaned the bike against the tree, fixed a friendly smile on his face, and strolled across to join them; Kisek's eyes watched his approach with the unswerving stare of a suspicious guard dog. Pony seized him by the arm, and eagerly shepherded him toward Kisek. "This is my Grandad, Matt," he said, "And Grandad, this is Matt, Matt Hegarty."

Then he stood back, eyes anxiously darting from one man to the other. "I told him, Matt, all of it."

"Pleased to meet you, Mr. Kisek," said Hegarty cordially. He made as if to extend his hand, but stopped when he saw no sign of any answering response. For a moment he wondered if Kisek was going to answer him at all, but he matched the man's disconcerting scrutiny with a steady gaze of his own. "I guess Pony hasn't had the chance to really tell you all about me yet," he said.

Kisek nodded slowly. "Much the boy has been trying to tell me; too much in such a short time."

He had a deep gritty German-accented voice, and spoke in overly precise English that reminded Hegarty of Pony's manner of speaking. He placed an arm fondly about Pony's shoulders, and for the first time there was a faint suggestion of a smile. "You seem to have been, ah . . . exciting his imagination, Mr. Hegarty," he said drily, "and all his words are running together without making much sense."

"Hey, Grandad, I told you about what happened to Schon, about the big croc in the lagoon, and how Matt killed it, and about Matt being a helicopter mustering pilot—all of it I reckon."

"Ja, ja, and not once stopping for breath," declared Kisek impatiently. "So I'm not knowing if perhaps the crocodile was the helicopter pilot."

"Jeez, c'mon, Grandad," said Pony indignantly.

Kisek motioned to Hegarty with his hat. "Perhaps it might be wiser if we hear it all from Mr. Hegarty, ja?" It came out like a curt order, his head cocked mockingly to one side, piercing eyes never deviating.

Hegarty shrugged assent, then launched into an explanation of how he'd been at the lagoon, and shot the crocodile as it was about to attack Schon. Also, that he was an American helicopter mustering pilot, looking for work. He'd heard there was a muster on at Cathedral Rock, and that there was a helicopter, but no pilot. So he'd come out from Normanton, hoping for a job. Through all this Pony was unable to constrain himself, enthusiastically peppering Hegarty's story with interjections of corroboration.

"Well isn't that just what I was telling you, Grandad?" asked Pony, as soon as Hegarty had finished. "Don't you reckon Matt'd be just great around Cathedral Rock. Terrific I reckon. We never got around to using the helicopter, and it'd be great if Matt could helicopter muster for us, just great. What d'you say, Grandad?"

"Like I said, I've worked as a ringer too, Mr. Kisek," added Hegarty. "All over—Texas, South America—as well as helicopter mustering.".

"Matt's been everywhere," interjected Pony, "just everywhere, all around the world." He shook Kisek's arm. "It's better than the helicopter just sitting over there in the shed, and never getting off the ground."

"Hush, boy, hush," commanded Kisek sternly. He pointed to Schon. "A horseman shouldn't be allowing his horse to stand around like that. Unsaddling him you should be, and turning him out."

Pony hesitated, threw a guilty look toward the horse, then looked back to Kisek. "It's just that I . . .," he began, but Kisek cut him off with a curt motion of his hand.

"I'll be the one talking to Mr. Hegarty. You go and tend to Schon."

Rebellion flushed momentarily into Pony's face, then he kicked disconsolately at the ground and backed off toward the horse. "Schon'd be dead if it wasn't for Matt," he muttered.

"I'll be deciding about Mr. Hegarty," grunted Kisek.

"I still bet Matt'd be great around Cathedral Rock," persisted the boy. "Jeez, it's just crazy having that helicopter sitting there going rusty, 'cause I reckon that's all it's doing."

Kisek pointed threateningly toward the horse. "Go," he ordered. "Don't be disobeying me."

Pony shrugged, grimaced at Hegarty, then turned and slunk away toward Schon. Kisek waited until he had untethered the horse and led it away toward the corral, then he redirected his scowl at Hegarty.

"So you are liking to shoot, eh Mr. Hegarty?" he asked harshly.

Hegarty shrugged. "Sometimes it's useful to have a gun—specially if there's crocodiles around."

"You are always carrying a gun? Maybe you like to shoot more than crocodiles?"

The questions were fired in a provocative manner, as if trying to needle him, but Hegarty refused the bait.

"I just like it for protection. The world can sometimes be a dangerous place if you're traveling around a lot like I do."

Kisek merely grunted. "You are using the boy to get yourself a job," he sneered. "Not coming here like a man, but creeping in the boy's shadow."

Hegarty figured it'd be a bad mistake to let that jibe go by; maybe it wasn't good tactics to back away from a man like Kisek.

"I'm not using the boy for anything," he stated coldly. "I didn't set it up for his horse to be drinking at the lagoon, or for the crocodile to try and kill it. I just happened to be there, the same as Pony. I figure I'm as good a helicopter mustering pilot as you'll find around."

"And you are knowing cattle, ja?"

"Like I said before, I've worked all over . . . as well as helicopter mustering."

"They're saying old Dorf Kisek's crazy, eh; buying himself a helicopter and not using it? Is that what you're hearing?"

"All I heard was that there's a helicopter here waiting to be used," lied Hegarty.

Kisek snorted, and made a derisory gesture with his hat. "Let them think what they like. Dorf Kisek does things his own way—that's why I'm being so successful. I don't need to hire people; I'm never hiring people."

Hegarty felt a surge of anxiety that the chance was slipping away from him. "Well I hear you've got one hell of a big spread here for one man," he pointed out.

Kisek very deliberately placed his hat on his head, then

made a slow sweep of the horizon with his hand. "As far as the eye is seeing; over a thousand square miles."

"That's a lot of mustering area."

"Two strong daughters I've got; better than men with cattle. And I've got some good black ringers—good workers, and giving me no trouble."

Hegarty frowned. The sonofabitch was proving every bit as difficult as he'd been led to believe. "You'd cut your mustering time to nothing using the helicopter," he said. "And I don't figure on sticking around for long. Maybe I could give some flying lessons to your daughter."

Hegarty merely threw it in as extra bait, but he saw at once the suggestion made an impact. Kisek thoughtfully pawed at his beard. "You've been hearing about Pony's mother's plan to fly it?"

"Pony told me."

"She was the one so anxious to buy it, always pushing me, and now she's not finding the time to learn; so it just sits there."

"There must be some good pilots around?"

"None that I'm trusting," growled Kisek.

Hegarty quickly built on the idea. "Maybe after the muster I could give her some lessons," he offered. "At least get her started."

For the first time there was a hint of indecision in Kisek's face, the piercing eyes taking on a strange glaze, as if trying to camouflage his thoughts. "I'm not liking strangers around Cathedral Rock," he muttered. It was more like a muffled whisper to himself than something said to Hegarty.

"I guess we're all strangers in the beginning, Mr. Kisek," murmured Hegarty. He held himself in tight, gently nudging; he could see the first glimmer that it was going to happen: Kisek would hire him. The man was clearly fond of Pony, anxious to please the boy, and the combination of an offer to give flying lessons to his daughter was obviously a strong temptation.

"I'm only having your word you can helicopter muster," he muttered.

"It'd be a stupid claim to make if it wasn't true. I don't aim to kill myself getting into a machine I can't fly."

The big man tugged at his hat, his face a portrait of conflicting emotions. "My grandson seems to be liking you very much, ja?"

"I like him too. He's a fine boy."

"Ja, and loving Cathedral Rock. One day it will all be his."

He was stalling, and Hegarty gambled on pushing it hard. "What about the job, Mr. Kisek?" he asked bluntly.

Kisek hesitated one last time, "Well . . . all right. But for Pony you understand, and not for long—just this muster. We'll see how it is working out for the first few days. If you're not proving yourself, than you're out, whether Pony is approving or not."

"Don't worry, I'll prove myself, Mr. Kisek," said Hegarty confidently. He fought to keep the tremendous elation from showing in his face. He was in; the gamble had worked, the mustering stint with Bobo Walters in Texas had paid off. Reine would be delighted. And Jules. He tried to dampen his jubilation with the realization that this was only the first step.

"I meant what I said about giving your daughter flying lessons, Mr. Kisek," he added. "Then you won't need to be hiring anyone in the future."

Kisek nodded approval. "Ja, that's being a very good idea." Then he jabbed a gnarled finger at Hegarty. "But I'm expecting more than flying from you, Hegarty. Mustering will not be starting for, oh, a few days, and I'll be wanting other work that needs to be done around the place."

He paused to gauge Hegarty's reaction, eyes intently on his face. Maybe it was a test; maybe he already regretted his decision and wanted to see if a pilot would indignantly refuse other work.

Hegarty shrugged. "That's okay; I'm easy," he agreed. "I just want to earn myself a stake before I push on again."

"Forty dollars a day, and your keep, when you're working around the place. Three hundred dollars a day and your keep when you are flying," said Kisek.

The offer was aggressively put, and deliberately low, as if again challenging him to decline, but Hegarty grinned acceptance. "Suits me. I figure there's not too many options around here for a pilot without a helicopter."

"Then you can start now?"

"Sure, why not. I guess the first thing I'd better do is take a look at the helicopter. Pony tells me it's a Bell."

"That's right. I'm expecting you'll want to test it out."

Hegarty glanced toward the setting sun. "I'd say that's something for first thing in the morning; it's going to be dark soon."

"As you wish." Kisek pointed to one of the large outbuildings. "Over there is where it's kept. I'm not knowing anything about the machine, so you won't be needing me for the time being. There's a room beside where the helicopter is kept. You can stay there."

"Suits me fine. What about meals?"

"There's being no fancy cooking here."

"I've still got to eat."

The old man cleared his throat harshly, spat forcefully to the ground, and squinted to an orange-tinted sky, where the sun balanced like a giant red bauble on the horizon. "I'm thinking Pony would maybe like it if you ate with us tonight," he muttered. He turned abruptly on his heels, and strode toward the house. "In the house, at eight o'clock," he flung back over his shoulder.

The invitation was surly, Hegarty suspected, because the man was disturbed at breaking his own rules. "Thanks, I appreciate that," he accepted.

Kisek was already halfway to the house, and gave no indication he'd heard. Hegarty waited until the door closed behind the German, then shrugged it off, went back to the Kawasaki, and wheeled it across to the shed. Kisek could be as much of an unpleasant sonofabitch as he liked, nothing could spoil the relish he felt at being in at Cathedral Rock. And if Kisek was actually Leiman, he'd make certain the bastard had just made the worst decision of his life.

He leaned the bike against the wall, and examined the helicopter. The time in Texas had been well planned; it was a Bell 47, identical to the one Bobo Walters had taught him with. It was like an overgrown insect, the glassed-in cockpit resembling a huge, voracious head with a spindly tail attached. It was an excellent workhorse for cattle herding, zippy, and highly maneuverable. Maybe he'd take Pony up with him tomorrow morning as a guide; it was already forming in his mind to make it an opportunity to see if Jules was safely located. He stood back and ran a critical eye along the fuselage. Christ, it was near to brand new. When Milhesco had first told him about the helicopter it had sounded like the simplest means to use if they decided to take Kisek out, but he could see now it was much too small, with limited range; it wouldn't work even if they brought the ship further into the Gulf. Better to let the plan stand as it was, for he was sure Jules wouldn't agree to taking unnecessary risks.

He checked around to make sure there was ample fuel, then went to the small room attached to the shed. He paused before opening the door as two figures strolled past heading toward the house. They were too distant to hear voices, and the quickening dusk made it difficult to distinguish features, but there was no mistaking the female outlines. They didn't see him, and he kept silent as they passed, then went inside pondering whether one of them was Pony's mother. He knew Kisek was widowed, so it obviously couldn't be his wife. Doubtless he'd find out in time.

It was a pleasant room, clearly little used, and much more than he'd expected for a hired hand. Bare, stained floor boards, with a few bright-colored rugs, single bed, closet, a cupboard with drawers, plus a small table and two chairs in matching dark-stained wood. There was a nicely executed painting of Cathedral Rock on the wall. Another door at the rear led to a tiny bathroom, complete with shower and toilet. It had the feel of a woman's touch. He'd been prepared to accept whatever he got in a way of accommodation, but this wasn't bad—not bad at all. Yet, in spite of the newness there was a film of dust over everything, so Christ knows when it had been last used, if ever.

He dropped the backpack to the floor, took out the Colt, and balanced it in his hand. It had been bloody essential for the emergency with the crocodile, but if he played his hand right at Cathedral Rock maybe it wouldn't be needed again. He wrapped it carefully in a small hand towel, then placed it in the bottom drawer of the cupboard. There were coffee facilities, so he quickly made himself a cup, then took out the old photograph of Leiman given him by Milhesco, laid it on the table, and carefully studied it. The print was frayed at the edges, and yellowing with age, but the image of the burly, uniformed young man with the grim expression was still clear enough. It told him absolutely nothing. There was no linking identification to tell him that the elderly, white-haired son-of-a-bitch who'd just hired him was the same man. He ran his fingers through his hair; could they possibly be wrong? Five years of meticulous work had gone into finally tracking this bastard down, and yet . . .? He had to reinforce himself with some of Reine's unshakable confidence, make himself utterly believe, but he hoped to Christ Brandt really did have Leiman's fingerprints.

Staring at the photograph did nothing to alleviate his doubts, so he put it away, took out his map of the area, and spread it out on the table. It didn't take him long to pinpoint the place where Jules was supposed to be located. That problem he'd resolve tomorrow.

He folded the map, leaned back in the chair, and slowly sipped his coffee, watching through the small window as the fast-disappearing sun flooded the landscape with the most vivid shades of red he'd ever seen. He sensed a strange empathy with this country, the vastness, the silence, combined with a raw beauty he found compelling. He might appreciate it, but it could never be more than incidental to what he was there for.

Chapter 3

He didn't know whether to knock, but no one seemed to be around, so he let himself quietly into the house. He was taken aback by the interior. The outside of the house looked impressive enough, and it was Australian in character; but to step inside was like entering an eighteenth-century European drawing room. The floor was laid out in a patterned tile mosaic, with rugs he guessed to be of Indian or Persian origin. The accompanying furniture was ornately carved chests of drawers and small tables in beautifully figured, highly polished woods, with matching chairs and sofas covered in rich plum velvet, standing on elaborately carved cabriole legs. Around the walls were gilt-framed paintings of all sizes, from small portraits to large landscapes, all in the old European tradition. A wide, intricately-carved cornicework formed the juncture where walls and ceiling met, and heavy drapes at the windows were tastefully coordinated with the plum furniture. On a small table to his left, exquisite ebony chess pieces were set out in position for play. A magnificent decorative antique piano that looked as if it could have come from some European palace sat in an alcove to his right. Overhead an elegant crystal chandelier presided over the room. He was amazed. He had the feeling of having wandered onto an extravagant film set for a movie about a French king. It was pleasantly cool after the outside heat, so there was obviously some form of air conditioning.

He just stood and gaped for a moment. For all its grandeur it had the feel of a museum: unlived in, untouched by human warmth. Double doors decoratively enscribed in white and gold scrolls were set into the far wall. One of them suddenly opened, and a young woman stepped into the room. She was perhaps twenty-five, with long fair hair and a tanned, thin face dominated by large, inquisitive blue eyes. In almost bizarre comparison to the room her garb of black-and-white checked shirt, jeans, and riding boots made her look like a time-traveler back to the eighteenth century. He guessed he probably looked the same.

She didn't say anything, closed the door softly behind her, all the while keeping her eyes focused on him in a way that reminded him of Kisek; then she sauntered across the room, hips swinging like a model on a runway. She stopped close in front of him, pouted her sullen mouth, then slowly circled him as if inspecting a prize bull.

"Hi," he said awkwardly, to break the silence. "Name's Hegarty, Matt Hegarty."

She didn't answer, just softly hummed a tune as she kept circling; then she halted in front of him again. She was tall, not as tall as he, but she compensated with arrogance.

"I know," she murmured. "I'm still getting over the shock of my father actually hiring someone, especially someone like you. Welcome to the museum, Hegarty. I've been hearing all about you. You look like a real prize stud to me."

He figured she wasn't old enough to be Pony's mother. He dipped his head, and grinned. "Well thank you, ma'am, I always aim to please, but I don't figure that's what your father hired me for. I'd say he wants me working cattle, not his daughter."

She tapped him gently on the chest with a long finger. "Well we'll see what you're hired for, Hegarty—we'll see."

That precise manner of speaking seemed to run right through the family. She flicked her hair back over her shoulder with a quick motion of her hand. He could feel the heat coming off her like sun-roasted earth, then she smiled, turned away, and with the same exaggerated rolling of her hips walked back toward the door. She paused and beckoned to him.

"Come on in to dinner, Hegarty—if you're up to risking being the main course."

Then she was gone. He grinned, shook his head, and walked slowly across to the door, heels rapping sharply on the tiled floor. He'd met women like that before, all come-on and sexual innuendo, but who froze if you took up the challenge. He didn't know if she fitted into that category, but he'd see. He was prepared to use anyone who could give him information about Kisek, the way he'd used Pony.

The dining room matched the other room in style, with heavy drapes at the window, high-backed maroon-colored chairs set around a magnificent rosewood table all laid out for a meal. An ornamental overhead lamp threw glistening reflections off a silver candelabra in the center of the table. In such an atmosphere he half expected Kisek to be decked out in a dinner jacket, but the four people seated around the table looked equally incongruous in their Gulf Country cattle clothes. They all turned in unison to look as he entered, Kisek at the head of the table, the girl Matt had just met to his right, Pony to his left, and beside him a woman as dark as the others were fair, but with her hair close-cropped. She was older than the other girl, perhaps in her early thirties, tanned nut-brown with a sprinkling of freckles across her cheeks, brown eyes crinkled from long hours squinting at the bright Gulf Country sun. Not beautiful, but strikingly attractive. She wore a black tank top like Pony, with the difference that she filled it out with lovely curves. If this was the other daughter, and Pony's mother, then she must be as much like her mother as her sister seemed to be like Kisek. A cliche, "earth woman," slid into his mind, but that was the effect she had on him. He couldn't help staring at her, and she knew it, looking away with a faint smile. There were several vacant chairs, the closest to him being at the opposite end of the table from Kisek.

"Sit down, Hegarty, sit down," growled Kisek impatiently.

"Thanks," he said, and seated himself.

"How's it going, Matt, are you all settled in?" chirped up Pony.

"Yes, everything's working out fine, thanks Pony. I figure my room's going to be very comfortable."

"It should be, it's hardly been over used," drily observed the fair girl. Kisek silenced her with an irritable wave of his hand.

"This is being Ingrid, my youngest daughter," he muttered.

Hegarty inclined his head. "Yes, we've just met," he said, with an edge of irony.

She gave a sly smile, but said nothing.

Kisek gestured to the other woman. "And this is Anna, my eldest daughter, and Pony's mother."

"Welcome to Cathedral Rock, Mr. Hegarty," she said warmly, with that same precise manner of speech. She picked up a nearby bottle of white wine and raised it toward Hegarty. "Would you like some wine, Mr. Hegarty?"

Hegarty nodded, and held out his glass to her.

"Matt," interrupted Pony. "He likes all his friends to call him Matt."

She lifted her eyebrows in the act of pouring, and Hegarty gave a smile of approval.

"Matt it is then," she said. She paused until his glass was filled, then sat the bottle back on the table. "Pony told me all about you saving Schon from the crocodile, and I want to thank you, too. We'd both hate to have lost Schon, especially like that."

"Fair dinkum, the croc was a real big bugger, wasn't it, Matt?" said Pony. "The biggest bugger croc I've seen in a long time."

"Do you have to use that language?" frowned her mother.

"He's picking it up from the black ringers," scowled Kisek. "Riding out with them is a good way to learn, but he doesn't have to be picking up their talk." He motioned with his glass to Pony. "You should be learning how to act like a boss, Pony. Ja, like a boss."

"Well, he *was* a big croc," insisted Pony. "Wasn't he, Matt?"

"He sure was, Pony," Hegarty said with a grin. "I don't figure Schon would have had much chance if the croc had got hold of him."

"Then I'm just glad you happened to be there," said Anna.

"And I'm just glad you happen to be *here*," added Ingrid mockingly.

The inference was so obvious that Hegarty shifted awkwardly on his chair, and sampled the white wine to cover his discomfort. It was delicious, and chilled just the way he liked it.

"What you have to watch out for around the Gulf Country is the human crocodiles," Ingrid added. She gave a brittle laugh, and snapped her fingers in the air. "Grab you like that. Take an arm or a leg before you know it." Her gaze shifted to Anna. "Isn't that right, Anna?" There was an underlying emphasis close to spite, and Hegarty had the feeling the sisters were unalike in more ways than appearance.

"I'm sure Matt can handle any sort of crocodile," said Anna.

"You bet," enthused Pony, "and he's going to teach you to fly the helicopter, Mum."

Anna cast surprised eyes from Hegarty to her father. "Is he now?"

"Maybe he can show me too," put in Ingrid. "What do you say, Hegarty?"

"We're only needing one pilot for now," said Kisek curtly.

"And naturally it's Anna," snapped Ingrid.

Kisek ignored her and offered Anna an apologetic shrug. "I was going to be talking to you about it later. I thought you'd be pleased. Perhaps after the muster."

"I am pleased; I think it's a great idea," said Anna. She turned with a regretful smile to Hegarty. "I just haven't had the time to get around to learning. But with you here Matt, I think it's a fine idea."

"And I'm going to fly too, aren't I Matt," added Pony. "You promised you'd take me up with you."

Hegarty could feel Kisek's jaundiced gaze on him, but he kept his gaze directed at Pony. Kisek had already accused him of manipulating the boy, and he didn't want to add to his suspicions. But Pony could be an asset to him in the helicopter.

"We'll see about that," said Anna quickly.

"But Matt promised," protested Pony.

"Well sure I did, but I guess it's up to your mother," said Hegarty.

"Hey, that's a backdown, Matt," complained the boy.

Hegarty looked to Anna for help. "I did say I'd take him—if it's okay with you." He could understand her reluctance. He suspected she'd want to know more about his ability before she committed Pony to flying with him.

She glanced tentatively from her son to her father, but Kisek merely glowered over his wine.

"I thought you'd want to try out the helicopter first?" she suggested.

"That's what I'm intending first thing tomorrow morning. There shouldn't be any problems; it's scarcely been used."

"Cathedral Rock's most expensive ornament," sneered Ingrid.

"Why don't we come and watch. Then I'll see about Pony," said Anna.

"Jeez," muttered Pony disgustedly.

"Okay. I figure I'll be ready to fly around eight o'clock." Matt smiled. "Don't worry, I know what I'm doing."

"I'm sure you do," said Anna.

"You're jealous I might learn to fly before you," growled Pony.

"Quiet your mouth, boy," interjected Kisek.

"That's a stupid thing to say," added his mother sharply.

Pony folded his arms over the table and lapsed into sullen silence.

The door behind Kisek partially opened, and an elderly black woman leaned through the opening. She wasn't a full-blooded black, but her racial features were still apparent in her thin face. Her gray hair was neatly pulled back in a bun. A simple white dress accentuated the darkness of her skin.

"You ready for dinner, Mr. Kisek?" she asked.

Kisek hesitated and glanced at the door behind Hegarty. "Just one moment, Zara." He looked about the table. "Anyone know if Carl is coming into dinner?"

"I haven't seen him, Mr. Kisek," said Zara.

"God, whoever does see Carl?" grunted Ingrid.

Hegarty didn't look up from his wine. Who the hell was Carl? Had Milhesco missed out on someone else at Cathedral Rock besides Pony?

"I saw him over by the corral about an hour ago," murmured Anna.

"I wish someone'd tell me," said Zara in exasperation.

"You'd better serve, Zara," said Anna.

Zara gave a disdainful sniff and disappeared behind the door.

"Carl should let Zara know," said Anna.

"He's old—getting forgetful," muttered Kisek.

"You know, I don't ever remember when Carl wasn't old," declared Ingrid. "I think someone like Carl was born old; all the time when we were growing up, he never seemed any different. He gives me the creeps; always did."

"You don't have any feeling for loyalty," rasped Kisek. "In the old days I couldn't have started Cathedral Rock without him."

"You'll be apologizing for Carl until the day you die, Dad," retorted Ingrid.

"I'm owing him something—you are all owing him something."

They all fell suddenly quiet, their eyes directed to a point behind Hegarty. He half turned in his chair as a gaunt figure shuffled past him and eased carefully into the seat beside Anna. The man was older than Kisek, maybe once had been as tall before age bent his spine. He moved like someone for whom the vigor of life had gone, now shriveled and merely seeing out his time. Unlike the others, his thin body was clad in an immaculately pressed white shirt and black trousers.

But it was his face that made a lasting impression. Hegarty had seen burn victims, and this man had been severely burned about the face, perhaps a long time ago. He'd been left with flat, blotchy skin, so that the puffy eyes, thin mouth, and misshapen nose were like features painted on parchment. He was bald, with white wisps of hair about his large ears. It was impossible to gauge his age; he could have been anywhere between sixty and eighty.

"G'day, Carl," piped Pony.

Carl's mouth moved in a slight smile, and he nodded to the boy. "Pony," he muttered. He glanced slowly about the table, speaking in turn to everyone, "Anna . . . Dorf . . . Ingrid," until his pale eyes finally came to rest on Hegarty. His lips scarcely moved when he spoke, the voice hoarse, as if straining with difficulty from his throat, and accented like Kisek's.

"This is Matt Hegarty, Carl," said Kisek. "He's going to be doing some helicopter mustering for us."

"Ah, at last; the helicopter," murmured Carl.

Hegarty extended his hand, and Carl responded with a limp shake. He kept his grip light; the bones of the man's hand protruded sharply through the skin as if they might snap under pressure.

"Carl Beaunig," he said, inclining his head. Hegarty had the impression he would have clicked his heels under the table if it were possible.

"Matt's from Texas," boasted Pony. "And from all over the world as well, aren't you, Matt?"

"I travel around," Hegarty shrugged.

"Carl is keeper of the museum, aren't you, Carl?" said Ingrid. "And something of a museum piece himself. Been around here longer than me, longer than Anna. Forever, eh Carl?"

"That's enough, Ingrid," snapped Kisek. He paused and looked at Hegarty. "Carl and I, we're both coming out from Germany together after the war," he explained. "Carl is helping me . . . ," he raised his arms and gestured to the ceiling, "build all this. Cathedral Rock. Without Carl perhaps I would not have done it."

Beaunig merely shrugged, offered a bleak smile, and poured himself a glass of wine. His hand trembled, spilling the wine about the table, but he ignored it and no one else took any notice.

The door behind Kisek thumped open, and Zara bustled into the room, carrying a silver tray loaded with plates of steaming food. She put the tray down on the nearby buffet, then circled the table, placing a meal in turn in front of everyone, all the time muttering indistinguishable words under her breath. Anna glanced at Hegarty with a wry smile.

"Thank you, Zara," she said, with exaggerated appreciation.

Zara didn't answer, merely picked up the tray and exited in the same manner, banging the door behind her.

"Zara's a woman of few words," apologized Anna, "but she's been cooking for us for a long time."

"Everything around here is forever," put in Ingrid. "You're like a breath of fresh air through the museum, Hegarty." She picked up her cutlery and turned over the food with distaste. It was typical of what Hegarty had seen in the country so far: grilled steak, with three or four vegetables. "Maybe one day we'll get a cook who can do something different."

"There's being nothing wrong with Zara," growled Kisek. "Perhaps one day you'll have to do the cooking yourself."

"You can count me out on that one," declared Ingrid sharply. "That'll be up to Anna; she's more the hausfrau type."

"I'm no cook," countered Anna. "My job's handling cattle, not cooking them. You'd all starve if I was ever expected to play chef."

"Just let's get on with dinner," Kisek interrupted brusquely. "Zara isn't going anywhere right now."

The rebuff had the desired effect. For a time there was only the clink of cutlery, the soft sounds of chewing, and polite inquiries about Hegarty's trip from Cairns on the Kawasaki. He took the opportunity to observe them all. Ingrid was prickly as a cactus, and all come-on, but Anna had no need to work at it; he'd never seen a woman so naturally and unself-consciously sensuous. He couldn't believe a kid as bright as Pony wasn't aware of the undercurrent of tension between his mother and Ingrid. Maybe he could make the conflict work for him. The elderly Carl was an enigma; he'd obviously been here as long as Kisek, yet Milhesco had failed to pick it up. As he had Pony. Carl took no part in the conversation, head down over his meal, mouth moving with the chomping rhythm of the aged, isolating himself from his surroundings.

Having refreshed his mind with the old photograph of Leiman before dinner, Matt now took the chance to study Kisek more closely, but identification was still impossible; the picture would be useless in court as proof of identity. He just had to find something else. Kisek's paranoia about strangers could be a starting point, it had the feel of a man still afraid, still hiding, even after forty years of safety.

He tried to involve himself more in the conversation. "You've got quite a house here, Mr. Kisek," he flattered. "My God, it's something of a surprise in country like this when you walk through the door, and . . ." He glanced around. "I guess it's like stepping into one of those stately old homes in England."

"Or Germany," suggested Kisek sourly.

"Sure, Germany, or anywhere else in Europe, I guess. But it's one hell of a surprise out here."

"Oh, you're taken with our museum," said Ingrid blithely. "Carl keeps it spotless. We don't charge admission, but you should feel privileged to see it, just as long as you don't have to live in it."

"Just because one is living in a harsh country there is no reason to live like a savage," said Kisek. "It wasn't always like this. First I'm living in what you call a shack, while Carl and I are starting up this place. Ja, a shack. And out chasing wild steers."

Anna turned to Hegarty. "Dad never went back to Europe, even for a visit. I suppose he's created his own piece of Europe out here."

"Only bad memories I have of Europe," muttered Kisek. "Bad memories. This is my home, and this is the way I'm liking it."

There was an inference that those who didn't agree could just leave, and Hegarty decided to abandon the subject.

"You're originally from Texas, Matt?" asked Anna.

"No, I was born in California. Just a college kid who got the wanderlust a long time ago."

"Tell them about all the places you've been, Matt," urged Pony. "Go on, tell them."

"You've been specializing in stud farms, I'll bet," slyly insinuated Ingrid.

He smiled the comment away, pushed his empty plate aside, and patted at his mouth with a napkin. She was like a bitch in heat.

"You told me you worked cattle in Argentina, ja?" queried Kisek.

"Sure, but cattle are cattle. Argentina, Brazil, Honduras."

"What about those other places you told me about?" prodded Pony. "Y'know, Matt, those places like Paris and London."

"Well they were great. But there's not too many cattle around Picadilly Circus."

"What did you do there?" asked Ingrid.

"Anything I could get. I drove a taxi in London for a time; worked on the roads in France, things like that."

He had the feeling he was being subtly grilled. If Kisek was Leiman, it was going to take time to figure out if his daughters knew. Kisek wasn't asking many of the questions, but he was listening attentively to the answers. Carl still seemed oblivious to it all, but doubtless he was tuned in.

"Mum's terrific with cattle," proclaimed Pony with pride. "And Ingrid," he added quickly.

"Why thank you, Pony," said Ingrid, with heavy irony.

"That's what I've been hearing," said Hegarty.

"We manage," said Anna with modesty.

"Seems as if you like to spread yourself around, Hegarty," observed Ingrid. "Are you going to shake us off just as fast?" She glanced pointedly at her father. "We don't see any new faces around Cathedral Rock." His gaze moved to Anna and Pony. "Matter of fact we haven't had anyone staying on here for about, oh, maybe twelve or thirteen years, wouldn't you say, Anna?"

There was awkward pause Hegarty failed to comprehend, except that for a moment Anna's face was suffused with anger.

"I figure I'll just be doing what your father hired me for," put in Hegarty quickly. "I'm not looking past that for the time being."

No one said anything. Zara came in and hustled around the table to pick up the empty plates, and was quickly gone. Kisek introduced a heavy claret to the table, declaring it the best in the country, and insisted that Hegarty's glass remained full. It was sour to the palate, with a heady feel, but he knew how to handle alcohol if Kisek figured it as a tactic to loosen his tongue.

"When are you planning on starting your muster, Mr. Kisek?" he asked.

Kisek shrugged. "Maybe another day."

"Then it'll give me a good chance to get the feel of the helicopter."

"If you are feeling the need," Kisek frowned. "Other things there are to be doing about the place."

"Well I'll be looking forward to those lessons," smiled

Anna. For whatever reason Ingrid's comment had angered her, she had quickly recovered composure.

"God, that stupid damn helicopter has just been sitting there," Ingrid blurted out. "You'd think we all had this bloody AIDS the way we never hire anyone. We could have been cutting our mustering time to nothing." She turned to Hegarty with a tart grin. "You must have cast some magic spell to be here, Hegarty."

"He saved Schon," said Pony.

Kisek scowled at Ingrid. "We've managed without the helicopter," he growled. "And we're having good black ringers to help with the cattle. I haven't heard Anna complaining."

"I'm not complaining," flared Ingrid. "It's just been so damn stupid to have it sitting there without being used, that's all."

"I'm sure Matt doesn't want to hear about our problems," declared Anna hastily.

Hegarty covered it with an easy smile. "Hey listen, all I'm interested in is doing some helicopter mustering for you." He glanced around the table. "Okay?"

Pony seized on it as an opportunity to push again for flying with Hegarty. "Then please let me go with Matt tomorrow, pleeze Mum?" he pleaded. "Honest, I've sat in the helicopter sometimes, and imagined how terrific it'd be to fly around in it."

"I said we'd see," said Anna firmly.

"Like I said, it's okay with me," interceded Hegarty. "I figure I need a good copilot to familiarize myself with the property."

It put Anna off. "We'll still wait until the morning," she restated sharply.

Hegarty backed off. He didn't want to offend Anna, but Pony's knowledge of the area could be valuable when it came to pinpointing Jules's location.

"You be fancying yourself a pilot, Pony?" asked Kisek, smiling indulgently.

"Why not? I could take over the mustering when I'm older." He grinned at Hegarty for affirmation. "Isn't that right, Matt?"

Kisek lifted an admonishing finger. "You should be taking

your time, boy. Rich you are in time, so you should use it well."

"Okay, okay, just as long as I can go."

"If it's being all right with your mother, then it's all right with me," said Kisek.

"Hey, how about that, Matt?" cried the boy excitedly. "Maybe I'll be your copilot after all."

"I'll be looking forward to it," said Hegarty with a grin.

Anna frowned, biting at her lip as if to control anger, but said nothing.

Ingrid stretched, with a contrived expression of indifference. "Maybe we could all take turns," she murmured. "I'm sure we could all show Hegarty some special corner of Cathedral Rock where there might be some stray cattle."

Hegarty took a mouthful of claret, acknowledging the suggestion with a vague smile. He still couldn't quite figure Ingrid, but there was clearly conflict here, an antagonism cutting three ways, and it could prove fertile ground for him to work on. He glanced at Carl, still as inscrutable as ever, to all intent deaf to the words flying around him. Did the old man take sides, or remain as aloof as he appeared? And how much should he be taken into consideration? If he'd come out from Germany with Kisek, maybe they'd worked in the concentration camps together. He'd have to talk to Jules about it.

The talk switched to cattle, and for the first time there was an agreeable common topic around the table; even Pony contributed to the discussion about various breeds of cattle that were suitable for the Gulf Country. There was the problem of months that could be so dry water holes dried up and the rivers ceased to run, then the wet season of November to January, when the country could become like a vast sea. That was when movement from place to place was virtually impossible, with rivers sometimes breaking their banks, and stock drowned. Even then Carl contributed nothing. He occasionally nodded or faintly smiled agreement, but he was generally ignored, as if that was the normal pattern.

Maybe Kisek was guilty of being a human monster, but Hegarty had to admit it would have taken a lot of guts and determination to make such a success of Cathedral Rock. Yet it must have also put the man in a permanent conflict situation, with his success at odds with an obsessive desire for anonymity.

Whatever their previous sniping at each other suggested, he was quick to realize that love of Cathedral Rock bound this group tighter than any personal animosity. Just to watch their faces, avid with the pleasure of discussing the way they lived, was a warning that he'd be stupid to assume driving a wedge between them would be easy. He seized the opportunity of a break in the conversation to push himself to his feet, and gave an apologetic smile. The claret must have had more kick than he realized, for he felt slightly light-headed.

"It's been a big day," he said, "and it'll probably be a bigger one tomorrow." He nodded around the table. "Thank you for the dinner, and the conversation, but I think I'd better get some shut-eye."

"I suppose when we get onto cattle and Cathedral Rock we don't know when to stop," Anna said with a smile.

He offered a gesture of appreciation. "Not at all, I enjoyed it. Sounds like you've got one hell of a place here. I can't wait to get a look at it tomorrow." He winked at Pony. "But I've got to be at my top just in case I've got a copilot flying with me."

"What time'll you be starting Matt?" asked Pony eagerly.

"I figure around seven-thirty."

Anna cut him off. "I'll see you get some breakfast sent over," she said, half rising from her chair, but Ingrid was quicker. She thrust her chair back and was halfway to Hegarty before he moved.

"I'll see you out, Hegarty," she offered. She took his arm before he could decline and guided him toward the door. "Just to make sure you don't steal any of the silver on the way out," she said with a laugh. "I don't get many chances to see visitors out of the museum."

"Good night," he managed, before she maneuvered him through the door.

"See you in the morning, Matt," Pony called.

Ingrid's fingers held firmly to his arm as they crossed to the front door, their footsteps tapping hollowly in unison. She kept herself close, breathing softly, and he caught the aroma of enticing perfume he hadn't noticed before. It was difficult not to be attracted, even if he had the feeling of being targeted by

a hungry piranha, but she was asking to be the first daughter
he worked on. He opened the door and slipped smoothly from
her grasp.

"Thanks Ingrid," he murmured. "You want to search me
for silver?"

"That's an invitation that's hard to refuse." She pushed
herself close, until her mouth was only inches from his. It was
an invitation to kiss, but he let it go. If she was that anxious it
might be smarter to let her dangle for a while.

"I guess we'll see plenty of each other around," he said,
grinning.

"You can bet on it, Hegarty," she whispered. The warmth
of her breath fanned over his face. "God, it's fantastic to have
someone like you here. This place is like a bloody morgue at
times."

"I guess you could always leave," he suggested.

"And go where? I'm part of this place; it's all I've ever
known, all I've ever wanted. Forget this museum." She pulled
back, with an unreadable smile, stroked at her hair, and
pointed through the door. "Out there's where I live; where I
breathe. It's only when I'm in the house I get so uptight. Dad
persists with his crazy obsession of trying to cut us off from the
rest of the world, like himself. Even when we were at school
he'd never come to visit."

"Doesn't he ever leave the place?"

"Never. He's a recluse. But he always was, even when my
mother was alive."

"Don't you go visiting?"

She shrugged. "At times. Brisbane, Sydney. That's not
satisfying; those places choke me. All those people going
through their lives like wind-up dolls." She grinned, her head
tilted to one side. "Mixed up, aren't I?"

"Aren't we all."

"Not you, Hegarty, not you, baby. I don't buy all that
wandering around the world bullshit. You know where you're
going, and what you're doing."

He was taken aback that she'd read him so quickly. She
was attractive, and earthy, but also goddamn shrewd. He'd
have to watch himself with her. He tried to laugh it aside.
"Hey, I'm just Hegarty. Don't try and big-deal me. What you

see is what you get: just a pretty hot helicopter mustering pilot." He grinned a farewell and eased himself out the door.

"Yeah, sure. Well we'll see, Hegarty. I like a challenge." She turned and left him, striding back toward the dining room.

He walked slowly back to his room, made uneasy by her perception. And he had the feeling Anna could be the same; he'd have to handle them carefully. He was certain in some way they could help him nail down Kisek. Perhaps it was too soon, but already he was getting the strong feeling the girls were totally ignorant of their father's past. It wouldn't make sense for Kisek to tell them anyway, it would only increase the risk of his being exposed. And Carl had to fit in somewhere. If Kisek was Leiman . . . ? He grimaced. Fuck it; he was going to have to stop thinking like that. He'd read the goddamn report. He had to force himself to be positive like Reine, or he'd never be able to pull this off. *Kisek is Leiman, Kisek is Leiman*, he savagely repeated to himself.

A full moon held sway in a cloudless sky, rendering the landscape in sharp black shadows and clear white light. Gaunt trees stood dark against the sky, posed like macabre sculptures. The air was sharp, but still, as if the countryside had gone into hibernation to await a new day. It wasn't like Texas; wasn't like any place he'd ever been. And yet he experienced again a disturbing feeling of arriving home—the pilgrim who finally discovers his place of peace in a strange land. He angrily shook the mood aside and went into his room.

The room was the same, yet subtly different; it was a perception learned from experience. His backpack had been moved only marginally, but enough for him to know. His clothes were folded, but not quite the same. He went swiftly to the bottom drawer of the cupboard. The Colt was still there, but now the fold in the hand towel was lapped in the opposite direction. It had been carefully done, and would have gone unnoticed but for his trained eye. Kisek knew he had a gun. Pony had told the old man about Matt shooting the croc. Kisek had asked him if he liked to shoot during their first conversation. Would it seem a strange weapon for him to be carrying? Would it cause any suspicion? There was no doubt someone had been taking a look at his possessions. But who? The only one absent from the dining room at any time was the aged

Carl. Would he come prying into Matt's room, when supposedly he didn't know Kisek had hired him? Supposedly? He sat down on the bed, and thoughtfully lit up a cigar. Obviously it was an attempt to check him out; that fitted in with Kisek's paranoia. It would be better to say nothing, and safer; just let them think they'd got away with it. But it was a warning for him to move with caution. He might be through the gate at Cathedral Rock, but that was all; clearly he was still regarded with suspicion. He sat for a time smoking, planning his tactics. If it worked out for Pony to fly with him tomorrow, he'd see what he could get out of the boy. And then Ingrid was practically asking to be next. She was like a mare fretting to be turned loose with a stallion. He didn't want to drag this out; he was going to have to discuss timing with Jules, but knowing Jules's temperament he'd doubtless want to move fast.

Matt decided to take a look around outside before he settled down for the night, just to satisfy himself no one was skulking about. He went out the door, closed it softly behind him, prowled past the helicopter squatting like a sleeping bug, and slipped silently around the shed. There was nothing, no betraying movement of shadows, only a static night. A silhouetted line of birds bisected the moon, and the beat of their wings came faintly. He went on past the shed and warily followed the line of eucalyptus trees toward the house. He was probably only wasting his time, whoever had gone through his room wasn't going to hang around.

He caught the sound of low, bitter voices, and stopped in the shadow of the trees just short of the house. He recognized Anna's voice, not soft and caressing as over the diner table, but like the snap of a whip.

"I'm just warning you, Ingrid," she was saying through clenched teeth. "Don't ever make a crack like that again about Pony; it was unforgivable, especially in front of a stranger. Pony's no fool; you make smart quips about no one being around Cathedral Rock for twelve or thirteen years, and he's quick enough to realize that's his age."

"Then why don't you tell him the truth about his father?" came Ingrid's sneering rejoinder. "Tell him he was just some bum who came wandering in here for a job when Dad was sick in hospital, and you hired the creep. You took one look and couldn't wait to get into bed with him."

"Do you have to be such a bitch? It wasn't like that, and you know it."

"It's still the truth."

"I'll tell Pony when I'm good and ready."

"Why let him go on believing all that bullshit about his father being drowned before he was born."

"Drop it," fumed Anna.

"I'll drop it when you stop giving Hegarty that how'd-you-like-to-get-into-my-pants? look."

"My God, you can be a crude bitch—you know that."

"Well it's true."

"That's really funny. *I'm* looking at Hegarty like that? You were so obvious about making yourself available it was positively embarrassing."

"Hands off, Anna. Hegarty's the best thing to come around Cathedral Rock in a long time; perhaps ever. Just keep your hot little hands off him, that's all. I'm warning you. You don't fool me with your sweet innocence act."

"You're crazy," scoffed Anna. "Pony's taken quite a liking to the man, so why shouldn't I be friendly?"

"Sure, friendly like a fox—maybe looking for a father for Pony."

"You're talking rubbish."

There was a pause in the cat fight. Hegarty could just distinguish the outline of the two women standing in the corner of the veranda, and the blinking red tip of a cigarette one of them was smoking.

"I'm not going to have Pony hurt," declared Anna forcefully.

"I'm not trying to hurt him; I'm just telling you to keep clear of Hegarty."

"For God's sake, Ingrid, the man's only just got here. I haven't got any feeling about him at all."

"Well I'm just warning you, Anna, this is one time you're not going to push me aside."

"And I'm telling you you're talking nonsense."

"Maybe. But I know Hegarty." The red tip of the cigarette blinked furiously like a warning light, and he knew it had to be

Ingrid. "Sure, I know Hegarty. I can tell about a man like that." Ingrid's voice fell away, and he strained to catch the words. "I'm going to have Hegarty, even if he doesn't know about it. Christ, you had your chance, Anna, and you made a mess of it, picking up with a creep who ran out on you when you were pregnant. Okay, you got Pony, but I want a promise you'll keep your eyes off Hegarty."

"You're making yourself ridiculous," retorted Anna. "God, how can you go on like that about a man who's a total stranger?"

There was a further pause, and the red ash vanished. "He's not a stranger to me," muttered Ingrid. "I knew everything I wanted to know about Hegarty the moment I set eyes on him."

"I think you're talking like a fool," rasped Anna. "And I'm not going to listen to any more of this."

There was the rustling sound of someone stirring, followed by sharp footsteps as one of the figures disappeared from the veranda. Hegarty waited for a while, but there was no further movement; then he carefully backed away under the cover of the trees and made his way back to the room. He didn't know whether to feel flattered or apprehensive over Ingrid's ferocious attraction, and he had a sneaking suspicion he would have preferred such a passionate declaration from Anna. Did it matter? The important thing was having it reaffirmed that Ingrid was smitten with him; that was going to make it much easier to extract any information from her about her father. He turned it over in his mind while he undressed and climbed into bed. He half wished he could respond to Ingrid in kind, but he hadn't loved anyone fiercely in a long time. He guessed it was because his father had trained him from childhood to an almost obsessive dedication, one that allowed little room for a lasting relationship. "It's your duty to the memory of your murdered family," the old man had kept hammering into him, until it was ingrained in his personality. But after Kisek, what then? Was he just going to go on until the inevitable retirement pension, fighting it like Andre Reine? His eyes wandered the room until they came to rest on the painting of Cathedral Rock. Nice picture. His boyhood bedroom had been lined with pictures, and it would have been nice if there had been just one with the modest intention of doing nothing more than please the eye.

But they'd all been stark black and white portraits, grainy and fading, faces with fixed smiles, others with brooding solemnity, as if intuitively sensing their terrible fate. People he'd never met, all hung there at his father's insistence, and he could still recite their names like a well-trained parrot: Matthew, Aunt Tatania, Uncle Efram, Aunt Bella, Uncle Januse; his cousins, Esther, Ida, Harriet, Moses, Abe, Rachel, Benjamin, Moshe, Maritza. And others who'd been old friends of his father—Greensperg, man and wife; Kalmann, man and wife—all long ago gassed and incinerated, yet held in perpetual memory by his father. And passed on to become engraved in his mind. With the clarity of instant recall, he could picture his father coming into his bedroom: tall, eyes pouched and deep-set under heavy brows, great mane of gray hair like an aging lion refusing to give up the hunt, never able to appease his hunger, yet with a fierce love for his son and only child, who would be his instrument of vengeance.

It was a morning ritual when he was about Pony's age, his father moving from picture to picture, pointing to each in turn, while his son called out the name from memory. Maybe it was obsessive, but by the time it was all firmly set in his mind, it would have seemed like betraying his father not to go on. Anyway, he too was fired by the horror, told over and over, was equally zealous for revenge. When he was still a boy his name was put down for the Mossad, like some fathers put their son's name down at birth for a place in an exclusive school.

But his parents fought about it, until eventually it drove his mother from the marriage.

"I don't agree with what you're doing, and I won't have it," she screamed. "You're obsessed. You can't sacrifice his future for your past."

"The boy has character; believe me: he understands, he wants to do this, to become involved."

"He's doing it because he loves you, not for himself."

"Wrong, Mimi—wrong, wrong, wrong. He wants to help bring the Nazi monsters to justice. He wants to do it."

"I'm sorry all your family are dead, Mordecai, but I can't

bring them back; your son can't bring them back. I've got a life to lead, I refuse to live in the past."

There were variations to the argument, but the form was always the same. He sympathized with his mother, but surely she should try and understand her husband's fierce desire to bring such animals to justice. In the end she just walked out. He still saw her from time to time, remarried, happy with her new life. She had too much natural gaiety to forever live out her life in the shadows of concentration camp horror, she was American-born and had married his father when he escaped from Germany, so she hadn't shared his front seat at the decimation of his family; it gave her a different perspective. It was over for her, but it would never be over for his father; and perhaps also never for him. She mourned for Matt, and it made him uncomfortable: "Where is the wife you should be having, the children, the happiness?" He assured her he was happy, but he doubted he believed it himself. But he took her name. When he was stationed in America for the Mossad, and moving around on international assignments, Hegarty seemed less a giveaway than Schickel.

He turned restlessly on the bed, he didn't want to think about those things now, all he wanted to think about was Kisek, that *Kisek was Leiman*, and he was going to screw all he could out of Kisek's goddamn family to give him unshakable proof.

Chapter 4

He rose about daybreak, showered, shaved, put on a fresh shirt, had a quick cup of coffee, then went out to the helicopter. There was a magical stillness about the countryside bathed in the sharp light of early morning, every detail etched with needlepoint clarity. He glanced at the house, but there was no sign of life. The yellow fuselage of the helicopter seemed brighter than yesterday. He ran his hand over the smooth curve of the bubble canopy as he walked around the machine, his fingers leaving trails of fine dust. The trip out to Cathedral Rock had probably been its only flight, but he was trained to the necessity of a preflight check. He untethered the main rotor blades and they turned easily under his hand, then he took a close look at the rudder blades, but there was no sign of any abrasions. The pitch chain linkage was normal, oil and fuel levels okay, so someone had been keeping it ready for flight. He seated himself in the cockpit, cyclic lever between his legs, feet resting lightly on the torque control pedals. There was a smell of newness, and the dash gleamed like polished silver. The cyclic and the collective lever at his side both moved easily, without any impediments. He picked up the maintenance release sheet from the other seat and carefully checked it through, but there were no problems; then he settled back for a few moments, familiarizing himself, remembering the jovial Bobo Walters instructing him in an identical machine back in Texas. All he had to do now was make sure he located Jules.

When he went back to his room there was a breakfast tray waiting on the doorstep. Orange juice, cereal, eggs and bacon, toast, and an elaborate silver coffee pot. He guessed Zara had brought it.

He breakfasted quickly, took a Canon 35mm camera from his backpack, loaded it with film, then slipped a tiny electronic homing device into his jeans pocket. That would be one sure way he'd know if Jules had arrived. He put on the cowboy hat he'd brought from Texas and went back to the helicopter.

Pony and his mother were already waiting there, standing by the cabin, both dressed in jeans and tank tops, Anna's white, and the boy's bright red. Pony was holding a small knapsack, and his face brightened to rival the rays of the morning sun when he saw Hegarty.

"Hey, Matt—hey, Matt, I'm ready," he called excitedly.

Hegarty looked uncertainly to Anna. "Morning Pony, morning Anna. I'm not too sure we agreed . . ."

"Mum said I can go, Matt, she said it's okay," Pony cut in.

Hegarty smiled at Anna. "Well, that sure is fine; I hope you thanked your mother?"

"Sure I did. I'll be able to tell her what a terrific pilot you are."

She returned the smile. She looked terrific the way the white tank top set off her tanned skin. "Thanks for letting him come," Matt said. "I'm looking forward to it."

"I'm trusting you, Matt," she said, "I didn't want to disappoint him."

"I won't let you down," he replied with a smile.

She gestured to the knapsack in Pony's hand. "I made up a few sandwiches, just in case you get hungry. I thought you might be gone a while."

"Why that's mighty nice of you, Anna, and thanks again."

In the harsh early morning light the spidery lines about her eyes were more noticeable; she could be a few years older than he figured last night, but it merely seemed to enhance the fact she was an incredibly handsome woman. In spite of the bitter argument she'd had with Ingrid, she seemed so relaxed, so easy with life, yet so subtly accessible, without the need of her sister's aggressive horniness.

She nodded to the helicopter. "It sounds kind of ridiculous, but my father kept it ready, then would never hire anyone to fly it." She pointed to his camera. "You're going to take some pictures?"

"Yeah, it's sort of a hobby of mine. I try and take pictures of wherever I go, like a record." He shrugged. "I don't know if they'd be good enough, but one day I'd like to try to put them together in a book."

"Bet they're terrific," declared Pony. He took Anna impulsively by the arm and dragged her closer to the helicopter. "Take one of me and Mum in front of the helicopter, Matt. Please, just one . . . go on."

It was all the cue Hegarty needed. Headquarters was going to want photographs of all the family.

"No Pony," Anna protested. "Matt doesn't want to photograph us."

"Sure I do," said Hegarty. "Go on, both of you stand in front of the cabin."

They posed for him, Pony like a peacock, Anna reluctantly, and he clicked off a few shots. He dropped the camera on the seat of the helicopter. "Come on, Pony," he said, "let's get it out and go take a look at this Cathedral Rock of yours."

Pony ran to help. "Sure Matt; c'mon Mum, give us a hand."

Hegarty grinned at Anna, and shook his head. "No, I figure the men can manage this one, Pony."

They pushed it out into the open space between the shed and the stockyards, Anna walking at Hegarty's side. After what he'd overheard last night he was surprised Ingrid wasn't there too. Pony was clambering into the seat almost before they brought the helicopter to a halt.

"C'mon Matt, let's take her up," he shouted.

"Easy Pony, easy," laughed Hegarty, "we've got all day." He turned to Anna. "Your turn'll be next—when we get around to the lessons."

"I'll be looking forward to that," she said. She clasped her hands awkwardly and inclined her head toward Pony. "You're carrying special cargo."

He patted her arm reassuringly. It felt firm, even muscular. "I know, and don't worry. I'm a careful pilot."

She nodded, stepped back with a smile, and raised her hand. "Have a good time, Pony," she called.

Hegarty had the feeling she was letting Pony come against her better judgment; the boy must have put a lot of pressure on her. They donned helmets, and strapped on safety belts, with Pony too excited to answer his mother, just waving his arms. Hegarty primed the engine with the throttle, then pressed the starter button. The rotor blades began to whirr. It turned over sweetly while he ran it up to flight idle, as he expected from a new machine, but he still took it cautiously, raising the collective and easing the cyclic forward until they were moving slowly at about ten feet off the ground. He saw Anna retreat from the downdraft as he began to climb, and caught a glimpse of Ingrid watching from the veranda, until the roof line cut her from sight. The machine handled beautifully, impressive enough for him to level off at around three hundred feet and go barreling confidently out across the savanna.

Conversation was close to impossible, so he and Pony exchanged grins of approval, the boy almost hypnotized with delight. The kid was so likable, so natural and unspoiled, though a little headstrong. It was a pity he'd probably be badly hurt by the time all this was over. There was clearly a strong rapport between him and Kisek; it would come as a stunning shock to know his grandfather was a wanted criminal. Hegarty shrugged it off; he couldn't afford to take that into consideration.

He kept heading south, even though the deserted house where Jules had planned to establish a base was to the west. Since Pony was pretty sharp, it might be a mistake to immediately make for the location.

It was from the air that the vastness and flatness of the Gulf savanna could be really comprehended, an immense tableland of light-brown grass, patches of red earth, scraggly trees, and in places lines of spidery cattle and vehicle tracks, as if drawn with a palsied hand. Only Cathedral Rock broke the monotony, thrusting up out of the earth like a giant red blister. To the north was the glittering water of the Gulf of Carpentaria, and by the river the cluster of buildings marking Normanton. He dropped down again, buzzing close to the ground, giving the helicopter full bore, catching Pony's rapt expression as the boy pointed out the boundaries of the property. At times he made a point of taking photographs, holding the cyclic between his legs and steadying the Canon against his face. The pictures could be useful when it came time to take Kisek out, and it helped to establish he liked to use the camera.

Occasionally they came across straggling cattle, which Hegarty used to demonstrate his mustering skills, maneuvering the helicopter this way and that like a fluttering butterfly, until he had the cattle bunched and running for him, to Pony's enthusiastic plaudits.

He tired of that, and decided to put down for a while, because he wanted to take the chance of talking to Pony. He circled until he spotted a good landing site, then eased the Bell softly to the ground and cut the motor. For a moment there was just the slowing swish of the rotor blades, then they were absorbed by the pervasive silence of the country. He grinned, and tapped the knapsack beside Pony.

"How about we try some of those sandwiches your mother made, eh Pony?"

"Sure Matt, sounds like a great idea," Pony agreed with alacrity. He gave a breathless giggle and slapped his hand on the knapsack. "Golly, the way you got those shorthorns running was really something Matt, really something. You can make the helicopter dance for you, Matt. That's what it's like, just as if it's bloody dancing for you."

Hegarty couldn't help but wince at the unstinting admiration, yet he couldn't deny the warmth it gave him.

"But not like Schon, eh Pony?"

"No; I reckon it's just . . . different from Schon." He hesitated, as if concerned he might be disloyal to his horse. "But I reckon Schon can be exciting too," he added.

"Well let's eat before we do any more dancing."

They could have been at the center of the Sahara, it seemed so remote from anything. Without the protection of the cooling in-flight air stream they felt the sun burning with a fierce intensity, and heat rose from the earth like an open fire. They settled under the scant foliage of a nearby tree, where Pony unwrapped the sandwiches, solemnly divided them, and passed over Hegarty's share. Hegarty was surprised to find himself so hungry, and the sandwiches were delicious, thick slices of beef coated with a tangy sauce, set between slabs of wholegrain bread.

"Your mother makes a great sandwich," said Hegarty appreciatively.

"She sure does," agreed Pony.

A crow skimmed the grass, feathering the air with its spread wings as it soared to an overhead branch, and perched there to enviously watch them eat.

"Y'know, I reckon this is my most exciting day ever," declared Pony.

"I hope there'll be a lot more of them, Pony."

"Jeez, so do I. I hope you'll stay a long, long time."

"I'm only here for the muster," Hegarty warned.

Pony munched disconsolately for a moment. "Yeah, I suppose so."

"You really like this place, don't you?"

Pony gazed out over the shimmering grass lands. "I reckon I can't imagine living anywhere else." He shook his head. "Mum took me to Sydney once. Jeez, all those people, and all those tall buildings. I tell you, Matt, I couldn't breathe properly."

"I guess Cathedral Rock will be yours one day."

"I s'pose so. Maybe I can stop Mum and Ingrid fighting over it."

Hegarty figured Pony would be aware of the friction between Anna and Ingrid. Was the inheritance of Cathedral Rock what it was really all about?

"Your grandfather's very fond of you."

"Grandad's okay, but I tell you Matt, he can be pretty tough . . . real tough. And I don't reckon he likes people very much. But I guess you've found that out anyway."

"Maybe he figures he has to take your father's place."

Pony shrugged. "Maybe."

Hegarty finished his sandwich and took a swig from the water bottle.

"Your grandfather's done pretty well since he came out from Germany," he said casually, wiping at his mouth.

"Yeah, I reckon so. It all happened before I was born. Jeez, he must of worked like buggery."

"Do you remember your grandmother?"

"No, she died before I was born too."

"I guess she came out from Germany with him?"

"No, Mum told me she was an Australian. I think she came from Darwin, or somewhere around there. There's a photograph I can show you at home if you're interested."

"With your grandfather?"

"No, just by herself." He frowned. "There's no pictures of Grandad anywhere." He shrugged. "I don't know why."

"Carl helps your grandad with Cathedral Rock, eh?"

"Not much now; I reckon he's too old. He looks after the house, and things like that." He cleared his mouth of the last of his sandwich and brushed crumbs from his mouth. "Jeez, I've known Carl all my life, and I don't know him at all, y'know? He's a funny sorta bugger. Never talks, not that he ever did. I can remember him helping me with Schon once, but," he shrugged, "but not much else. I think he talks to Grandad, but that's all." He gave a nonplused grin. "Mum's known him longer than me, and she says he was always like that."

"Your grandfather never talks about Germany?"

"No, at least not to me. I reckon that big war must have been pretty bad for him. Perhaps it's why he doesn't like people any more."

"Could be," reflected Hegarty.

They both fell silent. Hegarty suspected he wasn't going to extract much information from Pony, because the boy knew little of value. He hoped probing the daughters proved more rewarding.

"You're interested in Grandad?" asked Pony suddenly.

Hegarty offered his most disarming smile. "Oh he just seems like such an interesting old guy, that's all, Pony. I meet lots of people when I'm traveling around, and I guess I'm just a curious sort of guy."

It seemed to satisfy Pony, his attention now taken by a point at the ground where he was idly scratching with a twig.

"There's one of those Tarantula Hawks, Matt," he said, pointing to the earth in front of him. "See her? She's a big bugger."

It was a red-bodied insect, about the size of an overgrown

locust, black wings sheathed back along its body. It ignored Pony's twig, probing at a small hole in the ground.

"Tarantula Hawk?" queried Hegarty.

"Yeah; bet there's a bloody whopper of a tarantula down in that hole."

"She's after the spider?"

"She's after the spider all right. She'll get down in that hole, and sting the spider, and that'll be the end of him."

"She'll eat it?"

"Oh, she's smarter than that. She'll sting him so he becomes paralyzed, and he'll stay that way for a long time. Then she'll lay her eggs on him, and just leave, and when all the little Tarantula Hawks hatch out they'll feed on the spider. Poor bugger gets eaten alive. That's the way it works out."

"Sounds kinda tough on the tarantula."

"I s'pose." He tossed the twig aside. "Grandad says that's just nature, and we shouldn't interfere with nature. Sometimes it's for the best that some things eat others, it keeps the breed strong." Hegarty gave a blank-faced nod; that philosophy fitted in with Leiman. "And he says some people are like that," continued Pony. "Y'know, get right inside you without you knowing, then just eat you away." He shrugged. "Maybe it was the war that makes him say things like that."

"You could be right," said Hegarty slowly.

He was sure it was only coincidence, the boy wouldn't consciously make an analogy between him and the murderous lifestyle of an insect. But it prickled him with unease to recognize the similarity. Christ, it was ridiculous to feel like that. Kisek was Leiman, someone had to play Tarantula Hawk, and if a few innocent people got eaten along the way, then that was the price that had to be paid.

The Tarantula Hawk had already disappeared into the hole when he stood to his feet and beckoned to Pony. "Time we were shoving off, copilot," he grinned.

Pony clambered to his feet and moved to the tree. "Better water the horse first," he said.

"Water the horse?"

Pony already had his fly undone and was urinating into the grass.

"Then I'd better water the horse too," laughed Hegarty.

He joined Pony, making his contribution, until the grass sparkled wetly in the sun.

"Ritchie says two blokes pissing together is the beginning of a real friendship," said Pony happily.

"Who's Ritchie?"

"He's Grandad's head ringer, and the best rider in the Gulf Country I reckon. He's with a horse like you are with the helicopter, Matt."

"Ritchie sounds like a pretty smart fella to me."

They boarded the helicopter again, and Hegarty headed west, mustering a few more stray cattle at Pony's enthusiastic urging. While the boy's attention was distracted, he slipped the homing device from his pocket and secured it against his thigh on the opposite side of the seat. He managed to position it so he could see the tiny blinking red light, then he checked his compass reading. He figured if he held to this heading for another ten minutes, then turned northeast, it would bring him back on a sweeping curve to Cathedral Rock and also, he hoped, over the position he estimated the abandoned house would be at.

It went just as he anticipated. He banked northeast, dropped down to a few hundred feet, and before long spotted the clutter of bricks and debris that marked the remains of a large house.

"Grandad's old house," shouted Pony, pointing down, "where he lived before he built the one we've got now."

Hegarty nodded. It was all the confirmation he needed. "Let's go take a look at it," he hollered back.

He dropped lower, coming around in a tight circle. Forlorn ruins of fencing and outbuildings were scattered about the main house like decayed sentry posts, but there was more of the house standing than he first realized, with part walls that still supported sections of rusted sheet-iron roofing. The pulse rate of the red light on the homing device began to slow dramatically, and by the time he was directly overhead it had stopped altogether. He gave a grunt of satisfaction; Jules had arrived, and was somewhere in the house. Across to the east he could see the outlines of the Cathedral Rock homestead, and he was surprised there seemed to be only a few miles separating the two buildings. It seemed risky for Jules to be so close, but he guessed he knew what he was doing. A track straggled away from the house to connect to the main road several miles away, and he figured that had to be the best way for him to get from Cathedral Rock to the place on the Kawasaki. Somehow he was going to try to make contact with Jules tonight. There were important things to talk about, and he needed to know the latest on the supposed fingerprints of Leiman that Eli Brandt claimed to have found in Berlin. If that really turned out to be true, it would alter the whole picture.

"I never lived there," shouted Pony. "Mum and Ingrid did, but they all moved long before I was born."

"I'll try and take a proper look at it from the ground when I get the chance," bawled Hegarty. "Looks like it'd make an interesting photograph."

Pony grinned understanding. Hegarty had the feeling that whatever he wanted to do was okay by the boy. He thumbed toward Cathedral Rock. "Time we were heading back," he called.

Pony nodded agreement, and Matt set a line for the homestead, hugging close to the ground, leaving furrows of windblown grass from the downdraft, while Pony chortled with pleasure. Hegarty experienced a sense of satisfaction; everything was running for him, everything slotting into place. But he hoped Eli Brandt really had found Leiman's fingerprints. If just for once Eli had actually pulled off something spectacular, it meant they could probably wrap this up fast, and get Kisek out of the Gulf Country. Somehow he feared his involvement with the Kisek family becoming too complicated, especially where this likable kid alongside him was concerned.

Chapter 5

London.

Andre Reine was not unused to the sight of corpses, but he felt infinitely saddened at having to identify Eli Brandt's body. Not that they'd worked together that often over the years, and of late he'd become increasingly irritated at Eli's tendency to misread signs that led to bad decisions; but he'd always thought of the man as one with a great ability to survive. He knew many placed himself at the top of that category, and he ignored it with conscious self-effacement, while secretly acknowledging its truth.

He had taught Eli the safety of ordinariness, of anonymity, and while it had carried him to his sixty-fourth year, for some reason the trick had eventually failed for Eli—Eli, who lay there on the slab, his skin white and flabby from the time his body had spent immersed in the flooded quarry . . . after someone had put a bullet in his brain. Except for an anonymous tip to the police, Brandt's body might never have been found. Even more odd, sufficient identification had been left on the body for the police to call Reine; but there was no sign of Eli's copy of the Leiman file.

Andre sighed, nodded confirmation to the mortuary attendant, and walked out into the rain that so often afflicts London summers. For all of Eli's blunders and misjudgments, he had at least remained professional to the end, leaving a second copy of the Leiman file for him in the safe of the Cumberland Hotel. Although why he'd held back that all-important final piece of verification from the Berlin police files baffled him. None of them had known of Leiman's being

fingerprinted as a young man, when he'd been arrested in a
Berlin street riot. If Eli had only sent on that extra piece of
verification, maybe his word would have been accepted at
headquarters that he did indeed have Leiman's fingerprints.

He mournfully shook his head. He suspected Eli had
indulged in a fatal piece of the departmental politics that had
much to do with his declining reputation as a reliable agent.
Maybe he saw it as a desperate ploy to restore his prestige
within the Mossad. Of course Andre would have to recheck it
with the Berlin police, but it did appear now that Brandt had
really pulled off a coup, that the fingerprints would prove
beyond legal doubt that the man calling himself Kisek in
Australia was the Nazi monster Horst Leiman. Jules would be
delighted. And Hegarty. Although he had no intention of
changing Hegarty's brief; he would still need him to keep
digging away at Kisek until the fingerprints were proved valid.

He considered calling a taxi, but he had an umbrella, and
he always found walking in the rain a stimulus to thinking. He
dawdled, not conscious of any direction, occasionally turning
abruptly to glance behind him. It was purely instinctive; he'd
been followed many times, and there was a bristling at the
nape of his neck, but there was no one. Perhaps it was merely
regret at what had happened to Brandt. He finally found
himself overlooking the Thames. To his right was Westminster
Bridge, the span like a live thing with traffic, and across the
gray water speckled with rain were the stately Houses of
Parliament, as if guarding the ancient river as much as the
democratic traditions of England. Those traditions held true
for Israel too, demanding justice for horrendous crimes, no
matter how long the passage of time. Five years it had taken
the Wiesenthal people, since they'd first discovered that faint
trace of Leiman's trail, five years of tediously assembling
fragments that had eventually led to the man in Australia
calling himself Kisek. And now the man who had in all
probability found the final conclusive proof for them was dead.
Murdered. Of course it would prove an irony if the fingerprints were to exonerate this Kisek, but Andre didn't believe
that for a moment, refused to even consider it. The circumstantial evidence was too strong.

He resumed walking, holding the umbrella low to his

head so the rain didn't fall on his immaculately pressed clothes. Of course the ultimate question denied all attempts to answer. Why in God's name was Eli Brandt killed? And by whom? That baffled him. The entire Kisek operation had been such a close secret, known only to the few personally involved, yet someone knew enough to kill Brandt for the Leiman file. Of what possible interest could the bringing of Leiman to justice after all these years have for anyone else? Oh there were still pockets of old guard Nazi sympathizers in Germany, who would certainly resist the idea of Leiman being brought to trial, but they were kept under surveillance, and there were no reports of any interest stirring. And he had to face the fact that if he took up the running for Eli, he would expose himself to the same risk of being killed. People ruthless enough to kill once would have no hesitation about killing again. Yet he could feel close to a surge of adrenaline at the thought; he craved the active involvement, the exhilaration of being at the heart of the action again. The trick of staying alive might have deserted Eli, but the craft was still strong in him. Andre would never confess it to his wife, but he dreaded the prospect of retirement, feared it as the first step on a slide to a doddering death. His mind was as clear and sharp as ever, yet encased in an aging body; he was like a trained athlete trapped on a doomed, sinking ship.

He frowned and quickened his step. He would need to be firm, even adamant, push his seniority to the limit, because Favett would no doubt attempt to dissuade him, pointing out that there were other, younger men more able to undertake the hazardous task of getting the fingerprints to Grubin in Australia. But this was his operation, even if so far in only an administrative sense—most likely the last he would carry out for the Mossad, and he was determined to see it through. If he had to end his working life, then seeing Leiman at the end of a rope would be an exquisite finale.

He called Favett from his hotel room.

"It was Eli," he reported soberly.

"Do you have any idea who killed him? Or why?" There was no expression of sympathy, of compassion. Favett's voice always sounded so young, but then he was young, a dynamic blend of youth and cunning beyond his years.

"I've no idea who killed him, but it was obviously for Leiman's fingerprints."

"Could it have been engineered by Leiman himself?"

"From Australia?"

"Such things are possible."

"I don't see how. We're positive he hasn't the faintest idea his trail has been picked up. Otherwise he would have bolted."

"You think Brandt made another . . . misjudgment? His murder had nothing to do with the operation?"

"In that case they would scarcely have stolen the file containing Leiman's fingerprints," Andre answered tartly.

Favett didn't take offense. "I expect you're right," he replied blandly.

"We're fortunate Eli left a copy for me in the safe of the hotel where he was staying."

"Thank God for that. Why didn't he leave both copies in the safe?"

Reine didn't know the answer to that. Maybe Eli hadn't been thinking straight because of the personal pressure he was under.

"Only Eli would know why," he said tersely. He paused. "There is further verification of the fingerprints we hadn't seen before; from a Berlin police file. Eli held it back."

Favett gave a grunt of exasperation. "The man was playing games, Andre. He couldn't have gone on with us much longer. No wonder we couldn't trust him anymore."

"I'll have to doublecheck it with Berlin, but it'll only take a phone call. If it checks out it will mean the fingerprints are definitely genuine."

"Then why don't we just bring Kisek out now?"

"The fingerprints may exonerate him."

"Surely you don't believe that?"

"I suppose anything's possible. We would look extremely stupid if we brought him out and that happened. Far better to prove it in Australia."

He knew he was playing the devil's advocate. Perhaps he wanted the involvement just as desperately as he wanted Leiman.

Favett fell silent, except for a thoughtful clucking of his tongue.

"Yes, you're right, Andre. Let it stand the way it is. You've done a good job. Why don't you stay put in London until I get a man out to take the Leiman fingerprints to Grubin in Australia."

Reine braced himself. "That won't be necessary," he said boldly.

"I don't understand."

"I'll take them myself."

"For God's sake Andre, Brandt's been murdered by Christ knows who, and now you have Leiman's fingerprints. Don't you realize it makes you a target too?"

"I think I've proved I'm a difficult man to kill."

"But it's unfair when you're so near to retirement. I can't allow you to take that sort of risk. It's too dangerous."

Reine bit down hard to hold back his anger. Favett considered anyone over fifty near to senility. He wasn't going to be brushed aside, certainly not by a political string-puller who had used connections to get himself the top job over more experienced men.

"This is my operation," he said, gritting his teeth. "I've handled all the details, all the planning. It would be absurd to hand it over to someone else at this crucial stage. Remember, we're always facing the risk of someone warning Leiman, especially now after what's happened to Eli Brandt. We need to move quickly."

"But why would you want to run such a risk, Andre?" persisted Favett. "You've done enough for Israel, for the Mossad."

Because I want to feel alive, thought Reine. Because I need this one last assignment, like an addict craves one more needle; it may have to last forever.

"I believe this entire operation could be put in jeopardy unless someone with my experience sees it through," he declared harshly. "There are too many things only I know; too many important details." He paused to add one more shot that he was sure would carry weight with an opportunist like Favett. "There could be very awkward questions asked about the organization in high places, if somehow Leiman escaped our noose," he stated meaningfully.

There was a further pondering silence from Favett.

Failure could be very damaging for someone with Favett's political ambitions.

"Then I suppose I should take the advice of someone with your extensive experience, Andre," he murmured finally.

Reine breathed a sigh of relief. He hadn't won many battles since Favett had taken over, but this was one victory he needed.

"You won't regret it," he said shortly.

"I'm sure I won't." There was the clucking sound of his tongue again. "Of course you realize you assume full responsibility. If Leiman were to escape, I would hate to think what a sad end it would be to a long career. A real blot, Andre."

Reine knew he was being set up in case anything went wrong, but he didn't care. And Favett was laying the groundwork to put himself in the clear—of course.

"It won't happen," he stated confidently.

"Then I wish you a successful trip to Australia."

"I'll need a cover. It would be too dangerous, too obvious, to just go to this Normanton and openly contact Jules. Or Hegarty. And I could risk breaking their cover. I'll arrange to travel as a tourist. I understand from my information Normanton is a place tourists visit."

"That sounds like a good idea."

"Can I leave it with you to let Jules know I'm coming?"

"I'll need all the relevant details."

"I'll call you again as soon as I know." He paused. "You've heard nothing yet as to whether Hegarty has managed to infiltrate Kisek's place?"

"No. It's probably too soon. Doubtless Jules will let us know." He cleared his throat. "You're taking care of Brandt's body?"

"Yes, I've arranged for it to be sent to Tel Aviv. You'll tell his family?"

"Of course. That will be . . . distasteful; but then we have to expect such things in this business. You know that more than anybody, Andre."

What was there to answer? Of course he knew, that's why it was so important he go to Australia.

"I'm going to assign someone to try and run down Brandt's killer," said Favett. "It's important we know."

"I'd handle that with great care."

"What do you mean?"

"I'm sure whoever killed Brandt believes they've achieved their objective. They wouldn't know there were two copies of Leiman's fingerprints. It would be to my advantage if they remained believing they'd destroyed the only copy. And my safety," he added heavily.

"Don't worry, I'll see it's handled with great caution," Favett assured him. "Just be very, very careful, Andre. I'm counting on you."

He made it sound almost like a patronizing vote of no confidence, and once again Reine had to restrain a feeling of irritation. He was sure Favett was more galled at having to give way than he was troubled by any lack of confidence in Reine's ability.

"I've never let the Mossad down yet," he replied stiffly, and hung up.

He poured himself a brandy to settle his aggravation, switched on the television news, and settled down in a chair. The progression of trivia on the screen made no impression, his thoughts were more of his coming trip to Australia. He might be annoyed by Favett's patronizing attitude, but the man was right, he would need to move with great caution. Andre might hope that Brandt's killers believed they'd done their job, but he'd be a fool to accept it as fact.

He thought of his home in Tel Aviv, where Lea had been redecorating the spare room, as a place where he would have more space for his Egyptology research during retirement. She would be aghast that he was setting off for Australia, that he was becoming actively involved in the operation. It would be impossible to explain it to her, she would never understand; maybe it would be for the best if he didn't tell her until he got back.

Chapter 6

Hegarty brought the helicopter in slowly to the Cathedral Rock homestead, easing down with a slight bump into the clearing at the right of the shed, dust swirling up to fog the canopy. He switched off, waited until the whirling blades had quieted to a muffled swish, swish, then grinned at Pony as one would to a boon companion sharing a great adventure.

"Well, how was that, copilot?" he asked with a broad smile.

Pony wrapped his arms about his body, hugging himself. "Fabulous, Matt, just bloody fabulous. I reckon this is the best day ever in my whole life," he declared fervently, "the best day ever." He hesitated. "Well, apart from the day I got Schon, but nearly as good."

"Maybe we'll be able to do it again—maybe during the muster."

"Golly, I hope so, Matt, I really do." The sun poked burning holes through the clearing dust, highlighting the sparkle in the boy's eyes. "I'll bet I do like you said, Matt, and fly it myself one day."

"I'll bet you do too, Pony," Hegarty agreed.

"Bet if my Dad was still alive he'd teach me. You could pretend you was like him, Matt, and teach me. You talked about that back at the lagoon."

Hegarty unclipped his safety belt, his face expressing doubt. For Chrissake, the last thing he wanted was Pony thinking about him as a substitute father. "I can teach you like me, not like your father," he said sharply. "And your mother's got to come first anyway."

The boy was taken aback by the tart retort, then he

grinned. "Okay, Matt, okay; just so long as you can teach me too."

"Just remember your grandfather didn't hire me as a flying instructor."

Pony gave a glum shrug. "Yeah, I s'pose so."

In spite of himself Hegarty tried to soften the boy's disappointment. "Well, we'll see how I'm doing for time."

"Maybe I could come out on the muster with you the first day."

"If it's okay with your mother."

"I reckon she won't mind, not when she sees how we went today."

"We'll see." He'd have to think about that. Keeping close to the boy meant getting close to Kisek, but he needed time with the women too. He picked up his camera and tapped the boy on the shoulder. "C'mon, let's get out. We'll see if the muster's on tomorrow."

It wasn't until he stepped out of the helicopter that he saw Ingrid, standing over by the shed together with a short, thickset aboriginal man. He secured the helicopter blades before he responded to her beckoning arm. The black man watched his approach with cautious eyes. He was a full blood, wide nose, full mouth, eyes set deep under protruding brows, a white stubble like snow on his black skin. He wore the usual dust-smothered jeans, a bright yellow tank top, and a large stockman's hat over shoulder-length hair. His muscled arms glistened in the sun as he smoked a limp, hand-rolled cigarette. He was somewhere between forty and fifty.

Ingrid greeted Matt with the mocking smile he was coming to know. The jeans and boots she wore were the same, but the bright checked shirt was too casually opened down the front to expose the rim of her small breasts. She didn't have Anna's curves, but she looked good just the same.

"Welcome back, Chief Pilot Hegarty," she bantered. "You approve of our helicopter?"

"Flew like a bird. Terrific machine."

"And you liked what you saw of Cathedral Rock?"

"One hell of a property. There's a lot of mustering to do out there."

"That's why we need you, Hegarty." She paused. "One of the reasons," she murmured silkily.

Hegarty ignored the inference, and looked back to the house. "I need to talk to your father."

She gestured vaguely to the countryside. "He's somewhere out there. Maybe seeing if there's any more crocs in the lagoon."

"G'day, Ritchie," said Pony from behind Matt.

The native took the cigarette from his mouth, and grinned at the boy. The impassive face was converted by affection into flashing white teeth and wrinkles of pleasure.

"G'day y'self, Pony. You been havin' y'self an exciting time in that whirligig, eh?"

"You bet," said Pony enthusiastically. "You should see Matt fly it, Ritchie. Jeez, I loved the way we went whizzing through the air."

"Better than Schon, eh mate?"

"Well . . . different, that's all."

"No way you'd get me up in one of those bloody things, no way. Give me a good horse any day."

Pony put his hands on his hips, and swaggered about in a small circle. "I'm going to fly it myself one day, betcha, Ritchie. Matt'll teach me." He glanced at Hegarty. "After Mum that is."

Ingrid glanced quizzically from Pony to Hegarty. "Don't be so anxious to work yourself out of a job, Hegarty," she murmured.

Hegarty shrugged. "It depends on how I'm doing for time," he muttered.

Ingrid gestured to Ritchie. "Anyway, this is Ritchie, our head stockman."

Hegarty extended his hand in a cordial handshake. "Matt's the name, Ritchie."

"Pleased to meetcha, Matt. I've been hearin' about you comin' all the way from America to muster for us in the whirligig."

"That's right."

"Miss Ingrid wanted me to talk to you about it," said the black.

Hegarty glanced to her in mock surprise. "Miss Ingrid?"

"Dad doesn't deal with the ringers; he leaves it to me, and Anna," she stated brusquely. She shuffled her feet impatiently in the dirt. "You make arrangements with Ritchie, Hegarty. We'll be mustering cattle to the north tomorrow morning." She motioned to the stockyards. "I'll be over there when you're through with Ritchie. There's some work needs doing on the yards. You may as well fill out the day there."

It was like a sharp command, as if to remind him he was just a hired hand. Maybe she'd be like that in bed—go here, touch me there, kiss me this way. He wondered where Anna was. He'd been sure she'd be anxiously waiting to greet Pony when he got back. He gave Ingrid an exaggerated bow, and touched his forelock in a gesture of mock subservience. "I'll be right with you, boss lady," he said softly.

She paused, irritably flicking at her long blonde hair, then motioned impatiently to Pony. "You'd better come with me, Pony. You can help too."

"Where's Mum?"

"Out checking the water hole toward Tulawanta. She heard it was dry, so she won't be back until later today."

She turned on her heels and strode toward the stockyards, but Pony hesitated, looking to Hegarty as if for guidance. She stopped, and beckoned imperiously. "Come on, Pony."

Hegarty nodded to the boy. "Go on; I'll be across in a minute."

"Okay Matt; see you later, Ritchie."

"Catch up with you, mate."

Both men watched them go in silence. Ritchie put the cigarette back in his mouth and scratched at the hair around the nape of his neck; a knowing smile spread on his face.

"You got Miss Kisek all het up, Matt," he remarked.

"She's got herself all het up over nothing," retorted Hegarty.

"Mebbe. We don't get too many fellas out here like you. Matter of bloody fact none at all. I reckon someone musta held a bloody gun at ole Kisek's head to get him to hire you."

Hegarty thumbed toward the helicopter. "There was no gun involved, just the fact I could fly that."

"It'd take more than that." Ritchie grinned. "Maybe the girls liked the look of you."

Hegarty didn't want to go through the crocodile story again; he figured Pony would eventually tell Ritchie. He shrugged. "Maybe. Kisek struck me as a pretty strange sort of guy. I understand he never hires anyone."

"Only blacks, like me. The ole bugger prefers us, I s'pose." He scowled. "Not that he has anything to do with us. All the orders come through the women." He shrugged. "Suits me. No one could ever work out ole Kisek anyway, not in a month of bloody Sundays. The way he acts you'd think us blacks were goin' to contaminate him or somethin', y'know. I hear it's always been the same, even before I came to work here. It don't bother me none; I stay around because he pays better for blacks than anyone else. Some of the cattle places in this country have been exploiting blacks for years, y'know, paying 'em nothin', but it don't happen here. Bugger him; if he don't like the color of our skin, then that's his bloody problem."

The way it gushed out with sudden vehemence, Hegarty had a shrewd notion it was a problem for the aborigine too, but he'd learned to live with it. Yet Ritchie's words were like the circumstantial evidence in the Wiesenthal report, another brick with which to build. A Nazi war criminal hiding out here would be too paranoid to risk hiring whites, but he would figure he was safe with blacks, even if his Nazi philosophy regarded them as an inferior, subhuman race. Untouchable. It would account for Kisek's attitude to them. He must have hated having to deal with them before he off-loaded the responsibility onto his daughters.

"Hey, I've been sayin' too much," grinned Ritchie. "Specially to a stranger."

Hegarty didn't want to dam the impulsive flow. "That's okay, Ritchie. Kisek might be a bit offbeat, but Christ, not like the guy I met last night they call Carl."

Ritchie removed his hat, and ran his fingers through his thick hair. "Shit, now there's a real weird bloke. Gives me the bloody creeps, y'know. Never speaks to me, never comes near me. Came close once an' just looked through me as if I bloody well wasn't there. I reckon if he was givin' out the orders, I'd be pissin' off outa the place. I don't know nothin' about him, an' I don't want to."

Hegarty nodded toward Ingrid. "The women seem okay."

"Oh sure, bloody all right, specially Anna. I guess you met her?"

"Yes. The sisters are . . . different."

"Bloody oath. But they're better than their old man."

"Listen, where are we starting in the morning anyway?" Hegarty cut in.

Ritchie dropped his hat back on his head, squatted down on his heels, and traced out a map in the dirt with his finger. "This here's Inverleigh, to the north," he pointed out. "An' here's Cathedral Rock back here. I reckon we'll start somewheres in between. I'll take a few of the boys out tonight, and we'll camp there. You should be able to spot us easy from the air, there's a stockyard there. Lotta stock around; bullocks, steers, cows, heifers. We can draft 'em out there for brandin' and truckin' off to the abbatoirs."

"I'll find it. What time are you starting?"

"We like to start moving around daybreak."

"I'll be there; maybe with Pony," said Hegarty.

Ritchie glanced at him in surprise. "Pony always rides with me."

Hegarty had sensed the strong friendship between Ritchie and Pony, even if it was obvious from the dinner conversation that Kisek disapproved.

"I guess he's kind of taken with the helicopter for now," Hegarty said, with a note of apology.

Ritchie brusquely scuffed out the map with his hand to conceal his disappointment, and stood up again.

"I reckon Pony's entitled to do what he likes," he said. "I s'pose a helicopter's more excitin' that some old horse, even Schon."

"No. I get the idea nothing's more important than Schon."

The aborigine's face was carefully impassive again. "That's the way it's always been before."

Hegarty slapped him on the shoulder. "It hasn't changed. I'll only be here for a short time, and Pony wants to learn as much about the helicopter as he can. Schon still comes first."

He thumbed toward the stockyards. "I'd better get on over there. I'll see you in the morning, Ritchie."

Ritchie dropped his cigarette to the ground and very deliberately ground it under his heel.

"You can be boss man to her, if you want," he said softly.

Ritchie didn't miss much. "I'm just here to do a job," Matt said.

Ritchie merely put his fingers to his mouth, and brought forth a shrill whistle. A saddled quarter horse trotted around from the other side of the shed and came to a halt by the aborigine, pawing at the ground, wide eyes nervously on the helicopter. Ritchie took hold of the reins, making gentle soothing sounds as he stroked the horse's nose, then he swung smoothly into the saddle.

"We all just do a job Matt, we just do it . . . different."

Hegarty thoughtfully watched him ride away. Ritchie might be very fond of Pony, but obviously had no great liking for Kisek. It could be worthwhile talking to him again; even if he had no contact with Kisek, there might be something important he could have seen, without even realizing it.

He glanced back to the house and saw the elderly Carl standing by the veranda, staring at him. Even from a distance there was no mistaking the malevolence. He still looked incongruous in white shirt and black pants. He'd have to talk to Jules about him—he might have some idea where the old man fitted into the picture. Matt shrugged and turned away. When he reached the stockyards he looked back, but Carl had vanished, as if abruptly incinerated by the hot earth. He moved surprisingly fast for an old man.

The stockyards were constructed mainly of metal, with upright iron stanchions set into the ground, and a combination of wooden planks and metal pipe bolted horizontally to form the walls. Pony and Ingrid were stacking lengths of pipe by a section of wall that had collapsed, dropping them in place with a reverberating clang. The sun was a white, fiery glare in the blue sky, so he took off his shirt, and put it down with his camera beside one of the stanchions. The iron felt like a heated stove to the touch.

"Some big bugger bullock charged the wall the other day, and knocked it clear down," explained Pony.

"How's the bullock?" grinned Hegarty.

"In better shape than the wall," retorted Ingrid.

She paused, letting her eyes linger on his bare torso, pink tongue languidly polishing her lips, making him feel like he was hung out in a meat market. He didn't look away, but let his own tongue flicker about his lips in silent communication. She stroked her thighs, and gently rolled her hips in answering body language.

"I guess you'd like me to fix it," he said.

She nodded. "That was the general idea. I know it's a comedown from buzzing around the country like a hotshot eagle, but that's the way of a cattle station."

It was as if she felt it necessary to put her tart words and her enticing body language in conflict, trying to conceal the obvious.

"Doesn't bother me none," he said easily. "Got any tools?"

She pointed to a canvas bag lying by one of the stanchions. "Everything you need should be there."

"We work together, we'll knock it off in a coupla hours, Matt," said Pony cheerfully.

"Get a water bag from the house, Pony," instructed Ingrid, glancing into the sky. "It's going to be hot work."

Pony scowled. "Why can't I stay with Matt?"

"You can stay with him as long as you want when you get back. But you're going to need something to drink. Now will you please go get a water bag."

Revolt simmered momentarily in the boy's face, then he relented, turned away, and trotted toward the house. "Don't start until I get back, Matt," he called.

"You've made quite an impression on Pony, Hegarty," she observed drily. "But then I suppose he's never met a big ringer from Texas before."

"He's a terrific kid."

"Don't make it too hard for him, Hegarty."

"What do you mean, too hard?"

"You're only here for a few days. It'll be short-term hero worship."

"I don't need any hero worship."

"That's the way it's looking to me."

"Maybe I can teach him a thing or two."

She laughed, a low throaty, taunting sound. "Are you aiming to teach us all a thing or two?"

He hid behind a grin. It was a reminder he needed to tread carefully with this woman, and he wondered if he might be making a mistake choosing her over Anna. He squatted by the tool bag, and nodded to the helicopter. "That's all the teaching I'm figuring to do."

She fell silent as he laid out the tools—hacksaw, drill, wrench, hammer, bolts. From the corner of his eye he could see her boots restlessly stirring the loose earth. "This is good country if a man wanted to stop wandering," she said. "It's dry now, but you should see it after the wet; green like you can't imagine, and teeming with life, birds everywhere."

She'd given him the opening he was looking for. He made a slow survey of the countryside. "Well, you could be right," he said. He lifted his gaze to her face. "There's a lot of things here to attract a man getting tired of being footloose."

She flicked her hair back with that characteristic movement of her hand. "You don't know the half of it."

He was beginning to see why she'd got rid of Pony. "I guess I should find out."

"Maybe." She half smiled, watching him intently, then glanced again to the sky. "You're going to raise quite a sweat fixing the yard, so how about taking a swim with me later today?"

"Sure, sounds great. Whereabouts?"

"Across at the lagoon."

He laughed, and shook his head. "You've got to be joking; you mean you want to play tag with the crocodiles?"

"No. There's a small separate pool at the west end of the lagoon. There aren't any there. You probably didn't see it when you shot the croc. We swim there all the time."

"Okay, if you say so."

"I'll be there around six."

"I'll be looking forward to it."

There followed an awkward silence, as if she felt she'd pushed it too fast. He didn't want to risk the possibility of her backing out, so he busied himself with a length of pipe, dropping it by the broken wall.

"Well, I'll leave you to it, Hegarty," she said, "I've got to go check out some horses for tomorrow."

He heard the thrum of an approaching vehicle, and saw a jeep swing around the far corner of the house, blurred by the swirl of accompanying dust as it drove slowly toward the stockyards. The bulky figure of Kisek at the wheel seemed to diminish the size of the jeep. Ingrid gave it a cursory glance, then turned back to Hegarty.

"You're coming out on the muster?" he asked.

"Not tomorrow. Anna's going out."

"Then I guess we've got to make the most of today."

Her tongue gave off signals again, accompanied by a hungry smile. "That's what I thought," she said.

The jeep stopped short of the yards. Kisek cut the motor, squeezed himself out from behind the wheel, and walked ponderously toward them. He carried a coiled bullwhip in his hand.

Hegarty picked up the camera. Of all the photographs he needed, Kisek's was the one headquarters would consider the most important, and this was probably the best chance he'd get.

"I saw the camera; you like to take pictures, Hegarty?" asked Ingrid.

"Right; it's kind of a hobby of mine, just taking pictures of everywhere I've been. Sort of a record. I was telling Pony I'm hoping to put them all into a book one day."

"That sounds like an interesting idea."

"I took Anna and Pony's photograph, so I guess I should take yours too," he offered.

She was suddenly surprisingly coy. "You really want to?"

"Sure, why not?"

"You might get a better shot at the pool," she suggested archly.

Kisek came to a halt just behind her. "Maybe there too," said Hegarty, grinning. "You'd look good no matter where."

The compliment pleased her. She lifted her head and involuntarily brushed again at her hair. "Okay, how's this?"

He focused on her. "That's fine." He was aware of Kisek scowling disagreeably in the background, but he took no notice and clicked off several shots.

Kisek grunted and pointed to the broken wall with the whip. "I'm wanting that fixed by tonight," he exclaimed surlily.

Ingrid ignored him. "You've got to give me one, Hegarty," she said.

He nodded. "Sure." Then he stepped abruptly to one side, moved forward with the camera still raised in a shooting position, and directed it at Kisek. "May as well get one of you for my collection, Mr. Kisek," he said, taking two quick shots.

He was prepared to risk some sort of reaction from Kisek, but it was like he'd jabbed a needle into the exposed nerve of a tooth, and the vehemence took him by surprise. A guttural roar as if from an enraged tiger gushed from Kisek's throat, the whip uncoiled menacingly as he raised a threatening hand trembling with fury toward the camera, and for a moment Hegarty feared he was going to use the whip. He knew a smattering of German, but he could only guess at the furious stream of unintelligible words spluttering from Kisek's mouth. He instinctively stepped back, caught his heel on a length of pipe, and would have fallen if one of the yard stanchions hadn't been within reach.

Kisek's anger finally translated into English. "How dare you taking my photograph without my permission?" he screamed. "How dare you are doing such a thing? Never am I allowing such insolence—never, never! I'm not caring if you are flying the helicopter or not, you are getting out of Cathedral Rock, you hear? Out, out—out!" His voice rose to a high, strained pitch. "Are you understanding, Hegarty, are you understanding? Get your stupid motorbike, and get out." The sun-browned texture of his face had converted to a blue-tinged red, as if apoplexy threatened, the words fused by an incoherent spluttering that spattered his beard with saliva.

Hegarty went fast into apologetic retreat. With Kisek's paranoia he'd figured on an element of risk in taking his photograph, but he hadn't considered it might end in his being thrown out of Cathedral Rock. Christ, after the trouble it took to get himself hired, he couldn't afford to let that happen. How could he possibly tell Reine? Or Jules?

"Wait on, wait—please, Mr. Kisek," he pleaded. "I was just . . ."

Kisek took several menacing steps forward, the whip

trailing through the dust at his feet, head drawn into his bulky shoulders like a bull about to charge. "Out! Out!" he bellowed. "No one is taking my photograph without asking. There's being no place for you here at Cathedral Rock, Hegarty."

Ingrid seemed as stunned by the reaction as Hegarty, but she recovered quickly, stepping to her father and trying to restrain him. "For God's sake Dad, will you just calm down," she demanded shrilly. "Christ, it's only a bloody photograph."

Kisek angrily shook her aside. "He has no right to be doing such a thing without asking," he blurted. "No right, and I'm not wanting him around Cathedral Rock. The hell with the helicopter."

Pony had come quietly up behind Kisek, water bag in his hand forming droplets in the black earth, his startled eyes darting back and forth from his grandfather to Hegarty.

"And I'm telling you to calm down. You want to give yourself a heart attack?" shouted Ingrid, with matching vehemence.

Hegarty held the camera out toward Kisek. "It's just a hobby of mine, Mr. Kisek," he appealed. "Taking photographs as I travel around is just something I like to do, something I've been doing for a long time. I didn't think you'd mind." He pointed to Pony. "I've been taking photographs of Pony; and his mother." He turned to the boy. "That's right, isn't it, Pony?"

"And mine," added Ingrid. "For Chrissake, what's so important about a measly photograph anyway? It won't kill you. Maybe it's time you had one taken."

Kisek's rush of venomous words were starting to falter, but his face showed no lessening of anger. "I'm the one who is saying when mein photograph is being taken," he choked.

"Oh my God," said Ingrid in exasperation. "Are you just going to let the helicopter rot in the shed forever?" she fumed. "Pass up the chance to finally get some damn value out of it? For Chrissake, we need Hegarty, Dad." She shook his arm. "Don't you see, we need him?"

Kisek glared at her, his voice finally dropping to a more temperate tone.

"No one is taking photographs at Cathedral Rock I'm not wanting," he persisted, breathing hard.

"What's wrong with taking a photograph?" intervened Pony with hostility.

"You are minding your own damn business, Pony," muttered Kisek.

"I don't want Matt leaving like that, Grandad."

"I'm still running Cathedral Rock, not you, not yet," rasped Kisek.

Pony thrust his chin pugnaciously toward his grandfather. "But it's not fair. I reckon if Matt goes, then I'll go with him," he threatened.

Kisek dropped the whip, raised his hand as if to strike Pony, hesitated, then let it fall to his side. "You'll be doing what you're told," he declared fiercely.

"My God, let's just drop it," urged Ingrid. "Please Dad, just drop it. Can't you see, it's all just a misunderstanding. I want to see that damn helicopter being used at last, and Hegarty's the only one to do it. I just can't understand you getting yourself so worked up over a bloody photograph."

"I've a right to my anger, and you watch your tongue. You're not speaking to me like that."

Pony slipped past Kisek and defiantly positioned himself at Hegarty's side. "I asked Matt to take some pictures, and anyway I'd like one of you, 'cause there's none anywhere, and that's no reason to throw Matt out," he challenged in a high-pitched voice. "I mean it. If Matt goes, then I'll go with him."

Hegarty was concerned Pony's defiance might only inflame Kisek further; there had to be a better way to make peace.

"Take it easy, Pony," he warned. "Don't speak to your grandfather like that. I'll handle it."

The dismay Kisek felt at Pony's rebellious defense of Hegarty clearly showed in his face, dousing his anger.

"Well . . . I'm not having my photograph taken unless I'm asking for it," he growled. "And you'll not be going anywhere, Pony."

Hegarty turned abruptly from Kisek, quickly rewinding the film. He opened the camera back and with apparent clumsiness let the cassette fall to the ground. As he knelt to recover it, his back still to Kisek, he surreptitiously exchanged it for an unused cassette from his shirt pocket. Then he stood to face Kisek, closed the camera, and held forth the unused film as if offering an olive branch.

"Believe me, Mr. Kisek, I didn't have any intention of upsetting you," he said with sincerity. "I guess I figured you'd appreciate a photograph. But if you resent it so much, then here's the film. Do what you like with it."

The offer was followed by a brooding silence. Over toward the house the elderly Carl had materialized again, and stood intently watching the confrontation. There was only the sound of the constant wind flushing the grasslands, tugging at their clothes, teasing their hair. Then Kisek bent slowly, as if rusted at the joints, retrieved his whip, and coiled it deliberately in his hands.

"Go on, take the damn thing if it'll make you happy," snapped Ingrid. "Just get off Hegarty's back."

Kisek didn't answer, contenting himself with a scowl. Then he stepped forward and took the cassette from Hegarty. He held it a moment, turning it over in his gnarled fingers, squinting, frowning, then just as deliberately went to the tools Hegarty had laid out, picked up the hammer, placed the film on the ground, and with one accurate blow flattened the cassette. He picked it up and handed it back, his eyes aggressively focused on Hegarty.

"I'm not liking my photograph taken without permission," he muttered. "You're remembering that, Hegarty."

"Sure, sure, Mr. Kisek," said Hegarty quickly. "It won't happen again."

"Matt's still mustering for us, Grandad?" asked Pony anxiously.

Kisek didn't answer. He turned away and lumbered back toward the jeep, passing Ingrid, who stood aggressively with legs apart and hands on her hips, as if she didn't exist.

"Be sure you're meeting up with the blacks when the muster starts in the morning, Hegarty," he grunted, without looking back.

They watched wordlessly as he got back in the jeep and drove toward the waiting Carl.

"Jesus Christ," muttered Hegarty, letting the expletive out like a gush of released steam.

"Are you okay?" inquired Ingrid.

"Sure. Christ, that was one sticky situation with your father."

Ingrid nodded. "Maybe I should have warned you, Hegarty. Dad's got so many hangups about what he imagines is someone butting into his precious privacy; it's like a crazy obsession." She frowned, and gazed after Kisek. "Dammit, I think he's getting worse as he gets older, y'know that? Sometimes I feel he's like a stranger I don't know at all. I once saw him order a bloke off Cathedral Rock at gun point, when he came looking for stray cattle. He really goes off." She gave a nervous, shaky laugh. "My God, I thought he was going to use that whip on you."

"I had the same feeling," confessed Hegarty.

"It was the war," said Pony defensively, "it was that war Grandad was in, that's what makes him act up like that."

Hegarty rubbed reflectively at his chin. "I guess you could be right, Pony." He grinned at the two of them. "Hey, I owe you both. I figure if you both hadn't been here, I'd be on my way back to Normanton right now." He tousled Pony's hair. "You helped me get the job, and now this, hey copilot?" He put out his hand. "I figure that makes us real mates now, eh Pony?"

The boy hesitated, then shook his hand. Hegarty had the feeling the boy was troubled by a divided sense of loyalty.

"You got to get to understand Grandad," he said. "You get to know him, and he can be terrific."

"Well I'm sure he can," Hegarty quickly agreed.

"If you two *mates* don't mind, I've got things to do," said Ingrid drily.

Hegarty ducked his head in apology. "Thanks to you also, Ingrid," he added. "You really stood by me."

"That makes us mates too, eh Hegarty?" she mocked.

He grinned. "Something like that."

"I'll still see you later?"

"Sure; I'll be there."

Pony looked inquisitively from one to the other, but asked no questions, then Ingrid was gone, striding in her purposeful way toward the house. The jeep was parked outside, but there was no sign of Kisek or Carl. She started up the jeep and drove off toward the east, accompanied by the usual trail of dust. Because of the flatness of the country she stayed in sight a long time, until she finally blended with the shimmering grass.

The temperature rose as the sun slow-baked the earth, casting hard-edged black shadows, coating their skins with running perspiration. Buzzing, circling flies constantly prospected for the sticky moisture, with irritating persistence, and Hegarty was grateful for the protection of his Texas hat.

The iron pipes burned to the touch, forcing Pony to hold them in place with his shirt wrapped around his hands. It was made bearable by the breeze fanning in from the north, with a faint tang of the sea.

It was coming together fast. Hegarty felt he already had a circumstantial frame fitted around Kisek, but no more concrete than the Wiesenthal report. Not yet. Kisek might live like a recluse, with an obsessive desire for anonymity; he might distrust strangers, hate blacks according to Ritchie, have a maniacal fear of being photographed—maybe that was the pattern of a man hiding out, but it was scarcely conclusive evidence that would stand up in court. Yet it was encouraging, and sufficient to reinforce Matt's conviction that Kisek was Leiman. He might get something more conclusive from Ingrid, if he handled her right.

"You didn't really give Grandad the film, did you Matt?" accused Pony suddenly.

Hegarty didn't look up from where he was bolting the pipe to the stanchion. The boy was certainly sharp; it was goddamn lucky he hadn't blurted it out before Kisek left, but it might be wiser to level with him.

"If you say so, Pony," he replied casually.

"I saw you swap it for the one out of your pocket."

Hegarty considered his answer. If Pony took the story of his sleight of hand back to Kisek, there wouldn't be any second chance; he'd be thrown out of Cathedral Rock on his neck. He played it easy, turning to Pony and holding out his hand.

"You got another bolt there, Pony?"

Pony dropped it into his hand. "You're my mate, Matt, but I don't like you tricking Grandad," he said. "He might act sorta funny at times, but I don't like him being tricked, y'know."

Hegarty positioned the new bolt, and began tightening it with the wrench. "Well, I'll tell you, Pony, I wasn't exactly leveling with you about that book of my photographs I was telling you about."

"How do you mean?"

"It's not just an idea, but it's important to me, very important. I've already spoken to a publisher about it. I really want to get it published, Pony."

"You can't put Grandad in the book."

"Believe me, I've no intention of doing so." He finished off the bolt, and turned solemn-faced to the boy for another. "But all the photographs I've taken since I left Cairns are on that film. They would have all been destroyed too, if I'd given them to your grandfather. You have to believe me when I tell you I won't use the ones of him, but I sure as hell need the others."

"You mean I'll be in your book, Matt?"

"If you want, Pony."

"And Mum, and Ingrid?"

"Only if they want to be."

Elation swept doubt from Pony's face. "Golly, Matt, that'd be terrific. Wait'll I tell Mum."

"Well I think you and I should keep it to ourselves for now," said Hegarty quickly. "Let's wait until I'm leaving Cathedral Rock, then we'll ask them how they feel about it. Sort of give them a surprise."

"Okay, Matt." The boy slapped his hands against the pipe with excitement. "I can just imagine showing the book to the kids at school; jeez, they'd be so jealous."

"Hey, it's going to take quite a time before the book's published," Hegarty cautioned.

The warning pricked some of Pony's enthusiasm. "Yeah . . . and you'll be gone from here by then."

"Don't worry, I'll be keeping in touch. Even send you a book."

"Jeez, that'd be great. And you won't use Grandad's picture."

"Absolutely promise, mate. Absolutely. You've got my word on that."

"I guess Grandad'd understand," murmured the boy.

"Sure he will. Bet he'd be real proud to see you in the book."

Pony's face brightened again. "Hey, I reckon you're right; yeah, I bet he will. And Mum, and Ingrid."

Hegarty was irritated at having to lie to the boy, but for Christ's sake, he had to get his priorities right. He was a practiced expert at twisting the truth when the stakes were high, yet why did it make him feel like a heel with Pony? He let it settle for a while, keeping the conversation to comments about the repairs, just grateful Pony had accepted the story about the film.

It went fast, Pony holding a length of pipe at one end, while Hegarty bolted it to the stanchion at the other.

"Bet you've worked on stockyards before, haven't you, Matt?" remarked Pony.

Hegarty tipped back his hat, and smeared his face with sweaty grime. "You mean I look like I know what I'm doing?" he asked with a grin.

"Something like that, I s'pose."

"I once built a stockyard in Argentina by myself."

"That musta taken a time."

"Yeah, well I had plenty of time on my hands right then. This rancher who lived in Buenos Aires sent me out to the pampas on my own."

"The pampas?"

Hegarty made a sweeping gesture to the surrounding country. "Yeah; it's what they call country something like the savanna here—a big plain, with plenty of grass, and lots of cattle." His hands waved about in the air as if trying to swat a persistent fly, and he assumed an exaggerated Argentinian accent. "'You eez building eet where zee Colorado and Salado rivaires eez joining. You eez finding the timbaire there,' he told me."

"Did he really sound like that?" Pony asked with a giggle.

"Well, a little like that. Big fat guy, handlebar mustache, never saw him without a big cigar stuck in his mouth. He gave me a Ford truck to work with, so off I went."

"How long did it take you?"

"I figure I was there a coupla months. I liked it. Sometimes it's good to be alone, work hard, make yourself sweat.

Your muscles ache, but you sleep like a baby. I dug holes, sawed timber, lugged it into position, slept in the truck, and ate at a little village a couple of miles away. The people were friendly, the girls . . . ," he paused and winked, "very friendly, and beautiful. I didn't hurry myself."

"Was the rancher pleased?"

Hegarty shrugged, and winked again. "Not exactly. Came out from Buenos Aires in a car looked about ninety feet long. Seems they'd stacked the timber on the wrong side of the river."

Pony's eyes widened in disbelief. "You're kidding me, Matt. You didn't . . . ?"

"Yep; the man said build it where they stacked the timber, and that's what I did."

"Bugger me, what'd he say?"

"My Spanish isn't so hot, and he went on for about ten minutes without me understanding a word."

Pony chuckled. "Something like Grandad."

"Something like that. The sonofabitch didn't want to pay me."

"I'll bet. What'd you do?"

"I started to drive off in the truck. Told him he wouldn't get it back until he paid up. He finally paid."

"Jeez, that's a crazy story, Matt." Pony could hardly talk for laughing. "You sure you're not pulling my leg?"

"It's as true as I'm working here at Cathedral Rock," maintained Hegarty, with mock solemnity.

Pony's shoulders shook with involuntary giggling. "Jeez, I can imagine how Grandad'd be, if someone built one of our stockyards in the wrong place."

Hegarty didn't leave it there. The story had taken the boy's mind off the film switch, and he was anxious to make sure it stayed that way. Besides, he had a feeling Pony was the key to what he needed to achieve at Cathedral Rock, and any time spent binding the boy to him was well spent. He had a fund of stories, and he kept the boy enthralled while they sweated together in the heat as they worked through the day.

Late in the afternoon Pony looked up to see clouds of dust in the distance. "Someone's comin'," he announced, and as the vehicle became visible, added, "It's Mum." He turned his attention back to Hegarty. "I don't reckon I've ever met someone like you, y'know that, Matt?"

"I'm not so special."

"I reckon you are." He climbed onto the stockyard wall and positioned himself close to Hegarty, arms draped over the top rail. "I wish you could stay around here, y'know that? I bet you'd be the best mustering pilot in the Gulf. And you'd make a lot of money. You wouldn't just have to work for Cathedral Rock. Bet you could even buy your own helicopter after a while. I bet you could."

Hegarty laughed it off. "No, I like to move around, Pony."

The boy jumped to the ground as the dust-grimed ranch wagon swung around the stockyards and pulled up a few yards away. Anna waved to them through the window.

"I see you two workers have got the yard fixed," she called, as she opened the door and stepped out.

Hegarty glanced at his watch. It was five-thirty, with the shadows already lengthening, but he figured there was plenty of time before darkness. He wasn't figuring on groping around in the blackness of a nighttime lagoon to find Ingrid. He strolled across to Anna, with Pony at his side.

She looked weary, her hair dank, the lines in her face deepened with perspiration, but it didn't matter, she wore it in the way other women enhanced their appearance with make-up. He placed a hand on Pony's shoulder.

"We make a good team," he said, smiling. "He's not only a good copilot, he's also pretty damn hot at repairing stock-yards."

"Just let any old bugger bullock try and knock it down now," boasted Pony.

She offered a tired smile. "How'd the flight go this morning?"

Hegarty opened his mouth to reply, but Pony was too quick for him.

"Terrific, Mum, just terrific," he claimed excitedly. "Jeez, you should see the way Matt flies the helicopter." He shuffled about in a circle, his hands describing sweeping curves through the air, his tongue vibrating in imitation of the rotor blades. "This way and that way, any way you want to go," he exclaimed rapturously. "You should have seen us, should have been there. We mustered some cattle, flew over the old house; Matt can make it do anything he wants."

"Sounds like it went pretty well," she said, with gentle irony.

"I had the best day of my life," added Pony eagerly. "Except when I got Schon."

She smiled, leaned on the wagon, and mopped languidly at her face. "I take it you're pleased with the helicopter, Matt?"

"It went pretty much the way Pony said. I figure I can do a good mustering job with it."

"I'm glad. From what I've seen around the Gulf it'll cut our mustering time by weeks. You've talked to Ritchie?"

"Yeah, I met him this afternoon. It's all set for tomorrow morning."

"You won't go wrong with Ritchie. Been here ten years, and I think he's one of the best ringers in the Gulf. Just as well; Dad won't have any white ringers on the place, for God knows what reason."

"Can I go out with Matt again tomorrow?" asked Pony eagerly.

She looked uncertainly to Hegarty. "I think that depends on Matt. I thought you were going out on Schon with Ritchie."

"That was before I knew about the helicopter, and Schon could do with a spell." He spread his hands imploringly. "C'mon, Mum, please."

Hegarty shrugged. Maybe it would be a good idea to keep Pony close to him. "It's okay with me, Anna."

She nodded agreement. "All right. You'd better let Ritchie know."

"I already have," said Hegarty.

She smiled uneasily. "You must have been pretty sure I'd agree."

"I figured you'd think it was good experience for the boy."

"Maybe," she said, with an abrupt change of mood. Maybe she figured he was taking too much for granted. She glanced into the sky, then turned back to the wagon. "I hope it's cooler tomorrow; it's not usually this hot at this time of year. I'm beat." She opened the wagon door. "I'm going to get myself cleaned up for dinner." She gestured to Pony. "Come on Pony, you may as well come too—if you can drag yourself away from Matt," she concluded sharply.

Pony took a few halting steps, then stopped. "Are you coming to dinner tonight, Matt?"

Hegarty took off his hat, and combed his fingers through his hair, feeling the caking effect of dust and sweat. He needed that swim, apart from meeting Ingrid, but he wasn't going to tell Anna about that; or Pony.

"Dinner may not be such a good idea, Pony," he said.

Anna shrugged. "You're welcome."

"You could tell us some more stories, Matt," Pony urged. "Matt's been telling me some terrific stories about the places he's been."

"No, I don't think I should come," persisted Hegarty.

"What's the problem?" queried Anna.

"Well . . . I had a bit of a misunderstanding with your father this afternoon."

"A misunderstanding? What sort of misunderstanding?"

"Grandad bloody near fired Matt this afternoon," piped up Pony indignantly.

Anna's eyes widened with astonishment. "Fired you? For God's sake, what for? You haven't even started mustering yet."

"Like I said, it was a misunderstanding. It's over now, but I don't figure dinner would be a good idea."

"Damn it, I want to hear about it."

It was Hegarty's turn to glance to where the sun was already homing toward the horizon. He wanted more than swimming time with Ingrid, and he had to make the attempt to get to Jules sometime tonight.

"Why don't I let Pony tell you; you'll get a more unbiased viewpoint."

"My God, I doubt it."

"Well, I figure it's just best to forget the whole goddamn thing."

"You don't want to talk about it?"

"Not now."

She shrugged. "Then I'll get it from Dad I guess."

"I don't figure he'll want to talk about it either. Like I keep saying, it was a misunderstanding."

"Okay, if that's the way you want it," she muttered in

resignation. "But I'll probably bring it up with Dad anyway."
She clambered into the wagon. "Come on, Pony."

Pony reluctantly followed. "I still wish you'd come, Matt,"
he tried again.

"Maybe another night," said Hegarty. "Best to let the dust
settle for now." He gave Pony a slow, deliberate wink. "You
know what I mean." It was an attempt to instill in the boy a
need to keep his confidence about the sleight of hand with the
film; he hoped to Christ he wouldn't say anything about it to
Anna. But Pony seemed to understand, and returned a
conspiratorial wink.

"Okay Matt, if that's the way you want it," he acknowledged cheerfully. "I'll see you in the morning."

Hegarty stepped back and raised his hand as Anna started
the motor. "In the morning, mate," he called.

He averted his face from the dust as they drove away. He
hated to admit it, but in a short space of time the boy had made
quite an impact on him. Perhaps if he hadn't lived his life on
such a narrow, dedicated path, he might have a son about
Pony's age. He turned away, and headed toward the shed
where his Kawasaki sat. Did it matter? He could think of other
possibilities he'd had for a lasting relationship along the way.
He'd managed to put them out of his mind okay, and there was
nothing to say this wouldn't be the same.

He took an indirect route to the lagoon, circling wide of
the buildings, even though the buzzing sound of the motorcycle would doubtless carry to the house. He was late, but the
terrain dictated his speed, and he didn't want to take another
spill. The air flowing past dried the sweat on his body, and by
the time he reached the lagoon he felt refreshed. He slowed to
a halt and looked around. He was again struck by the sense of
tranquility, with the soft drone of insects, the rush of passing
birds overhead, the necklace of green trees around the still
water that he now knew might well be a facade for a savage
death lurking beneath the surface. Still, there were hoof marks
at the water's edge, with no sign of any dead cattle, so maybe
the croc he'd shot had been the sole inhabitant. He turned
west, as Ingrid had instructed, and cautiously guided the bike
around rocks and trees, following the shoreline. It ended

where a strip of grassed earth formed a dam between the lagoon and another much smaller, irregularly shaped pool that was almost completely screened by whitewood trees and jumbled rock, except for an opening like a narrow beach at one side. He rode slowly around to the opening, braked to a stop, turned off the motor, then dismounted and propped the bike by a small pile of clothes draped on a large rock. Ingrid's bright checked shirt lay among the garments, as recognizable as a calling card. He could see the jeep, parked amid the trees at the far end of the pool. The pool was about fifty feet across, with the surface sharply divided into two contrasting colors, dark green where the trees cast a canopy of shade at the far side, and burnished gold where unimpeded sunlight shone on the water in front of him. It looked quite deep.

He didn't see Ingrid at first, then there was a sudden swirl of water and a flash of brown and white skin as she launched out from behind a tree on the far side. He waited, grinning, hands on hips, while she swam in a leisurely breast stroke toward him. She stopped a few feet from the bank, gently circling with her arms as she treaded water, mouth slightly parted in a mocking smile. Her long hair trailed on the surface like fronds; he could see where the brown of her shoulders marked the shape of a tank top, and below that the sudden whiteness of her breasts and body that gradually blended with the color of the water.

"I thought you were going to let me down, Hegarty," she murmured.

He squatted at the edge, elbows resting on his knees. "Now why would I want to do that?" He grinned at her. "I always keep my word."

"Is that a fact now?" She flicked water in his face, and it felt deliciously cool. "Then come on in," she invited, "the water's beautiful."

"That's why I'm here."

"You're wasting precious time."

He nodded toward the lagoon. "I don't see why the crocs can't cross over here."

"They never do. Nothing in here for them to feed on, I suppose."

"You can guarantee that?"

"I'm in here, aren't I." She flicked water at him again. "You scared of the crocs or of me?"

"You don't scare me."

"Then come on in."

She suddenly launched herself away with the action of a graceful back dive, arms outstretched above her head, arching across the water like a playful dolphin, in a fast unfolding sequence of brown shoulders, white breasts, firm belly, and saturated pubic hair momentarily glittering with promise in the sunlight. Then it all slid beneath the water, until her head surfaced again in the middle of the pool. She pinched at her nose, and mopped water from her eyes.

"Stop acting like a chicken, Hegarty," she called laughingly. "I won't bite."

He quickly shed his clothes. He was going to have to work her with subtleness, take her a step at a time until she was willing to answer anything he asked her. It would take care; he had the feeling she could unsheath claws if crossed.

He had a good physique, muscle-hardened by the way he'd lived, and he knew she was watching, appreciating. He cleaved the water in a shallow dive; the sudden coldness took his breath, and he threshed about for a moment to pump up his circulation, then swam unhurriedly toward her. She backed away, arms sculling, the same tantalizing smile fixed on her face.

"Didn't I say it was great?" she said.

"Hell, it's cold at first," he gasped.

"You'll get used to it."

He reached to touch her, but she twisted away like a slippery fish and headed in the other direction. He tried again, and once more she slithered out of reach, with a sharp kick of her legs. He was surprised, wondering if his first impression had been right, she was all tantalizing tease but no action.

"What's the matter; scared I'll bite?" he mimicked her.

"You don't scare me," she mimicked back.

But she slowly allowed him to close the gap; after each evasion she made he found himself a little closer, until they were touching, her hands on his shoulders, his arms moving in circles about her to keep them afloat, their bodies irresistibly fusing as if by magnetic attraction. There was too much blood pulsing for him to feel cold now, he felt himself harden against her belly, and she felt it too, sliding her hands down about his buttocks, and pulling him tight to her. He could feel her warm, quick breath on his face, while her smile remained, more intense, even yearning.

"Maybe this is all happening too fast, but there's never been anyone at Cathedral Rock like you, Hegarty," she whispered breathlessly.

"Time's got nothing to do with it," he murmured.

"You're right. Take what you can, when you can."

"While you can," he echoed.

She crushed her mouth to his, sliding a frantic tongue into his mouth, and he found himself forced to move his arms faster to prevent them sinking. He broke free of her mouth.

"Let's get out on the bank," he panted.

"This is more exciting," she breathed.

She pressed herself tight to him, wet skin clamping like suction, mouth close to his ear, blocking everything except her rapid breath, while her fingers pried down between them until they were clasped feverishly about his rigid stem.

"Put it in me," she whispered urgently. "Put it in me, Hegarty, put it in me." She raised her legs, and scissored them about his waist, frantically trying to guide him into her. The way she'd imprisoned him he couldn't move his arms, there was nothing to keep them afloat.

"Jesus Christ," he managed to gurgle, before he sank beneath the surface. He could feel her going down with him, but she seemed too absorbed to notice; already she had him partway into her, legs clamped fiercely about him in a wrestler's hold that felt like she'd never let go until he either surrendered or drowned. He was vaguely aware of the watery sunlight disappearing overhead as they sank toward the dank green underneath. He was prepared to do whatever was needed to open her up, but he wasn't into drowning while fucking. He forcefully extricated his head from her arms, kicked himself loose, and bobbed to the surface, spewing water. She was still smiling in a crazy, irrational way when she too emerged a few feet from him.

"Christ, are you trying to drown me?" he spluttered.

She giggled and spurted a stream of water from her mouth into his face.

"All you had to do was hold your breath a bit, Hegarty; no one was going to drown. I reckoned you'd be one bloke who'd like to try something different."

He stroked away from her, heading for the bank. He'd marked her down as hard to figure, but there was a crazy streak in this girl.

"Different, okay, but impossible—forget it," he panted.

"We've got some unfinished business," she simpered.

"Not in the water, baby."

He clambered out onto the bank and stood brushing water from his body, watching her glide toward him. The warmth of the sun and the hot rocks underfoot felt like stepping from a winter night into a heated room. She stood knee-deep at the edge of the pool, wringing out her hair, water flowing in myriad rivulets over her small breasts and down her body. Her bemused expression was focused on his groin.

"I hope the way you're losing weight down there is only temporary," she murmured.

"There's only one way you're going to find out."

She shrugged, stepped out of the water, and came slowly toward him, rolling her hips the way he'd seen before, her nakedness making each movement more salacious. He held her close for a while, standing and sharing their wetness, until the sun warmed them.

"See, it was only temporary," he whispered.

"Then let's do it now," she breathed huskily.

He brushed her mouth with his lips. "Yes, let's do it now," he agreed.

He laid her down by her clothes on the flat, warm rock, without any preamble, which was neither needed or wanted. Her legs spread eagerly for him as he thrust into her. Maybe he was only using her, but it was what he was trained for, and she was craving to be used. Yet the excitement of sex with a girl like her could never be more than a bonus for why he was at Cathedral Rock. He worked her hard, just as she wanted, to the sucking sounds of their wet flesh in motion, her moans increasing in volume like a singer moving up the scales, their bodies gathering feverish momentum, until they joined in a duet of frenzied orgasm.

It was over quickly; they'd both been on a hair trigger. He didn't know about her, but it had been quite a time for him, and in a peculiar way he was already wishing it'd been Anna. They lay silently for a while, she still on her back, he on his stomach just as he'd sprawled when he lifted off her, basking in the dying sunlight. He felt her fingers trickling down his spine.

"I knew you were a stud the moment I laid eyes on you, darlin' Hegarty," she murmured. "It's going to be quite a mustering time."

He debated if it was wise to let her think like that, that there was going to be as much screwing as mustering. He rolled to his side, propped his head on his hand, and studied her face. It was like peering through a gauze mask, her expression so soft, so relaxed, so free of rancor.

"It's going to be a busy time," he said. "Don't let's be greedy."

"Who's being greedy; that was terrific, Hegarty." She brushed aside her wet hair, then leaned to him and kissed him without passion on the mouth. "I want you to do it to me again, and again, and again."

It sounded vaguely like a command, and it made him feel uneasy.

"I figure a good-looking girl like you could get all the men she wanted."

She frowned, eased over on to her stomach, and laid her head on her crossed arms. "God, there's nothing around here; so help me I sometimes feel envious when I see the cows being mounted. Crazy eh? Playing with myself is the only thing I've got around here."

"Like I said before, you could go somewhere else."

"Cathedral Rock might be lousy for screwing, but I do love this country." She pouted. "I guess it sounds like I'm having a tug of war with myself." She studied him a moment, with that same penetrating look she'd inherited from her father. "You're needed around here, Hegarty. I need you. You could stay around the Gulf Country and helicopter muster; make yourself a good living, y'know that."

He'd already had that from Pony, but there were too many questions he wanted answered.

"That's something I'd have to think about. Maybe it could be a good idea."

"It'd be a fabulous idea. You got anything you've got to go back to America for?"

"I reckon not."

"Another woman?"

He laughed easily. "No, nothing like that."

"Just a lot of lonely beds, eh Hegarty?"

"I don't ask you about other men."

She shrugged. "What about a family?"

"A father." He traced abstract lines on the rock face. "Your father might object to his daughter screwing around with the hired help."

"The hell with him. He's had his life, he's not going to turn me into a hermit like him; and creepy Carl."

"What makes your father like that? I mean he's so goddamn uptight about it, so . . . vehement. Christ, look at the way he reacted when I took his photograph. I mean it was nothing, yet he went off like a crazy man."

She sighed, eyes absently to the sky, as if searching for an answer.

"I honestly don't know, but he's always been the same. I mean, God, he's never ill-treated me, or anything like that." She hesitated. "He's got no warmth, y'know. Just no bloody warmth; hasn't got the faintest idea how to show affection." She scowled. "At least not to me. I reckon he's too busy worshipping Pony to have anything left over for me." She shrugged. "Not that it was much different before Pony came along. Anna's closer to him than me, always was. I reckon they've got something special, and I just can't get into it, even though he went to no end of trouble to teach me all about running Cathedral Rock." She was meandering, reliving bitterness, and he let her go on. "And he can be cruel, the way he uses that bullwhip. I remember seeing him use it on a black once, not that he knew I was around. I thought he was going to kill him, honest to God. He always tried to make sure we weren't around when anything like that happened; although I figure my mother must have seen plenty."

"She was different than he is?" asked Hegarty.

"Oh sure. God knows how they ever married. She was a . . . free spirit, y'know? I can remember the way she was when we were kids, always laughing, ready to have fun. But in the end he made her like himself; locked her up like a bird with wings clipped so it can't fly. I reckon that's why she died when we were still young, just gave up and faded away."

"Pony keeps saying going through the war in Germany made him like that."

"Maybe, but God, it's over forty years ago," she protested.

"Something like that can leave a scar that never goes away."

She cast a moody glance toward the lagoon. "Perhaps. He's never talked about it—at least not to me. Once I overheard him describing to my mother what it was like; how he was desperate to get out of Europe when it was over, to get anywhere."

"I wonder what made him choose Australia?"

"I think it was someone he met in Germany, an Australian. At least that's what Mum told me."

"It wouldn't have been easy. I mean getting a passport or an immigration visa after being in the German army. There'd have been a lot of bitterness in Australia, the same as everywhere."

"I don't know that he was in the army."

"What do you mean?"

"Oh he was in the war all right, but it could have been the navy or the air force for all I know. But I know he had a passport all right to get out here."

"You saw the passport?"

"Once; when I was a kid. God, he looked so young, you wouldn't know it was the same man to see him now." She smiled lazily, eyes half-closed, lost in nostalgia. "I was home from school in Cairns, just fooling around, y'know, and I came across it in a bottom drawer." She grimaced. "He caught me."

"You mean he was upset?"

She didn't immediately answer, but edged toward him so her thigh touched his in enticement. He didn't offer any reaction; he didn't want to make love to her again, not when he had the conversation running this way. Christ, he'd like to get his hands on that passport. He levered himself up on his elbows, and glanced across the savanna to where the sun was within touching distance of the horizon, tinting everything with an orange glow. He was cautious of pushing too hard, but maybe he'd never have her in this communicative mood again.

"He reacted something like you saw today," she said finally.

"That must have been tough."

"I was terrified. I think he would have belted me for the first time if my mother hadn't stopped him."

He contrived a yawn, as if this was merely trite conversation between couplings. But in fact the passport sounded important. Reine would be delighted if he got something like that, but he had the disappointing feeling she knew little more than Pony about her father's history.

She shaded her eyes and squinted at the distant sky flushed with red. "That's something you should photograph, Hegarty," she murmured. "God, this is unpredictable country, either drowning in torrential rain, or bone-dry with drought, then you see it like this, and it's something to believe in." She turned suddenly to him. "What do you believe in, Hegarty?"

She took him by surprise, and he was stunned that he didn't have a ready answer, even for himself. Justice maybe? His father's preoccupation with vengeance? It wasn't a question he asked himself any more.

"Oh, many things," he answered evasively.

"I'm not talking about God and stuff like that; I'm talking about an aiming point. You've got to have an aiming point, otherwise you're just walking around in circles."

He didn't want the conversation deflected away from Kisek. "Staying alive," he said drily.

She gave a short laugh. "We're all into that."

"It means something if you're moving around."

She shrugged. "Well, I suppose it's better than nothing."

"Your father's managed it pretty successfully. Maybe it changed him from the passport photograph you were talking about, but he's survived in a tough country."

For the first time she appraised him with a curious stare. "We're back on him again. What is with you and my father?"

"Nothing. I just find him an interesting man."

"More interesting than me?" She trailed her fingers across her breasts, and down over her stomach, as if to emphasize the point.

He made a joke of it. "I can't imagine swimming naked with him."

"I get the feeling you'd like to see that passport photograph."

He laughed to hide his discomfort, and fondled her hair. She was sharp. "It's no big deal; photography's my thing, that's all. Old photographs interest me, people interest me. I've got a picture at home of my old man when he was sixteen. It can tell you what they've done with their life."

"You want to see an old photograph of me? See what I've done with my life?"

"Sure; if you've got one."

"I wouldn't have the faintest idea where Dad's passport is anyway," she said. "For all I know he could have destroyed it." She shrugged. "And I don't think I'd be interested in looking; I mean you've seen what he's like when he's angry. Why bother, just to satisfy a little bit of curiosity."

"That's okay," he said easily. "If you happened across it I just thought it sounded interesting, like so many things around here—because they're so different, I guess. The country, Cathedral Rock, the people, you, Pony, your father, Carl." He deliberately held back Anna's name; he suspected it might create a sour reaction.

"Carl?" she scoffed in disbelief. "You find Carl interesting?"

"Sure. Why not?"

"Sometimes I wonder if Carl's really a zombie these days. He only seems half alive. You'd never know with Carl. God, I've known him all my life, and I can't tell you a thing about him. Oh, he was active enough around Cathedral Rock until he got too old, but he was always more interested in the cattle than any of us."

"You know how his face got like that?"

"An accident back in the early days before we were born. They were out chasing wild steers, and Dad rolled the truck

over. It exploded; Dad got out, but evidently Carl got caught.
At least that's the story my mother told me."

"I guess he and your father must have been close friends
back in Germany?"

"Something like that I suppose, or they wouldn't have
come out here together. I know they worked their asses off
getting the place started."

"Is he like your father; I mean does he ever leave
Cathedral Rock?"

She shrugged. "Well, he doesn't carry on like Dad,
but . . . I don't think I can ever remember him leaving the
place." She gave an embarrassed laugh. "Crazy isn't it. And
I'm sure he's got some sort of share in Cathedral Rock."

"You mean you don't know?"

She frowned. "I guess I should know; and Anna. Dad just
keeps avoiding the subject." She gazed morosely to the pool.
"Unless Anna knows, and isn't saying anything," she added
peevishly.

"Perhaps you should ask her, and about the passport.
Unless you'd rather I asked her?"

As he suspected, raising the subject of her sister sparked
immediate rancor.

"Christ, you're an inquisitive bastard, Hegarty, you know
that? What the hell are we doing lying here naked and talking
about someone like Carl for? Or Anna?" she flared. "I'm sure
you're just itching for an excuse to ask her something."

He had tried to make it sound like a relaxed, incidental
conversation, but he realized he'd pushed too hard. "Hell no,
that's not true; it's just that you mentioned Anna was maybe
closer to your father." He rubbed softly at her stomach, edging
up toward her breasts. "Let's forget the whole thing. Being
here with you is the most interesting thing to happen to me at
Cathedral Rock."

But he'd obviously rubbed a sore, and it brought an
abrupt change of mood. She pushed his hand aside, sat up on
her haunches, and clasped her hands about her legs.

"I've seen the way she's been looking at you, making cow
eyes over the dinner table, and using Pony to get close. My
God, I've seen her in action enough before to know the signs,"
she fumed. "And you wouldn't miss it, Hegarty, not you."

"Come on, you're imagining things."

"The hell I am. You wouldn't want to get yourself mixed up with Anna, believe me; she can be trouble, real trouble."

Maybe he knew the score between the two sisters after overhearing last night's conversation on the veranda, but he was amazed that the mere mention of Anna's name provoked such malice.

"It's you I've been swimming with, making love to, not Anna," he pointed out.

"And probably wishing it was her," she accused, with more perception than she could have realized. "You might be here with me now, but that's something she'll try and change. God, how I know her; Dad's little pet. She got Pony by screwing with some bum who wandered into Cathedral Rock. She's anybody's who'll have her, Hegarty, just ask around Normanton. The only reason she occasionally goes down south is to find someone to bed down with. My God, you want to watch yourself with her."

It was uncontrolled bitchiness. He didn't believe her ranting, wasn't even sure she believed it herself; she was breathing hard, mouth trembling, eyes dilated. Whatever inspired the jealousy she had for her older sister, it was felt with a passion difficult to handle. Perhaps there was some way to tap into that and make it work for him, but for the moment he opted to try to calm her down.

"Well she's your sister, so I guess you'd know," he soothed. "I'll watch out for her like you said."

"If she wanted you, Hegarty, she'd just as soon get pregnant again to keep you here, and I reckon you wouldn't want that. Just swallow you like a croc."

"Believe me, that won't happen."

She fell silent, taking deep breaths as if to get herself under control, and when she turned her face to him again, it was softer, more relaxed, with the hint of a smile.

"You got any baby seeds to spread around, then make sure you plant them in me, darling," she teased.

He felt a spark of alarm that she might be using him as the means to emulate her sister; it was possible, given the way she felt about Anna.

"That'd be a crazy thing to happen," he said sternly.

The storm had abated; she even managed a laugh as she tossed back her hair. "Don't worry, I know how to take care of myself," she pouted. "I'd want to make sure the man was going to stay around before I got myself in the family way." There was a trace of guilt in her voice, now that she was calmer. "It'll be better when just Anna and I are running Cathedral Rock," she mused. "Sometimes I suspect Dad sets us against each other." She paused, face sober, perhaps regretting the harsh accusations against her sister. "Things just seem to happen for Anna," she murmured. She shrugged, leaned across and kissed him lightly on the mouth, then glanced to where the horizon was already beginning to digest the crimson sun. For a moment she let her eyes linger longingly on the length of his body, but gave a slight shake of her head, and clambered to her feet.

"It'd be beautiful to just stay here and make love all night, Hegarty, but I'd better be getting back."

He nodded, and scrambled upright to join her. The warmth of the sun and the rock had completely dried them, and now the cool breeze riffling across the savanna prickled their skins, pushing them shivering into a close embrace. He was sure if he made the move he could make love to her again, but he merely returned her casual kiss.

"Maybe again tomorrow?" she whispered.

Perhaps he'd inherited too much ice water in his veins from his father, but he couldn't feel anything but disappointment and frustration that the assignation had yielded so little information about her father. Whether he would do any better by playing off one sister against the other he didn't know, but he couldn't afford to spend any more time with this girl, she knew too little. Except for the passport, and that seemed unattainable unless he risked searching the house. There had to be a chance Anna knew more, if she was closer to her father as Ingrid claimed.

"What are you thinking?" asked Ingrid. "Don't you think you can make it tomorrow?"

He gave an offhanded shrug, broke away, and began to slip into his clothes. "Let's see how the day works out," he grunted. "A lot'll depend on Ritchie and his ringers. It might be late before I get back."

She watched him a moment, her expression confused, then she too began to dress. "I reckon you could make it if you really wanted," she softly challenged.

"I said I'd give it my best shot," he replied sharply.

She zipped up her jeans, and gestured to the rock. "There's lots of other exciting things we can do," she tempted. "Today was just an appetizer."

He smiled without warmth. Maybe, but she'd got as much out of this as he had, even more. But he was going to have to be ruthless; she'd have to learn this was all there was going to be. Already he was convinced he'd made a mistake. Instinct had told him Anna was the better deal, and foolishly, maybe because of time, he'd opted for the easier target.

She placed a pleading hand on his arm. "I'll come here anyway," she promised.

He felt a twinge of guilt, it wasn't her fault she'd been fathered by a monster, and he consolingly patted her hand.

"Okay; you were great, honey," he praised. "Really something, you know that."

"My God, so were you, darling Hegarty, so were you," she breathed.

He picked up his hat, dusted off his jeans, and nodded to the jeep in the trees. "You go on ahead of me, and I'll wait here awhile. It'll look better that way."

"You're worried about Dad?"

"I've been fired once today; I don't want to risk it again."

She grinned, with the old taunting flair. "He might be a mean old bastard at times, but he's tolerant about things like this. He understands about . . . urges. He's been breeding cattle for long enough; he doesn't expect virgin daughters."

"Let's still do it my way," he insisted. He couldn't possibly risk riling Kisek again.

She hesitated, for a moment he thought she was going to kiss him again, then she turned and went rapidly to the jeep without looking back. He sat back on the rock, watching the jeep threading its way through the trees and grass until it seemed to be swallowed by the fiery horizon. For some reason he remembered Pony's Tarantula Hawk. Kisek was the one he wanted to sting, yet it seemed inevitable Ingrid had to finish up being eaten along with her father.

* * *

There was no sign of Ingrid's jeep when he ran the Kawasaki into the shed, so he figured she'd gone into the house. It was dusk, but like he'd never seen before, as if the sky was reflecting a gigantic fire burning on the other side of the world. When he went to his door he saw Anna approaching from the house, so he stopped and waited for her. It was a surprise, when she was so much on his mind. He hoped to Christ Ingrid wasn't watching from somewhere in the house, she'd probably read some paranoid meaning into the casual meeting.

"Hi there, Anna," he greeted her.

He leaned against the door, waiting, while she nervously cleared her throat. "I've been speaking to Pony, Matt," she said.

He nodded, without comment.

"About what happened this afternoon," she continued, "between you and Dad, and the trouble over the photograph."

He tensed, wondering if Pony had confided in her about the switch in the film.

"It's settled," he said. "I'm still mustering tomorrow."

"I'm glad. It sounded for a moment as if we weren't going to be able to prove to Dad how much time we can save using the helicopter."

"It's over," he said with a smile. "Your father destroyed the film, so there's no problem." He raised it deliberately, to see if she challenged him about the film.

"I . . . I wanted to make sure there were no bad feelings," she said, "not when we've all got to be working together."

He concealed his relief. Pony had kept silence. "I haven't got any bad feelings at all. I hope your father hasn't either."

She smiled. "Then why don't you come on over to the house for dinner. It might help to settle things down, and . . ." she gestured to the house; she was nervous, and he didn't quite know why, " . . . and I know Pony would love having you," she added. "He's done nothing but talk about you since I came home." There was a hint of reservation in her smile. "You've made quite a hit with my son."

"Well, I'll tell you Anna, it's certainly reciprocated."

"Then you'll come?"

He was sure it would be a mistake. Apart from anything else, he suspected Ingrid would seize such an opportunity to parade him like a conquest, for Anna's benefit. He didn't want that.

"I'm grateful for you asking, Anna, I really am, and I appreciate what you're trying to do, but . . ." He hesitated, and rubbed thoughtfully at his chin. "It's too soon, and I'm sure it'd make for an awkward dinner. Why don't we just let it sit for tonight?"

"It's okay with Dad, it really is," she assured him.

He didn't quite believe that, a raging bull didn't quiet that easily. He put his hand on the door and pushed it slightly ajar, to signify the end of the meeting. Being near her was quite different than with Ingrid, even her subtle perfume emphasized the contrast between the two sisters.

"You won't change your mind?" she asked.

"Like I said, I appreciate you asking, but I think we should leave it for now."

"Pony'll be disappointed."

"I'll see him tomorrow."

She hesitated. "I'll be disappointed."

"I'll see you tomorrow—at the muster, so I hear."

He failed to understand her sudden change of expression, from warmth, to surprise, to resentment in rapid sequence; her eyes flashed as she looked past him into his room. He turned quickly to follow her gaze and saw Ingrid sitting on the bed. He made a weak effort to cover his confusion.

"Christ, Ingrid! What are you doing in there?" he stuttered foolishly.

"You should have told me you had another engagement for the evening," said Anna coldly.

He struggled for the right words. "Wait, no, it's not like that Anna—I mean I didn't know Ingrid was . . ."

"You don't have to explain anything to me," she icily cut him off. "What you do in your own time is none of my business."

Goddamn it, how was he to know Ingrid would pull a stunt like this? He reached for Anna's arm, but she brushed his hand aside and spun around on her heels.

"For Chrissake, will you just listen to me, Anna?" he protested.

The words only fell on her back as she stalked away toward the house.

"Don't be late for the muster. We like to get a daybreak start," she curtly threw back at him, without turning her head.

"Shit," he spat furiously. He went into the room, kicked the door shut, and stood hands angrily on hips, glaring at Ingrid, sitting with fingers and legs clasped and an expression of virginal innocence on her face.

"What the hell are you doing in here?" he snarled

"Don't yell at me."

"Why the fuck shouldn't I? This isn't what we agreed back at the pool."

Her expression passed quickly from mock innocence to hostility. "You're a gullible prick, you know that, Hegarty? See, I told you Anna had plans for you." She grimaced. "'*I'll* be disappointed if you don't come to dinner'," she savagely mimicked Anna. "God, you have to ask why she was so upset at seeing me in here?"

"I still want to know what you're doing in here?"

"I . . . I just wanted to talk to you. I got to thinking about us at the pool when I was driving back, I mean your attitude, and the way we parted." She shrugged. "I guess I got the feeling now you'd . . . had me . . . I was just going to be brushed off."

Once again he was bemused by how accurate her perception could be, but it was a different Ingrid, the arrogant self-confidence subdued by an unsuspected insecurity.

"I thought we both had one hell of a good time," he blustered. "Jesus, Ingrid, we both *had* each other."

"I kept thinking of you out on the muster with Anna."

"We'll be busy working cattle, for Chrissake."

"She's a shrewd bitch."

"She's your sister."

She stood to her feet, close to him, hands clasping at his arms. He knew she was there looking for reassurance, but he couldn't give it to her, not now. He backed off, and it immediately sparked resentment.

"And I'd like to know why you're so all-fired upset over her being upset?" she demanded.

"I just don't want any trouble; I've got to work with her," he answered glibly.

There was more than animosity in her face, an expression he hadn't seen before; it was confirmation of his suspicion she had dangerous claws. Well, he'd have to live with that, she wasn't any use to him any more.

"Don't play me for a fool, Hegarty," she said venomously. "I don't let any man do that to me. I don't just brush off like some bloody bush fly, and I leave claw marks if anyone tries it, believe me."

He tried to pacify her enough to get her out of the room. "Look, you're not making a lot of sense; why don't we just leave it for now, we're both tired, and . . ."

"Don't fucking patronize me, Hegarty," she flared. "You're still on my payroll."

It was a crude attempt to put him down, and ridiculous after what had passed between them, but he accepted it with gratitude, because in a way it let him off the hook. He stepped away, and gave her a mocking bow.

"Then I think we'd better leave it at that, boss lady," he said.

It threw her; she was indecisive, tentative again, and she reached warily toward him once more, then let her hand fall away.

"We just got started," she muttered, "and I don't want it to end just like this. Not when it was so . . . so terrific."

"Just let's leave it," he repeated wearily.

She waited a moment, as if half hoping he'd take her in his arms, then she went reluctantly to the door. She paused, and attempted to retrieve the situation. "The pool tomorrow then?"

"Like I said before, if I can make it," he replied offhand-edly.

He was sure she knew he was lying, but at least she knew where she stood now.

"Bloody Anna," she muttered furiously.

He felt the small room quiver, she slammed the door with such force. He sat down on the bed. Goddamn it! Reine had chosen him for this assignment as much as anything else because he knew how to handle women, but so far his score wasn't too impressive. From now on he had to give Ingrid a wide berth. She was going to hate him for it, but he had no alternative; he had to try to mend fences with Anna.

Chapter 7

Washington, D.C.

Richard Gormane deemed himself fortunate that his wife was regarded by all as such an accomplished hostess, and that she shared his enjoyment of entertaining. It was a big plus in the Washington political circus. Their charming Georgetown apartment was within easy reach of the White House. The president liked to have his top security advisor within earshot to cope with a world constantly in ferment. Iran today, Russia tomorrow, the Pacific region next, in one perpetual pressure cycle.

But for now there was merely the pleasant buzz of conversation between fashionably dressed women and well-groomed men, accompanied by drink, good food, unobtrusive tasteful music. Yet if the party had not been arranged months ago, Gormane would have had no hesitation in canceling it. To observe him, sleek, balding, distinguished, clad in a superbly cut dinner jacket and making small talk with Zavlaska from the Russian Embassy, whom he knew to be KGB, one would have no clue that his mind was thousands of miles away. He was in his late sixties, medium height, betrayed by good living into signs of corpulence, with the lingering outlines of a once handsome youth now gradually collapsing like an unstable slag heap, enlarging the nose, dragging the flabby facial muscles toward his neck.

After a time he tired of pretending he found Zavlaska interesting, broke away with murmured apologies, took a fresh glass of Jack Daniels, and lit up a cigar. For him, cigars were like a baby's pacifier, a way of soothing nagging anxiety. His wife threaded her way through the guests toward him, dressed with the flair of a glittering Christmas bauble, offering passing smiles like a Pope dispensing blessings.

She was maturely beautiful; dark hair, with traces of gray expertly concealed, slim, an inch or two taller than he, ten years younger, and looking more like twenty. While he'd made a career in public service, she'd made a career of herself. Her tone was at variance with her smile.

"For God's sake, Dick, circulate, circulate," she urged frostily. "There are people here who want to meet you."

He sighed. He knew she was right, but his heart wasn't in it tonight. Most of them were only there to push a personal barrow anyway, knowing his influence with the president.

"I'm just taking a breather," he grumbled.

"Well it looks like bad manners." She smiled graciously to a passing couple. "Honestly, Dick, you've been like a bear all week. If you wanted me to cancel the party, you should have said so."

"No, no, I didn't want it canceled," he lied.

"Then something's bothering you."

That was the trouble; you lived with someone a long time, and you became as transparent as glass. "Nothing I can talk about, Lorene," he said.

"Oh, one of those again."

"You know the way it has to be."

His secretary made an unobtrusive appearance at his elbow. "Excuse me, sir, there's an international call for you in the study."

Gormane stared at him. Mike Whitney's smile was always so boyish, did he have to look so incredibly young? "International?" he queried, controlling the sudden tremor in his voice with difficulty. It had to be Corliss calling from London, and he hoped to Christ the man had good news for him.

"Yes—from London," Whitney added, as confirmation.

He clamped tight on his cigar. If it was bad news it would quickly wipe the smile from his wife's face.

"Perhaps someone's blown up all our bases in England," murmured Lorene mockingly.

He ignored the comment. "Okay Mike, I'll take it," he said.

"Don't be long," warned Lorene sharply.

He went swiftly to the study, and carefully closed the door behind him. The thick carpet, heavy drapes, and wood-paneled walls lined with books made excellent soundproofing. He slumped into the club chair and picked up the telephone.

"Is that you, Chip?" he rasped.

"Yes sir."

As usual Chip's voice was carefully controlled, masculine, yet deferential. Gormane could almost imagine him standing stiffly at attention, ribbons in place, while he spoke on the phone. There was a pause, as if each was waiting for the other to lead the conversation.

"You've got some news for me, Chip?" he asked impatiently.

"I believe we've managed to . . . prejudice the courier, sir," came the cautious answer.

Once he'd tried to impress on Corliss not to call him "sir," but the military background was too deeply ingrained.

"Good, Chip, good. I knew I could rely on you."

"Prejudice" could mean anything, but he didn't want to know details; that sort of information could be disturbing, and it was better not to know.

"I'm afraid I also believe that it's possibly only a temporary solution," added Corliss, in the same flat monotone.

It tempered some of Gormane's relief. "What do you mean only temporary?"

"The man's name was Brandt, and I understand . . ."

Gormane hastily cut him off. He didn't like the way Corliss used the past tense. "Never mind names," he ordered abrasively.

"Of course, I'm sorry, sir. Well, I understand the, ah, courier's organization has another copy of the information he obtained in Berlin."

"Christ, you're sure of that?"

"Yes, my informant is absolutely certain. He knows better than to lie."

"Jesus," muttered Gormane. He patted at his brow, feeling the dampness of perspiration. "The information was as damaging as I'd been led to believe?"

"Absolutely. I believe the verification with the fingerprints would guarantee identifying Kisek in Australia as Leiman."

"They're sure Kisek is their man."

"Positive. But they doubt that their evidence for identification would stand up in court. The fingerprints solve that problem."

The sudden flush that passed over Gormane's body forced him to undo his tie. Where in God's name had the Mossad agent managed to find something like fingerprints, after more than forty years?

"The existence of another copy makes the situation very difficult," he said.

"I don't think it gives us any alternative," replied Corliss.

"What do you mean?"

"I think I should try to get to this man calling himself Kisek first, if at all possible. Terminate the problem at its source. And that will be the end of your worries for all time."

Gormane tried to pretend he hadn't heard the word "terminate." "Can you do that? Australia is one hell of a big place. Does your informant have any idea where Kisek is located in Australia?"

"No, that's one thing he hasn't been able to find out."

"You think he's leveling with you?"

"Yes. As I said, he knows the consequences of lying."

"Then how are you going to find him?"

"I'm working on it, sir. I've a plan in operation now which I believe will bring us the information."

Gormane took a deep breath, then let the air escape slowly from his lungs. God, he felt so helpless. It was up to Chip, but the man had never let him down yet.

"Then I'll just have to leave it all in your capable hands, Chip," he concluded heavily.

"I think you can do that with confidence, sir."

"I know I can. I know I can."

He suddenly felt very weary. "You'll keep me informed?" he asked.

"As much as it's possible. If things go as I expect, I hope to be in Australia within the next few days, and it will be difficult to keep in touch."

"Okay. Good luck, Chip."

"Thank you, sir."

He hung up, but stayed there in the chair. His cigar had gone out, and he relit it, vaguely aware of the faint sounds of the party. He felt much too tense to rejoin his guests, but doubtless an exasperated Lorene would eventually come looking for him. He blew smoke to the ceiling, bleakly contemplating his predicament. Goddamn, it was unjust that an act carried out in good faith so many years ago, one that had almost passed from memory, could so abruptly emerge from the past to threaten his whole life. His career. His influence. Yet at the time, as a captain in the OSS in Germany just after war's end, it had seemed like a good deal to trade a passport to safety for Horst Leiman in exchange for valuable information the man had about Russian Intelligence. It had been Leiman's decision to go to Australia, which was about as far away from Germany as the Nazi could get, and Australian Intelligence had been very cooperative. Not that he'd had any doubts that Leiman was as guilty as hell of the atrocities in Treblinka, the man was clearly a human abomination, but one had to be realistic. It had not been difficult, even back in 1945, to recognize where the postwar battle lines would be drawn. God, he'd been right about that anyway. Of course he'd had superiors who'd gone along with him, but they were all dead, and it was his name alone on the documentation.

Yet he had learned almost by accident that the Wiesenthal people had picked up Leiman's trail and passed the information through to the Mossad. It had come in on just a routine report about the Israeli agency, mentioning in an offhand manner that the organization was sure Horst Leiman was still alive and well, living somewhere in Australia, and they were mounting an operation. A mere footnote mentioned the possibility that one of their agents had obtained a copy of Leiman's fingerprints in Berlin that would positively identify the man in Australia calling himself Kisek as the wanted Nazi war criminal. It stunned him. For a week Gormane had been in a daze, unable to function properly. He should have known that forty years meant nothing to the Nazi-hunters, they were like bull terriers. They would just keep at it and at it, until they put a noose around their quarry's neck. God, if he'd thought about Leiman at all in the intervening years, it had been only a passing, comforting reflection that he was probably dead. There had been occasional surges of anxiety when Adolf Eichmann was caught, and again with Klaus Barbie, but they had quickly passed.

Now a Leiman trial would attract world-wide attention, and there was nothing more certain than that they would dig up the name of the man who had masterminded the Nazi criminal's escape from justice. It would be a disaster: security advisor to the president revealed as the man who aided and abetted the escape of one of the Nazi monsters. Never mind that it was a different time, different circumstances back then, he'd be crucified. People never forgot. Look at the invective hurled at Austrian President Kurt Waldheim because of his past Nazi connections, and he was scarcely accused of Leiman's diabolical crimes.

It would be unjust for his career to end in disgrace, when he'd given unstintingly for his country. He didn't want to fade into the shadows. There would be prestigious university appointments available to him when he retired from the administration in a year or so, but not if his involvement with Leiman came out.

Sleepless nights and anxiety-ridden days had followed, which he failed to hide from his wife. Lorene was too astute for that, she recognized something was seriously wrong. But he couldn't bring himself to confide in her. He wrestled with the options of sitting tight and trusting to luck, or trying in some desperate way to influence the course of events, although he had no idea how. He even thought of approaching the White House, but rejected that as a risk of putting the president in a compromising situation.

In the end, out of sheer desperation, he had confided it all to his aide, Colonel Chip Corliss. It would have saved him sleepless nights if he'd decided on that course in the beginning. Chip revered him, asked no questions, gave unstinting loyalty; they were the very attributes that had influenced him to pluck the colonel from the army and give him political clout within the administration.

Chip was a patriot. Vietnam had taught him how to bend the rules, and he applied his talents with cunning vigor in his boss's interests. He found the elevation from a dreary peace-

time army routine to Washington's corridors of power heady
stuff indeed, and he was always eager to do anything possible
to express gratitude for what had been done for him by the
powerful presidential security advisor. It only served to make
Gormane realise how stupid he'd been not to immediately
confide in a man of action so completely devoted to him.

Of course Chip understood his problem. He'd sat opposite him in this very room, ramrod straight in the chair,
uniform immaculately pressed, short-cropped hair tinged with
gray, dark eyes exuding warmth from an otherwise expressionless face. Even at ease he looked superbly fit.

"I understand your decision about Leiman, sir," he'd said.
"It seems completely logical to me."

"You have to know the man was a monster—really, a
monster."

"History is crowded with monsters. Sometimes a great
country owes its beginnings to such monsters."

"Leiman was more than that."

"You did what was in our national interests, sir. I can only
applaud that."

"Leiman on trial before the world can destroy me, Chip."

"You mean the media vultures?"

"Exactly."

"Let me try to help you, sir. I owe it to you."

"Can you?"

"Not officially. But there are ways."

He didn't want to delve into ways and means. Chip
understood the darker maneuverings of power, and it was
wiser not to know.

"You realize how crucially confidential this all is, Chip?"

"Absolutely. What you've told me will never pass outside
this room." He was thoughtfully silent a moment. "I know a
man in the Mossad who was involved in a double play with the
Islamic Jihad." He smiled. "I like to keep files on such things.
The Mossad would be appalled to know of this agent's
involvement with the Jihad; it would in all probability lead to
the man's arrest and trial as a traitor." He nodded, still smiling
gently, "I'm sure he can be persuaded to give me any
information about this Leiman operation."

Gormane squirmed nervously in his chair. It was already

moving into an area he preferred not to know about. "How you operate is your concern, Chip," he muttered.

"Of course, that's understood. But you'd agree our main area of concern is the man who supposedly has Leiman's fingerprints?"

"Yes, yes I would. That's unbelievable, and it would be devastating."

"Then I think I should begin there. I think through my Mossad contact I should be able to locate this man, and perhaps persuade him that it's not in his interests, or in ours, to expose this Leiman after such a long time."

"There must be more than the fingerprints."

"Certainly; but let's start there, then I can follow through on any other developments."

Gormane was hunched morosely over his desk. God, what did he have to lose? There was no one he could trust more than Chip, even if he did have misgivings about terminology that implied blackmail and coercion.

He committed himself; he had to, or risk destruction. "Believe me, I'd be grateful for anything you can do on this one, Chip," he said.

Corliss nodded, and stood up. He gave the impression of rigid steel standing solidly in place.

"I'll leave in the morning, sir, probably for London first." He paused. "I have an open brief; I can handle this in my own way?"

Gormane nodded. If the worst came to the worst he could always claim Corliss was acting on his own initiative.

"Yes, yes, you have an open brief," he agreed.

"Just how long do you intend to sit there, Dick?" demanded his wife testily.

The caustic interruption jerked him abruptly from the past to the present.

She was framed in the partly open doorway, a glass in one hand, her red dress a blaze of color in contrast to the dark tones of the study.

"Have they really blown up our bases?" she bantered. "Have all those creeps running around with their placards actually gotten around to using bombs?"

He attempted to grin and pushed himself to his feet. "You

should know by now how these things are, Lorene," he gently protested. "They always take precedence over entertaining guests."

She relented, came halfway into the room to meet him, and linked her arm in his, guiding him toward the door. "For goodness sake, do up your tie." She stopped and fussed with it herself. "You work too hard, dear; you're like a soldier forever on duty."

"That's the way it has to be, honey."

She brushed his forehead with her lips. "Then I'm glad you only have a year to go for retirement. We need more time together, and we'll have it when you accept a university position. We'll be able to travel too, do some of the things we've always wanted to do."

They walked out of the study and he closed the door gently behind them. God, he wanted that too, but it all depended on Chip Corliss now. If he was crushed, he wondered if she'd stay at his side? "I don't know if I could tolerate it if you hadn't been so successful, Dick," she'd admitted to him once. "I'm like a gaudy butterfly, spreading my wings for everyone to admire, as I flutter around in my beautiful garden." He shrugged. He wondered how she'd react if the garden died.

Chapter 8

Dinner appeared on Hegarty's doorstep as mysteriously as breakfast had that morning. Zara moved as silently as a ghost, and she was obviously a woman of few words. He might have angered Anna, but it was encouraging that at least she wasn't going to let him starve. It was fish, probably the barramundi he'd heard so much about, complemented with a tomato salad. He hadn't realized he was so hungry, and he ate ravenously, relishing the flavor, then put the tray back on the doorstep. Darkness had come with the suddenness of a drawn curtain, glittering moonlight superseding the rich red patina of sunset. It was eight. He decided to wait a half-hour more before he set off to make contact with Jules. They had much to talk over, and he wanted to allow a few hours. If there were any questions from the Kiseks, then it might be a good idea to establish he liked to take moonlight rides on the Kawasaki.

He went carefully around the room, checking to see if the mysterious intruder had paid him another visit, but he found nothing. His clothes were exactly as he'd left them, the Colt wrapped the same, still in the bottom drawer. He hoped it was a sign he'd passed inspection and been accepted, although he'd still like to know who it had been. He studied the Colt a moment, pondering whether he should take it with him, but decided against it. He checked his watch and stretched out on the bed.

He never seemed able to put his mind in neutral. He thought of Ingrid, Pony, Anna, Carl, Kisek, living out a life that was going to be abruptly torn apart. Jesus, after more than forty years of living in peace and prosperity, and raising a family, it was hard not to see that in actual fact Leiman, under the name of Kisek, had got away with all his crimes. Putting his head in a noose could never be more than an anticlimax, when he'd had a harmonious three score and ten years anyway. It seemed to make punishment somehow meaningless. Such reflections would infuriate his father. "Time is running out for us, but we have to keep on and on," he'd said once. "These monsters have to be hunted like vermin until they draw their last breath. And even then we should dig up their bones and scatter them to vultures." Matt wondered if that sort of hatred was destructive in itself, but he understood it. Jules was like that; they tried to obliterate us once, and now nothing is more important than that we show the world we have teeth and are prepared to bite. Had he lost that commitment? It was all too much like a macabre card game: we'll up your ten murders with twenty of our own—and then they up the stake with thirty more. Oh, Israel would hang Leiman all right, and rightly, but he wondered what it would solve.

He shut it out, and tried to doze for a few minutes, but in the end he gave it up and went to the Kawasaki. There were lights in the house, but no sign of anyone, so he started up the motor and moved off slowly, without the headlight, relying on the bright moonlight to guide him over the terrain. He figured the sound of the bike would be difficult to pinpoint with accuracy, but the headlight could be seen for miles, and he didn't want to advertise his trip to the old house.

He followed the main road from Cathedral Rock, then turned off at the junction with the track he'd seen from the helicopter that led to the old house, and damn near getting bogged in loose sand, weaving drunkenly from side to side until the frantically spinning wheels finally gripped. But it was the only incident, and the jagged silhouette of the house soon came into view. He steered into what looked to have once been a driveway, now only marked by decayed fencing lining each side, ran the bike into the shadow of a large tree, and switched off the motor. Maybe it was the contrast between night and day, but there was an air of pathos about the dilapidated building.

He leaned the bike against the tree, and stood cautiously listening. The wind had risen, stirring the grass to a lively jig, beating the overhead branches into a drumming sound. Somewhere a piece of loose timber flapped with a repetitive rat tat tat. He didn't use the flashlight he'd brought, picking his way through the clutter of broken brick and twisted remnants of machinery. Something slithered by underfoot, and he froze. This was the land of venomous snakes, like the taipan Pony had mentioned, which he'd read struck with repeated viciousness, leaving multiple poisoned puncture wounds that brought quick death unless antivenom was administered immediately. He waited until it passed, then tentatively moved to where he could see a doorway set into the part of the house that was still standing. The timber was badly eroded, the door merely propped into position by a length of forked branch. To the right the remains of a window was sealed with iron sheeting. Wind funneling through the holes in the wall gave off an eerie moan of longing. If there were ghosts on the savanna, this is where they'd spend their nights.

He pushed aside the branch, opened the door, switched on the flashlight, and swept the beam about the interior. The floor was spotted with various shafts of moonlight shaped by the holes in the roof. The flashlight revealed dirt, cobwebs, rotted flooring, wood stacked against the far wall, and directly ahead a pile of old newspapers and partially filled bags. There were the scuttling sounds of night creatures fleeing the intrusion. He closed the door and stood uncertainly in the darkness, still probing about with the flashlight for some sign of habitation. Could he possibly be wrong about Jules? Yet there was no chance he'd misread the homing device, and Milhesco had been quite positive about his instructions; this was where he was supposed to find Jules.

He hadn't heard a sound, so the touch of cold, hard metal against the nape of his neck came as an unpleasant surprise.

"Don't move," hissed a voice.

He knew it was Jules, so cool, so composed, with no hint of tension, yet giving the unmistakable promise of violence.

"Jules?" he whispered.

"Matt? Hegarty?"

"Who the fuck else are you expecting?"

He turned slowly, it wasn't wise to startle someone like Jules when he had a gun at your neck, and cast the beam of the flashlight in the other man's face.

"Hi Jules," he grinned. "You're a long way from New York."

Jules dropped the gun away, and slapped him on the shoulder. "I thought it might be my favorite meshuga American."

There were still traces of accent from the Polish of his childhood, before his surviving relatives had gotten him into Israel.

"I figure we're both a little crazy to be here like this, Jules."

He kept the beam on Jules's face. It had been a year since they'd last worked together, but his memory of the man as a throwback to a seventeenth-century swashbuckling pirate remained constant. He'd heard some people call him the Buccaneer, and although Jules didn't use the nickname Hegarty was sure he approved because that was his self-image. Maybe it was partly cultivated, but he could have stepped straight out of a Sabatini novel: strong-boned, angular face, hawkish nose, long black hair, sharp eyes beneath heavy brows, abundant black beard partly concealing a thin, ruthless mouth, all given dramatic emphasis by the harsh shadows cast by the flashlight. He was about forty, but no one was sure. Self-doubt was not part of Jules Grubin's makeup; friends called him dedicated, enemies labeled him a zealot, but none quibbled over the fact that he was brutally effective. He wasn't as tall as Hegarty, but equally lean, with quick supple movements that denoted a fierce energy.

"I was wishing there was some way I could have warned you I was coming," apologized Hegarty. He gestured to the gun. "To avoid this."

Jules firmly pushed the flashlight aside. "Put it out," he said. "I don't want the slightest risk of a light being seen in here."

Hegarty flicked off the switch, and there were only the meager arrows of moonlight filtering through the roof.

"It was you in the helicopter this morning?" asked Jules.

"Right. I picked up your signal. I was checking to see if you'd arrived."

Jules chuckled. "I guessed it was you." He nodded to the outside. "I was taking some air when I saw you pull up on the bike tonight." He slapped the gun into the palm of his hand. "I was just polishing up my skills, seeing what a sitting duck you'd be."

"You aiming to kill someone?"

"Only if they get in the way of taking Leiman back to Israel."

That sounded like the Jules he knew. He felt the man's hand at his elbow, urging him forward.

"No point standing here in the dark," said Jules. "We've got some talking to do. You'd better come down into my hole."

"Hole?"

"That's right. Too risky setting up in one of these old rooms, even if it's only for a short time." He paused. "At least I hope it's only for a short time."

Hegarty asked no further questions, just allowed himself to be led, treading cautiously across the cracking floor and through the sagging opening of another doorway into a smaller room, where Jules brought him to a halt.

"Wait," cautioned Grubin.

In the dim light he watched Jules crouch to the floor, lift a small trapdoor, switch on his own flashlight, then point the beam into the dark hole. "This is where I'm set up, Matt. Much less risk than up here. It's lucky Kisek had a European liking for cellars when he built the place." He maneuvered himself around and carefully began to descend. "That's one of the reasons Milhesco picked out this place for me." He paused and tapped the rim of the opening. "Watch yourself on these steps. I had to do some repair work before I could use them."

Hegarty waited until Grubin had disappeared, then warily followed, using his own flashlight. The steps were set very steep, forcing him to grip the side rails with both hands, the worn wood spongy under his weight. Cobwebs brushed his face, and he felt a sudden coolness of the air, accompanied by the smell of must.

"Pull it shut after you," hissed Jules.

He reached up, groped about the trapdoor until he made contact with a handle, then pulled it down after him. He missed the bottom step, slipping the last few feet, and jarred down on hard stone. Except for the narrow beams of the two flashlights, the surrounding blackness had the solidity of a wall of coal.

"For Chrissake," he muttered.

"Over here," called Jules.

There was the flare of a match, the grating sound of glass on metal, then a small core of light that began to expand to the swish, swish pumping action of a kerosene pressure lamp. Jules raised the hissing light in his hand, swinging it slowly about in an arc, so that all the shadows seemed to vibrate in a macabre dance. He wore a kind of black track suit, which enhanced his appearance as the keeper of an eerie nether region.

Hegarty switched off his flashlight and glanced around. It was a small room, the brick walls fractured with myriads of cracks, and raddled heavy timber beams forming the ceiling. Underfoot irregular flagstones were set in a patchwork pattern. Where Jules stood was a folding chair set at a small table, which held a transmitter and several items of electronic gear unfamiliar to Hegarty. There were also eating utensils, a bottle of wine, and the remains of a meal. In the opposite corner was a spread of blankets for sleeping, and further along two crates stacked on top of each other.

Jules gave a wry grin, and placed the lamp on the table. "Not exactly four-star accommodation, my friend, but it's a palace compared to the rathole I operated from in Lebanon." He pointed to the chair. "Sit down, sit down. I can put my ass on the table."

Hegarty nodded, still peering about as he crossed to the chair.

"How long have you been here?"

Grubin shrugged. "Going on four days. Milhesco did a good job finding it for me."

"They flew you in from the ship?"

"Yes," he gestured to the transmitter, "with the equipment." He glanced to the other items. "And whatever I need to survive for a time."

"There were no problems? I mean no one spotted the helicopter?"

"No."

"The ship's going to wait around?"

"Yes, for as long as it takes; they're cruising around just

north of the Gulf." He pointed to the transmitter. "We keep in touch. As soon as we figure we've got what we need to take Kisek out—or Leiman, if you prefer to call him by his real name—it'll only take a call and they'll come in with the helicopter to take him out. And us." He gave a wolfish grin of satisfaction, levered his haunches up on the bench, and picked up the bottle of wine. "So we're all waiting for you, my friend."

"I can't make it happen overnight, Jules. I know everything's set up with the ship, but you're going to have to give me a little time. I'm making progress, but if I push too hard and too fast I'll risk making them suspicious."

"I understand that, but you know how impatient Reine is."

"Andre's impatient because he feels he's running out of time," replied Hegarty sharply. "He's been after Leiman so long, and now he's this close he's frightened retirement will beat him."

Grubin shrugged. "He's just going to have to wait." He grinned. "I take it by the fact you were flying around in the helicopter that you succeeded in getting Kisek to hire you?"

"Right. I had a few lucky breaks, which was just as well; the sonofabitch is absolutely paranoid about strangers, or anyone else for that matter."

"That would figure for a man hiding out."

"It's working well for me, Jules."

"Great. I'd have guessed it was more than luck, just the same." He poured two glasses of wine, and held one out to Hegarty. "I take it Milhesco was right, the helicopter instruction in Texas paid off. You're a good operator, Matt." He nodded to the wine. "It's a nice white." He glanced around the walls, and smirked. "Even in a place like this I like my comforts." He held up his glass. "Take it as a congratulatory drink. Here's to justice for that scum over at Cathedral Rock."

Hegarty responded to the toast. He drank more than he intended, not realizing how dry he was until the wine moistened his throat. He put the glass down and wiped at his mouth.

"Let's just hope I can get something that will prove he's Leiman."

Grubin misunderstood the intonation in his voice.

"You read the Wiesenthal report the same as I did, Matt," he snorted. "My God, surely you haven't got any doubts." He made an exasperated gesture about the cellar. "Christ, not at this stage."

Hegarty felt the need to make his denial as vehement as possible. Maybe he had slivers of doubt, but it wouldn't be wise to expose them to Jules.

"Don't be goddamn crazy," he responded hotly. "What the fuck would I be doing here, if I had doubts? I'm talking about the proof Reine wants, something that's indisputable in court."

Grubin raised his hands defensively. "Okay, Matt, okay; you're right, I'm sorry. I just thought you sounded a little . . . unsure."

"Well forget it."

"Okay." Grubin hesitated, slightly embarrassed. "Reine wants a daily report relayed to him. Have you got any information I can send him about Cathedral Rock?"

"Sure, I figure it's looking promising. But have you got any information for me? What about Eli Brandt, and his claim about having a set of Leiman's fingerprints?"

Grubin hesitated again. "I'd like to get down the material on Cathedral Rock first," he said.

"Jules, if Eli's really got Leiman's fingerprints, then it's the most important thing to what I'm trying to do at Cathedral Rock."

Grubin wiped his mouth and put his wine glass down on the table.

"Brandt's dead," he said flatly.

Hegarty stared at him as if he hadn't grasped the words. "Dead?"

"Yes. Murdered in London."

Hegarty shook his head in disbelief. He recalled the defensive man who looked so much like an innocuous clerk, and felt a wave of pity. First Eli had lost his reputation, and now his life.

"For Chrissake. Do we know who killed him; or why?"

"We don't know who, but we know why."

"The fingerprints? Leiman's fingerprints? Brandt really had found them, and he was killed for them?"

"That's the story relayed to me by the ship, from Reine. It seems they've been verified as belonging to Leiman."

"Jesus, that doesn't make a lot of sense, Jules. Who would kill to protect Leiman, after more than forty years?"

"Favett's working on it. He suspects Nazi sympathizers still around in Germany."

"But how would they find out about the prints?"

"Maybe Brandt was careless about covering his tracks." He shrugged. "You know Eli."

"Then you're telling me we don't have the fingerprints?"

"Yes we do. At least Brandt redeemed himself by making sure Reine got a copy."

The words were coldly dispassionate. It made Hegarty realize how little he really knew about Jules, except that he'd worked through the Middle East conducting preemptive strikes against suspected terrorists, which was another way of saying assassination. He wondered if Jules would express any more emotion if he, Matt, were terminated? Probably not, which was perhaps why he was such a superb professional.

"Then we need them here, not in London; and fast," he said curtly.

"Reine's bringing them."

Hegarty was surprised a second time. "Reine's bringing them? When he's so close to retirement? After Brandt being murdered I would have thought Favett considered it too dangerous. I mean, why take such a risk with Reine's life at this stage?"

Grubin allowed a faint smile. "You know Reine; he sees retirement as death. He craves to be at the center, always did. I'll bet he fought with Favett over it, but he's coming."

"How soon before he arrives?"

"Two days, maybe three. He's coming to Normanton as a tourist."

"Then I'll need to meet him, and bring the fingerprints to you. You're the expert in that field, Jules. It'll be up to me to somehow get a copy of Kisek's prints for matching." He glanced around the cellar. "Will you be able to do a comparison test here?"

"Certainly. I have everything I need."

Hegarty pinched at his nose, and hunched in the chair. It

was cold in the cellar, but it was more the challenge posed by obtaining Kisek's fingerprints, especially when the sonofabitch was so antagonistic. It would have to be planned carefully.

"You'll have to let me know when Reine's due to arrive."

"That can be arranged."

Hegarty nodded, considering a moment. "Reine wants me to keep on with what I'm doing at Cathedral Rock? I mean, the fingerprints'll be the ultimate proof."

Grubin gave a sardonic smile. "Reine impressed on me that he wants you to keep digging at Cathedral Rock. Poor old Brandt's reputation was really shit, you know. I guess Reine wants to keep all his options open until he's absolutely sure the fingerprints are going to work." He paused. "Anyway, let's have your information on Cathedral Rock, so I can pass it through to him."

The request was made rather like a waiter asking for the food order. Hegarty suspected Jules felt slightly chastened about having challenged him over his conviction Kisek was Leiman. They were of equal rank in the Mossad, but cooperation between them was absolutely essential.

Hegarty told him everything from the time he got off the train at Normanton: meeting Pony, saving Schon, how it got him the job, Kisek's quirks of character that appeared to link him so strongly to Leiman, the strange Carl Beaunig who had immigrated to Australia with Kisek, his progress in extracting information from the daughters—although he skimmed over the sexual details of his time with Ingrid—the passport, and the fact he hadn't had the chance to work on Anna yet.

Some things Matt omitted. Reine regarded personal feelings as inexplicable, and dangerous; it would only disturb him to know of the strong empathy between himself and Pony, and his attraction to Anna. He had no doubts he could handle it, he was a professional; nothing would get in the way of bringing Leiman to justice.

Grubin listened intently, occasionally taking notes, and showed a mocking smile at the end. "I'm told the daughters are very attractive," he jibed. "I like to see a man enjoying his work." He frowned. "I take it Milhesco was right, there's no possibility Leiman can be identified from old photographs?"

"Absolutely not. I checked my photograph to refresh my

memory, and he's changed beyond recognition." He took the film cassette from his pocket and dropped it on the table. "I managed to get a few shots of him."

Grubin gave an approving nod. "Excellent. Headquarters will want those."

"It very nearly got me thrown out of the goddamn place. The bastard almost went berserk at having his photograph taken."

"What I'd expect from scum trying to hide from his crimes. It's a wonder he kept the passport."

"I don't figure he'd have any option; he'd need some form of identification as Kisek, even for something like taxation, or he'd risk having his background checked in Germany. He couldn't afford to take a chance like that."

"Do you think you could get hold of it? It'd have his photograph as a young man on it, and Reine would consider it invaluable."

Hegarty grimaced. "I've been thinking about it. I'd have to pick the right time to search the house. If I get caught there won't be any second chance, I'll be thrown out on my ear, or worse."

"It's essential you stay there, Matt, especially now that we need his fingerprints."

Hegarty drummed his fingers reflectively on the side of the chair. "I've got to find a way. God, you should see the damn house, like a replica of a seventeenth-century European palace. The sonofabitch's made a lot of money in Australia."

"The bastard won't enjoy it much longer. Maybe the daughter Anna can help you?"

"Maybe; if I handle her right. I'm almost sure the daughters know nothing of their father's past. I've been working on the theory they must inadvertently know something that would betray Kisek, something he could have told them, if I can jog it out of their memory. Forty years is a long time to keep a secret without letting something slip, especially with your children."

Grubin gave a sly grin. "I'm sure you'll get something out of her." He paused, and frowned. "I'm surprised Milhesco failed to find out about the grandson and this Carl Beaunig. He's always so efficient."

Hegarty scowled. "I resent holes in a brief, but . . ." He shrugged it aside. "The boy's proved invaluable, but I don't figure where Beaunig fits."

"His appearance means nothing to you?"

"Not with his face so badly scarred; and of course his age."

Grubin nodded thoughtfully, then put his notes on the table, picked up a briefcase from beside the transmitter, took out a manila folder, and extracted several photographs that he held out to Hegarty.

"These are some more old photographs of Leiman as an SS officer you haven't seen. You can see he's standing with another SS man. They're both about the same build, except the other man is obviously older."

"I should have been shown these," growled Hegarty.

"I'm sorry, Matt, I only got them myself the day before I left Tel Aviv."

"Who's the other man?"

"Stauffer—Max Stauffer, Leiman's aide at Treblinka. They were close friends. Stauffer vanished about the same time as Leiman."

"You think Beaunig could be Stauffer?"

"I don't know. I'm just saying it's a possibility."

Hegarty pursed his lips, squinting in the dim light. "We get two sons of bitches instead of one."

"No, Reine's not interested in Stauffer. He's only small fry; Leiman's the big fish we want to hook."

Hegarty silently studied the photographs. If it was impossible to identify Kisek as Leiman from old photographs, then it was equally impossible to identify Beaunig as Stauffer. He pointed to the whip Leiman held in his hand. "The bastard still carries a whip," he muttered. "I thought he was going to use it on me when I took his photograph."

Grubin took the photographs back, and somberly examined them. "You're lucky he didn't. Leiman was an expert with a whip." He shook his head. "What makes people scum like that? They called him the Whipmaster at Treblinka, you know, Matt," he grated, "him and his fucking whip. There was a path that led from the barracks to the gas chambers. The Nazis called it the Road to Heaven. Leiman used to make his victims run to the gas chambers by flogging them with his whip." He growled deep in his chest, like a maddened dog, and flung the prints down on the table. "Can you imagine it, like a scene from hell; the bastards knew that exhausted lungs succumb much quicker to gas. Christ, at times I get the feeling it'd be so much easier to just go over there and put a bullet in that monster's head; except that'd be too easy for him, much too easy. Better to watch him sweat through a trial and finish up with his head in a noose."

Hegarty frowned. He hoped he wasn't forced into restraining Jules's assassination urge. Reine was a stickler for the conventions; only a trial would satisfy him. And Favett would enjoy the political kudos. But he'd never heard Jules vent his emotions like that. Did Jules have to memorize pictures on his bedroom wall when he was a child? Was there a memorial to his family in the Yad Vashem, the Museum of the Holocaust in Jerusalem?

"Strange a man like that should be so successful at raising cattle," he observed, veering away to another tack.

"Not so strange. The Nazi party attracted all types. Leiman's family raised cattle around Wismar in northern Germany before the war. Remember, Himmler was once a chicken farmer. It didn't stop them turning into animals themselves."

There was a brief period of brooding silence, then Grubin indicated the wine bottle. "You want another drink before you go, Matt?"

"No thanks." He paused. "It's going to be tough on the daughters; and the grandson. They were born here, raised here. They only know the sonofabitch as their father."

Grubin's face took on the rigid texture of the surrounding brick walls.

"You're only assuming that," he said coldly.

"No, I'm pretty sure."

"Then they'll manage to survive. Murderer's relatives generally do," he said curtly. "Which is more than the thousands Leiman butchered in Treblinka managed to do."

"You can't blame them for that; they weren't born then."

"No matter; that's not our concern, never has been. God, you know that, Matt. They'll get a shock to find out they were fathered by a monster, but they'll have to live with it. That's the way it is."

Hegarty backed off. Maybe Jules was right, but it didn't stop him from imagining the look on Anna's face when she found out. And Ingrid's. And Pony's. Fuck it! What was the matter with him? Jules was right; it was irrelevant, and he'd been stupid to even raise the subject.

Grubin seemed to sense his thoughts. "We've got enough problems bringing Leiman to trial," he grunted. "Don't get involved with the family."

"Don't tell me my goddamn job," Hegarty replied coldly.

It was undeserved, but Grubin merely smiled. "I wouldn't presume to do that, Matt. You know what's expected of you."

As if to end the subject he picked up the photographs and returned them to the briefcase. Then he took up a rectangular black object about the size of a small transistor radio and handed it to Hegarty.

"You've a room of your own at Cathedral Rock?"

"Yes."

Grubin pointed to a switch at the side, and the small circular light at the top righthand corner. "Keep this switched on by the side of your bed. When I know the time of Reine's arrival I'll transmit a signal, and the red light'll come on. That way you'll know to come here again, and I'll give you all the details. Okay?"

"Sure," agreed Hegarty. He slipped the receiver into his pocket, then got to his feet. His shadow moved in sinister accord, cast in gross proportions on the wall as he headed for the steps.

"I'd better get back," he said. "This first time there might be a few questions asked, but I want them to get used to the idea I like to take the bike out at night. That way it'll make it easier when I have to see you again."

"Sounds like a good idea," agreed Grubin. He turned the lamp down to a pale glow, leaving just enough light for them to move around, and the hissing sound of the pressurized kerosene faded to a whisper. He gestured to the ceiling. "I don't want any light to show when you lift the trapdoor."

Hegarty paused at the bottom of the steps. "Brandt being

killed makes it a different ball game, Jules," he warned. "Not knowing who murdered him bothers the hell out of me, especially if they traced Leiman here. It's something else we're going to have to watch for."

"I don't believe it's a worry," said Grubin confidently. "I'm sure Favett can contain it in Europe. If they'd known Leiman was in Australia they would have warned him to bolt long ago."

It made sense, but Hegarty wasn't convinced. "I hope you're right." He put his foot on the bottom rung, and gripped Grubin's hand. "I won't let you down, Jules."

"I know that, Matt. Reine picked the right man. You'd better stay well clear of here until you get my signal."

"Okay. There's no point in my bringing Kisek's finger-prints until we can match them against the ones Reine's bringing." He hesitated. "I hope none of the family come prowling around. You're pretty close to Cathedral Rock."

Grubin patted him on the shoulder. "Then I'll make like a mouse, and stay in my hole until they go. Why should they anyway?"

Hegarty shrugged. "No reason, I guess." He paused. "Reine wouldn't be too pleased about any innocent people getting hurt."

Grubin's grin resembled a wolf protecting its lair. "Don't worry, I'm not planning to shoot anybody. Nothing's going to happen down here, unless a snake tries to keep me company." He shrugged. "I know there's an element of risk being this close, but I think it's worth it so we're not too far apart. One time I considered Normanton as a base, but I think I would have been too easily noticed." He shook his head. "This is better, as long as we're quick."

"I'll buy you a dinner at the Piroshki when this is over," said Hegarty with a grin.

"I'll hold you to that."

Hegarty nodded farewell, then climbed to the trapdoor, the steps creaking threateningly under his weight. He pushed it open and peered cautiously about the room. There was only silent darkness, and overhead, moonlight sieving through the hole-pocked ceiling. He levered himself out, crouched at the opening, and peered down to Grubin.

"I'll wait for your signal," he whispered.

Grubin raised a hand in acknowledgment. "Okay. Good luck, Matt."

Hegarty carefully lowered the trapdoor, then crept warily through the old rooms and out into the night.

The ground ran at a slight incline away from the house, and he let the Kawasaki run free to the bottom before starting the motor. He figured it would be safer if the sound didn't connect to the ruined house. The wind had taken on a keener edge, chilling his face, and the countryside danced to its beat as if to offset the cold. His shadow moved in tandem, a black companion set against a moonlight-frosted background. The potholes in the track were harder to see with his back to the moon, and when he was well clear of the house he switched on the headlight. Maybe it didn't matter now, and he didn't want to risk a spill. But he rode slowly as he considered the problem of getting Kisek's fingerprints. Reine's impending arrival locked him into a time frame, and he needed to figure an angle pretty quickly. It was too risky now to try and use Ingrid; better to try some devious way with Pony. Or Anna—which wasn't going to be easy. He hoped to Christ she didn't put a wall between them over the business of Ingrid in his room. He had to convince her he was the innocent party on that score, do whatever was needed to win back her confidence—lie, connive, invent, ply her with charm. He had to persuade her to ask him to dinner at the house again, and then find a pretext for getting hold of a drinking glass Kisek had used.

He was jolted from introspection by a glimpse of a fleeting shape set apart from the landscape. Then it was just as quickly gone, cut off by a group of trees, it might have been a trick of light. Then he spotted it again, clearer this time, the dramatic silhouette of a horse and rider, pacing on a parallel path several hundred feet off the track that led to the road. He throttled back, cutting the sound of the motor to a throaty murmur, just holding sufficient speed to maintain balance. Faintly came the drumming of hooves, mingling with the burble of the Kawasaki, and the rush of wind. Maybe it was Pony and Schon, and he hoped to Christ he hadn't been seen at the house. The incident with the film had shown it wasn't easy to lie to Pony; he would need to find a convincing excuse. He held to the dawdling speed except when he came to the loose sand where he'd nearly gotten bogged down on the way in, and he opened the throttle to take him on an evasive route through the side grass. He stopped at the junction, switched off the motor, and sat waiting astride the bike. Someone had obviously seen him, and he decided it was better to face them here than back at the house.

He was forced to turn his head when a sudden gust of wind scuffed dust into his face, and when he looked back the horse was only a few feet away, snorting and shying as it sidled from the cover of the trees. It was Schon, but Anna in the saddle instead of Pony. She walked the horse slowly to the bike, reined to a halt, then impassively studied him. The white blouse she wore glowed in the moonlight, accentuating her darkness. The angry words from their last meeting made for a standoff of awkward silence.

"You like to do some night riding, Anna?" he asked, probing for an opening.

She leaned forward and patted the horse's neck for a time.

"I could say the same about you, Hegarty," she answered coldly.

Calling him Hegarty instead of Matt made her sound like Ingrid, and she used it like a form of reproach. It was an indication she was still irritated over Ingrid's being in his room, yet he had a strong hunch she'd come looking for him.

"It's just something I like to do," he said. He gestured to the savanna. "I like the feeling, out by myself, burning along in country like this; as if I'm the only man on earth. Free, no ties, no worries, just going."

In a way it was partly true.

"A stranger could get himself lost out here at night," she warned.

"I've got a good sense of direction, and I've been sticking to the roads." He paused. "You like to ride at night for the same reason?"

Schon jigged edgily, and she quieted him with a tug of the reins, then appraised Hegarty with her father's challenging stare. The wind teased at her hair, pressing the blouse tight to her breasts, and again he had the powerful instinct she'd be really something to know, to feel, to make love to.

"Perhaps," she murmured. "Pony generally rides Schon every day, but he's been so taken with you and the helicopter the horse hasn't been out. I thought I'd give him some exercise."

"You saw me on the road?"

"I heard the bike."

"That's all?"

She tossed her head with irritation. "Of course that's damn all." She glanced around. "Unless you're out here waiting for Ingrid," she added maliciously.

"You know that's not true."

"Do I? Like I said before, it's none of my business."

Her expression, and the strength of her denial, belied her words.

"I told you before, and I'll tell you again, I didn't know she was in my room."

"You're telling me she invited herself?" she scoffed.

"That's the way it was. She wasn't the reason I turned down your dinner invitation. Dammit Anna, you know why I couldn't come."

"Are you collecting scalps, Hegarty?"

"What's that supposed to mean?"

"Scalps. Ingrid's. Pony's. Mine, if I was stupid enough to give you the chance."

"Hey, that's bullshit," he protested.

"Maybe. It's been a long time since there was anyone like you around Cathedral Rock. Perhaps never. I'm just warning you not to take advantage of it."

"That's not the way it is," he lied. He shrugged, and spread his hands, remembering the conversation he'd overheard between the two sisters. For sure Anna had Ingrid's implied intention concerning him in her mind.

"Okay, okay, look, maybe Ingrid does have some sort of . . . itch about me," he admitted. "I mean I'm flattered, of course," he added quickly, "but she's going to have to forget it, I don't want that sort of involvement." He paused, watching her. "At least not with Ingrid."

Maybe the innuendo was a mistake, but she didn't react, merely reflected for a moment. "What Ingrid does is her affair," she muttered finally.

"Not when it concerns me. I don't want her making bad blood between us—not when we'll be working together."

"Why should it?" she said defensively.

"You tell me."

She moved uneasily in the saddle. "You're your own man, Matt."

She was back to calling him Matt again, the aggravation filtered from her voice, and he figured she wanted to believe him.

She began to have trouble holding Schon again, the horse was nervous about the Kawasaki and kept shying away. He dismounted from the bike, propped it up, then took hold of the horse's bridle, offering soothing words.

"Why don't you get down for a while," he suggested.

She hesitated. "I should be getting back."

"It's hard to talk like this."

"You want to talk?"

He grinned up at her. "Well, now that we've accidently bumped into each other, why not?"

She relented, with an answering smile. "All right." She shrugged. "Maybe I was hoping to run into you," she admitted.

She slid down into his arms, then stepped quickly away and took hold of the reins, as if wary of the enforced closeness.

"You saw me ride out of Cathedral Rock?" he asked.

"Yes; but I didn't know where you'd gone. I was just riding around, and I saw your headlight."

He held back a sigh of relief. She hadn't seen him come from the old house.

"I was just cruising around enjoying myself," he said.

He ran his hands gently over the horse's flanks, aware that she was watching, doubt still on her face.

"I wanted to talk to you about Pony," she said.

"We could have talked back at the house or out on the muster."

"Not without Pony." She uttered a soft laugh. "He'll scarcely let you out of his sight."

"I think he's a great kid."

"You know he's in the first stages of hero worship."

He tried to laugh it aside. "I'm delighted he likes me, but I don't know about hero worship."

"Oh, that's what it is. I listen to him, watch him with you. He's never seen anyone like you."

"Maybe I can teach him a thing or two. I figure he'll be running this place one day."

"That's what's worrying me."

"I don't get you. How's it worrying you? I think the boy's terrific."

"Well, you're short term, Matt." She paused, her eyes on the horse. He knew she could sense the ambiance rising between them like a heat haze. Then she focused that penetrating gaze on his face again. "For all of us," she added.

"I guess everything's short term, if that's the way you want to look at it," he replied cautiously. "So I figure you've got to make the most of it, learn from the contact. Pony's bright, he'll learn—and I'll learn from him."

"As long as he doesn't get hurt."

"You want me to lay off, keep him out of the helicopter, make like I think he's suddenly someone I don't want to know any more? I figure that'd really hurt him."

She bit down on her lip, stirring at the track with her foot. "You go from one extreme to the other. I'm not too sure how he'll handle it when you've gone. He's never had a father."

"I know."

"His father was drowned before Pony was born." She swept her arm around. "It's hard to imagine what this is like during the wet, but a man can get drowned if he's unlucky."

He knew she was lying, but he merely grunted.

"I'm not trying to be a father. That's not what I want," he said.

"Maybe, but it makes him vulnerable to someone like you."

He considered before answering. He needed Pony, didn't want anything to disturb what he had going with the boy, especially the way he could influence his grandfather.

"Why not let it run the way it's going? I can enjoy Pony's company, and he can enjoy mine," he urged persuasively. "Kids his age are flexible; he knows it's like you said, only short term. He'll adjust when I'm gone."

She fell silent. Schon fidgeted again, and when he settled down they were standing closer together. She didn't appear to notice.

"Perhaps you're right. But there's his grandfather."

"Surely he's not against my friendship with the boy?"

She gave a hesitant shrug. "I think he's a little jealous. He feels very strongly about Pony, you know, with him set to inherit the place and all."

"I don't think your father will miss me," he said with irony.

"That isn't what I mean. Dad's tried to be like a father to him." Her mouth trembled, and a troubled expression clouded her face, which he failed to comprehend. "He can't get near Pony since you arrived."

"That isn't deliberate. Christ, I'm trying my best not to rile your father in any way."

She placed a placating hand on his arm. "I know that, Matt. But it's important you understand, just in case it comes up."

"What do you mean?"

She shrugged. "I don't know; I've seen him watching you and Pony. I just want you to be aware of it."

He reached for her hand, but she swiftly withdrew it.

"Thanks anyway," he said. "I'll watch myself with Pony when your father's around."

"Thank you," she murmured. "That's all I'm asking."

There was a silent pause. She shivered under a sudden gust of wind and he wondered how she'd react if he placed his arm about her for warmth. She turned away before he had time to put thought into action, and glanced back along the track. "You must have come past the old house," she murmured.

He casually nodded. "Yes. I took a look. I passed over it earlier today in the helicopter. You get the right sort of light and old ruins like that can make a terrific photograph."

"I suppose so. We used to live there."

"Yes I know; Pony told me." He thought about Jules. "You ever go there?"

She shook her head. "Hardly ever. It makes me kind of . . ." she hesitated, ". . . sad I suppose. Like watching someone you love aging; just gradually falling apart. I had some happy times there."

"Before Pony?"

"Yes. When my mother was alive."

"It would have been nothing like the palace you live in now."

She shrugged. "Nothing at all. Mum would have hated the . . . palace, as you call it. That's all Dad's idea. I think he had the urge to build some sort of monument to his success in the Gulf Country."

"He and Carl?"

"Yes, Carl too, I suppose. He worked just as hard as Dad back in those days."

"But no one ever sees his monument, except the family."

She uttered a self-conscious laugh. "You saw it."

"Yeah, but I gather I was a surprise exception."

"Right. A surprise for all of us."

"But it's still an unseen monument," he persisted.

She leaned against Schon, her expression wistful. "Don't ask me to explain it. I would have been just as happy staying in the old place. I love my father, but he has some strange ways; I suppose you've realized he doesn't like people very much."

Hegarty pursed his lips and nodded. It was hard to imagine anyone loving a monster, but then as Jules had reminded him, some of the worst Nazis had been devoted family men.

"I sort of figured that out," he commented drily. "But I guess the . . . palace fulfils some sort of need. He couldn't have had much back in Germany."

She frowned. "The war must have been terrible, but before that I don't think it was too bad. His family raised cattle in a place called Wismar. That's how he knew about cattle before he came to Australia."

She surprised him, knowing about Wismar and the cattle background. Maybe Ingrid was right, Anna was closer to her father, he confided in her more than anyone else. He cursed himself again for wasting time with Ingrid.

"I guess Carl doesn't like people too much either."

She gave a derisive chuckle. "How would anyone know

what Carl liked or disliked? God, what he thought about anything? You know I've known him all my life, yet I know nothing about him."

It was a repeat of what he'd heard from Pony. And Ingrid.

"He must talk to your father."

"Oh sure; when no one else is around." She reflected a moment, combing her fingers along Schon's neck. "I think Mum was always a little frightened of Carl. She never said much, but I think she felt he was like a barrier between her and Dad." She checked herself with a sudden grimace of embarrassment, and took hold of the reins. "Good God, why am I boring you with all this family stuff? I'm absolutely sure it's of no interest to you."

He didn't want her to stop. "Not at all," he assured her. "I'm always interested in the different ways people live their lives. I'm interested in anything you want to talk about."

She dipped her head. "Why thank you," she said, pleased.

Schon impatiently stamped his feet, swinging his head about, nudging her closer to Hegarty. Matt could feel her quick breath, their closeness, and knew she sensed it too. If it had been Ingrid he would have picked her up and laid her in the grass, but this woman required more subtlety.

"I'd better be moving," she breathed unsteadily, backing away. She put her foot into the stirrup and swung quickly up into the saddle. He held the bridle to control the horse's nervous jigging.

"It was great meeting you like this," he said. "It gave me the chance to straighten a few things out."

She smiled down at him. "I'm glad too, Matt; so you'd know how I felt about Pony."

"Don't worry too much about Pony. The kid knows how to handle himself."

The horse broke free, prancing sideways, snorting, and she let him go, raising her hand in farewell as they headed for the savanna.

"That's the way I'm trying to raise him," she called back.

Then she kicked at Schon's flanks, and the colt took off as if from a starting stall, deftly leaping a narrow channel along the side of the track and drumming away across the savanna until it was only a dark shape, then a receding beat, then nothing. She knew how to handle the colt; the animal had a lot of spirit, it could kill someone who didn't know what they were doing. He remained watching even after there was nothing more to see, hands thrust in his pockets, then finally went slowly back to the Kawasaki. Christ, the woman disturbed him, he'd be a fool to deny it. And her son. He started up the bike and headed down the road toward Cathedral Rock. For some reason his mind went back to the Tarantula Hawk Pony had shown him, and he felt close to a sense of envy for the insect. The Hawk wasn't troubled by anything so irrelevant as concern for the spider, no emotion like he felt stirring for Anna. Or Pony. The survival of his species was all that mattered to the Hawk. Jules was like that, and once Matt had prided himself on being the same. Whatever had brought the change, he had no doubt it was given added impetus by the brief encounter with Anna and Pony.

Kisek sank into the soft leather club chair, while Carl poured two glasses of schnapps. He loved the feel of the old chair, that embraced him like a favorite coat.

It was late; the silent house exaggerating the clink of the bottle against the rim of the glass, produced by the tremor of Carl's hand. It was unspoken, but of late Kisek had begun to wonder how much longer his partner would live. Over the last few months the process of decay seemed to have accelerated, even if Carl's mind was still sharp. But there were legal problems to be resolved over the property, and the time was coming when they'd have to be broached. It was stupid not to have settled it long ago. It was Carl who'd suggested this late night drink, so perhaps he wanted to raise the subject himself.

Carl ignored the splattering of schnapps about the table, delivered one glass to Kisek, then went and carefully lowered himself into the matching chair opposite. He half lifted the schnapps to his mouth, then hesitated, and glanced about the room.

"To comfort," he toasted, with barbed irony.

Kisek followed his gaze. It wasn't a large room, but a good place to be alone, to shut out the world. Deep carpet underfoot, a small rosewood antique table separating the two chairs, a magnificent old Victorian-style desk positioned in front of a large window that gave an unimpeded view of the savanna. The only concession to modernity was several metal filing cabinets, containing all the breeding records. Around the walls were framed paintings and photographs of Germany in the thirties, illustrating the way Kisek liked to remember the fatherland. The only light came from a small desk lamp, highlighting Kisek's face, keeping Carl's features in shadow.

"There's being nothing wrong with comfort," Kisek growled.

"Then to Germany," Carl conceded. "As she was, as we like to remember her, ja, Colonel?"

"Enough of that," Kisek sharply cut him off. "Enough, Carl." He straightened in the chair and motioned irritably with his glass. "Even here, even now, we should never be using anything but our chosen names. That was agreed over forty years ago—never to be changed. You know the rules. What if the girls were to overhear, even Pony? It's not worth it, even now."

Carl scowled, took a sip of schnapps, and rolled it about his mouth before swallowing. "You're right, of course, Dorf," he wheezed apologetically. He attempted to form his scarred face into a smile. "Forgive my age, my doddering old body. It's been a long time since I made such a slip, ja, a long time. You have to admit that."

Kisek sullenly studied his glass. Doddering he might be, but Carl never did anything without reason.

"Perhaps it's because of the danger I see you are allowing at Cathedral Rock," Carl continued. "Ja, if we are talking about iron rules laid down long ago, then surely you are breaking the most important of all." He tilted his head quizzically to one side. "Ja, the most important of all."

"What are you talking about? What rule? What danger?"

Carl held back answering, finishing his schnapps with tantalizing deliberation, then placing the empty glass with contrived care on the table.

"You know I'm talking about the American," he said. "The rule of no strangers at Cathedral Rock, of no strangers anyplace where we've been breeding cattle in the Gulf Country." He picked up the glass again, and softly beat it on the table in rhythmn with his words. "Never, never, no strangers, no strangers, trusting no one, ja, that was the rule. It has kept us safe for over forty years, so why in God's name break it now?"

Kisek gave a snort of disagreement. "Carl, the man is nothing but what he seems; just a helicopter mustering pilot. Too long the helicopter has been gathering dust in the shed, too long I've been waiting for Anna to learn to fly it. This Hegarty can be a great help to us." He shook his head. "You are jumping at shadows, ja, shadows. After all this time, and at your age, it's being ridiculous. We've beaten them, don't you understand? We've beaten them." He drained his schnapps and thumped the glass down beside Carl's. "Don't be worrying, you'll die in bed," he jeered. "We both will."

Carl clasped his hands and placed them thoughtfully to his chin. Only the eyes seemed alive in his scarred face.

"I have a nose for Jews," he muttered. "Something you learn, and never forget, like walking, and breathing. Hegarty has the smell of Jew about him."

"Ingrid says it better than I, but you're talking bullshit," declared Kisek derisively.

"The man carries a strange weapon, for a helicopter mustering pilot," persisted Carl.

"What of it? Americans carry such guns, and it saved Pony's horse. And you found nothing in his room to back your suspicions. Let it be, Carl. The man will be gone in a few days."

Carl tapped his nose. "And I tell you he has the smell of Jew. Time may have dulled your senses, but I've never forgotten."

"I haven't forgotten."

"The man comes here as a savior of Pony's horse, and it's like a blindfold thrown over your instinct for survival."

"My instinct for survival has managed very well over the last forty years," retorted Kisek tartly.

"It's too dangerous. The man should go."

"And I say he's no threat." Kisek twisted irritably in the chair. "Mein Gott, tired I am of treating the whole world as our enemy, seeing every stranger as an avenging executioner. Safe we've been here for a lifetime, and a lone man like Hegarty isn't going to be changing it. Not now. I keep telling you Carl, we've beaten them."

Carl retreated into sullen silence. Outside the rising wind buffeted the house and stirred the savanna to a sound like someone weeping.

"Ingrid is making cow eyes at him," Carl began again. "Have you thought of that problem?"

"Ingrid can look after herself. A man might take the sharp edge off her tongue."

"Surely you're not meaning a man like that? A wanderer, with no roots? Maybe Anna is needing a man too?"

"Anna needs no one; she has Pony," Kisek flared. "She knows better than to make use of a man like Hegarty."

"Once we would have discussed a decision like Hegarty," muttered Carl.

"You said yourself you're too old now for Cathedral Rock. The helicopter will be making a big difference."

"You let the boy twist you," accused Carl, with sudden venom. "You want his love so badly, it makes you fear to discipline him. He says he wants the man Hegarty, and you turn to jelly."

The accusation cut into an exposed nerve. "You are talking nonsense," protested Kisek angrily. "God, I discipline the boy more than his mother; I don't have to beg for his love, he gives it to me without question. He's in my blood; don't be blaming him for this."

"Back in the old days a mere boy wouldn't have been allowed to stand in the way."

"Are you comparing Pony to those at Treblinka?"

"No, no, of course not," said Carl hastily. "But I think he makes you weak."

"That's not true."

"I see him with Hegarty."

"Hegarty's new, different. It's natural the boy is attracted. It'll wear off once the man is gone."

Carl gave a gesture of defeat, pushed himself wearily out of the chair, and poured another schnapps. As an indication of displeasure he didn't fill Kisek's glass. He retreated to the chair, fondling the drink, absently contemplating space. "Wrong it was from the very beginning," he mused. "So easy

it would have been to melt into the big cities; leave no trace.
That was our original idea. It was what we planned on the boat
coming over. But you had to marry Julia, and all the old
ambitions came back, the way it was raising cattle at Wismar in
the old days; you had to be the big cattleman again. We were
too successful, Dorf, and it made us forever on guard, never
feeling safe, living like hermits. Then your children coming to
complicate life further, more ears that could hear secrets, and
betray us."

"Never betray you, Carl," sneered Kisek, "never, not
when you're treating them like they don't exist."

"One of us had to be making sure of safety. Better only
one mouth to risk the slip of a betraying secret. Ja, only one
mouth is safer." Carl mournfully shook his head. "Better we
should have stayed with our original plan, and not spend our
life suspicious of every shadow. Julia found out, and it
destroyed her. Never could you be making her understand."

"Leave Julia out of this."

"It's part of it."

"You were willing enough," stated Kisek coldly. He
gestured about the room. "You've enjoyed what it gave us."

"I'm not enjoying what it did to my face."

"Don't be throwing that up at me. You know it was an
accident."

"Ja, an accident; chasing steers like a madman you were."

Kisek leaned forward in an attitude of contrition. "Carl,
don't let's argue like this. We're safe now, believe me, we're
safe. This American Hegarty is nothing—nothing. Stupid it is
to be having regrets after more than forty years."

"I'm not having regrets about the great days in Germany."

"Better if you're forgetting them."

"Never. Always I am seeing the cattle, and thinking of the
days with the Jews." For a moment the aged quaver went out
of his voice. "Ja, cattle, only fit for slaughter; that's how it was,
cleansing the world we were." He stopped, breathing deeply,
then the sudden flame in his eyes gradually dimmed. "And
we've spent our lives fearing them, ja, there's the irony."

Kisek furiously shook his fist in the air. "Ah, fear has only
been part of it. You're forgetting the enjoyment, the freedom,
God, the success," he hissed irately. "Mein Gott, will you be

shutting up, Carl! Not for years have I heard you bring up the old days like this. Are you out of your mind? It was agreed, damn you, it was agreed: forget the past. No more. You hear? No more."

Carl slumped back in the chair. "You're getting rid of Hegarty, and it'll be the same again."

Kisek stood abruptly to his feet, glowering down at Carl. "Hegarty stays," he declared harshly. "I refuse to be jumping any more at shadows that aren't there."

"Better it would have been if you'd used your whip on Hegarty at the stockyards," wheezed Carl. "Ja, I was watching. You are being a fool, Dorf, believe me, a fool."

Kisek turned on his heels, and strode angrily toward the door. "That's the end of it," he snarled. "I'm going to bed. If Hegarty frightens you, then why don't you hide under your bed until he's gone."

He wanted to slam the door after him, but he closed it with care, anxious not to disturb the sleeping house. He didn't want his daughters, or Pony, to come running to ask what was going on. But he needed a place to calm himself, to expunge the rancor simmering within. He went softly through the living room, let himself out the front door, walked slowly to the corral, and leaned heavily on the railing. Ritchie had already gone with the ringers to establish camp for the morning muster, and there was only a lone horse remaining. It raised its head, snickering nervously as it pawed the ground, but stayed on the far side. He breathed deeply, then turned to look back at the house. Nothing soothed him more than to be out here alone in the night, surrounded by the savanna glistening in the moonlight, listening to the wind stir the grass with a husky whispering sound. To see Cathedral Rock hovering over the house like a giant protector, the Rock as nature's monument, the homestead as his.

It was a night like this when Julia had died, and he rode the savanna for hours, not knowing or caring where he was headed, letting the horse take him, until by daylight he'd found himself at the summit of Cathedral Rock. That's when he'd decided on the location for the new house. He suspected the girls thought he'd dominated their mother, and perhaps they were right, but he'd loved Julia as much as he was capable. The time in Germany had put a steel casing around his heart, and the role of gentle lover was beyond him. He'd never understood how she found out; there were times he suspected Carl was responsible, that Carl had decided she was too dangerous, but he had no proof, and even hated having such a suspicion.

He could feel the tension bleeding from him, even though the conflict with Carl was unresolved. God, he couldn't recall the last time the old days in Germany had been raised. Right from the beginning in Australia he and Carl had taken an oath that any reference to the old days was forbidden, a closed chapter; to even speak of it was to risk the dangerous possibility of being overheard. It wasn't an act of approaching senility in Carl, he'd seen nothing to indicate Carl had lost any sharpness of mind. But Carl had cried wolf before, and been wrong, yet perhaps he shouldn't be so contemptuous; they'd had their disagreements, but through the years they'd remained close, Cathedral Rock would have been impossible without him. Carl had spoken uncomfortable truths. It was true Kisek had broken the rigid rule of no strangers, but Pony had caught him off guard. Did he crave Pony's love so much he was prepared to endanger them, rather than deny the boy anything? Recalling past disciplines, his first instinct was to reject the idea; yet watching Pony's sudden rush of idolatry toward Hegarty stirred feelings of jealousy he'd never experienced before, made more intense by the boy's aggressive defense of the American over the photography incident. He would need to guard himself against any further such outbursts, because he would only risk antagonizing the boy further.

He sighed, placed his hands behind his back, and began a slow circuit of the corral. The horse broke into a canter, hooves softly drumming, then halted in a stirring of dust, watching like a suspicious sentry. When Kisek thought back to those early days in the Gulf, the work, the sweat, running down unbranded cattle with the old four wheel drive, it seemed ludicrous that a stray American was going to threaten them after a near-lifetime of safety. God, surely there was nothing to fear now? He stopped at the far side of the corral, watching the white grass curling before the wind like an incoming tide. There was no denying he had broken the iron rule, and he'd be relieved when the helicopter mustering was finished and Hegarty was only a memory. Both for himself and Pony.

Chapter 9

London.

Sam Jaroff morosely studied the view from the window of the apartment overlooking Baker Street. The traffic tooted and start-stopped below, moving like blood laboring through a clogged artery. People scurried aimlessly along the sidewalks, some ignoring the safety of traffic lights, ducking and weaving through the vehicles. Here and there the lumbering red double-decker buses, so symbolic of London, dwarfed their competitors as they disdainfully forced their way through the congestion. He scowled at a group of laughing, jeans-clad kids, their hair garishly colored, and spiked up like a goddamn crazy cockscomb. Creeps. He rubbed his large hands together relishing the feel of the sun on his face, appreciating the warmth after the last few dreary days.

Physically he was an odd contrast to Corliss. About five-foot-six, his broad shoulders and thick torso made him seem shorter. He'd been a hell of a tackle in his school days, which had first earned him the nickname of Tank. It followed him to Vietnam, where he was known more as Tank than as Sergeant Jaroff, but he took pleasure in the name, with its allusion to charging through and flattening all opposition.

He was in his mid forties, like Corliss, black hair tinged with gray. He took pride in the fact he was part Navaho, and walked proudly everywhere. Even so, his hawk nose, black eyes, truculent mouth, and craggy lines seemed more attuned to the harsh Arizona terrain of his forefathers than the civilized clutter of London.

He'd been gunned down in ambush during the Tet

disaster, and Corliss had come charging through the carnage in a jeep to pull him out. He gave his blood to the Colonel from that day, he figured Corliss had given him a second life, and in gratitude he handed it back to the Colonel to use as he saw fit. Anything Corliss asked, anytime, anywhere, he was available, no questions asked. There had been times when the debt was called in, and he'd responded gladly—when things needed to be done outside the squeamish liberal commie rules they operated under in Washington. He had it figured this was one of those things.

He knew Corliss was in some sort of loyalty hock to one of the big shots in Washington. Jesus, he didn't dig those guys, they were all shit as far as he was concerned, who'd stabbed them in the back over Nam. But that was the Colonel's business; his loyalty was to Corliss, not to any of the Washington jerks.

He ran his fingers around his buttoned-up shirt collar, and self-consciously adjusted the tie. He still felt a jerk dressed up in a business suit the same as the Colonel; jeans and an old shirt was all he ever wore driving his truck, but the Colonel claimed a business suit was needed to make this job look right, and an order was an order.

"You know, Colonel, I saw a plaque in the roadway in front of Marble Arch yesterday . . ." he still deferred to Corliss as "Colonel," even though his army days were far behind him, ". . . which said it was the site of the old Tyburn gallows, where they used to string up the criminals." He turned and grinned at Corliss, and drew a finger across his throat. "Jesus, they didn't pussyfoot around in those days, no sir. It was all so simple then, like in Nam: just point the gun, pull the trigger, and blow the sonofabitch away."

Corliss glanced up from where he was making notes at the small table, took the cigar from his mouth, and offered a bleak smile.

"Nothing's that simple any more, Sam," he remarked. He never referred to Jaroff as Tank. "Nothing. Certainly not what we're trying to do here."

Jaroff wasn't exactly sure what they were trying to do. Like a good soldier he didn't ask questions; he knew the Colonel would fill him in on whatever was necessary at the right time. But he did know there was some creep called Kisek who was a dangerous threat to their country's security. For Chrissake, why did the politicians make it so fucked-up complicated? If the sonofabitch was a threat, then just cross the bastard off, and have done with it. But Corliss had also hinted that the Mossad was involved, and the Washington guys were always leery about offending the Israelis, just in case it cost them the Jewish vote.

"Tipping off the cops about finding Brandt where we dumped him wasn't simple, Colonel."

"But very necessary, Sam. Circumstances changed after we got rid of the body."

"You sure your information about this Mossad guy Reine coming to London to identify the body is on the level?"

"Absolutely. I'm told he's already here. We need Reine, Sam. If we're ever going to find out the location of the man Kisek, then I figure Reine can lead us to him."

"Maybe we should have tried to squeeze it out of Brandt before we iced him. After all, he was a Mossad guy too."

"He wouldn't have known."

"It might have been worth a try."

"No," stated Corliss firmly.

"There was nothing in the papers you took from Brandt?"

Corliss shrugged. "They concerned Kisek, but not where he is."

"And you figure this Reine knows?"

Corliss thoughtfully shuffled through his notes. "That's my information, Sam. Let's leave it for now, and see if the morgue attendant calls."

"You think he will?"

"I figure he's a guy who could be bought if the money was right."

"You read a guy pretty well, Colonel."

"If Reine goes to the morgue to identify Brandt then I'm sure the man will call."

"He knows about you now though, Colonel. I mean, I guess that couldn't be helped, but it's sort of awkward."

Corliss leaned back in the spindly chair, drew on the cigar, then drifted smoke to the ceiling as he glanced about the room. Christ, it was a shabby dive, cracked walls, peeling paint, drab furniture, but he'd used it before and found the location ideal.

"That was a problem I was hoping you'd take care of for me, Sam," he said.

Jaroff moved from the window, and dropped untidily into a nearby chair. "Sure, Colonel, if that's what you want."

"Like the old days, Sam, remember? Never leave a trail for Charlie to follow."

Jaroff scowled at the memory. "Yeah, right. You want I should arrange something now?"

Corliss gave a negative gesture of the cigar. "Later. Let's wait until he calls."

Jaroff choked off an ugly snigger. "You know, my old lady gets really frayed when I take off with you like this; figures I'm away having it off with a dame somewhere." He disdainfully surveyed the room. "That's a laugh, eh Colonel?"

"Things have to be done, Sam."

"Hey, I'm not complaining, no sir, you know the way it is with me where you're concerned. How's it with your family?"

"My wife's used to it. She doesn't ask any more. Was a time she did, but she gave up when she never got any answers."

"She's got your kids to keep her busy. They must be growing up now."

"One at college, the other getting set to . . ." The jangle of the telephone cut him off. He let it ring several times, then picked up the receiver and answered by giving only the number, no name.

"Is that Mr. Humphrey?" asked a cautious voice.

The asthmatic wheeze gave Corliss an instant image of the pimply faced morgue attendant. Humphrey was the name he'd used when offering the bribe.

"This is Humphrey," he answered curtly.

"The Mr. Andre Reine you wanted to know about?"

"He came to the morgue?"

"Yeah, like you said, to identify the man taken out of the quarry. His name was Brandt."

"Forget him. Did Reine leave a London address?"

"When do I get the money?" the attendant countered.

"I'll see you get it tonight."

"How can I be sure?" asked the attendant suspiciously.

"One half of a hundred pound note is no more use to me than you," sneered Corliss.

There was a snuffling pause. Then, "Okay. You'll bring it to me here at the morgue?"

"Yes, someone will bring it," said Corliss impatiently. "Now, can I have Reine's address?"

"Okay, he's staying at the Cumberland Hotel."

Corliss grimaced. He should have figured he'd stay in the same place as Brandt, maybe in the same room just to sniff around. "What room?"

"520."

It was the same room. "Thanks. I'll see you get what's coming to you."

"You'd better, mister, you just bloody well better."

Corliss dismissed the feeble threat, and hung up. He opened the London telephone directory and quickly located the Cumberland Hotel number.

"It was the guy from the morgue?" asked Jaroff.

"The same. I told him you'd take care of him tonight."

Jaroff grinned. "I'll handle it. He told you where . . . ?"

Corliss held up his hand for silence as he rapidly dialed the number.

"He's staying in the same room at the Cumberland that Brandt used."

"He won't find anything there," said Jaroff.

"We know that, but he doesn't." He turned away. "Hello, Cumberland Hotel?"

"Yes sir, may I help you?" came a manicured voice.

"My name is Glass, Franklin Glass," Corliss said silkily. "My wife and I stayed at the Cumberland some time ago, and had such a pleasant stay I wondered if it were possible for us to have the same room again. Just for sentimental reasons. It looked over Hyde Park, and we thought it charming."

"If the room is available we'd be delighted, Mr. Glass. What number was it?"

"520."

There was a brief pause. "I'm very sorry, Mr. Glass, but the room's taken. However we have other excellent rooms available."

Corliss clucked his tongue. "I'm disappointed. Perhaps we could get close by, say a room next door."

There was another pause. "518 is also taken, but 522 is available. An excellent room, which also looks out on to Hyde Park."

"That will be fine."

"Good. When may we expect you, Mr. Glass?"

"I'd say about an hour."

"Then we'll look forward to seeing you, sir."

Corliss hung up, and grinned at Jaroff. "We're in, Sam, right in the next room to the sonofabitch. You can make yourself scarce in the lobby while I check in—unless you want to make like you're my wife?"

Jaroff tittered, and swung his hips in a parody of female impersonation. "I don't think I'm the type, Colonel."

Corliss stood, picked up the suitcase from the floor, dropped it on the bed, and opened the lid. "Pack all the bugging gear, Sam. We'll set it up so we can hear every breath he takes, every telephone call, every fart he makes."

"How are we gonna know him?"

"He's got to leave his room some time, to eat, or whatever. We can watch for him, drop a few tips around to set it up. I know about Andre Reine, even if I've never seen him; he's something of a famed institution in the Mossad." He slowly began to pack clothes in the suitcase. "Christ, he's been around a long time, he must be on in years now. I'm surprised he'd be involved in an operation like this. I thought he'd be sunning himself on a Tel Aviv beach, or watching the pretty girls in Dizengoff Square, while younger guys took the risks."

"Sounds like you've been there, Colonel."

"There was a time," Corliss murmured, with an expression that cautioned against further questions.

Jaroff got the message, and turned to open another suitcase and start packing the bugging equipment between his clothes.

"I don't quite know what the operation is, Colonel," he said tentatively.

Corliss offered an appreciative grin. "That's what I like about you, Sam; I just point the way, and you don't ask, just do it. You're something special, y'know that?"

Jaroff glowed in the praise. "Sorry, Colonel; I just wondered what direction we're headed?"

"How about Australia, Sam?"

Jaroff froze in mid motion, mouth open, eyes wide. "Australia?"

"That's where Kisek is. But Australia's one hell of a big place, and I've got it figured only Reine can give us a lead on where in Australia."

"Then we go there and waste this Kisek?"

"That's the idea."

"He can really make a heap of trouble for our country?"

"He can stir up some very dangerous shit, Sam."

"Kisek's his real name?"

"Let's leave it that way for now."

"Why don't we just take Reine like we did Brandt; screw the information out of him. If he's ancient like you say, it shouldn't be too hard."

Corliss grimaced. Sometimes Sam's simplistic, brutal approach needed muzzling.

"That would risk alerting too many people, maybe even Kisek. Reine's a big wheel, not like Brandt. It's better this way."

Jaroff shrugged and returned to his packing. "Jesus. Australia for Chrissake. The old lady would never believe it."

"Don't ever tell her," Corliss warned. "This is just between the two of us, now and forever."

Jaroff knew that also included the big shot in Washington, but he didn't say so.

"You know I can keep my mouth shut, Colonel," he grunted.

Corliss gave an appreciative nod. "I know, Sam."

And he figured so did Gormane, if he wanted to survive. The security advisor had enemies in Washington who'd make hay with the Leiman thing if it ever came out. Not that he had any illusions about Gormane and his hypocritical pretense of maintaining ignorance about the solution to Leiman. He'd known people like that in Nam. Giving orders for him to go out and risk his ass, while they sat down to a good goddamn dinner. If you pulled it off, and got back in one piece, maybe a medal for you, and a medal for them. Shitheads. But he'd grown expert at interpreting the politician's crazy double-talk, that camouflage for grubby reality.

Sure he owed the security advisor, even if he'd never really understood why. Gormane had plucked him from the army and given him access to playing the political power game he wouldn't have dreamed possible in the Nam days. He had a shrewd suspicion Gormane didn't understand it himself. Sure he had a great army record, but there had been moments when Gormane touched him in a certain way, to express comradely affection, that made him wonder if there was a gay urge lurking deep that the guy couldn't even acknowledge to himself. But he'd made it work for him, just as long as Gormane didn't get any ideas about going past the touching stage.

Yet if he fouled up on Leiman he knew the security advisor would head for the hills, deny all knowledge, dump him like a barrel of radioactive waste. That was okay, he accepted that, but he wouldn't foul up. Gormane was approaching retirement, and Corliss wasn't going to risk being tossed out onto the trash heap when the security advisor quit the administration. Apart from any act of loyalty, this Leiman job was his insurance policy, just to make sure Gormane was still in his corner, and was prepared to wield influence on his behalf. When he got back to the States he'd find a way of reminding Gormane of his indebtedness, just so he knew the score.

It couldn't have run smoother at the Cumberland. They set up the bug on the wall adjoining Reine's room, and worked shifts keeping tab with the earphones. Except for the few hours Jaroff went to pay off the morgue attendant.

"Any problems?" asked Corliss, when he returned.

Jaroff responded with an expressionless shake of his head. "No, it went easy."

It was all that needed to be said. They were totally unalike, yet combined in a tandem understanding that required few words.

The sensitivity of the bug proved to be everything Corliss had said, they could actually distinguish sounds Reine made in the bathroom.

"Old sonofabitch's constipated," observed Jaroff laconically.

Corliss was on shift when Reine called the Australian airline, Qantas.

"I wish to book a flight to Australia as soon as possible," he heard Reine say.

"Yes sir, we have a flight out of Heathrow at five o'clock tomorrow afternoon," answered the reservation clerk.

"Nothing sooner?"

"I'm afraid not."

"Very well, I'll take that."

"Tourist or first class?"

"First class." Reine believed in flying in comfort.

"Your name sir?" inquired the clerk.

"Reine, Andre Reine. R-E-I-N-E. What time will that get me to Sydney?"

"Ah, leaving Wednesday at 5:00 P.M. you'll arrive in Sydney at approximately 6:10 A.M. Thursday morning."

"I want to fly on from Sydney to the northern town of Cairns as quickly as possible. Can you arrange that?" inquired Reine.

"Certainly. We can book you on a domestic flight. Just a moment." During the pause the eavesdropping Corliss had an image of the airlines clerk rapidly tapping computer keys. "How will you be paying, Mr. Reine?"

"American Express." Reine gave him the card details. "And I understand there are tours that leave Cairns and travel across to the town of Normanton in the Queensland Gulf Country. Do you know of such tours?"

"I'm afraid not, sir. If you wanted to book such a tour, it would have to be done through the Australian Tourism office here in London."

"Where's that?"

"I believe their office is in Savile Row."

"Do you have the telephone number?"

There was a tolerant sigh from the clerk, then a period of silence, and finally the number.

"Thank you, you're very kind," said Reine.

"Not at all. Just to confirm, Mr. Reine. I have you on Qantas Flight 7024 leaving London at 1700 hours tomorrow

afternoon. Then I have you on Flight 534 of Australian
Airlines, which leaves Sydney at 9:30 Thursday morning, and
arrives in Cairns at noon. Is that satisfactory?"

"Yes, that's fine."

"You may pick up your tickets at the Qantas desk at
Heathrow. Please be there two hours before flight time. Do
you have a place where you can be contacted in London?"

"Yes. I'm at the Cumberland Hotel. Room 520. The
number is 262-1234."

"Thank you, Mr. Reine. We're glad you chose Qantas, and
have a nice flight."

There was the click of the phone disconnecting, then
quickly the burr of another number being dialed. Jaroff poured
them each a beer, but Corliss impatiently brushed it aside,
hastily checking through the flight times he'd noted down.

"You got something good, Colonel?" asked Jaroff.

Corliss motioned Jaroff into silence. "Australian Tourism,"
he heard a brisk, accented female voice answer.

"I wish to join one of your tours that operates in the north
of Australia," said Reine. "I understand it goes from Cairns to
the town of Normanton in the Queensland Gulf Country."

"Just a moment, please." Again Corliss imagined fingers
flying over computer keys. "That's correct, sir. There's a rail
coach tour of three days, with an adult fare of about five
hundred dollars Australian."

"Would there be a tour leaving at the end of this week?"

"Yes, there's one that departs at eight o'clock on Friday
morning."

"What time would that get to Normanton?"

"Ah, around noon on the Saturday; that would be the, ah,
sixth of July."

"I'm flying out to Australia tomorrow, and I would like to
join that tour please."

"I'll have to confirm it back to you, sir. May I have your
name, and where you can be contacted in London?"

Reine quickly gave her all the details.

"I think that should be all right, Mr. Reine. I'll confirm it
for you within the hour. How will you be paying?"

"American Express." Once again he provided details.

"I'll call back as soon as it's confirmed, Mr. Reine."

"Thank you," responded Reine.

The phone went dead. For a moment there were only the sounds of Reine shuffling about the room, then silence. Corliss removed the earphones and ran his fingers through his hair as he grinned with satisfaction.

"You look like the cat that just got the canary, Colonel," said Jaroff.

"I've got the location of Kisek in Australia, Sam. Some town called Normanton, in what's known as the Queensland Gulf Country. That's where Reine's going, and that's where Kisek's got to be. Reine's got to be taking a copy of the fingerprints we found on Brandt to a Mossad agent in Normanton."

Jaroff studied his beer for a moment, then looked questioningly at Corliss. "The Mossad are after this Kisek too, Colonel?"

Corliss rubbed thoughtfully at his chin. Gormane wouldn't like it, but the time was coming to take Sam completely into his confidence. He knew he could trust Sam implicitly, and it would make for a tighter operation. He went part of the way.

"Yes, they are, Sam."

Jaroff gave a knowing smile. "I figured that. This Kisek has some information the Mossad want, that could put the squeeze on our country, eh Colonel?"

"Something like that. We've got to shut his mouth before they get to him. I figure the Mossad are aiming to kidnap him."

"We'll get him, Colonel. Count on me. Those fingerprints are important?"

"Proof of identity." He paused. "He's a Nazi war criminal, Sam. Real name's Leiman."

Jaroff's eyes widened. "One of those creeps." Then he shrugged. "The sonofabitch has got it coming to him then, right Colonel?"

"That's what I figure," agreed Corliss. He held out the earphones. "Take over will you? I've got to make some phone calls. From now on we're going to live in Reine's pocket, until he leads us to Leiman."

Corliss duplicated everything he'd overheard from Reine, booking the two of them on the same Qantas and Australian

Airlines flights, and also on the same tour from Cairns to
Normanton. He didn't quite understand the tour, but he
reasoned Reine was probably playing safe by using it as a
cover. If the Mossad had been trying to run down Leiman ever
since the war, they'd be almost paranoid about losing him
again when they were this close. But why would a man Reine's
age take on an operation like this? He shrugged it aside, it was
irrelevant. If Gormane's information was right, that the Mossad had an operation mounted to kidnap Leiman, then for sure
they already had agents in the Normanton area, watching
Leiman. So it had to be that Reine was acting as a courier,
taking the fingerprints to other Mossad agents. It was the only
thing that made sense; they wouldn't have an old man like
Reine playing a key role in the actual kidnapping.

He took a small atlas from his case and located Normanton, noting it was by a body of water called the Gulf of Carpentaria. The town was obviously very small, with no airport
that could be used by an international jet, so the Israelis
probably had a ship waiting in the Gulf to take Leiman out.
Maybe he was playing hunches, but that's the way he'd do it.

"Someone from the Australian Tourism office is confirm-
ing Reine's booking on a tour to Normanton in Australia,"
muttered Jaroff, his fingers pressed against the earphones.

Corliss put aside the atlas, eyes intently on Jaroff.

"Now Reine's calling long distance, Colonel . . . someone in Tel Aviv."

Corliss went swiftly to Jaroff and took the earphones.
"This I want to hear myself, Sam," he said brusquely. "It could
confirm what I think's going on."

He heard Reine talking to a man he called Favett, giving
him the details of his travel arrangements to Australia, and
Normanton.

"You'll radio Grubin, and tell him I'll be in Normanton
around noon, on Saturday the sixth of July," Reine continued,
"I understand it will be by train."

"Hegarty will probably meet you. It'll be wiser if Grubin
stays under cover."

"Hegarty or Grubin, it doesn't matter," replied Reine
testily. "Instruct Hegarty not to approach me, not to give any
sign of recognition at all. I'll find a way to get him the

fingerprints. Just tell him to watch me. I'm using the tour as a cover, and I want it kept that way. We can't be too careful; for all we know Leiman may have informants in Normanton."

"Don't worry, Andre," said Favett, "Hegarty will know what to do; you just take care. Leave it to Hegarty and Grubin to handle Leiman. The ship's waiting. It will only take a call from Grubin when it's set, and they'll send in the helicopter."

"I just hope to God the fingerprints confirm the identity," muttered Reine.

"But you've verified them, Andre."

"The Berlin police seemed sure enough. I suppose there's always an element of doubt."

"I'm sure the fingerprints will match."

"Is there any contingency plan if they don't?"

"Let's worry about that if it happens," answered Favett evasively. "Don't prolong your stay in Australia."

"I don't intend to," said Reine curtly. "I'll be heading straight back to Tel Aviv."

"Get a good night's sleep, Andre. You've got a long flight ahead of you."

"That's what I intend. I'll have an early dinner, then sleep as long as I can."

"You're wise."

The man Favett sounded rather patronizing, as if he didn't quite have complete faith in Reine, and the elderly agent noted it also.

"Thank you for your concern," Reine concluded frostily, and hung up.

Corliss waited, listening to the sounds of Reine moving about the room and the opening and closing of doors. He was probably dressing to go to dinner. He took off the earphones, and pointed urgently to the door.

"I think Reine's getting ready to go down to dinner, Sam," he said. "Get out in the hall and tail him until you get a good look at him. We'll be doing quite some traveling together, so don't let your face register with him. Once we're on a 747 there won't be any problem of keeping out of his way. I don't want him aware of us at all until we join the tour." He gave a sharp nod. "Okay?"

Jaroff had already slipped into his jacket, and was on his way to the door. "Gotcha, Colonel."

He waited until Jaroff was gone, then he lit a cigar and wandered to the window overlooking Oxford Street. The traffic below resembled a millipede that frantically split in two around Hyde Park, one section heading straight on to Bayswater Road, the other squirming into real estate rich Park Lane. The green stretch of the park was like a sanctuary from the frenzy. Christ, what a sanctuary Leiman must have found in Australia; after more than forty years of safety he would think it inconceivable the Mossad could have tracked him down. Well, killing Leiman would save the Israelis the cost of prosecution, although he was sure they'd rather parade a Nazi criminal like Leiman before the world in a showpiece trial. Even that would be poor consolation for them, after the goddamn sonofabitch had got away with it for half a lifetime. Of course that was beside the point as far as Gormane was concerned, he was only concerned with saving his own skin.

But the phone conversation he'd overheard between Reine and Favett confirmed everything that had only been a hunch before. Reine was playing courier with the fingerprints, there were Mossad agents in the Gulf, there was a ship waiting with a helicopter to take Leiman out. They must have some way figured out to get a set of Leiman's fingerprints to compare with the ones Reine had. He gazed thoughtfully across the park to where he could see small boats dotting the Serpentine, pondering on the recollection of Reine's measure of doubt over the fingerprints, then impatiently brushed it aside. Christ, if the Mossad were sure enough to set up a kidnap operation, that was good enough for him. But once the fingerprints confirmed beyond legal doubt that Kisek was Leiman, there was nothing surer than that they'd move fast to pull the Nazi out. It was going to be tricky beating them to it, but he had surprise on his side.

Chapter 10

Cathedral Rock Station.

It was like a window blind being imperceptibly raised along the horizon, permitting just a sliver of light to mark the approach of a new day. Although the moon was gone, the stars still paraded, but with lessening glitter as the night sky gave way to dawn. The sharp air carried the sweet tang of fresh earth as Hegarty went to the helicopter. Pony was already waiting, jacket buttoned to the neck, arms clasped about his body, face bright with expectancy in the faint light.

"G'day there, copilot," said Hegarty with a grin.

"G'day, Matt."

The boy's voice was still thready with sleep. Hegarty wondered how long he'd been there. "You should have knocked on my door, Pony."

"No, I reckoned you'd be here soon." He hugged close to the helicopter in an unconscious gesture of longing. "Betcha we muster more cattle today than Ritchie and the ringers would do in a month."

"Maybe," said Hegarty, untethering the rotor blades. He glanced toward the widening band of dawn light. "I'll set a course for Inverleigh, but I need a little light to be able to see where Ritchie's set up."

"Don't worry, I know the place, Matt. I could find it with both eyes shut."

"Then we'd better be moving." He looked to the house. "I guess your mother's already gone."

"Yeah, coupla hours ago I'd reckon, in the four-wheel drive. She'd be there now."

Hegarty wondered about Ingrid, but he didn't ask. There was no sign of Kisek. Or Carl. He tried to suppress anxiety; this was taking him away from Cathedral Rock, lessening his time of getting Kisek's fingerprints, yet he had no option but to act out his mustering pilot role. Maybe the chance would come if he could wangle a dinner invitation tonight. There had to be a way. He tousled Pony's hair, and thumbed toward the cockpit.

"Let's go and join them, mate."

They donned their helmets, strapped in, and were quickly airborne. Hegarty held it at two hundred feet, giving himself ample visibility to spot the stockyards Ritchie had told him to watch for. The gray terrain rushed past underneath, blossoming with specks of light as the horizon rapidly brightened. They were going to be late for a daybreak start, but he'd hesitated at trying to find the location in total darkness. Pony was silent, his rapt expression making words unnecessary, occasionally moving his body in concert with the motion of the helicopter, as if he were flying it. After about thirty minutes, he suddenly pointed down.

"There they are, Matt," he shouted. "See, just ahead."

Hegarty nodded. He could see the patchwork grid of the stockyards close to a clump of eucalyptus, to one side the narrow swimming trough for dipping the cattle, to the other parked vehicles and a collection of men, some standing, others mounted on horses. Smoke from the remnants of a campfire wisped lazily into the pale light. One of the mounted men broke away, gesturing with his hat to a clearing away to the right of the stockyards.

"It's Ritchie," called Pony excitedly. "He's showing us where they've marked it out for us to land, Matt." He motioned to where Ritchie was indicating. "See, over there by the four-wheel drive and those fuel drums. Mum's there too."

Hegarty banked right and throttled back. The site was about five hundred yards from the stockyards; Anna knew what she was doing. Bobo Walters had always stressed keeping the landing and refueling site away from the cattle holding area.

He set it down easy, switched off, slipped off his helmet, took the radio transceiver from the side pocket, then nudged

Pony to follow as he stepped out of the cockpit. Anna came to meet them, broad-brimmed leather stockman's hat in hand, a smile of welcome on her face.

"Hi there, you two; I'm glad you found us okay," she said. "Ritchie and the boys are all ready to go." She laughed. "They're looking forward to finally working with a helicopter at Cathedral Rock."

Hegarty patted Pony on the shoulder. "How could we miss with my copilot-navigator here?"

Anna laughed again. She was obviously in good humor. "Well, I've told them all they'll be working with a hot pilot."

Hegarty managed a self-effacing grin. There was a subtle difference to her this morning; she was dressed much the same, blue checked shirt, jeans, boots, but there was a sparkle he hoped was lit by their meeting last night. It might be a good omen, that she'd be receptive if the chance came to pry for any more information.

Ritchie came hustling up on his quarter horse in a swirl of dust, as if leading a cavalry charge, hat perched back on his head, perennial spindly cigarette dangling from his grinning mouth. He pulled to a halt just short of them, took the cigarette from his mouth, gave a flash of white teeth, and mopped his brow. His bright yellow tank top made a match with the helicopter. He sat the horse as if cast from the same mold.

"G'day Matt, g'day Pony," he said. "You didn't have any trouble findin' us?"

Hegarty again referred to Pony. "Not with a good navigator."

Ritchie grinned, relit his cigarette, and glanced into the fast-brightening sky.

"You all set to go, Matt?"

"Whenever you're ready, Ritchie. You've worked with a helicopter before?"

"Not for a long time, mate. How d'you want to handle it—you want to bring 'em right to the yard, or work 'em to a point where we can take over?"

Hegarty pointed to a grass-denuded track obviously worn by the movement of stock.

"Why don't I herd them to a point about a mile down the track, then you and the ringers can bring them in from there."

Ritchie nodded agreement. "That's okay by me, that's the way it's usually done around here." He glanced back toward the camp. "I reckon some of the boys were worryin' there wasn't goin' to be much for 'em to do with the whirligig." He shrugged to hide his own concern. "But we get on to the dippin' and brandin' in the yards, and I reckon they'll soon get over it." He looked to Pony. "You goin' up with Matt, Pony?"

"You betcha," cried Pony enthusiastically.

The casual manner in which Ritchie expelled cigarette smoke failed to conceal his disappointment. "I brought Schon out with us, just in case you change your mind," he grunted.

The boy was quick to recognize the letdown in his friend. "There'll be other times, Ritchie," he consoled, with a tinge of guilt.

Ritchie nodded. "Sure, Pony, yeah, sure there will."

Hegarty held out the transceiver to Ritchie. "Know how to use one of these to make contact with me?"

The aborigine leaned down from his saddle and took it from Hegarty. "I've seen 'em plenty of times, Matt. I reckon I can do it okay."

"I'll want to call you, too," said Hegarty. He pointed to the switches. "This position for when I'm talking to you, then flick it to the right so you can answer. Okay?"

"She'll be right, mate," cheerfully replied the black. "Though I reckon you'll be doin' all the talkin'. You'll be seein' the cattle better up there than me." He turned in the saddle and made a sweep of his arm to the north. "Out there is where you'll be startin', mate. There's a hundred square mile paddock, with about four thousand head. How long d'you reckon it'll take with the whirligig?"

Hegarty shrugged, and studied the countryside. The wind of the night had died, the vegetation was hushed with the stillness of daybreak.

"Well it doesn't look like I'm going to be worried about any downwind turns for now, but . . . maybe a couple of days."

Ritchie gave a bleak grin, and backed the horse away. "I reckon it'd take us ringers a coupla weeks, y'know." He urged the horse into a trot. "I'll be waitin' to hear from you, mate," he called back.

They silently watched Ritchie canter back to the camp.

"I think Ritchie feels perhaps you'll put him out of a job, too," said Anna.

"Hey, Ritchie doesn't have to bother himself about a thing like that," protested Pony.

"I won't be around long enough to put anyone out of a job," declared Hegarty. He took Pony's arm and steered him toward the helicopter. "We'd better get moving, copilot." He smiled at Anna. "See you when we get back for refueling."

There was no denying the increased warmth of her answering smile. He was sure the chance meeting last night had not only straightened out the hassle about Ingrid, but also sparked a quickening interest that he could exploit.

"Good mustering," she said.

"See you later, Mum," called Pony.

The cattle were spread over a wide area, and Hegarty gave the mustering all his concentration, shutting his mind to Kisek, Jules, Reine, Anna, the fingerprints. He had to do this job well; he suspected it wouldn't take much for Kisek to use incompetence as an excuse to get rid of him, especially after the incident with the camera. If it hadn't been for Pony he might have been gone already. It was absolutely crucial he stay on until Reine arrived.

So he gave it everything he had, and Bobo Walters would have been proud of him. Visibility improved as the sun breasted the horizon and climbed quickly into the sky, bringing with its bright glare a sharp breeze that forced him to guard against downwind turns.

Pony played scout, watching for cattle, avidly pointing out those sheltering in small clumps of trees. After a time Hegarty began to enjoy himself, satisfied he was performing up to Pony's claim he could make the Bell 47 "bloody dance" around the sky, delicately coordinating the cyclic and collective as he weaved and circled above the savanna, using the noise of the helicopter to gently maneuver the cattle toward the stockyards. Gradually a herd—what Ritchie and the other ringers called a mob—began to form, even the cows with attached calves moving easily, with only an occasional bull obstinately trying to go his own way.

It went on hour after hour, with only a break now and then to refuel and gulp down an enamel mug of potent tea, while between mouthfuls Pony enthusiastically exalted Hegarty's skill to his mother. Hegarty laughed it aside, but he did nothing to discourage the boy, noting it was adding to the light forming in Anna's eyes, not a sexually aggressive gleam as with Ingrid, but certainly something for him to build on. Common sense warned him to snuff out the disconcerting fire building in himself for her.

Fueled up, they'd be off again, scouring the savanna, working mainly to the east side of the paddock, until there was finally a well-disciplined mob of fair size moving at a steady pace down the track toward the stockyards.

Ritchie called on the transceiver.

"Bloody terrific, Matt, that's about all the yard'll take t'day. Me and the boys'll take 'em from here."

"They're all yours, mate," he answered, and banked away, seeing below the ringers already sweeping around to encircle the mob, while Ritchie waved his hat in acknowledgment.

Anna was waiting again by the ranch wagon when he put down at the refueling area. Helicopter mustering wasn't exactly the sort of activity that insurance companies liked covering, and even if she respected his ability, he figured she still felt anxiety about her son. He switched off; the two fliers doffed their helmets and went across to the mugs of hot tea set out on a small folding table. Anna smiled a greeting as she handed one to Hegarty.

"I guess you would have preferred a beer now you're finished flying," she apologized.

"No that's okay, Anna. Maybe we'll have a beer later."

She indicated the wagon. "There's a Coke over there if you like, Pony."

"Jeez yeah, I reckon I've had enough tea for one day," said Pony.

He crossed quickly to the wagon, while Anna took up the other mug of tea and glanced to where the first of the cattle were already lumbering toward the stockyards.

"My god, Matt, that was so quick," she complimented.

"We should have done this years ago." She took a sip of tea and gave an apologetic shrug. "I guess it's my fault really, for putting off learning to fly for so long."

"I'm still aiming to teach you," said Hegarty.

"Hey, me too," interrupted Pony.

"Don't rush it; you've got a few years to go yet," warned Anna.

"So what? Wouldn't hurt if Matt showed me a few things now, then I'd be ready when I'm old enough." He waved the can of Coke toward the stockyards. "Golly, look at that, betcha it would have taken Ritchie and the ringers days to do that." He took a swig from the can, then pawed hurriedly at his mouth. "Schon's over there; I'm going to go over and give Ritchie a hand, Mum."

"All right then." Her voice rose as he began to run toward the stockyards. "Are you flying back with Matt tonight?"

"Jeez yeah, you bet." He gestured at Hegarty. "Don't you go leaving without me, Matt."

"Don't worry," Hegarty reassured him with a grin.

After Pony had gone, they drank quietly for a time, exchanging small talk about the technique of helicopter mustering and planning some flying lessons for her which he knew would never happen.

She nodded to where the cattle were beginning to thread through the open gate of the forcing yard. "God, this should convince Dad hiring you was one of the best things he ever did," she murmured.

"Well, you'll be doing it one day."

"That might take some time." She hesitated. "Maybe you'd like to stay on a while longer?"

He kept poker-faced, inwardly smiling. He had to be doing something right, that suggestion had already come from Pony and Ingrid.

"That's mighty nice of you, but I figure to move on."

He expected persuasion, but she let it go. He gestured to the cattle. "You've got things to do over there?"

She inclined her head to the ranch wagon. "I've got a hypodermic ready there. We always innoculate against tick fever."

"That's a lot of cattle to stick with a hypodermic."

"I can get through pretty fast." She shrugged. "Anyway Ritchie always lets them calm down for about an hour before we do anything."

He paused, then crouched down and sat on the ground, with his back against the wagon. He looked up with an inviting smile. "Might as well be comfortable then. That wind's pretty fresh, and it's warmer down here, Anna."

She hesitated, then accepted, moving into a sitting position beside him, but not touching, consciously or not, just close enough for him to catch her aroma.

"We've got some culling to do, but the road train to take away the cattle won't be here until tomorrow afternoon, so there's no hurry," she remarked, but self-consciously, as if she really didn't want to discuss cattle.

He pointed to the helicopter. "Everytime I fly over this place I realize what a terrific spread you've got here," he said.

"We think it's something special."

In the distance they could see Pony already mounted on Schon, hand raised in the air as he trotted beside the mob.

"It'll be really something for Pony one day," he said.

"Yes. Luckily he loves the place."

"It's great the way a guy like your father can come out here as an immigrant from Germany after the war, and create all this."

"It wasn't easy."

"I can believe it. This is tough country. But then I guess the war made him tough, or he wouldn't have survived."

"You could say that," she said reflectively. "But the struggle left its mark. I mean the way you see him now. It aged him."

Maybe he was courting trouble to raise Ingrid's name, but he went ahead anyway. "Ingrid said something like that. She told me about a photograph she's seen of him as a young man. Claimed you wouldn't know it was the same person."

She frowned, and for a disturbing moment he thought he was going to get an angry reaction from the mention of her sister's name.

"Photograph?" she questioned.

"That's what she said."

"She must mean the old passport he keeps in his desk in the study."

He hadn't expected to score so easily; so quickly. At least he had a location now for the passport.

"Something like that I guess," he said casually.

"I haven't looked at it in ages, but yes . . ." She picked thoughtfully at her lip. "I guess I never thought about it, but no, you'd never recognize him now from what I remember of that picture."

"Maybe it was the memory of what he went through in the war that changed him as much as this country."

She shrugged. "Perhaps. He's never talked about it that much." She paused. "Although once he told me about his brother." She stopped, and drank from the mug until it was empty. He thought back to Reine's brief. There had been something about a brother, but all the Leiman family were dead: mother, father, a brother, and a sister. Anna broke off his train of thought as she glanced across to the cattle and said, "I've never seen them move so easily. And I can't see any calves separated from the cows. We have trouble that way sometimes." She smiled. "I wish Dad was here to see this."

He restrained impatience at the divergence.

"Perhaps he'll get the chance tomorrow."

"He was supposed to be coming out later today."

"There's still time."

He held back for a period of silence.

"It's a wonder your father's brother didn't come out to Australia with him," he tentatively tried again. "I guess he was involved in the family cattle business in Wismar, before the war."

She glanced sharply at him. "How did you know about that?"

"You told me, last night."

She laughed. It was a nice sound. "You're right, so I did." She raised her eyebrows questioningly. "You're thinking about the Gulf Country? How to breed cattle here?"

"Maybe," he said offhandedly, offering it as bait. "I'm just fascinated by what a guy like your father's managed to achieve here, I guess."

He saw that the remark pleased her, and it lured her into continuing openness.

"A brother would have been better than Carl." She gave a scornful giggle. "God yes."

"Then I take it the brother died during the war?"

"Yes. Dad told me the story a long time ago. He was shot by the Russians."

"They took him prisoner?"

"Well . . . ," again she hesitated. "Dad was ashamed of his brother, if you want to know."

"Why ashamed?"

"They had these camps in Poland; concentration camps. You must have heard about them, where all the Jews were murdered." She gave an involuntary shudder. "It sounds ghastly. But this brother was evidently in charge of one of them. That's why the Russians shot him."

He didn't look at her for fear the consternation flooding his mind showed in his face.

"He was executed as a war criminal I suppose?"

"I guess it must have been something like that."

"Toward the end of the war. That's when that sort of thing was happening."

"Yes." She gave him a curious glance. "You know about those things? I mean I've read about how they still catch them, even after all this time."

With a concentrated effort of will he managed to pass it off with a nonchalant shrug. "Oh, I've read about it too, that's all. It's interesting to hear of someone directly involved."

"I don't know the details," she said. "I just know Dad was ashamed of what his brother had done."

He nodded, put the mug of tea to his mouth, and drank deeply. Jesus Christ, it was a horrendous thought, but had the Wiesenthal people somehow been misled into tracking down the wrong Leiman brother? Had the real Whipmaster of Treblinka been executed by the Russians all those years ago? The Wiesenthal organization didn't usually make mistakes like that, but perhaps it could happen? Yet it was also possible she was telling him some phony story fed to her by her father, when he'd felt the need for a cover. Or to avoid awkward questions. Christ, and he was compounding it with an inkling that he would like to believe the story, because of what he could feel building in him for her. He couldn't afford that. He put the empty mug aside as she continued.

"I don't know why I told you such a terrible story," she apologized. "It's all so long ago, and has nothing to do with Cathedral Rock." She gave a wan smile. "Dad told me about it at a time when we were just feeling . . . sort of close, I guess, but he's never mentioned it again." She suddenly laughed. "Hey, I'll have to watch myself with you, Matt Hegarty; you have a knack of drawing people out, y'know that?"

The easy grin he managed bore no relation to the turmoil he felt. For Chrissake, if there was any truth in it, what a goddamn irony after years of digging, and him coming half way around the world to infiltrate the Kisek family, if Horst Leiman had been dead for over forty years.

"I always seem to be getting on to my family when we talk," she said, "I'm sorry—like I did last night. You must find it awfully boring."

"Hell no, Anna," he said with warmth. "I haven't met anyone in a long long time who would bore me less than you do."

To his surprise the skin beneath her brown freckles took on a pink flush. "Why that's a very kind thing to say, Matt," she murmured. "I . . . I could say the same about you—I'm glad you're at Cathedral Rock."

She paused, leaving a vacuum that demanded to be filled, but he held back. He knew it was there if he wanted to go for it, but it wouldn't be like Ingrid; he was wary of an emotional involvement that would be plain lunacy. Maybe he'd drawn all he could from her; after all, he now knew where the passport was, if he was prepared to risk making a try for it. And he had to talk to Jules about this executed brother story.

"I'm glad to be here, too, Anna," he felt impelled to answer. "You love this place, don't you?"

"Yes." She gazed to some unseen point on the horizon. "I suppose it's in my blood," she mused. "At times it's so hot, then so wet, then so dry, you wonder why. Then a time comes when you're out here alone, and the whole country's glowing red from the setting sun, and the grass is like it's whispering secrets, and you stand there feeling like the freest creature on earth. And you can think about things, like in a book I once read by a man called Kenneth Clark; love is better than hatred, forgiveness better than vengeance, gentleness better than violence." She gave a self-conscious smile. "I reckon it must be hard to have those thoughts in the bustle of a big city." She fell silent for a time, then followed with a wry grin. "Loving Cathedral Rock is about the only thing I've got in common with Ingrid."

"You make me feel envious," he admitted.

"You've got to have roots; or wander forever," she said quietly.

Maybe she didn't consciously mean him, but the inference was there. He got up abruptly, unable to sit with her any longer. There was something about her feelings for Cathedral Rock, or the way she spoke about them, that made him realize with an unaccustomed longing that he'd been looking for a woman like this all his life. And he felt anger with himself, because it could blind him to reality—like the story of the executed brother, which had to be some shit cover Leiman had planted on his daughter. The Wiesenthal people wouldn't get it that wrong, not after years of work. The fingerprints would resolve it beyond all doubt.

He cleared his throat, and thumbed toward the stockyard. "Think I might wander over and have a look at the guys working," he said.

His abrupt cutaway disappointed her, but she shrugged acceptance. "Okay; I've got to get the serum ready anyway. I'll see you over there later."

"Sure," he said, and turned away.

He could feel her puzzled eyes following him, but he didn't look back. He wondered what his father would have said about forgiveness being better than vengeance? Ask six million ghosts, he would have fumed.

He watched as a bystander, while Anna and the ringers went about the cattle with the sureness of experience. Pony was enthusiastically joining in, hollering and waving his arms to help drive the cattle from the forcing yard into the crush, where Anna went from beast to beast, dexterously wielding the hypodermic. Then the repetitive splash of the cattle leaping one by one into the disinfectant dip, a concrete-walled channel set into the ground, just wide enough for each beast to swim through in turn, head held high, and snorting in protest, until it emerged dripping, into the draining yard. Other ringers guided them through the raceway for culling, running the calves into the branding cradle, locking each in place, dropping the cradle into a horizontal position for quick application of the branding iron—sizzle and smoke rose from the hide to the bawling accompaniment of the animal.

It was a welter of sights and sounds: shouting, gesticulating ringers dodging the occasional aggressive bull with practiced skill, calves hugging close to cows, lumbering fat bullocks, the hiss of the branding iron and the smell of scorched hide, and over all a haze of dust that blended the colors of the scene like a gray filter.

Between each operation Pony trotted over to Hegarty with happy asides, all in the same vein.

"Hey, Mum says it's just terrific the way you mustered the cattle, Matt."

Then, "Betcha you could learn Mum to be just as good as you, Matt."

And again, "Mum thinks you're the best bloody thing ever happened at Cathedral Rock, Matt. So do I—I really do, mate."

Even, "I reckon you and Mum'd make a great team, Matt, yeah a real beaut team."

Hegarty grinned and tousled the boy's hair, but avoided answering. What could he say? Hero worship Anna had called it, and he didn't need to be clairvoyant to realize what was passing through the boy's mind. He didn't want to hurt the boy, but if the operation ran smoothly, Pony would be brought back to earth with a mind-snapping jolt. There were many past times when Matt had needed to be ruthless, but there was always the justification of seeing himself as some angel of vengeance. But no one had ever made him feel like a conniving son-of-a-bitch before. He hoped seeing Leiman standing in an Israel courtroom would prove a sufficient, soothing balm.

* * *

It was near dusk when they finished with the cattle. Hegarty knew he'd impressed everyone, and made his mustering job secure at Cathedral Rock. That was all that really mattered for now.

The black dust-smothered ringers drifted away back to their campsite, with the exception of Ritchie, who waited with Anna and Pony. There was a bulbous cloud bank to the west, dimming the usual sunset splendor, but the wind had died, leaving the savanna as motionless as a becalmed sailing ship.

Hegarty lit a cigar and strolled across to join them.

"That was really somethin' t'day, Matt," said Ritchie with an approving grin. A crumpled cigarette bobbed in his mouth. "Fair dinkum, really bloody somethin'. Would've taken us days without the whirligig."

"That's what I told him, Ritchie," Anna smilingly agreed.

"Bet we clear out that paddock tomorrow," added Pony. "Just bet we do."

Hegarty shrugged. "Maybe. You coming out with me again tomorrow?"

"I'll say," said the boy with alacrity. "Jeez, today was even better than yesterday."

Hegarty glanced into the sky. "I guess we'd better be getting back to the homestead, Pony."

Ritchie turned away toward the camp. "We'll be staying here tonight, Matt. I'll be watching out for you in the morning."

"I'll be here."

Ritchie pointed to Schon. "You'd better be turnin' out Schon before you quit, Pony."

"Yeah, okay, Ritchie." The boy turned to Hegarty. "Are you coming to dinner tonight, Matt?"

Hegarty glanced uncertainly to Anna. "I'm not sure I'm invited."

"I'm inviting you, mate."

Hegarty wanted the invitation badly, but it had to come from Anna. "I figure that's up to your mother," he said.

"Go and attend to Schon like Ritchie said," rebuked Anna sharply.

The boy paused, scowling. "You asked him last night."

Anna thrust a pointing finger toward the horse. "Go and

fix Schon, or you're the one who won't be coming to dinner," she threatened.

The boy pouted, thrust his hands angrily into his pockets, then slunk after Ritchie, kicking rebelliously at the ground.

"Promise you'll come if you can, Matt," he called back.

"If I can," replied Hegarty.

There followed an awkward silence. There was something here he didn't quite understand, and it made him regret last night's refusal, but a dinner invitation had to be his best chance of getting Kisek's fingerprints. He'd been so sure she'd ask him, but the way she obviously wanted Pony out of the way raised doubts.

"I don't think it'd be such a good idea tonight," she finally muttered, her eyes following Pony instead of looking at Matt.

He was taken aback. He knew from experience the chemistry between them was running strong, so why the refusal? He tried to push it.

"Ah, I thought it would be a good chance to tell your father how successful the helicopter mustering had gone," he suggested.

"I'll tell him," she said shortly.

"I figured it'd be better coming from the pilot."

"You can catch up with him some time tomorrow maybe."

He couldn't comprehend. "You're still upset over Ingrid?"

"Ingrid's got nothing to do with it. I just don't think it's a good idea right now."

"You told me last night he'd got over the ruckus with the photograph."

"He has, but . . ." She paused, tentatively plucking at her mouth.

It mystified him; she'd practically begged him last night, and the only thing since then was a growing yen he thought was mutual.

"I figured we were getting on pretty well," he suggested.

"We are; you know that."

"Maybe that's the problem," he said. Ingrid seemed contemptuously indifferent to what her father thought about her screwing around, but perhaps it was a changed ball game with Anna; another point of contrast between the sisters.

"No, no," she said, but too quickly.

She lied badly, even if he couldn't understand why it was a problem.

"It's, ah . . . Pony," she added. "What I talked to you about last night. I know Pony'd be like some sort of adoring fan if you came to dinner, and it'd only upset Dad. I know it would." She suddenly showed irritation at her embarrassment. "God, is it that important to you?" she flared. "I'll make sure Zara brings you over a good dinner."

He didn't believe her excuse over Pony, but he had to let it go, she gave him no option. Christ, was he going to have to break into the goddamn house to get the fingerprints?

"That's okay," he said, "it's your house."

She impulsively took his arm in an expression of contrition. "Perhaps another night, Matt. When the muster's over."

That didn't make sense either. "Sure, I'll look forward to it," he said offhandedly.

There was an uncomfortable pause, her hand dropped away, and her gaze went to Pony unsaddling Schon.

"Would you mind telling Pony you can't come?" she asked.

"If that's what you'd like."

"I'd very much appreciate it." She gave a wry smile. "I guess he's been a bit spoiled. He can throw quite a temper when things don't work out the way he likes. I mean he just wouldn't understand."

Neither did Hegarty, but he went along with her. "That's okay, I'll tell him I've got other more important things to do."

"I appreciate it, Matt. You're very kind."

He didn't feel kind at all. There was the quick motion of her hand at his arm again. He was as sure as he could be of anything about what they had going between them, and that only puzzled him more.

He thought about it flying back to the homestead, only vaguely listening to Pony's shouted enthusiasms for the day. There were streams running deep in Anna he hadn't reached, maybe never would, so anything was possible. She could even know the truth about her father's real identity, and love him enough to want to protect him—tell a stranger like himself that phony story about the executed brother just to play safe, even if she knew it was a lie. Yet he knew getting close to her had taken on an urgency beyond why he was here. He tried to shut out the crazy murmurings at the back of his mind, suggesting there could be some future for him with Anna and Pony after they'd kidnapped Leiman. Such idiotic, wistful dreams belonged in cloud cuckoo land.

It was close to dusk when he set the Bell down at the homestead. He sat with Pony awhile, their helmets off, listening to the swish of the slowing rotor blades.

"Wait 'til you tell Grandad over dinner how the muster went," said Pony. "Jeez, I bet that opens his eyes."

Hegarty unbuckled, and gave a hesitant shrug. "I'm not going to be able to make dinner tonight, mate. I've got a few things I just have to do."

Disappointment covered the boy's face like a shadow. "There'll be other nights," Hegarty added.

"But jeez, Grandad'll want to know," the boy protested.

"You're the copilot, you'll be able to tell him as well as I could."

"Bugger no," insisted Pony, "he'll want to hear it from you, Matt."

"Then I'll tell him tomorrow."

The boy sullenly rapped his fingers on his helmet. "I was sort of looking forward to us both telling him, y'know."

"Next time. Anyway he'll see for himself if he comes out on the muster tomorrow."

Pony cast him a suspicious glance. "Mum did ask you, didn't she? I mean, she promised."

"Sure she did. She's disappointed too." Hegarty gave him a consoling pat on the shoulder. "Hey, don't forget we're going out again tomorrow. That's more important than an old dinner, for sure."

"Yeah, okay, Matt," the boy muttered.

They clambered out, Pony still scowling.

"Come on kid, the sun'll rise again tomorrow morning," Hegarty remonstrated. "You're flying mustering. Must be lots of kids around the Gulf who'd envy the chance you're getting. Think of that."

Pony hesitated, then ducked his head, with a shamefaced

grin. "You're right, Matt. Jeez, I'm sorry. I'll see you in the morning; same time."

"Yeah, same time. I'll be looking forward to it."

The boy gave a brief wave, then trotted away toward the house. "Bet we clear that paddock tomorrow, bet we do Matt," he shouted back.

Hegarty waved, then began to tether the rotor blades. They probably would clear the paddock tomorrow, and he had a hunch it would be his last day of mustering at Cathedral Rock.

Zara maintained her wraithlike style of meal delivery. There was a slight knock on the door, and when he answered there was a dinner waiting on the step—grilled steak, vegetables, apple pie, coffee, all set on a silver tray, but no sign of the cook. Whether it was shyness, or whatever, there was something eerie about her ability to vanish so quickly.

Over the meal he considered the fingerprint problem again. He could wait another day, and hope for an opportunity to arise, or risk breaking into the house later tonight, when everyone was asleep, and try searching for something that could have Kisek's prints on it. Maybe in the study Anna had talked about—a letter, a drinking glass, anything. It was a hell of a risk, but without the dinner invitation, what alternative did he have?

He finished dinner and made ready to go out on the Kawasaki again. It was important he establish the nighttime bike riding routine, for when he had to return to Jules. When he got back he'd make a decision about the break-in.

He opened the door to put the meal tray back on the step, and found Ingrid standing there, eyes wary, her expression a strange confection of invitation and caution. Her white shirt was open almost to the waist, just concealing her nipples. If she was figuring to turn him on, she was too late, much too late, he only had Anna on his mind.

She held out a bottle of liquor. "Scotch," she said. "The best. I went to the pool, and waited." She shrugged. "I thought maybe we could have a . . . sort of peace drink; get us back on the right track, how about it, Hegarty?"

He hesitated over a brutal refusal. She seemed calm

enough, maybe she'd accepted the situation; he couldn't afford
to have a dangerous enemy, and he was sure she had a
vindictive streak. But he didn't want to jeopardize what he had
going with Anna.

She took the decision out of his hands, slipping past him
into the room, as he peered anxiously toward the house.

"Don't worry, no one knows I'm here," she murmured.

He stood by the door, without closing it. "There was no
way I could make it to the pool, I was mustering all day."

It was a stupid excuse, she knew he was lying.

"A man like you can do anything if he wants to badly
enough, Hegarty," she said.

She sat down on the bed, nursing the scotch on her lap.

"I'm just on my way to take the cycle out," he said. "I like
to ride around at night, and there's a few bugs in the motor I
want to check out."

"You're not going anywhere special, darling, so does it
matter?" She held the bottle upright in her crotch, like a
phallic symbol, and offered a more confident smile. "Besides,
I heard you go out on your bike last night."

He still remained by the door, cursing to himself, unsure
whether to shut it or leave it open. If Anna saw them it could
put him right back to square one.

"I heard over the dinner table you were a real star today,
Hegarty."

"It went well enough," he said casually.

"My, such modesty. Pony made it sound like we should
strike some sort of Gulf Country medal in your honor."

"Pony gets a little carried away."

"You were a star yesterday too, down at the lagoon."

He hesitated over a reply. Maybe there was still some way
he could use her. "You were something of a star yourself," he
said glibly.

She tried an enticing smile, and caressed the bottle
erotically. "Just a small drink? What harm is there in that?"

If he relented there'd be no holding her; there would be
war between the sisters, and that would be a bad tactical error.
He'd already learned that if rebuffed she could turn like the
wind from a soft breeze to a roaring cyclone, but maybe there

was no way of letting her down gently. He had to extricate himself as diplomatically as possible.

"Perhaps another night," he lied.

"Time's short, like life, Hegarty. You're not going to be around much longer."

"Like I said yesterday, I'd be crazy to risk provoking your father again. I need this job."

"That's not a reason, the hell with him." Her breath quickened, and there was a light in her eyes like lightning warning of a coming storm. He knew from experience she had a short fuse.

"Christ, it wasn't easy for me, coming here like this," she muttered. "Not after the last time I was here—having you stand over there like I've got some damn contagious disease."

"It's not like that. Let's talk about it tomorrow."

"I won't see you tomorrow. I've got to go across to Burketown."

She stood up and moved about the room with that seductive roll of her hips he'd seen before, but it changed nothing.

"I've got to go, Ingrid," he said curtly.

A sullen cloud obscured the last remnants of enticement. "You're going off somewhere fucking with Anna, aren't you, you bastard," she accused maliciously.

He cast another anxious glance to the house. The wind had changed direction with a vengeance, and he didn't want any screams of rage carrying across the yard. Christ, he'd misread this woman right from the beginning.

"For Chrissake, that's crazy talk, Ingrid. I'm just going out on the goddamn bike."

"Is it crazy talk? Is it? What about out on the muster today? Where were you poking her, Hegarty? Over in the trees by the stockyards? With Pony watching, I'll bet."

"You know you're talking shit, Ingrid. Will you please calm down. Look, I'll have a quick drink if you like, and . . ."

"I must be out of my mind letting a bastard like you get under my skin," she shrilly cut him off. "Demeaning myself, coming here almost . . . almost damn begging." She shook her head, tears of rage welling.

He began to move toward her, shushing her with his hands. "You're not demeaning yourself," he attempted to placate her, "I appreciate you coming, Ingrid, I really do, but it's the wrong time. If you'll just . . ."

It was shit, and she knew it. She threw the scotch at him. He wasn't a bad outfielder once, his reflexes were still sharp, and he didn't want the bottle smashing against the wall. He shot out a hand and made a deft catch that would have drawn praise from his old coach.

"Let's call it a night," he said evenly. "For both our sakes."

"My God, don't think I'll ever come here again," she fumed.

It was a threat that was no threat; she knew he didn't give a damn, and at once she realized how ridiculous it sounded.

He put the scotch down carefully on the small dresser. "Why can't we just be friends?" he said gently.

Her high-pitched laugh had an edge of hysteria. "You bastard. After what happened between us? You must think I'm some sort of an idiot."

He lost patience. He was sorry, but he just hadn't figured she'd take it so seriously. He hadn't figured on a lot of things about her, like her jealousy of Anna.

"Look I've got to go," he said bluntly. He motioned to the door. "Close it when you leave, will you?"

"Jesus, I'll make you bloody regret this, Hegarty," she said, gritting her teeth. "You and Anna, my God, yes. Don't kid yourself I can't do it."

He refused to be flustered. He couldn't afford her as an enemy; it was a complication, but he'd just have to live it.

"I just don't want any trouble, Ingrid," he said coolly.

She stalked to the door, thrusting him forcefully aside as she swept past. "Go to hell," she snarled.

He leaned in the doorway, watching as she stormed angrily back toward the house, head down, arms swinging, heels thumping the ground with each long stride, until she disappeared into the eucalyptus. He sighed, went outside, and closed the door behind him. He had really opened up a can of neurotic worms when he involved himself with her. He went slowly to the Kawasaki. It was hard to see how her threats could mean anything to him, but her vehemence made him uneasy, and he resolved to keep out of her way as much as possible until they took Leiman out.

The weather was a replay of the previous night, overhead a full moon riding on a black velvet sky that looked as if it had been dusted with diamonds. The wind had returned, cold in his face, rustling the grass. Again he didn't require the headlight, it was enough that they heard him go out, without revealing any direction.

He took a different track that wound around the back of the house and ran toward the towering, shadowed mass of Cathedral Rock. He rode in an aimless fashion, trying to come to a decision about breaking into the house, just letting the track lead him, and it wasn't until he hit the first steep, winding gradient on the other side of the monolith that he realized he was heading up the Rock. It hadn't occurred to him that there was some way to the top; where it backed the house it was sheer cliffs, but here it ascended in craggy waves, like steps hacked out by timeless erosion.

Curiosity pushed him on; if he went to the top maybe he'd learn something from the view. He needed the headlight here; the higher he went, the narrower the track became, strewn with rocks of varying shapes and sizes that could slew his front wheel and spill him over the edge. But he kept at it, managing to hold enough speed to maintain balance, until he finally came out to a small, flat clearing.

It wasn't the actual summit, the spire that gave the Rock its name still soared overhead at one side, but it was clearly as high as he could get. He cut the motor, propped the bike against the rock face, and walked across to the side overlooking the house. It was like being in the helicopter, the house and outbuildings spread out beneath in miniature, the savanna stretching with silver luminosity to the dark horizon. It was somehow moving, breathtakingly beautiful. Everyone claimed it was harsh country, and it had to be goddamn difficult raising cattle here, but a feeling of belonging obviously flowed with the blood in the veins of the Kiseks. Perhaps from up here it was easier to see why, even feel it himself.

He moved slowly along the edge, until he was stopped by piled rocks. He glanced down with the intention of skirting the pile, and saw it had the shape of something constructed by hand. Peering closer, he realized it was some form of cairn, with a cross fixed at one end. At the same time he heard the snicker of a horse. He straightened in alarm, squinting over to the large boulders in the shadows on the opposite side of the clearing. Vaguely he could see the shape of the horse moving, hear the jingle of harness, then the figure of a large man detached itself from the shadows and moved ponderously toward him. The horse followed, head down, hooves beating hollowly on the rocky surface.

It was Kisek, somehow made even larger by the night, like an ancient prophet with his white beard speckled with moonlight. One who had preached violent death to thousands of Jews.

"This is being a private place, Hegarty," he stated.

"I just followed a track, and it brought me here," said Hegarty.

"Ah yes, the nighttime riding. I have been hearing about that."

"It's something I like to do."

"It shouldn't be bringing you to this place. This is my place."

There was an awkward silence. The wind was stronger up on the Rock, swirling into the clearing like a breaking wave to wash against the opposite wall.

"This is my wife's place too," added Kisek, gesturing to the grave.

"I'm sorry, I had no idea," Hegarty apologized.

Kisek shrugged. "You wouldn't be knowing."

It was a Kisek Hegarty hadn't seen before, the aggressive edge sheathed, tolerant, subdued. He moved close to the grave, staring down, hands clasped before him, white hair whipping about his face. Then he lifted his hand, and made a slow sweep of the countryside.

"Life was perhaps too hard for her, coping with the Gulf Country." He tapped his chest. "Coping with me, ja, I never learned to be a good husband. You understand? When war hardens the heart, perhaps for some it never softens again. The children were the best thing to happen for her."

He fell silent once more, and Hegarty wondered if he should just quietly leave. He was like Ingrid, his mood could change swiftly from calm to storm, and the last thing Hegarty wanted was another hassle.

"Ingrid is being difficult for me," Kisek began again. "But Julia would have straightened her, ja . . . not like Anna, there's being a real woman, eh Hegarty?"

"Yes, a real woman," Hegarty guardedly agreed.

"Proud, Julia would have been." He bobbed his head, and muttered something Hegarty failed to catch.

"But Julia was never understanding the Gulf Country," Kisek continued. "Always she feared it—feared it when it was green, and running with water, feared it when it turned dry, and the grass shriveled." He coughed harshly, and spat. "You fear the Gulf, it kills you; you become part of it, it rewards you well. If you understand its moods, and build strength in your cattle, in yourself, then you'll beat it. She never grasped that." He shuffled his feet. "Up here at least she's being safe from the savanna she feared, from the wet, the dry, the heat."

To listen to the man's reflections was to once again raise Hegarty's doubts, to revive the story of the executed brother. Maybe time had mellowed him, but he just didn't sound like what one would expect from a human monster like the Whip-master of Treblinka. Was he being naive? Was he listening to a carefully rehearsed facade, perfected over more than forty years? He had to remind himself again that the Wiesenthal organization had tracked this man down, and how meticulous they were.

"You're thinking it's a strange place for a man to bury his wife, ja, Hegarty?"

"No. It's rather . . . beautiful. Do you come up here often?"

"Now not. But this is being the anniversary of her death."

"Then I'm sorry for intruding."

"I can see you're understanding."

"Of course."

"You're never marrying?"

"No. Maybe one day." Hegarty paused, thinking of the scotch Ingrid had brought to his room. Maybe this was the opportunity he was looking for. "Well I'll be heading down," he said. "Why don't you call at my room when you get back, and let me offer you a drink." He nodded to the grave. "In her memory," he added. "And it'll help settle our . . . misunderstanding yesterday, too."

"That's forgotten," said Kisek.

"Sure, but let's seal it with a drink. It always helps." He smiled encouragingly. "And there's still a lot of mustering to do."

Kisek pawed thoughtfully at his beard, gaze concentrated on the grave. "I'm hearing the helicopter mustering is going well, ja?"

"Ritchie seemed to think so, and Anna."

"Saving us much time. And money. Anna was also claiming the cattle were much easier to handle, and the calves."

"The helicopter handled well, too. The Bell 47's a good machine."

Kisek nodded. "Perhaps I'm calling in for a drink," he said cautiously.

Hegarty kept the elation out of his voice. "That's great; I'll look forward to it."

He waited a moment, but Kisek turned away to stare mutely out to the horizon, as a signal the conversation had ended. It made him doubt the man meant it, but he hesitated to push it any further. He just hoped to Christ he came.

He went back to the Kawasaki, feet scrunching on the loose rock. When he started the motor, the racketing clamor reverberated around the rocky walls. He glanced back just before he set the bike on the downward track, but Kisek was still standing there, apparently oblivious to the noise, his bulk seeming as solidified as the rock about him.

As soon as Hegarty got back he opened the scotch, placed it with two glasses and a jug of water on the small table, then sat down to wait. Perhaps meeting Kisek atop Cathedral Rock was as much a lucky break as saving Schon from the crocodile, especially catching him at such a sentimental moment. He'd acted with appropriate respect, and it gave him reason for optimism that Kisek would keep his word. Even so, he felt as jittery as an expectant father, unable to stay put for any length of time, going to the bathroom, then to the door, then the window, watching, hoping, listening. There was so much hanging on it, and even when an hour passed with no sign of Kisek, he refused to give up hope. Christ, he had to come. He'd just gone back to the table when the door suddenly opened without the preamble of any knock, and Kisek was standing there. Perhaps he figured it was his property anyhow, and he was entitled to just walk in unannounced.

Hegarty was at once composed, playing the smiling host, extending his hands in a gesture of welcome.

"I'm glad you decided to come, Mr. Kisek," he said.

Kisek nodded, but remained at the door, his eyes rapidly traversing the room before coming to rest on the scotch and glasses. Hegarty hoped he didn't recognize it as liquor from his own house. He gave a curt grunt, stepped heavily into the room, and shut the door. It was done with the attitude of a man half regretting his own actions.

Hegarty picked up the bottle, and indicated a chair.

"Why don't you sit down. I'm sorry I haven't got any soda, but if you like it with a little water . . . ?"

Kisek ignored the invitation to sit down. "Just a little water will be fine," he said. The words were strained, the voice stilted. He glanced about the room again, more slowly this time, while Hegarty poured. His uncertainty came across like a strong odor. "You are being comfortable here?" he asked.

"Best I've ever had."

"It's never been used before."

Hegarty handed him a glass. "I figured it must be new."

"Not new; just never used before."

Hegarty raised his own glass. "To the memory of your wife, Mr. Kisek."

Kisek accepted the toast without expression. "Ja. Thank you." He put the glass to his mouth, then lowered it again. "And to a continuing good muster with the helicopter," he added.

It seemed odd linking the two disparate thoughts, but both men drank deeply. Half the whiskey in his glass was gone when Kisek lowered it, and he uttered a grunt of satisfaction, wiping at his beard.

"Good whiskey, ja."

"Yes, very good," agreed Hegarty.

Kisek nodded his head, swirling the whiskey about in the glass as if searching for words, then drank again. There were questions Hegarty could have tried, perhaps to verify what he'd learned from the daughters, but why should he risk making him suspicious? The fingerprints Kisek was leaving on the whiskey glass were the only thing that mattered.

"Pony's getting a terrific kick out of flying in the helicopter," he said instead.

"You are flying careful with the boy?"

"I don't take risks."

"Pony's admiring you."

"And you. He talks about his grandfather all the time," Hegarty flattered.

Kisek shrugged it aside. "He's being an impressionable age." He looked at Hegarty. "You should be remembering that."

Hegarty remembered Anna's warning, knew it was a veiled rebuke.

"I'm just something new passing through. He'll forget me soon enough when I'm gone," he murmured.

"Ja, perhaps. The boy has not been seeing a man like you before."

"He's a great kid. Maybe I can teach him a thing or two. And he can teach me. He knows about cattle, and he's got the Gulf Country in his blood."

"Ja . . . like his mother."

"I was watching her with the cattle today too. Better than a man. She knows what she's doing."

Hegarty found himself subjected to that intense probing scrutiny again. "You are still intending to teach her to fly the helicopter, ja?"

"Sure, soon as the muster's over," Hegarty lied.

"I think she is admiring you too, like her son."

Hegarty smiled it easily aside. For reasons he didn't quite understand he suspected it was dangerous ground. "And forgetting me just as quickly," he said.

Kisek's stare assumed the penetration of a laser beam. "That's what I'd be hoping," he stated forcefully. "Better for her if she's not showing interest in a . . . a wanderer. Not easy it's been for her with men. She's vulnerable, like her son. Out here both of them are not seeing many like you."

The blunt warning puzzled Hegarty. Anna was a fully grown, mature woman, not a young teenager in need of parental protection. Was that why Anna wouldn't invite him to dinner, for fear her father might sense the growing attraction between them. So what? Why so much concern for Anna, and so little for Ingrid?

"She's a fine woman," he passed it off.

"And staying that way. She has enough with Pony."

"Sure, sure," Hegarty frowned. "I'm not for changing anything. Why should I?"

"She's liking you."

"And I'm liking her. And Pony. And Ingrid. It makes for easy living when you're working with people you like."

"I'm not wanting her hurt," persisted Kisek.

Hegarty took another mouthful of whiskey, trying to suppress irritation. The friendly drink was running the risk of turning into an intense third degree, and he didn't want that, didn't want anything that would upset Kisek. What was it with him and Anna?

"Look Mr. Kisek, the last thing I'd want to do is hurt Anna."

"Hurting my blood is hurting me. Ja, I'm not a forgiving man, you're understanding?"

"Dammit Mr. Kisek, all I'm aiming for is a good muster. Then Anna can take over when I'm gone. That's all there is to concern you. Okay?" He tried a reassuring smile. "I honestly don't see what you're getting at."

Kisek didn't answer. He suddenly dropped the subject, drained his whiskey, and put the glass down heavily on the table.

"You're clearing the north paddock tomorrow?" he asked.

Hegarty felt relief at the change of subject. "If it goes as well as today, then I figure we should."

Kisek nodded. "Good." The intimidating probe had gone from his eyes like a switched off light. "Then you'll be moving south of the homestead. Ritchie knows." He gestured to the empty glass. "I'm thanking you for the whiskey, Hegarty. Perhaps I'm seeing you out on the muster sometime tomorrow."

He turned on his heels without another word, and strode from the room, the door closing behind him like the crack of a whip. The room seemed larger with him gone.

Hegarty lowered himself into the chair, and lovingly

contemplated Kisek's empty glass. The business with Anna mystified him. Maybe Kisek's accepting his invitation for a drink had been more an opportunity to warn him off his daughter than any attempt at reconciliation. The hell with it, the important thing was that he had the man's fingerprints all over the glass. Now he only had to wait for Reine.

He savored it awhile, until another itch began to niggle him. Jesus, what a prize if he could have both the fingerprints and the passport. Anna had told him where it was. If even at this late stage Reine was still plagued by doubts over Eli Brandt's reliability, then surely the passport could be an invaluable backup. He thought it over while he carefully placed the glass upside down in the special carton he'd brought with him, securing it in position with tape in a pattern across the inverted bottom that carried no risk of smudging the fingerprints. Then he sat considering things for a long time, slowly drinking and smoking cigars steadily. Why not the passport? It wouldn't be the first time he'd been a burglar.

His mind made up, he sealed the carton with its fingerprint-laden glass and put it into his backpack; then he switched off the light, stretched out on the bed, and dozed for a time. When he next checked his watch it was two o'clock. He sat up and dry-wiped his face. Then he went to the door and quietly eased it open. The clouds had multiplied, merging shadows and highlights into a joint blackness. No lights showed anywhere in the house. It was perfect.

He took a pencil flashlight from the backpack, slipped out of his boots and socks, and padded barefoot across the yard to the house. The wind whined through the eucalyptus like a banshee sounding a warning. He shut his ears. Was he taking a risk like this for Reine, or for Anna, hoping in some goddamn stupid way the passport photograph would clear her father, not incriminate him? He furiously brushed it aside; for Chrissake, he was Mossad. He was doing it for Reine—Kisek was Leiman, *Kisek was Leiman*.

He opted for boldness; slithering around the house searching for an open window would only be asking for trouble. Maybe they didn't lock their doors in the Gulf Country. Why should they, who was there out here to rob them?

He went up the front steps with the tread of a wary cat,

cautiously tried the handle of the front door, and breathed easy when it opened for him. He slipped quickly inside, closed it quietly behind him, and stood for a moment to accustom his eyes to the darkness. Ingrid had labeled it a museum, and he recalled the musty aroma of unused things, surfaces that knew only the touch of dust.

Which way? He knew the door directly opposite led to the dining room, and from there to the kitchen. He cast the flashlight beam in a fast arc about the room, then flicked it off. His only other choice was a single door to the left he hadn't noticed before. He crossed swiftly, went through, and found himself in a hallway, thick carpet underfoot absorbing his weight like a sponge. He risked another fast dart of light, like a lightning flash that reveals everything in a garish split second. Pictures lining the walls, four doors, two to the right, one to the left, one at the end of the passage. He was going to have to gamble. If he chose either of the girl's rooms, lust was an easy alibi, even with Pony he could contrive some story; but Carl would be a big problem, and Kisek would be a disaster, especially after the warning about Anna. He hesitated, considering retreat. He was never foolhardy. Of necessity he took risks, but always carefully calculated, and although he might try to blind himself to it, he knew concern for Anna was pushing him just as hard as a sense of mission for Reine.

Christ, it was worth a try. He decided for the end door, it seemed to make sense that the study would be toward the rear of the house. He went soundlessly along the passage and gently opened the door just enough to squeeze through, then flattened himself to the wall, stifling his lungs, straining to hear if there was the breathing rhythm of someone sleeping. There was only silence. The clouds conspired with him, opening to permit wan moonlight through a window opposite to briefly illuminate a desk, chairs, filing cabinets, and another door in the wall to the right.

It brought forth a nervous snicker of breath; maybe it was more luck than he deserved, he'd shuffled the deck and the ace had fallen for him. He switched on the flashlight again, and went quickly to the desk. It was obviously antique, large and ornamental, in character with the rest of the house. There was nothing on the top of interest: telephone, date pad, strewn papers, a newspaper, a farming magazine. The top drawer opened easily, and with practiced skill he sifted through the contents, making sure it looked undisturbed. A diary, checkbook, a clipped sheaf of accounts, notes in German on a pad. But no sign of anything resembling a passport.

The second drawer was also unlocked, but once more he drew a blank. A calculator, loose ballpoint pens, paper clips, a glass paperweight in the shape of a shorthorn bull. He moved down to the bottom drawer, and found it locked. He hesitated, then withdrew the middle drawer completely from the desk and laid it softly on the floor. It failed to give him acess to the bottom drawer, which was roofed over with the metal covering, to make it like a small safe. He quietly cursed. It was long ago, but perhaps Ingrid's accidently coming across the passport had made Kisek put it under lock and key. A man in his position would leave nothing to chance, yet he must have shown it to Anna. It was another indication of how he discriminated between his two daughters.

Hegarty knew about locks, and he focused the flashlight beam on the catch, trying to see where it connected, whether there was any way of prying it loose. He tried gently to force it, but it refused to budge. Suddenly he became aware of a sound like the buzzing of a fly trapped in a web, frantically beating its wings in an attempt to escape. He raised his head, listening, then he saw the light, a small orb of red blinking above the door on the other side. He froze, certain it hadn't been there before. The buzzing had to be an alarm, sounding a warning somewhere in the house. Shit, he must be losing his touch, it hadn't occurred to him the son-of-a-bitch would have the drawer wired. Then light flared under the bottom of the second door in the room. He quickly pushed the middle drawer back into place, moved rapidly to the door through which he'd entered, closed it softly behind him as he stepped back into the hallway, then paced silently toward the living room entrance. For Chrissake, with what Kisek had at stake, he should have figured the drawer might be wired.

He was almost to the living room when a shaft of light flushed under that door. He jarred to an indecisive halt. Someone had switched on the light in the living room, if he opened the door he risked confronting Kisek, if he went back to the study he chanced the same thing. It left him no choice but to make a lottery of the other doors, gamble that whoever he chanced on was a heavy sleeper, and that there was an unlocked window which would give him an out.

Jesus, why the hell did he push himself out on a limb? He didn't even get a look at the passport, much less take it. He should have been satisfied with the fingerprints. Goddamn it, his mixed feelings about Anna had made him risk too much. The sound of the buzzer had stopped, but faintly he could hear footsteps, and he knew he had to make a fast choice. He wasn't clairvoyant, he needed blind luck again. He went for the door on the left, slipped inside, shut it behind him, and stood straining his eyes in the darkness. There was sufficient moonlight filtering through a large window dead in front to vaguely outline a bed and other items of bedroom furniture. He couldn't hear the sound of the regular breathing of sleep, but his nostrils suddenly caught the fragrance he recalled from being close to her. Anna's room. Then he was momentarily part-blinded when a lamp abruptly flicked on, and there was nowhere for him to hide. Everything about the room said "feminine"—the wide bed with the white and gold metal antique ends, the lace curtains, the Degas prints on the walls. But there was nothing soft about the expression on Anna's face, as she shrugged herself into a sitting position, one arm still outstretched toward the bedside lamp. Her hair was disheveled, eyes wide with disbelief, lips slightly parted with a suggestion of fear. White string straps stood out against brown shoulders spotted with freckles like her face.

"What the devil . . . ?" she muttered huskily.

Brashness had to be his only tactic, he didn't have the alternative of an apologetic retreat. Not without being faced with unanswerable questions.

Her arm dropped away from the lamp, and she pushed her fingers distractedly through her hair. "For God's sake, what the devil are you doing here, Matt?" she protested throatily. "You're crazy if you think you can . . ."

He reached the bed in a few quick strides and clamped his hand tightly over her mouth. It couldn't be helped, but he frightened her, her body squirming frantically under the covers, one hand desperately attempting to push him away, the other wrenching at his hand over her mouth.

"Please, Anna, please, I'm not going to hurt you," he whispered urgently. "I had to see you; I had to. Please don't call out." He tried to plead with his eyes. He had something going with this woman, and now he had to play it for all he was worth. "I went into the wrong room," he hissed into her ear. "It must have been your father's study, and I set off some sort of goddamn alarm." He slightly eased the pressure of his hand on her mouth. "I think I woke him." He paused. "I'm going to take my hand off your mouth. Okay? Okay? Please don't call out; just hear me out. I just had to see you, believe me." Even now, like this, he was so very aware of her aroma, the feel of her. He waited while the fear in her eyes dimmed, her hands fell away, and he felt her body gradually lose its tenseness. When he took his hand away she might scream bloody murder, but he had to chance that. As he warily let go, she pushed him back and wiped contemptuously at her mouth.

"I'm sorry," he said quietly but urgently.

"Get out of here, you bastard," she hissed fiercely. "Get the hell out!"

He glanced toward the door. "I can't; if I do I'll risk running into your father."

He was banking on whatever it was between Anna and father. If it meant she didn't want him at the dinner table, then sure as hell she wouldn't want Kisek to know he was in her room. Even if she was blameless. Her expression confirmed it.

"Then get out the bloody window," she ordered.

"He'll hear me."

"God, you've got a nerve, Hegarty," she whispered vehemently. "You think you can come creeping in here and I'll fall into your arms. My God, I'll . . ."

"It isn't like that," he interjected.

"Isn't it! You think I'm that naive? I know what you're after. Forget it, I'm not Ingrid."

"You've got it wrong."

"Really," she softly jeered. She glanced at the bedside clock. "God, it's after two o'clock."

There was a tentative knock at the door. It was the testing time. He focused intently on her face, as if willing her not to betray him. She hesitated, then indicated a door on the other side of the bedroom, her pointing finger wagging urgently.

He nodded understanding, crossed silently to the door, and passed through into a small bathroom. Before he closed the door he saw her pick up a book from the bedside stand. He stood listening, straining to hear over the thudding of his heart.

"Who is it?" he heard her call.

"Dad. Are you all right?" Kisek inquired.

There was the sound of an opening door, then Kisek's voice more clearly. "I saw your light on."

"I couldn't sleep. I was just having a read."

"Was you going into the study?"

"Yes. I remembered I left this book in there the other day. In the drawer where I put the accounts," she replied easily.

Hegarty couldn't repress a grin. She was as accomplished a liar as himself. Still, he didn't get it. Was she frightened of Kisek? No, she was her own woman. But why would she so readily lie for him?

"You was setting off the alarm," stated Kisek, in a grieved tone.

"I'm sorry, did I?"

"Didn't you see? Didn't you hear?"

"I guess I was a bit fuzzy from trying to get to sleep. I suppose I should have put the light on, instead of stumbling around in the dark. I'm sorry it woke you."

Kisek muttered something indistinguishable, and cleared his throat with a gritty rasp. "There is being the switch by the filing cabinet to turn the alarm off," he growled.

"I'm sorry, I forgot," replied Anna, in a sharper tone. "I don't know why you need an alarm anyway."

There was further inaudible muttering from Kisek, then a brusque goodnight, followed by the closing of the door.

Hegarty waited a moment, then stepped back into the bedroom, and quietly went back to the bed. Anna had lifted the pillow to support her shoulders, the book lay closed on her lap; she studied him with a reproachful expression. He thought right then she was close to being the most beautiful woman he'd ever seen.

"Thank you," he said simply.

"I don't like lying to my father," she muttered. "Why in God's name did I?"

"Maybe it was the lesser of two evils," he suggested.

"It wasn't for you, Hegarty."

She was back to calling him Hegarty again. "I know," he said.

"How do you know?"

He cautiously sat down beside her. "I've seen you have a special feeling for him. You wouldn't want him upset."

She grimaced. "Perhaps. How on earth did you set off the alarm in the study?"

"I don't know; it was dark in there. I know I stumbled against the desk, then the alarm started up. Is he frightened of thieves out here?"

"No . . . I don't know. He's funny about things like that." Her eyes narrowed with suspicion. "How did you know this was my room?"

"I didn't, it was just . . ." He shrugged. "Luck."

"What if it'd been Pony, or Ingrid—or Carl for God's sake?"

"It wasn't."

"Perhaps you wanted it to be Ingrid."

Christ, they were back to that. "You're the one I was looking for."

"So you say."

"It's the way it is."

Her dark, watchful eyes never left his face, then she picked up the book and indicated the window.

"Well, your luck's over. It's safe now, you can go out that way."

He'd failed with the passport, come damn close to getting caught, but he was only conscious of her closeness, her brown skin, her mouth, her marvelous eyes. Even then he couldn't stop the intrusion of the idea she might be able in some way to get the passport for him.

"I haven't told you why I wanted to see you," he protested.

"Tell me tomorrow; out on the muster."

"I can't tell you then." He was making it up as he went along, not too sure where it was going to lead.

"Why not?"

"No woman has made an impact on me like you have in a long, long time," he said softly. Should he be surprised it was true? She tried to derail him with a soft, cynical laugh.

"I told you I knew why you'd come. Leave off the pretty words, Matt."

At least it was Matt once more. "It's not just pretty words. You feel it too; I can tell."

"The voice of experience," she mocked.

"Maybe. But I know it's true."

"You think you know me better than I know myself?" she said, without conviction.

He suddenly leaned forward, and kissed her on the shoulder. Her skin felt cool, and smooth as polished opal.

"Don't do that," she hissed.

He waited for her to push him back, but it didn't happen, so he slid his mouth across onto her throat.

"No," she murmured. "No please, Matt."

He could feel her pulse fluttering under his lips, and then, ever so gently, her trembling hand on his back. He traveled softly down into the vee of her night gown, until his mouth found a hardening nipple.

"Oh, Jesus," she moaned.

He wanted her, and it had nothing to do with Reine, or Jules, or Favett, or Leiman, or why he was at Cathedral Rock. He hooked back the bed covers, probing down until he found the firm roundness of her belly, the triangle of soft hair, her legs spreading without persuasion for him to caress the opening, already awash with the urgent juices of desire. He lifted his head and kissed deep into her mouth, and her arms tightly encircled his neck, holding him there. Then she placed her hands on each side of his head, and held him back, an expression in her eyes of passionate yearning, her quick breath like fire on his face.

"You know," she breathed unsteadily. "You do know."

"I know for both of us," he answered tenderly.

"Love me," she whispered feverishly. "Love me, love me, love me—it's been so long; too long. Love me."

Maybe it was more a cry for understanding, but he was too caught up to pay heed. He wasn't even aware of the haste with which he discarded his clothes—as if by the wave of a wand they were suddenly locked in mutual nakedness. He was deep within her, then out, then in, with a continuous throbbing motion that seemed to have an energy of its own, while she moaned, and pulsated in unison under him. It bore no resemblance to the cool, detached way he'd used Ingrid, he was submerged in her so completely the world outside her had no meaning, everything was just being part of her, and her part of him, now, and now, and now, until dual orgasm was a delicious wrenching fulfillment, and he felt as if he didn't ever want to let her go.

But he knew he would. He hadn't expected to come halfway around the world and find the sort of woman he'd been looking for all his life, but he wasn't here to love her, it was to hang her father. Savage irony, but that was the only commitment he could allow himself. He couldn't be made vulnerable, no matter what he might feel for her, a lifetime's training had gone to making him inflexible where scum like Leiman were concerned. Or so he told himself.

He waited until her moans subsided and his heart steadied to a normal beat, then he eased off her, slipped his arm about her shoulders, and drew her close. She lay with legs entwined in his, arm loosely across him, her face on his chest.

"Oh, my God," she finally breathed softly.

"Amen to that," he whispered in reply.

"I felt it so quickly when I first saw you; but I knew you were only a passing thing, and I promised myself it wouldn't happen."

"I felt it too." Then it came unchecked from his mouth: "I love you."

"You don't have to say that."

He knew it, but the impulse to level with her on this at least was irresistible.

"It's the way I feel," he insisted.

"It'll pass."

"No. I know myself. It won't pass."

She fell silent, then raised herself on her elbow until their eyes were level. "And you'll pass."

"Maybe not. I only know I've come one hell of a long way to find someone like you."

He dropped easily into lying again. For Chrissake, why the hell was he persisting with this charade? It had to be wishful thinking leading his tongue. How could she love someone aiming to get her father hanged?

"You'd stay in the Gulf Country?" she asked.

She was wanting so badly to believe him. He sidestepped any commitment. "I love you," he repeated.

"Maybe I love you too."

"It could also pass for you."

She offered a throaty chuckle. "After what just happened between us, perhaps I should give my head time to clear, but . . ." she shook her head. "I know myself too. It won't pass for me. I know when it's right."

He placed a hand in her hair, and gently pressed her head back to his shoulder. "Then that's something we're going to have to think about very seriously," he murmured.

Christ, it was all bullshit, bullshit, but he felt ensnared in some magical aura, like a child wanting to believe in a fairy tale.

"I'd like to think so," she whispered. "I really would." She hesitated. "There might be some problems."

"You mean Pony?"

She laughed softly. "God, he'd be delirious with joy."

"Ingrid?" he tentatively queried.

"I know she likes you, but she'd get over it."

He thought of Ingrid at the lagoon, and the hurled whiskey bottle. The hell she would. Why should he care? It wasn't going to happen anyway, this unforgettable fragment was the only reality he would ever have with her.

"Your father?"

She didn't immediately answer.

"He's very fond of you," he added.

The way she stirred conveyed unease. "I guess you can get past any problem, if you want to badly enough," she muttered.

It was so ambiguous it could have meant anything. "I'd say your father and I weren't exactly bosom buddies, and I figure he's counting the days until I get lost. If it wasn't for Pony I'd probably already be gone."

"He's realized how valuable you are."

"He still hates my guts."

"It's not just you."

"Then what is it?"

She gently kissed his chest, as if to close the subject. "Let's worry about it later," she murmured. "I'm more interested in you; where you've come from, where you've been, what you've done."

"You heard it all at the dinner table. I'm a scrap of paper."

"What's that mean?"

"I get blown where the wind takes me. The wind drops, I settle. It springs up again, and I'm away, never knowing where I'm going to land next." Well, it was partly true, only there was nothing accidental about where the Mossad sent him.

"There must be more?"

"What about your problem?"

"It's nothing. Forget it."

She was adept as he at sidestepping. Was there some unbreakable bond between her and Kisek? Did she share the knowledge her father was Horst Leiman, and feared a commitment might betray him? If there was ever a ready-made moment for further probing about Kisek it was now, with her so soft and pliable, but he hesitated to use it. Christ, was he already letting her get in the way of the operation? He could almost hear Jules's contemptuous laughter. No. Now he had a clear pattern of a Nazi war criminal hiding out, and he'd settle for the fingerprints—the hell with the passport, and the hell with the phony story about the executed brother. Maybe he hadn't been able to pinpoint Carl, he was almost surely Leiman's aide from Treblinka, the man Stauffer Jules had spoken about. It was irrelevant; only Leiman mattered.

Her hand gently rubbed at his chest, then she lightly kissed him, and nodded to the window.

"I think you'd better go now," she murmured.

"It's fantastic just lying here with you."

"For me too." There was that unreadable expression again. "But I don't want to chance any more . . . interruptions."

"You're a big girl now, Anna. What you do is your own business."

She hesitated, then smiled. "It's not quite as easy as that. I'd rather Dad got used to the idea gradually. Believe me, I know the best way to handle him, and at times it's got to be done with kid gloves."

He wondered how it had been with Pony's father, but he didn't offer resistance, merely returned her light kiss, then eased himself out of bed and rapidly dressed. She lay back on the pillow, watching.

"It's best if you use the window," she warned softly.

"I intend to."

He kissed her. There was a suggestion of sadness in her farewell smile, and he sensed once more there were things about her he didn't know, would probably never know.

"I'll never forget tonight," she whispered. Then, "Don't say anything to Pony. It's too soon."

It was the last thing he wanted. "Don't worry, I won't."

He went to the window, and quietly eased it open. She lay on her side, head cradled on her arms, watching like a contented cat.

"Tomorrow," he whispered.

"I love you," she called quietly after him.

He went quickly out the window as she flicked out the light, and when he turned to close it, darkness had blotted her from sight. He shook his head. This had never happened to him before. Emotional involvements on an operation were absolutely taboo; he was going to have to discipline himself, get it firmly under control, be professional, even try to find some way to make it work for him.

He glanced about. He was on the other side of the house now, and he circled swiftly around the back, keeping to the deep shadows, trying to free himself from the images of Anna, the feel of her. Around here he was sheltered from the wind, that was why he came to an abrupt halt when he spotted a fluttering bush along the line of eucalyptus leading to his room. It was possibly a bird, or a night animal, but he decided for caution. He waited, not moving, blended with the shadows, focused on the bush. It shivered again, as an indistinguishable shape shifted position. It was someone watching his room; maybe Kisek hadn't believed Anna and was checking to see if he was in his room. He had no choice but to wait it out, there was no other way back to the room without risking being seen, and even to retreat could risk a betraying sound.

He stood there for nearly half an hour, allowing no movement except breathing, until the figure finally moved, leaving the cover of the trees and shuffling unsteadily back to the house. Christ, it was the elderly Carl, not Kisek. Had the old man also heard the alarm, spoken about it to Kisek, and decided to play spy just to make certain he wasn't involved? Maybe. It was a sobering indication that the attempt to get the passport had been an unnecessary and crazy risk. But then he wouldn't have made love to Anna. He allowed a sour grin; if he didn't watch himself that could prove to be just as big a risk.

He waited until he was sure he was in the clear, then padded rapidly to his room, went inside, and closed the door behind with a sense of relief. Jesus, he really would have had some explaining to do if he hadn't been lucky enough to see Carl.

It wasn't until he was in bed, and beginning to doze, that it suddenly hit him. Shit, had he been used, like he'd used Ingrid? Had he been sucked in by the oldest bait in the world, had an attempt been made to weaken his resolve by a woman fiercely determined to protect her father from the hangman? For Chrissake he actually loved her, didn't want to believe that, yet suspicion was part of his profession, and it had to be a consideration. Had he been just as much sucked in by male ego, the great lover sure the woman could scarcely wait to get him between her legs? If he was anywhere near right they knew everything, or at least suspected. He fought against it, debating it with insomniac intensity, until the first light of dawn filtered through the window. God, he hoped Reine came soon.

Sleep refused the comfort of peace to Ingrid. Those early battles with her mother had always revolved around a fierce wilfulness to get her own way, and a dogged persistence until she did. It beat her mother, and forced her father into indifferent retreat. Hegarty was something different, insinuating himself into her like a habitual drug, and she couldn't let go, wouldn't let go. He'd humbled her. God, she despised herself for crawling back to him like a lovesick idiot. And what was worse, she had the feeling of being used in a way she hadn't figured out yet, but by God somehow she'd bring him crawling back to her, burying his face in her crotch, saying please, please, then she'd laugh at him, tell him to get lost.

But she couldn't forget what had happened at the lagoon, she masturbated to the memory, moaning for him to be in her again, but sleep still failed her. The thought that he might have moved from riding her to Anna drove her crazy. Anna had Pony, their father's damn favor, did she have to have everything for herself at Cathedral Rock?

She finally gave up the attempt to find sleep, got out of bed, and crossed to the window, hoping the view of the savanna would ease the ache. The dark cloud made for little to see, and she closed her eyes as she rested her forehead against the glass, relishing the coolness. She was startled by a soft scraping sound from somewhere outside, and she cast a glance toward the window of Anna's room on the right. She saw a figure cautiously emerge, then slip past her so close, she could have put out a hand and touched him. Hegarty. God, Hegarty. Coming from Anna's bedroom. The lousy sex-hungry fucking bastard. She'd never experienced such intense rage, sweeping her like fever, choking her so she could scarcely breathe. She thought she was going to fall as she felt her way unsteadily back to the bed and slumped down on the edge. She didn't know how long she sat there, her mind crowded with uncontrollable hideous demons who with screaming obscenities demanded revenge. She didn't know what she'd do, or how she'd do it, but by God they'd both suffer! No one alive would humiliate her like this. And the worst humiliation was to still want the bastard, to know that if he came knocking at her window right now, she'd throw herself at him, do anything, give him anything he wanted.

The muster was a repeat of the previous day, and Hegarty tried not to think about Anna; he refused to plague himself with doubts any longer. But he was unsure how to react with her so he opted for caution, deciding to leave it in her corner and take his cue from her attitude. In the beginning there was no problem, because she didn't show for the early morning start of the muster.

The first few hours he spent with Pony in the Bell, sweeping back and forth across the northern section of the paddock, where the cattle seemed more numerous than yesterday. The early clouds quickly cleared, and soon they were flying under a great ceiling of brilliant blue stretching to the horizon in all directions, the brown grass cooking in the dry earth.

When he went back for his first refueling stop, Anna was waiting there. And so was Kisek. It only took a few moments to realize that doubts about his attitude to Anna had been taken out of his hands.

"Hi, Anna," he warmly greeted her. He knew there was an ingredient of intimate knowing in the sound of his voice. "Hi there, Mr. Kisek."

"G'day, Mum, g'day, Grandad," called Pony.

Kisek grunted acknowledgment, but Anna merely offered a cool glance of appraisal.

Pony was quickly at the fuel drum, setting up the manual pump, inserting the nozzle into the gas tank of the helicopter.

"I've got him well trained," grinned Hegarty.

"Sorry, I got held up, or I would have been here earlier," said Anna. "I hope it's going as well as yesterday?"

The words fell on the air like an icy breeze, devoid of warmth, an impersonal query from the boss to a hireling, as if last night was only a fantasy of his imagination. It was Kisek's presence, of course; it made her like a different woman. He glanced quickly to where Kisek was watching Pony, then back to her, but she simply returned a blank stare.

"Well, is it?" she asked curtly.

He tapped his brow in a mocking gesture of respect. "It's going pretty well," he said. "But I figure there's more stock where we're working this morning. It could take longer than yesterday."

"You think you'll clear them?" She disdained to even look at him, her eyes were on the cattle beginning to bunch out on the savanna.

"Yeah, I figure we'll still do it," he said laconically. If she wanted to play it like this, then he'd tag along. In spite of his resolve, the father-daughter relationship still intrigued him.

"I've been watching you," said Kisek, equally brusque.

The shared drink last night had done nothing to soften him either.

"It works well, ja, very good," added Kisek. "I can see how fast the cattle are coming together, and Ritchie is cooperating well."

"We're working together like a sweet-running machine," said Hegarty.

"Ja, I'm seeing that," replied Kisek absently. He pursed his mouth, studying the cattle. "They are looking down in condition, we are going to be losing some before the wet comes. Maybe we are shipping some south to better feed if it gets worse."

"As good cattle as I've seen anywhere, Mr. Kisek," Hegarty observed, flattering him.

Kisek was obviously pleased by the remark. "Breeding, that's being the secret, Hegarty. Breeding-in Santa Gertrudis for strength in the herd, like I was doing before anyone else was thinking of it."

"They look goddamn good to me," said Hegarty.

"You'd better keep moving, Matt, I want that paddock cleared today," Anna cut in sharply.

He refused to be ruffled, replying with a quizzical grin. She was working so hard at being deliberately offhand it was coming across as phony, and Kisek might just notice if she overplayed it. "Sure, yeah sure," he said. He turned to Pony. "How's it coming there, mate?"

Pony didn't look back from vigorously working the pump handle. "Almost there, Matt, almost there. Just a few secs more."

"Good man." Hegarty glanced at the sky, and put his helmet back on. "Well I'll be seeing you both later; we've got a great day for it."

Anna started to put out a hand, but stopped herself short. "Good flying; take care with Pony."

"I always take care," he said, smiling.

The brief conversation set the pattern for the day with her.

Pony never lost his enthusiasm. Every sweep, every turn, every delicate maneuver of the Bell was greeted with gleeful appreciation, and in between he never let up on his pro-

poganda barrage extolling his mother to Hegarty. He couldn't
know it wasn't needed any more.

But every time Hegarty landed, it was the same. Hot tea
would be waiting, accompanied by an inane, stilted conversation with Anna, until their feverish love-making last night
assumed the remoteness of an erotic dream.

Except for one passing moment, late in the day, when the
flying was finished, and he was leaning to the forcing yard, the
cattle bawling, milling, and stirring a stifling dust, that clogged
the skin and misted the air. He could see Kisek on the other
side of the yard, as if through a fog. Anna came and stood close,
watching the ringers working, not looking at him, arms folded
along the top railing.

"I love you," he said.

He wanted to hear her say something that related to last
night, even if it was like taunting a dog with a bone it couldn't
have.

She didn't respond, eyes still straight ahead, and he
thought maybe she hadn't heard above the stockyard ruction.

"I love you too," she finally answered.

"Today was like working with a stranger."

"I'm sorry about that," she muttered. "It's the way it has
to be for now. I need time. Please try and understand."

He played it her way, keeping his eyes on the cattle.

"I want to see you again tonight," he said.

"No, not tonight. I couldn't handle it."

"What that's supposed to mean?" he asked with irritation.
He might be gone by tomorrow, and he craved one more time
with her, he didn't give a damn if she knew about her father or
not.

"Give me time," she repeated.

"Then when?"

"I don't know. I don't want you coming to the house
again."

Christ, he was like a junkie wanting another hit. "Goddamn it, Anna, the hell with your fucking father," he said in
exasperation. "You're a grown woman, what you do is your
business."

"It's not as easy as that."

"It is if you love me—if I love you."

"I need to be . . . sure about that."

"You were sure last night."

"Dreams end; daylight comes." She shook her head. "Don't push me, Matt. Just let's leave it for now; let me work on it."

She was talking in circles, he couldn't figure the sudden change. Before he had a chance to reply she turned abruptly away to where the first of the cattle were being driven into the crush.

He stood looking after her, remembering the way she moved under him, and punched at the stockrail in frustration. He walked slowly back to the helicopter. Anna had touched him deep in a place he'd thought exclusively his own, and the role of thwarted lover was a new experience for him. Yet he'd be a fool not to accept it, let it lie, it was an element he had to force himself to push aside. Anyway love would turn to hatred when he put her father at the end of a rope. If there was no signal about Reine by tonight, he'd pay another visit to the old house. He needed the therapy of Jules's hard-edged ruthlessness.

Chapter 11

When he got back to his room the tiny red light was glowing in the receiver. Reine had arrived.

He felt enormous relief that the waiting was over; now things could move; he'd be too involved in setting up the kidnap details to tie himself in emotional knots over Anna.

Dinner materialized as usual on the doorstep in the form of another excellent steak, which he quickly consumed; then he waited impatiently for darkness. It had all worked for the best. Maybe he'd been frustrated by Anna's rejection of another night in her bed, but he would have had to bail out anyway. Leiman came first, and he was pleased to feel so positive about it.

When the day had expired in its usual flaming red mourning colors, he put the carton containing the glass with Kisek's fingerprints into a small denim bag with a pull string, hung it about his neck, and went out to the Kawasaki. He started it and headed toward the road, sure that the routine of taking the bike out each night would provoke no questions. That, and luck, had given him Kisek's fingerprints.

It went easily, with a friendly moon again providing glittering light that made the use of his headlight unnecessary. He would have to watch himself if the subject of Anna came up—falling in love on an operation, especially with the daughter of the target, would be inconceivable to Jules. He hoped Jules had some more information on Eli Brandt's murder; he'd been too busy to give it any thought, but it was still an uneasy gnawing at the back of his mind. Unresolved questions like that could be traps waiting to catch you if you put a foot wrong, yet he'd seen nothing to indicate the killer could have traced Leiman to Australia.

Matt leaned the bike against the same tree at the front of the house, then stopped, listening, wondering if Jules would again attempt to indulge his sardonic humor by pushing a gun into the back of his neck. The overhead leaves fluttered in the breeze, as if whispering in anticipation.

"I've been waiting for you, Matt," called Grubin softly.

Hegarty squinted uncertainly toward the jumbled shadows about the ruins.

"Goddamn it, where the fuck are you, Jules?" he hissed impatiently.

A figure detached itself from the decayed doorway and gestured to him.

"Don't get your balls in a knot, my meshuga friend. Over here."

There was no mistaking that ironic tone. In confirmation, the moonlight caught his face as Jules moved forward, exposing those grinning buccaneer features that would have relished some victims to send walking the plank. They briefly shook hands.

"I figured you'd come tonight," said Jules.

"I take it from your signal Andre Reine's at Normanton?"

"Not yet. He arrives tomorrow. I got a transmission from the ship this afternoon." He took a quick glance about the silvered countryside. "You're sure you weren't followed?"

"Why? Why the hell would anyone follow me? They don't suspect a goddamn thing. You know better than to ask that, Jules."

Grubin shrugged. "Just checking."

"You want to go down to the cellar?"

In answer Grubin took him by the arm and drew him into the shadows. "Let's just go into my front room," he said with a chuckle. "That's where I've decided to do all my entertaining. It's so God-awful stuffy down in that bloody hole, I'll be damn glad when I'm out of it."

Hegarty followed him into the ramshackle room, cautiously picking his way through the rubble. The news about Reine had obviously put Jules in good humor. They came to a halt, the perforated roof casting freckles of moonlight on their faces.

"Thank Christ Leiman'll soon be on his way to Israel, and I can shake off this fucking place," grunted Grubin.

Hegarty took the denim bag from around his neck, and handed it to Grubin. "Here's what I promised, Jules. Treat it like a precious jewel."

It was difficult to see Grubin's expression, but there was no mistaking the tone of excitement. "Kisek's fingerprints?"

"The same. They're on a drinking glass, so for Chrissake take care you don't smudge them. They weren't easy to get."

Grubin gave his arm a fierce squeeze of congratulations. "Jesus, great Matt, just great. Reine'll be delighted. You got them without him suspecting a thing?"

"He was a sitting duck. After more than forty years I figure he wouldn't believe he's not safe in the Gulf for as long as he lives."

"Maybe. From all you've told me about his paranoia though, it sounds like he's never relaxed his guard," said Grubin.

Hegarty shrugged. "He's been living like that for so long now, I figure it's second nature to him; he does it without thinking. I'd bet a year's salary he'll get the shock of his life when we take him."

Grubin slowly nodded his head. "Great work, Matt, absolutely fabulous. You'll be Favett's fair-haired boy after this."

"We've got to get Kisek out yet."

"That won't be a problem."

"I'm just hoping there'll be no problem about the fingerprints matching."

"Christ, you doubt it? I thought we'd been through that. You haven't seen anything at Cathedral Rock to give you doubts since we last met?"

Hegarty hesitated. "No, not really. I guess the man doesn't quite ring true, in some way; not what I'd expect from someone who behaved like an animal at Treblinka."

"It's a long time ago; he's perfected a facade. What else would you expect? And look at his paranoia. That says it all."

"There was something from the older daughter."

"Important?"

"Maybe. I've made up my mind about it, but you'd better hear it."

He told Grubin about the supposed executed brother, who had been a concentration camp commandant.

"It's a phony," Grubin declared without hesitation, once Hegarty had finished. "A fucking concoction Kisek fed his daughter, just in case anyone came nosing around asking awkward questions. Everything you've told me about the way the bastard lives indicates that's the sort of precaution he'd take."

Hegarty nodded slowly. "I figured the same," he said, "but I thought you should hear it."

"Forget it. It's bullshit. The Wiesenthal organization hasn't got anything on file about any Leiman execution at the end of the war. You still think the daughters have no idea he's Leiman?"

"I think so; but there's no way I can be absolutely sure."

"The eldest daughter told you the story. What about her?"

"It's possible, but I still don't think so."

"Watch her, just the same."

Hegarty grinned wryly in the dark. Christ, he could scarcely take his eyes off her.

"That won't be for much longer, it's nearly over, Jules. Don't worry, I'm still just a helicopter mustering pilot to them."

"At night too?"

"Nighttime I've been sleeping."

"Yeah, but with which daughter?" Grubin asked with a smirk. "What about the passport?"

"I made a try for it last night. I not only didn't get it, I nearly got caught."

"You knew where to look?"

"In the drawer of a desk in Kisek's study."

"The eldest daughter told you that too?"

"She mentioned it in passing."

Grubin laughed appreciatively. "Jesus, you must have her eating out of your hand. She can't know about her father to pass that on to you."

"Maybe. He had the goddamn drawer sealed up like a safe, and wired with an alarm. That's how I nearly got caught."

"Don't risk it again. With the fingerprints we can do without the passport."

Hegarty shrugged it off. Jules made it all sound so starkly simple. Would he have felt seeds of doubt if he'd been exposed to Kisek's complex personality? But then it was part Anna for him, and he couldn't confide that to Jules.

"What are the details on Reine?" he asked.

"He's traveling with a tour group as a cover, just to play safe. He arrives in Normanton by train tomorrow around midday."

"That'll be on the Gulflander."

"Gulflander?" queried Grubin.

"It's what they call the train. It's the way I came into Normanton."

"You can get away from Cathedral Rock okay?"

"I'll have to. Don't worry, I'll think of something. How do I get the fingerprints from Reine?" asked Hegarty.

"Be at the station, watch him. Reine doesn't want any recognition, no sign at all. He knows all the tricks, he'll get them to you."

"Then Reine'll continue on with the tour?"

"Right. He'll have done his part. You bring the prints back here, I match them, and then we set it up to take Leiman out."

"What if they don't match?"

Hegarty heard a quick intake of Grubin's breath that indicated suppressed anger. "It's a question that has to be asked, Jules," he added quickly. "Even if it's a remote possibility. You know the way it was with Eli Brandt. Jesus, we've got to have some contingency plan. What do we do?"

There was a short period of silence, as if Grubin were trying to swallow his rancor.

"Well, if you want to be pessimistic, the word from Favett is we still go ahead and bring him out," said Grubin.

"They'll put him on trial with what they have, and try for identification from concentration camp survivors?"

"That's the decision. What the hell else can we do; we can't let the bastard off the hook. Anyhow it won't arise; the prints will match."

It had become an article of faith with Jules. And Favett. And Reine. Hegarty realized it was stupid to even raise the question. The wind moaned through the cracks in the walls, and it was like he could hear Anna's moans, feel her feverish breath, her thighs heaving under him. He shuffled his feet irritably about the floor, blotting it out.

"You've got a problem?" queried Grubin.

Hegarty bottled a derisive laugh. "When do we take Leiman out?"

"The helicopter's on standby. It'll only take a call."

"When do you figure?"

"Tomorrow night."

It was as if part of Hegarty's brain had revolted against control, his thoughts went immediately to Anna. He was going to lose her that fast.

"So soon?" that section of his brain asked.

"The quicker the better. I'll know about the fingerprints by then. Surely you don't object, Matt?" He slapped Hegarty on the arm. "Let's get the hell out of here—don't forget that dinner you promised me at the Piroshki."

Hegarty nodded. How could he possibly object. "We'll take him from here?"

"That could be a problem, we'd have to get him here somehow. Better if we go straight for the Cathedral Rock house."

"You'll risk involving the family if you do that. Leiman may go quietly, and he may not. I don't want them caught in any crossfire."

"Jesus, Matt, you're on about the family again," said Grubin with exasperation. "Just let's concentrate on Leiman. No one else is going to get hurt. Not the daughters, or the grandson. The hell with them, I warned you about getting involved."

Hegarty knew a passionate defense of Pony and Anna could betray his feelings, there were better ways to manipulate Jules.

"Goddamn it, I'm not talking about involvement, Jules," he declared hotly. "You know Favett'd blow his top if innocent people got hurt in the operation; something like that happening could even prejudice the trial. How would that make us look?"

From Grubin's hesitation he knew the point hit home. "No one's at risk," Jules replied sullenly. "We'll take Leiman by surprise, there won't be need for any shooting."

"You can't guarantee that. He's going to hear the helicopter."

Grubin fell silent, leaning against the wall and crossing his arms. The house shivered in the wind, timbers creaking, iron rattling, like an aged crone whining for attention.

"Okay, I'll buy that," said Grubin finally. "But how do we get him here?"

"There's got to be a way."

"How?" demanded Grubin aggressively.

"Let's think about it," said Hegarty persuasively. "We've got some time before I get back from Normanton tomorrow, we don't have to make a decision until then. I only know Favett would have our ass if someone like the boy accidently stopped a bullet."

Grubin didn't challenge the point, merely cleared his throat with a disagreeable rasp. "Okay, let's see what we come up with. But by Christ, Matt, it's got to be something absolutely foolproof. Otherwise we go for Cathedral Rock. There isn't any other way."

Hegarty didn't push it any further. Maybe it was just that he didn't want to see the look on Pony's and Anna's faces when they took Leiman out.

"It won't take you long to do the comparison test?" he asked.

"No. When I get everything set up I'll be able to tell in a few minutes." He offered an apologetic shrug. "I'd go to Normanton myself, Matt, but I don't want to break cover." He spread his hands. "Besides, I haven't got any transport."

"Forget it, that's my job." At least he had Jules calmed down again. "Anything on who killed Eli Brandt yet?"

"No. I just don't think it's a factor to worry us here. Favett's sure it was someone run by a control in Europe."

"I hope to Christ he's right."

"You haven't seen anything to indicate otherwise have you?" questioned Grubin.

"No, everything's running smooth. They think I'm the best thing to ever hit Cathedral Rock."

"You talking about cattle or daughters?" Grubin bantered, all his good humor returning.

"I'm working both; that's why I'm there, remember." Grubin snickered lewdly in the pause. "I guess that's it then?" asked Hegarty.

"Pity about the passport; it could have been useful," reflected Grubin.

"I might have a chance to try for it again, if we weren't taking Leiman out tomorrow night—if it was worth the risk."

He knew it was a limp attempt at a stall. What was the point? Was another night with Anna going to resolve how he felt about her? It would probably only enmesh him deeper.

"We can't risk putting it off for something like that," said Grubin. "We've got everything running for us." He cocked his head to one side. "Any chance one of the daughters might get it for you? If you asked nicely?" he added with a chuckle.

"I don't know. I think it's too risky to ask. They could just say something to their father, and I'd hate to make the sonofabitch suspicious when we're this close."

"Then forget it," said Grubin. He dangled the denim bag in the air. "We've got his fingerprints, thanks to you, and that's the most important thing."

"I had a few breaks."

"A good agent makes his own breaks."

Hegarty shrugged it aside. Anna was one break he hadn't counted on. And Pony. "Is there anything else?"

"Nothing more on the old guy, the one calling himself Carl Beaunig?"

"No. He keeps pretty much out of sight, but I figure he's as paranoid as Leiman. I've seen him watching me at times, but I don't figure he'll give us any trouble when we take Leiman."

"Then forget him too. Maybe he is Leiman's aide from Treblinka, but we can't waste time trying to prove it. Favett only wants Leiman." Grubin paused, his fingers beating a tattoo against the wall. "There's another piece of information I heard that could help convict Leiman."

"What's that?"

"We've got a mole in AISO, the Australian intelligence organization. He's dug out some old files that indicate it was an American OSS officer who engineered Leiman's escape from Germany after the war. Seems Leiman bartered some intelligence about the Russians, in exchange for freedom. This American was working with Australian intelligence people at the time to arrange for Leiman to come to Australia."

"I've heard that's how some of the scum got away. Christ, it's hard to believe."

To Hegarty's surprise Grubin offered a gesture of tolerance. "I guess different times, Matt. We can all act like bastards when we think it's in our own interests."

"You've got the American's name?"

"Not yet, but our man's working on it."

"The man could be dead," cautioned Hegarty.

"Possibly. Leiman's still alive, why not him?"

Hegarty rubbed reflectively at his chin. "I wonder if that could have anything to do with Eli Brandt's murder?"

"That's a wild card. I don't see how."

"Yeah, I guess you're right; it just seemed to trigger something." The floor creaked under Hegarty's weight as he shifted position. "I don't know why."

"Let's see if our man comes up with a name, then we might have something going for us," said Grubin. He gave a malicious laugh. "Then we can stir the ghosts of some asshole's past. If he turned out to be any sort of public figure we'd screw the bastard into the ground."

The sounds of the house took over as they both dropped into pondering silence. Unseen things slithered and pattered in the darkness. It was no wonder Jules was anxious to be gone from this place, mused Hegarty.

"I guess I'd better get back to my rathole," Grubin said finally.

"No problems with anyone coming near here?"

"You've been my only guest, Matt."

They shook hands again.

"Watch yourself, Jules," said Hegarty.

"You too, my friend. You're the one taking the chances, not me playing messenger boy in my black hole."

Hegarty offered a sympathetic grin and turned away

toward the door. He ducked under one of the rotted timbers and glanced back to the dark shape still standing by the wall. "See you some time tomorrow afternoon," he called in a whisper.

"Right. And don't worry about the Kisek family. From what you've told me they'll manage well enough without that murdering bastard around."

Hegarty didn't answer, just gave a brief gesture of fare-well and walked quickly to the bike. The night still glittered, the contrasting shadows looking as if die-cut from carbon. At least he'd managed to discipline himself not to betray the fact that he'd fallen in love with Anna. Or felt so drawn to Pony. Not that it should give Jules cause for concern—nothing was going to stop him taking Kisek out.

When Kisek was aggravated he had a way of scowling that resembled a shaggy English sheep dog turned suddenly ferocious. He tugged the wide-brimmed stockman's hat down over his eyes, and growled some indecipherable German words deep in his throat. He was carrying the whip, carving swirls in the ground as he irritably flicked it about.

Hegarty leaned against the tail of the helicopter, deter-mined to be laconically at ease, watching, waiting. The cool breeze fanning in from the west tempered the sting of the early morning sun. He'd been checking over the Bell, and it was already close to ten-thirty. He could see Anna and Ingrid over by the corral, but on opposite sides as if deliberately creating space between them, the horses circling as if to a trained circus routine. Pony had gone off somewhere on Schon, and he rarely saw Carl anyway.

"Ritchie tells me they won't be ready to start mustering to the south until late this afternoon anyway, so I figure you won't be needing me today," Hegarty pressed.

"Maybe so, but there's being other things about the place you could be doing," muttered Kisek.

"Then don't pay me for the time I'm gone," offered Hegarty. "I'm sorry, but there's personal business I've just got to do in Normanton."

"You're not knowing anyone in Normanton."

"I'm not going to see anyone. There are things I have to buy . . . to send away."

"You should have been doing it before you came to Cathedral Rock."

"I guess I wasn't really expecting to get the job," Hegarty said, grinning. He straightened into a more upright stance. "I have to go, Mr. Kisek," he declared firmly.

"You'll not be going in the helicopter. How am I knowing you're coming back?"

"I'll be going on my motorcycle, and don't worry, I'll be back. I haven't been paid yet."

Kisek flicked the whip again, then abruptly turned away, with a shrug of his heavy shoulders. "If you have to be going, then go," he growled. "Just be making sure you're back for the south muster."

"I'll be back," Hegarty assured him, but Kisek was already lumbering toward the house, the trailing whip weaving lines on the ground. It brought visions of what it must have been like for the terrified victims of Treblinka under the lash of a whip like that, and he had a sudden vivid flash of the pictures on his boyhood bedroom wall. It swept away the last of his prickling doubts, there could be no mercy for such a monster.

He filled the gas tank of the Kawasaki, then as he wheeled it into the open he saw Anna coming toward him from the corral, a smile on her face, one hand raised in greeting. She looked fantastic, but maybe it was just the special aura she had for him now. Her warm expression said everything about the difference in her attitude when her father wasn't around. He could see Ingrid still over at the corral, watching them.

"Hi there," he said warily, feeling his way after yesterday.

"You look like you're going somewhere," she said with a smile.

"I have to go into Normanton."

She showed surprise. "Normanton? Something for Dad?"

"No, just some personal business. I checked it out with him. Ritchie says we won't be able to start the south muster until tomorrow."

"That's right." Anna cast him a questioning glance. Perhaps she was also wondering if he was coming back. "Will you be gone long?" she added.

"I should be back by late afternoon."

He mounted the bike, and put his foot on the kick-starter. She stepped forward and laid a hand over his on the handle-bars.

"I'll miss you," she murmured.

It was a reversal of yesterday; she blew hot and cold, and he had to take each mood as it came. He squeezed her hand in return and smiled.

"Maybe I'll see you tonight," she offered.

Jesus, it was sweet temptation; could he really make love to her, then get out of bed and go kidnap her father? He played along anyway.

"You've got something in mind?" he said. "I thought after yesterday . . ."

"Don't tease. I'm sorry about yesterday."

"Of course I'll come," he said. Would he? It wouldn't have mattered a damn if he didn't love her, but surely he risked becoming more screwed up over her than ever if he went.

"We can talk things over; about us," she said. "Have you been thinking about it?"

"All the time," he said, with some truth.

"I love you," she breathed.

"And I love you." He wished it could have been a lie, just a device. He thought of kissing her, but decided against it, especially with Ingrid watching. He could have real trouble from that quarter before he was through. He released her hand and kicked the motor into life; she stood clear, shading her eyes, an expression on her face close to yearning. It was the last sort of image he wanted troubling him on the way to Normanton.

"See you when I get back," he said.

He let out the clutch and eased away so as not to smother her with dust, but didn't look back. She'd obviously been doing some thinking, fitting him out to run Cathedral Rock with her, be a father for Pony—and goddamn it, that was what he would have wanted, too. That was an ache he was just going to have to live with.

Pony knew there would be no helicopter mustering that day, and he felt guilty over neglecting Schon, so he took the horse for an early morning run to the lagoon. In all his life he had never spent such exciting days as he did with Matt. He lay awake long into the night, reliving the thrill of riding the helicopter as it danced about the sky, impatiently waiting for the first dawn light so he could join Matt again.

Oh, Mum and Grandad were okay, even Ingrid at times, but it needed someone like Matt to understand his dreams, the way he really felt about things. Before Matt it had sometimes seemed like he was living by himself, the sky, the savanna, and Schon his only real friends. Schon understood, he could talk to Schon; maybe the horse couldn't answer back, but Pony could tell he knew by the way he shook his head. He was sure he even understood about Matt. Matt was more like a big brother, he didn't treat him like a kid, but a mate, a copilot, a special fair dinkum friend, ready to listen to anything, no matter how stupid it might be. He didn't want to believe Matt would ever go away, and maybe he wouldn't now. They didn't think a kid noticed, but he saw the way Matt and his mother looked at each other sometimes, fooling themselves that no one else could see, and jeez, for him it was just like the promise of an early Christmas present, the best he could ever wish for. He felt like he wanted to run around and yell and throw his arms up in the air, because if they loved each other then Matt would never leave, never, never, and having someone like Matt for a father would be the best thing that ever happened to him, the best ever. 'Course there was a time he thought Matt fancied Ingrid, but he knew that wasn't working out. Matt'd see Ingrid was too bitchy, she could be a real bugger sometimes. No, he and Mum and Matt'd run Cathedral Rock together, and he guessed Ingrid, too, and he'd get to be a helicopter pilot, with Matt sitting beside him and saying, "Pony, you're the best helicopter mustering pilot I've ever seen."

Perhaps he should just sort of let Matt know he could see the way it was, just so he'd know how pleased he was.

When he rode back into the yard, he saw his mother gazing after the long trail of dust that marked the departed Kawasaki. He reined in behind her, and she still stood watching as if she hadn't heard him.

"Where's Matt going?" he asked.

She turned toward him, and he could see that special look in her face again.

"He had to go into Normanton on some business for himself," she replied.

"Will he be gone long?"

"He'll be back this afternoon."

"He didn't say anything to me about going into Normanton."

She smiled. "He doesn't have to tell you everything."

"He could've said about going to Normanton."

"Well he didn't, did he."

He scowled, and ruffled Schon's mane.

"I'm glad to see you giving Schon a run," she added. "You've neglected him since Matt arrived."

"I've . . . I've been giving him a spell," said Pony defensively. "And I've got to learn about the helicopter I reckon."

"You've only got another week before school holidays end anyway."

"Maybe I'll be able to fly by then."

"I doubt it; I've got to learn to fly myself yet."

Pony hesitated. "You like him, don't you, Mum?"

She gave a half smile. "We all like Matt."

"Except Grandad. But I reckon you like him a lot."

She gave an evasive shrug. "He's a nice man."

"Oh I don't mind," put in the boy quickly. "Jeez, no. Fair dinkum, I wish he'd stay for ever and ever."

"I don't know how long he's going to stay," said Anna soberly.

"The rest of your bloody life if you had your way, you bloody bitch," spat Ingrid.

They both turned in surprise, not noticing that Ingrid had come up behind them. Pony had never seen Ingrid look like that, red-eyed, her face all screwed up sort of mad, like she wanted to fight the whole world.

Anna didn't answer for a moment, just coldly appraising her sister, then she motioned to Pony. "You'd better turn Schon out, Pony," she said quietly.

"Don't think you can ignore me, you damn slut," raged Ingrid.

The horse backed nervously away, as if sensing the hostility in Ingrid's voice.

"I think you'd better go somewhere and cool off, before you say something you'll regret," said Anna frostily.

"I don't need to go anywhere and cool off—and I'm not bloody blind, or stupid."

Anna started to walk away, but Ingrid grabbed savagely at her arm and wrenched her back. Anna angrily shook herself free.

"Take your hands off me," she said furiously.

Pony didn't know what to do. He'd seen his mother and aunt have arguments before, but this was different, he'd never seen Ingrid like this, she looked like she wanted to kill his mother. He backed Schon further away, and cast an anxious glance to where he could see his grandfather coming out of the house.

"You just couldn't keep your hands off him, could you, you damned tart," snarled Ingrid. "You fucking tramp, just couldn't help yourself, just had to wiggle your ass and spread your legs to prove you could take him away from your dumb bloody sister."

She was breathing so hard that the words came snorting out of her mouth with the sound of a distressed horse.

"Go and turn Schon out, Pony," demanded Anna.

"Let him stay and hear the truth," fumed Ingrid.

"You're talking like a fool."

"Oh yes, I'm a bloody fool all right; Christ yes, a damn bloody fool, to think you could resist the chance of adding another scalp to your . . . your screwing belt."

"You've got it all wrong, Ingrid. Matt makes up his own mind," replied Anna.

"Oh yeah? Hegarty's a randy asshole, he's like a fly to shit; he'll take any available crotch that waved in front of his eyes, and God, you've been waving yours."

Ingrid was so mad she scarcely knew what she was saying, but Pony understood all right, and Matt wasn't like that, he wasn't. He saw his grandfather had stopped short of the fierce confrontation, alarm on his face, eyes darting from one daughter to the other.

"Enough," shouted Kisek. "Enough, both of you—you are hearing me?"

They didn't hear him, failed to realize he was even there.

"Will you go, Pony," yelled Anna.

"You scared he might hear something you don't want him to know?" taunted Ingrid. "God you want everything, you damn bitch, Cathedral Rock, Hegarty, you've got your bastard son, what more do you want?"

The sudden charged silence was like the brief interval between lightning and the following peal of thunder. Pony backed Schon past his grandfather, he knew the row was in some way over Matt, but he also felt an unexplained fear there was something here he didn't want to hear, didn't want to know.

"Stop them, Grandad," he pleaded.

"Enough you crazy women," shouted Kisek.

Anna hit her sister, a sweeping blow flush into Ingrid's face. She was wrong if she thought it would stem the fire, it acted more like a dash of gasoline. Ingrid uttered a cry like an enraged animal, then lowered her head and charged into Anna's midsection, fists raining punches.

"You bitch! You rutting bitch," she screamed.

They fell to the ground, locked together, rolling over and over in the dirt, Ingrid totally out of control, arms flailing, screaming obscenities, while Anna's fingers clawed at her sister's hair, trying to hold her off.

"Stop them. Jeez, stop them," shouted Pony.

Kisek ran toward them, one hand seizing each woman like a referee trying to separate contestants gone beserk, adding his own German obscenities to the clamor, gradually forcing them to their feet and holding them apart so their heads were thrust back by the strength of his grip, their eyes directed to the sky.

"You crazy, crazy women—stop it, stop it," he bellowed. He shook them until their heads bobbed like puppets. "Mein own daughters behaving like savages—ja, savages. I'm not having it; enough, enough!" He glared from one to the other. "You're hearing me? You're understanding?"

Pony slid down off Schon and stood apprehensively holding the reins, tears welling in his eyes. This was terrible,

terrible, his mother and aunt fighting like wildcats, and he wondered if it'd ever be the same at Cathedral Rock again? "You're listening?" demanded Kisek.

Both sisters nodded as best they could, and Kisek gradually relaxed his grip, then finally let go altogether. Both women were disheveled, coated with dust, hair awry. There was blood on Anna's lip, and the strap of Ingrid's tank top was torn away. They didn't look at each other but glowered at the ground.

"Mein Gott, it's Hegarty, isn't it," said Kisek through gritted teeth. He waved an admonishing finger at each daughter. "You think I'm blind, ja? You think I'm not knowing the sort of man Hegarty is? Always such a man is playing games with stupid women like you—ja, dummkopf women." He gave an angry shake of his head and picked up his whip from where he'd dropped it on the ground. "Saying nothing I have been, hoping you have both sense to see him for what he is." He shook the whip at each in turn. "Using this on him I should have. . . . The hell with him. You think I am putting up with my two daughters behaving like animals to each other? No more, you hear? No more. I'm not caring if he's the best helicopter mustering pilot in the world." He furiously shook the whip in the air. "The best—I'm not caring! I made Cathedral Rock the best cattle station in the Gulf before he came; out of my mind I must have been to hire him, to think we were needing him. We mustered the old way before, and we can do it again. Ja, the hell with Hegarty and his kind. Nothing but trouble it's been for us since he arrived, filling Pony's head with nonsense, thinking my daughters are easy . . . easy tarts." He was working himself into a frenzy, arms waving, scarcely pausing for breath during the tirade. "He goes, you hear me? He goes. As soon as he gets back from Normanton I'm throwing him off Cathedral Rock. He goes, he goes, he goes!"

He glared wrathfully from one daughter to the other, as if daring them to challenge his decision, but neither spoke.

"No words, I'm not listening to anything," he spat at them. "He comes back, and he packs his things, and he gets out."

Ingrid turned abruptly on her heels and strode toward the house without uttering a word.

"OUT," Kisek shouted after her. He focused on Anna, his rage still simmering. "You I'm not understanding," he said with a rasp.

"What's there to understand?" she said rebelliously.

"You I thought would be seeing Hegarty for what he is."

"What is he? You tell me."

"I need to?"

"God, this can't go on; you just watch." She gave a bitter laugh. "You know, it's like coping with a jealous husband, I feel like I'm not my own woman. I'm not going to take it any more, I'll leave Cathedral Rock if I have to. Don't think because . . ."

"You can't take Pony away," he cut in.

"I'll take him any damn place I please."

A flush of anxiety shunted his anger aside. "All I want is to protect you from a man like Hegarty."

"Go to hell," she rebuked him.

She brushed angrily past, and stormed across the yard toward the corral. Kisek looked hesitantly after her, glanced mournfully at Pony, then went silently to the ranch wagon, climbed in, started the engine, and drove slowly away to the west. Gradually the wagon disappeared into the savanna, the sound of the engine faded, and there was just Pony and Schon, as if left stranded in a wasteland in the aftermath of battle.

Pony felt something like death in his heart, his dreams in ashes. The growing excitement that Matt would become his father was gone, shattered. There'd been an empty feeling inside him for a long time now, that he couldn't explain to anyone, like he was hungry, and it didn't matter how much he ate, it never went away. But it had disappeared when Matt arrived. He knew it was useless going to Grandad and pleading for Matt, like he had after Matt took those pictures; he'd never seen his grandfather so mad, he just knew he'd never change his mind.

Even if he maybe threatened to go away with Matt, it wouldn't mean anything, because he knew Matt would never take him. Perhaps after what Mum had said they might just all go away from Cathedral Rock together, but jeez, he'd really hate to leave this place, specially if they went and lived in some big city. If only there was some way he could talk to Matt before Grandad fired him, warn him about what was going to happen, then they might be able to work something out. Bugger; he felt tears again at the awful thought of never seeing Matt again, and he quickly wiped at his eyes.

He slowly walked Schon across to the corral while he thought about it. He couldn't ride Schon all the way into Normanton, bugger no, but maybe he could wait somewhere, and meet Matt as he was coming back. Grandad's old house could be just the place; he'd maybe hide there and watch back along the road, then when he saw Matt coming he'd ride out to meet him. He took the saddle off, and laid it by the side of the corral, excited by the idea. His mother was across on the other side of the corral, her back to him, just standing with her arms folded, staring out to the horizon. He reckoned he'd better leave her alone for now, she was probably pretty upset at what had happened. He couldn't imagine how her and Ingrid would ever make up after a fight like that. By the time he'd turned Schon into the corral his mind was made up. He'd do it all right, go over to the old house later on, but he wouldn't say anything to anyone, not even Mum, and just wait there for Matt. There had to be something they could work out together.

The entire house seemed to shudder, Ingrid slammed the study door so hard. She locked it, then went and slumped in the chair at the desk. She'd made no attempt to change or clean up after the fight, the broken strap still hung from her shoulder, her long hair tangled and laced with dust. She was conscious of a swelling under her left eye, but her fury anesthetized all pain.

She picked up the telephone, but her hand trembled so much she was forced to put it down a moment. She took a deep breath, and tried to bring herself under control. The bitch. The bitch! Even without Hegarty this explosion had been building for a long time, it had just taken the American bastard to bring it to a head. It had been damn impossible ever since she'd seen him coming out of Anna's bedroom; she'd scarcely been able to look at her sister, let alone speak to her. She wasn't going to spend the rest of her life letting Anna bloody well walk all over her; she and Hegarty screwing away like crazy, laughing at her, taking her for an idiot. And her father carrying on like some outraged sanctimonious clown. He didn't give a damn who Hegarty was screwing, he was just looking for an excuse to get rid of the American asshole.

All last night she'd lain awake, turning ideas over in her mind to get back at them, to make them pay for making a fool of her, yet resolved nothing, even frightened by some of the murderous thoughts eating like worms into her brain. But learning about Hegarty going into Normanton had sparked a marvelous idea, which would at least pay off part of what she owed that bastard. Anna could come later. God, she'd think of something to push her right out of Cathedral Rock—find a way to poison her father's doting faith in his eldest daughter. But for now it was a delicious thought to call Red Orton in Normanton, and tell him all about Hegarty and Anna screwing like a couple of dogs on heat. Orton would go off his head. As far as she was concerned Red was a hulking, muscle-bound buffoon, but he had the size to tear Hegarty to shreds. Everyone in Normanton knew about Red Orton's obsessive crush on Anna, going around boasting it was only a matter of time before Anna married him; they knew too that Anna despised him. It would have been funny, except that Orton threatened to crack the skull of any other man in the district who even looked at Anna. His crazy, aggressive jealousy was one of the reasons Anna rarely went to Normanton; she couldn't stand the man, even had the police warn him against pestering her, but he was too thick in the head to believe Anna was doing anything else but playing hard to get. At least he never came out to Cathedral Rock; he knew he risked a shotgun blast from her father. God, he'd want to kill Hegarty when he found out about Anna.

She took several deep breaths, picked up the phone again, ignored the quiver still in her hands, and dialed the number of the National Hotel. If she knew Orton, he'd be in the bar at this time of day.

"Yeah, Red's here," said the barman. "I'll get him for you."

She waited, rehearsing her words.

"Yeah, who is it?" growled Orton.

She had a quick image of the man, hairy-chested, cigarette dangling from his mouth, not only looking like an ape, but sounding like an ape, and she curbed her distaste.

"Ingrid Kisek," she murmured silkily, as if to a confidante. "From out at Cathedral Rock."

"G'day Ingrid. How's your beautiful sister out there? Haven't seen her for a while."

"That's what I'm calling about. I'm worried about her."

"If Anna's got some problem, then I'm the man to fix it; bloody oath."

She chose her words carefully. "I suppose you've heard about the American helicopter mustering pilot we've got working for us out here?"

"Jesus, who hasn't? That's a bloody surprise. Your old man must be getting soft in his old age. He's never hired any bastard for as long as I can remember."

"The Yank's hassling her, Red."

There was a pause at the other end of the line. "What d'you mean hassling?" asked Orton menacingly.

"Well, I don't want to be one telling tales, but . . . I think she's gone off her head where he's concerned."

A strangled quality came into Orton's voice. "Off her head? Christ, that doesn't sound like Anna."

"This Yank's making a fool of her, Red. We can all see it, and it's worrying us sick. He's just using her."

"Using her how?"

"He's . . . he's screwing her, Red." She managed to convey a feeling of distress. "He's just going to throw her aside like an old cow when he leaves, and she's going to be badly hurt."

There was a long pause. Orton was probably gripping the phone so tight, she wouldn't have been surprised to hear the sound of it splitting apart. "I'll come out there, and break the fuckin' bastard's neck," he finally managed to get out.

"You don't have to come all the way out here. The Yank's on his way into Normanton now."

"Then I'll break his neck when he gets here. I'll send him back to Yankland in a bloody box."

"Hey, don't get yourself into real trouble with a murder charge," she said quickly. "No killing, God, nothing like that. I'm just thinking of Anna, that's all. I just think it would be best for her, for all of us, if he doesn't come back to Cathedral Rock. You understand, Red?"

"Just leave him to me," said Orton thickly. She suppressed qualms from the ugliness in his voice. "I'll take the shithead apart," he added. "How'll I know him?"

"His name's Hegarty, Matt Hegarty. Tall thin guy in his mid thirties, black hair. He's wearing a blue checked shirt and jeans, and he's riding a Kawasaki motorbike. You should be able to see him from the hotel when he rides in."

"Gotcha," Orton said. "I'll fix it so he never bothers Anna, or anyone else for that matter. I'll stuff his bloody cock down his throat." An aggrieved tone entered his voice. "Jeez, it doesn't sound like Anna; the bastard must've really pitched her a line. No bloody Yank is going to treat my girl like she's some damn tart." He almost choked on the final sentence.

The term "my girl" was a figment of his imagination, but Ingrid knew this wasn't the time to refute it. "I really appreciate it, Red. I've been so worried about what's been going on."

"I'll fix the creep—an' thanks for tipping me off, Ingrid. Bloody oath."

She hung up, and sagged back in the chair. So much for smartass Hegarty. She'd seen Orton in a fight once, he was like a brawling gorilla, hamlike fists mercilessly pounding his opponent senseless. Yet now it was done she felt no sense of the satisfaction she expected from revenge. She knew it was Hegarty—it wasn't over, she wasn't cured. Damn him. Damn him! Why did he ever have to come here? It made no sense to both hate and want someone at the same time, but that was how she was caught. Wishing him to hell, yet aching with the thought of never seeing him again. Tears formed streaky rivulets through the grime on her face, and she was suddenly overwhelmed by misgivings for what she'd done. She stubbornly shut it out, angrily brushing away the tears. The bastard had it coming, she wasn't going to be tossed aside like an old used shoe. It'd be easier for her to get over it once he

was gone, she'd have to, even if she suspected he'd remain in
part of her mind like an irremovable stain. She had to concentrate on what to do about Anna now.

So much had happened, Hegarty found it hard to believe
it was only a few days since he'd traveled the Normanton road.
He knew he'd subtly changed since then, and not only because
of Anna and Pony. The emptiness and isolation that had struck
him so forcibly on the way out seemed irrelevant now; he felt
a sense of ease with the country, like the forming of a
friendship you know will endure. He shrugged. It could only
be another experience to slot away in his memory file.

He enjoyed the ride. A few lonely clouds straggled in the
sky, and again he found the breeze an effective cooling system,
clearing his mind. He wasn't too concerned about making the
contact with Reine. That wily old bird would have something
figured out.

As so often happens on a return journey, it seemed to go
faster this time, and he was soon back on the Cloncurry Road,
with the buildings of Normanton in sight, bracing himself
against the passing rush of monstrous road trains roaring south
with their multitrailer loads of cattle. It was just before noon
when he cruised into the main street, so he headed straight for
the railway station. The town still moved at a sedate country
pace, even if there seemed to be more curious eyes trailing
him this time. He guessed old Snowy Cutmore had probably
broken the story, over a beer or two, about the Yank helicopter
mustering pilot trying for a job with the eccentric German.
And the town mystified at his getting it.

The Gulflander was already in sight when he pulled up at
the station, weaving and swaying across the grasslands like a
threatened snake scuttling for cover. He propped the bike by
a parked bus, with a driver dozing at the wheel, then strolled
into the cavernous station and positioned himself near an
ancient seat. It was as he remembered: the great curving iron
roof, the overhead girders, the old posters on the wall, the
wind funneling through with a hollow drumming sound. There
was an elderly couple at the other end, appraising him with
curious stares, but he ignored them.

The clanking, wheezing train crawled into the station, its throbbing engine muted, passengers in obvious city clothes at the windows, cameras poised as the train squealed to a halt. Hegarty faked disinterest, examining an old Pears Soap poster, as the tourists spilled from the train, laughing, chattering, calling to each other. There appeared to be around twenty in the group, predominantly middle-aged, all in casual clothes, with a mixture of Australian, Japanese, and American accents.

He turned slightly, searching for the Mossad man, and just for a moment failed to recognize Reine circling the rim of the group, a folded newspaper under his arm. Hegarty restrained a grin. He'd never seen Reine in anything but a conservative business suit, and he looked so out of character in casual clothes. He knew Reine had seen him, even though he gave no outward sign.

A fiftyish man in shirt and tie held one hand aloft for attention. "Just a moment ladies and gentlemen, if you please," he called. He was obviously the tour leader. The chatter gradually subsided, and the tourists gathered about him. Reine was so close Hegarty could have touched him.

"Welcome to Normanton," began the tour leader, "the heart of the Gulf cattle industry, and the capital of the Gulf Country." He pointed to the roof. "If it seems a grandiose station for a small, once-a-week train, then we have to go back to 1889, when gold was discovered at Croydon, where we boarded the train. Normanton was the chief port then, and thousands of miners were rushing to the gold fields. This line was built to take them. Those were Normanton's great days, the streets were crowded with miners out to make their fortune."

Reine disdainfully dropped the newspaper on the seat, as if he had no further use for it, and moved to a different position. A tall, good-looking man about forty, who held himself like a soldier at attention, was standing close to Reine, and he glanced casually at the discarded newspaper, at Hegarty, then back at the tour leader. The tour leader continued on with the history of the station and the area, but none of the words registered with Hegarty; he was certain the Leiman fingerprint file was in the newspaper, but he forced himself not

to look at it. The man made him nervous, but he seemed to
take no further interest, concentrating his attention on the
tour leader.

"Now there's a bus waiting for us outside," said the tour
leader, "which will take us to visit all the interesting points of
this historic town. Then we'll be having lunch at one of
Normanton's best hotels."

The leader moved to the exit, with the tourists shuffling
dutifully in his wake, and again there was a buzz of conversation. Hegarty could see Reine in the center of the group,
animatedly talking to a silver-haired woman, making no attempt to look back, clearly confident Hegarty understood the
significance of the newspaper.

Hegarty waited until the last tourist had passed through
the door, then casually picked up the newspaper, placing it
under his arm so that just enough showed for Reine to see he
had it, and followed them out. They were already lining up at
the bus door, with Reine near the end of the line, and this time
the elderly agent permitted himself an indifferent glance at
Hegarty for confirmation, then turned quickly away. Yet there
was something in the glance Hegarty failed to grasp, until he
saw the Kawasaki lying on its side, and a large man standing
over it, muscular arms folded, one foot resting on the bike in
the stance of a hunter posing with his kill. The man gave the
impression of preparing to pound his chest and throw his head
back with a Tarzan cry of victory. He looked to be in his late
thirties, a thatch of unruly red hair topping a large head, set
with small, belligerent features, and a prominent jaw jutting
aggressively toward Hegarty. He had the color of a man who
spends his life in the sun. Heavy, scuffed boots, stained jeans,
and a tee shirt that had been once white covered a body that
obviously outweighed and outreached Hegarty. His distended
belly denoted an overfondness for beer. He could have been
hacked from the craggy cliffs of Cathedral Rock—just as tough,
just as mean.

The man made no attempt to move as Hegarty strolled
slowly to the bike, his scowl deepening, watching as if
counting every step. Hegarty stopped just short of the bike,
looked askance at the heavy boot planted on the gas tank, then
with deliberation raised his eyes to the man's face.

"Would you mind taking your goddamn foot off my bike?" he said with a rasp.

"You're the fuckin' Yank called Hegarty aren't you, who's workin' out at old Kisek's place," snarled the man.

Hegarty carefully took in the man before answering. He hadn't the remotest idea what this was all about, but the man was clearly out to make big trouble. If he had any brawling skill to go with his size, then Hegarty figured he could be in for a tough time. "Yes, that's me," he said. "Who wants to know?"

The man unfolded his arms and stabbed at his chest with a calloused thumb. "Red Orton, if it's anything to you, asshole."

Hegarty tried to ignore the provocation. A fight was the last thing he wanted, but what the hell was this all about?

"Well, you've obviously got a problem, Red," he said evenly. "Just take your foot off my bike, and maybe we can talk it over."

Hegarty was aware that the line of tourists had stopped moving toward the bus entrance, curiously watching the confrontation.

Orton kicked viciously at the bike. "No, *you've* got the fuckin' problem, Yank. One big fuckin' problem. You won't be needin' the bike any more."

"You aiming to steal it, Red?"

"No; I'm goin' to leave it here to bloody well rot, y'know that? Just as a warnin' to any other smartass Yank who thinks he can come into the fuckin' Gulf Country and start screwin' around with our women."

Our women? Did this obnoxious hulk know Ingrid? Or Anna? How the hell would he know what was going on at Cathedral Rock?

"I don't know what you're talking about," growled Hegarty. "Now get your goddamn boot off my bike."

"Bloody hell you don't know what I'm talkin' about. No one makes a fool outa my girl Anna while I'm around, bloody oath, an' if he does I'll beat him into a pile of shit."

Anna? His girl? Hegarty couldn't believe Anna would give a bullying hulk like this clown the time of day. It had to be Kisek's doing, this was a setup to get rid of him. It didn't make sense, why didn't Kisek just fire him?

"No one's making a fool of Anna," he retorted.

"Well, I know fuckin' different," snarled Orton. "You got two choices, shithead. You can plant your ass on the Gulf-lander, and wait until it carts you outa here, or I'll mash you into fuckin' pulp, and then *carry* you on the bloody train." His boot thudded into the Kawasaki again, small eyes rolling with malice, hands clenched into battering-ram fists, face florid, ugly mouth spitting out each threatening word like fired bullets. It forced Hegarty to realize that if he wanted the bike back he was going to have to fight for it, and he was going to have to win. There wasn't time to worry about who'd put the sonofabitch up to picking the fight with him. Orton was much bigger, but he had him figured for a street brawler, and he'd learned a long time ago how to counter those tactics. You had to get in first. That blown out belly had to be the weak point. He crouched down to carefully lodge the newspaper into some old rusted railing, then straightened, and stepped closer to the bike. He halted, and warily balanced himself.

"It'd take more than a loud-mouthed sonofabitch like you to run me out of Normanton," he said softly.

Orton gave a raucous laugh. "Jeez, so you want it the hard way, eh Yank?" He gloatingly rubbed his hands together. "I was hopin' you would, asshole; almost prayin' for it, you know that? Just so I could have the fun of makin' your face look like bloody chopped liver."

From behind, a woman squealed, while a man laughingly claimed it was all part of the tour. Then without warning Hegarty lashed out with his foot, the heel of his boot crunching against Orton's shin. The surprise on Orton's face registered as forcefully as the pain. Yet in a way the maneuver failed, for when Hegarty stepped across the bike to smash his fist into the man's belly he was out of range, staggering backward, clasping at his leg, mouth wide with a bellowing scream of agony, and he avoided the full impact of the punch.

"You fuckin' bastard," Orton ranted. "I'll kill you—bloody kill you." Rage seemed to deaden the pain in his leg. He twisted surprisingly fast for a man his size, and brought a haymaker swinging from somewhere behind his back, a giant fist rushing toward Hegarty's face like a runaway road train.

Hegarty ducked, but it still caught him a glancing blow on the shoulder, sending him sprawling to the ground. He rolled as he fell, avoiding a large boot whizzing past inches from his head, then Orton flung his great bulk down on him, pressing him into the dirt so he could scarcely breathe, huge hands locking about his throat, then dragging him up as if he was a helpless rabbit, and thumping his head repeatedly into the ground.

"You bastard. You fuckin' Yank asshole," he roared. "I'll beat the bloody life outa you."

"Stop him, please stop him!" a woman screamed.

Hegarty's brains scrambled with every jolt, but he fought to keep cool, breaking a hand free, stiffening it for a karate blow, then with all his force chopping viciously at the side of Orton's neck. Once. Twice. It had an immediate effect, Orton's eyes glazed, he moaned, then flopped to one side, coughing, spluttering blood, hands clasped at his neck. He attempted to unsteadily lever himself to his knees.

"Bloody Yank. I'll . . . I'll . . ." he moaned.

Hegarty knew it would be crazy to let the man get up. He could be as good a street fighter as anyone, and there was too much riding on this to give any quarter. Without pause he smashed his fist into Orton's face, again, and again, and again, until his hands were red with Orton's blood, then he pulled back, and with all his old football skill sent his boot thudding into the man's pudgy belly. Orton collapsed and lay softly moaning, a bloody halo forming on the ground about his head.

Hegarty staggered back apace, gasping for breath, aware the watching tourists had been stunned into silence. Even Reine failed to mask his concern.

"My God, oh my God," cried the silver-haired woman.

"Hey, does this happen for every tour group passing through Normanton?" asked an elderly man, with a shaky laugh.

"You sure put paid to that son-of-a-bitch's hash, bud," proclaimed a flat American accent from behind Hegarty.

Hegarty wiped at his face with the back of his hand, ran quivering fingers through his hair, and turned back to the Kawasaki. One of the tourists had lifted the bike to an upright position, a squat, broad-shouldered man, hair tinged gray with the onset of middle age, features vaguely reminiscent of the Indians Hegarty had seen around Arizona. He gave Hegarty a hawkish grin and held out the newspaper.

"Just thought I'd take care of this for you while you were handling that hoodlum." He gave a wink. "We Yanks have got to stick together, eh man?" he added softly.

Hegarty nodded thanks, took the newspaper, and accepted the weight of the bike. His neck muscles felt as if they'd been rubbed raw with sandpaper, and he'd be lucky if there wasn't any bruising.

"You gonna be okay, bud?" inquired the man solicitously.

Hegarty nodded again, and glanced back at the prostrate Orton. The other tourist he'd seen standing beside Reine earlier was now kneeling beside Orton, trying to prop him into a sitting position, and examining the man's bloodied face. Orton's eyes were closed, but his mouth moved with effort, dribbling blood and profane threats about Hegarty he was beyond putting into action.

"Maybe I should check and see if he's okay," muttered Hegarty. The last thing he wanted was any trouble with the local police if the man was seriously hurt; after all, he was an outsider.

The tourist slapped him reassuringly on the shoulder. "I happen to know that guy with the hoodlum knows a lot about things like that," he said. "Leave it to him, he'll take care of it." He offered a friendly grin. "Christ, you couldn't kill a sonofabitch like that with a goddamn axe. Why don't you play it smart, and get the hell out of here. I saw the way he picked the fight—the jerk had it coming."

Hegarty nodded uncertainly. Orton was shaking his head, still mumbling inaudible threats, spraying blood. The tourists gathered at the bus were still mute with shock, and there was an expression on Reine's face that told Hegarty the advice was sound, he should get the hell out of here.

The tour leader began to bustle about the group like a mustering ringer, waving his hands, clearly as taken aback by the fight as his charges.

"Come on, come on now, ladies and gentlemen, the

excitement's over. Believe me, Normanton's not like this, not at all, and we have a schedule to stick to. Please now, on the bus."

Hegarty carefully inserted the newspaper inside his shirt, straddled the bike, and started the motor. The American tourist again slapped him on the shoulder.

"Good luck to you, bud; you can bat on my team anytime. Hell yeah, any time at all."

Hegarty gave a pale smile of thanks, let in the clutch, and slowly rode around the bus, conscious of staring eyes following him, then headed toward the town. Christ, Reine would be furious; the last thing he'd want at the contact point would be a bloody dog fight like that attracting attention. He shook his head in bewilderment. The fight obviously had something to do with Anna, but who had set it up for the goddamn brawling gorilla to attack him? If it was Kisek, it made no sense for the German to be that vindictive, unless he was on to him, but he refused to believe that. Then who else? Ingrid? It was possible, he figured he'd made a bad enemy there, but was she venomous enough to pull a stunt like this? Maybe, with the way she felt about Anna. Someone was in for one hell of a disappointment when he showed up back at Cathedral Rock in one piece, but he decided against making an issue of it. He'd know soon enough by the look on their face who it was, but it'd be better to let it pass than brew up a storm that would only get in the way.

He stopped a mile past the Burketown turnoff, when he was a solitary figure on the landscape, took out the newspaper, and unfolded it. There was an envelope taped to one of the inside pages, and he quickly opened it. Inside were several sheets of paper, one showing a set of fingerprints, with a scrawled notation at the side:

"Matt: I've verified these fingerprints with Berlin police files. They were evidently taken when Leiman was arrested as a young man, when he was involved in a Berlin political street riot before the war. Poor Eli got it right, I'm certain they're Leiman's fingerprints. Good luck to you and Jules with the comparison test, and with the removal operation. Look forward to seeing you both in Tel Aviv. Regards, Andre."

The other pages were photocopies of the record of Leiman's arrest in Berlin.

Hegarty gave a grunt of satisfaction, even with the unexpected brawl, it had all turned out all right. But the mention of Eli Brandt revived that uneasy feeling. He still wished he knew who the hell had killed him. And why.

Chapter 12

The tour leader clucked his tongue impatiently, foot tapping, and gestured to Corliss, still kneeling by the battered Orton, helping to mop the blood from his face. Sometimes he wondered why he stayed with this job, people could be so damn difficult at times, everything had to go to schedule or the tour became a shambles.

"I'm sorry, but I think I should stay with this man a little longer," said Corliss. "Just to make sure he's okay. Believe me, I know about these things, and I wouldn't feel right if he had any serious injuries."

"It's not really any of our business, Mr. Corliss. If two hooligans decide they have to try and belt each other senseless, then that's their affair. I've got a tour to run."

Corliss nodded in the direction of the town. "Why don't you go on, and we'll catch up with you at the hotel. I can't just leave him lying here."

The tour leader glanced anxiously to the bus, where everyone else was seated waiting.

"Well, if you think it's absolutely necessary."

"I certainly do."

"I can send someone from the hospital."

"That's a good idea." Corliss indicated Jaroff. "My friend and I'll wait here until they come."

The tour leader reluctantly shrugged agreement. "It's all very responsible, Mr. Corliss, but I know how tough these people are, and . . ."

"I don't mind. I just think I should do it," replied Corliss sharply.

The tour leader hesitated a moment, then began to withdraw toward the bus. "All right, if you insist. I'll get someone up from the hospital as soon as I can." He gave a sour smile. "It's very good of both of you."

Corliss shrugged, and returned the smile.

The tour leader went to the bus, gave an uncertain wave before boarding, then the driver started the engine and maneuvered around the aftermath of the fight. Every pair of eyes on board was focused on the scene as if it were a television drama. Corliss watched as the bus drove slowly toward the center of the town.

"Let . . . let me get up on my fuckin' feet," growled Orton thickly, spitting blood.

"Just take it easy for a while," soothed Corliss.

"I ain't bloody well finished with that bastard Yank yet," muttered Orton. "Christ no." He wiped at his mouth with the back of his hand, then stared at the blood. "Fuckin' bastard took me by surprise. Jesus, I'll tell you, that wouldn't happen again; I'd use a bloody bottle on the shit next time."

"Who is he?" asked Corliss.

"Some Yank bastard called Hegarty." He glanced blearily at Corliss, then at Jaroff standing off to the side. "You sound like bloody Yanks yourselves."

"Sure, sure, but we're not all like that son-of-a-bitch," put in Jaroff. "No sir, we're just trying to make up for what the jerk did to you, ah, Mr. . . . ?"

"Red," muttered Orton, shaking his head, "Red Orton."

"Hegarty from around here, Red?" asked Corliss.

"Nah, came in here a coupla days ago. Been helicopter mustering out at a cattle station called Cathedral Rock. Fuckin' creep's been screwin' around with my girl out there."

"I can see why that pissed you off," said Jaroff. "Sure would me, I'll tell you. Hell yes."

"Bloody oath it did," growled Orton. "And I'll still finish the bastard. There'll be another time, and the bastard won't be so lucky, I'll make bloody sure of it." He squirmed around on his broad buttocks. "You two blokes gonna help me up?"

They positioned themselves at each side and heaved the bloodied hulk to his feet, as if pushing a massive rock into place, then tentatively supported him as he swayed unsteadily on his feet.

"You think you'll be okay?" asked Corliss.

Orton pawed at his face with red hands, but the bleeding had stopped. "My gut hurts," he groaned. "Jesus, I'll really clobber that bastard next time."

"You think he's coming back?" inquired Jaroff.

"He's got to come back sometime when he leaves the fuckin' Gulf. He can't hide out at old Kisek's place forever."

"Kisek?" asked Corliss.

"Yeah; he's the bloke owns Cathedral Rock station where Hegarty's mustering. Old German bastard, came out here years ago." He brushed his hands through his hair, then bent forward and rested his hands on his knees. "Old bastard's never hired anyone to work for him in his whole bloody life. I'll tell you, there's gotta be something fuckin' funny goin' on out there for him to take on Hegarty. Crazy old Kisek had a bloody helicopter out there for Christ knows how long, with no one flyin' the bloody thing, then he hires this Yank bastard to fly it for him. Bloody funny if you ask me."

"Your girl lives out at this Cathedral Rock, eh?" asked Corliss.

"Yeah. Kisek's got a coupla daughters out there, and one of 'em's my girl." Orton straightened, and glared from one man to the other. "I oughta go out there and blow the shit's head off with a shotgun." He irritably shook off their hands, and began to stumble toward the town.

"Hey, you'd better rest up here for a bit," Corliss called. "They're sending someone up from the hospital to take a look at you."

Orton waved a derisive paw back at them. "The hell with the bloody hospital, I don't need anyone. No Yank bastard's goin' to put me down for the count, not in a bloody month of Sundays. A coupla beers is all I need to fix me up—yeah, bloody oath."

Corliss and Jaroff stood and watched as he shambled unsteadily down the road, weaving from side to side, occasionally wiping at his face, leaving a trail of bloody spit in his wake.

"Crazy son-of-a-bitch," muttered Jaroff.

Corliss shrugged. "Let him go, Sam." He uttered a harsh laugh. "He can't tell us any more, but God, what a break." He thumbed toward the sky. "Someone up there is watching out for us, Sam, you'd think that fight was specially arranged for us. We hit the jackpot. Kisek's here all right, and running a cattle ranch called Cathedral Rock." He smacked his fist repeatedly into the palm of his hand. "What a break," he said gleefully. "Tailing Reine all the way from London really paid off; Christ, it's all set up for us, Sam."

"Maybe we should have got Orton to tell us where this Cathedral Rock is, Colonel."

"Doesn't matter. We'll make a few inquiries. Everyone's sure to know of the place, if Kisek's been around a long time. Hegarty has to be Reine's Mossad contact. Did you get a chance to look inside the newspaper?"

"There was an envelope taped to one of the pages."

"You left it there?"

"Sure. Like you said, sir: if I found anything, let it be." He gave Corliss a puzzled glance. "If it was the fingerprints maybe I should have taken it out. It would have stalled them for a while, really thrown 'em."

Corliss firmly shook his head. "No. Even without the fingerprints they'd still kidnap Kisek, or Leiman, if you want to call him that. We've got to put the sonofabitch away for keeps. That's all we're interested in, Sam. It's got to be the fingerprints you saw inside the newspaper."

"We go out to this Cathedral Rock, and blow him away, right Colonel?"

"It's got to be done right; it's got to be planned well. What about Hegarty's motorcycle?"

Jaroff sniggered. "No sweat. Those two jerks were so busy trying to beat the shit out of each other, it was dead easy to slip the bug under the back wheel guard. There's no way Hegarty's going to spot it, unless he goes looking for it, and he's got no reason to start looking."

Corliss gave a nod of approval. "You're the goddamn best, Sam. As far as possible, I want to know where this Hegarty is every moment until we terminate Leiman. From what I picked up from Reine's London call to Tel Aviv, there's another Mossad agent in this area working with Hegarty. We're going to have to watch ourselves with those guys. I don't want to tangle with the Mossad if I can possibly avoid it."

He fell pensively silent, staring down the road to where

the forlorn figure of Red Orton was still in sight, head bowed, but now walking a straighter path. He pointed in Orton's direction.

"I figure we're going to have to move fast, Sam," he muttered. "We can't afford to waste time hanging around Normanton."

"You figure the Mossad'll be aiming to take Leiman out fast?"

"Sure of it. They've got a ship waiting off the coast, with a helicopter ready to go. Once they've checked the finger-prints for a match, they'll move. For all we know, maybe even by tonight."

"That doesn't leave us much time. How do you want to play it, Colonel?"

"First we quit the tour, give the tour guy some story about how we find this place so interesting we want to stay on for a time—you know, see more of the country. Then we get ourselves a vehicle; there's got to be a rental place around here somewhere."

"The tour guy isn't going to like it."

"Tough. I'll leave it with you to find us a four-wheel drive, Sam. I figure that's what we'll need in this sort of country."

"Sure, Colonel. And I'll pick up our luggage." He grinned. "It was smart bringing the receiver, we sure as hell need it now, with the bug on Hegarty's bike." He glanced around. "You're right about the country, I've never seen anything like this; man, it seems to go on forever."

"We won't be hanging around, Sam. We do the job, and we get out."

Jaroff patted at his colored shirt and fawn pants. "Tell you, my old lady wouldn't believe it to see me in this gear we brought in Brisbane."

"It's important to look the part, Sam."

"Sure. I'm looking forward to trying out those .30/30 Winchesters. Jeez, they were as easy to buy here as back home; a lot of hunting out here, I guess."

"You'll get your chance, Sam."

Jaroff's mouth curved in an ugly grin. "Like the old Nam days, eh Colonel?"

"Yeah, but this one we win."

"Sure, but do we get any thanks this time?"

"Don't worry, it'll work for us, I'll make goddamn sure of it."

They began to move toward the town, walking at a steady pace, looking for all the world like avid Gulf Country tourists, in their casual clothes.

"That Hegarty's a tough sonofabitch," mused Jaroff. "Christ, he really handled that Orton character. He'll need some watching, Colonel."

"Like I said, I'm hoping we don't have to tangle with the Mossad guys. But if it comes to it, then we've got surprise on our side. They won't know what hit 'em."

Jaroff scrubbed thoughtfully at his chin. "You're right, dammit yeah. You and me, we can take anyone, Colonel."

They came to the sealed section of the road, then into the main street. The bus was in front of the Burns Philp Company building, and the tourists were grouped around the tour leader, who was gesturing to the nineteenth-century structure. Corliss could see Reine, leaning forward to pay attention, still playing the enthusiastic tourist. He even felt disappointed with the old guy: he had such a formidable reputation, but not for one moment had he got wise to the fact he was being tailed all the way from London. It was time the Mossad turned him out to grass.

Further down the street he could see the two-story building called the National Hotel. That would be the most likely place to make a few discreet enquiries about directions to Cathedral Rock. He experienced a warm feeling of well-being, that old instinct that told him an operation was going to succeed. He'd better send a wire to Gormane, to let him know he'd located Leiman. That should cure the security advisor's insomnia.

Pony kept to his decision to say nothing to anyone. He stayed in his room for a good part of the morning, telling his mother he was getting things ready for the start of school. Zara made him a sandwich, but no one else was in for lunch, and Carl was probably just sleeping. Grandad, Ingrid, and his mother were all off somewhere. The south paddock was short of water, so they were probably all over there trying to work something out.

The more he thought about Matt, the more determined he became to see him before Grandad had a chance to fire him. Jeez, he just couldn't let that happen; he wouldn't say it to his mother, but Matt meant almost as much to him as she did. Matt was smart, he'd know what to do, all he had to do was wait by the old house until he saw Matt coming.

There was still no one around when he saddled up Schon. The colt was skittish, throwing his head about, stamping impatiently with an eagerness to be going, as if looking forward to sharing the adventure. Once mounted, there was no need to spur the horse, just give him a direction, and let him go.

The joy Pony always felt on Schon deserted him this time, he could only think about Matt—him and Matt fixing the stockyards; him and Matt in the helicopter; Matt and his mother. Time passed without his knowing, the savanna flying past under Schon's hooves, then he was suddenly having to drag on the reins to stop Schon from galloping right on past the old house.

He coaxed the horse to a trot, then finally to a walk, letting him pick his own way through the old rotting fence posts, the tangle of rusting wire half-buried in the grass. He reined to a halt by the tree. The horse was breathing hard from the unrestrained dash across the savanna, and Pony spent time soothing him, scratching him around the ears the way he liked. Then he slid out of the saddle, tied the reins to one of the old posts, and rubbed at Schon's neck as he stood looking at the ruins.

It'd been a while since he was last here, but he remembered it had been with his mother, listening to her talk of the times she'd spent here when she was just his age. Then the old place had seemed exciting, full of dark secrets, maybe a hideout for bank robbers, or even ghosts. It could have been because of Matt, but now it just made him feel kind of sad; somehow it was like Carl, all lived out and rotting, and falling down, and no one caring any more. Maybe he should try and be nicer to Carl. Bugger—it couldn't be any fun having a scarred face like that.

There was no sign of a telltale spiral of dust that would

show Matt was coming. Pony was sure it would be some time yet. He went across to the dilapidated doorway and stepped inside. This was the room his mother told him she'd played games, and he tried to imagine what sort of games she played, what she'd looked like then. He went further into the room, peering around at the refuse, hearing things scuttling in the dark corners. He came to a wary halt. Snakes liked places like this, there was probably lots of rats and mice to catch. When he looked back to the doorway he could see his footprints in the thick dust—and alongside, other footprints, much larger than his. And just as fresh. That puzzled him. Grandad never came here; he'd once heard him tell his mother he liked to be forgetting the past. And the footprints looked too big to belong to Ingrid or his mother. Ghosts didn't leave footprints. Maybe there *were* bank robbers here, on the run from the cops down south.

He followed the footprints into the next room, where they stopped at the old trapdoor. He knew about the cellar, his mother had shown it to him, explained how Grandad had used it as some sort of freezer to keep the meat fresh. Now there was a light coming from somewhere down in the hole, shining through so it showed up the shape of the trapdoor. He hesitated. Maybe he shouldn't do anything, just go back and tell Grandad, and Ritchie; but then he wouldn't be able to wait here for Matt. He grinned. Mum was always telling him he had too much imagination, seeing things that weren't there, and it was probably a trick of the light in some way. He lifted up the trapdoor, and cautiously peered down into the cellar. He couldn't see anything, so he crouched low, craning his neck below floor level, until he could see blankets laid out like a bed, and there was some sort of equipment set up on a table.

Then something seized him from behind, something so strong, and so fierce, he couldn't move, couldn't struggle, dragging him back from the cellar, and his mind flooded with terror. Oh jeez, oh jeez, there were bank robbers here after all, he thought. He tried to struggle, but no one had ever held him so tightly, it was like being locked in Grandad's vice, and then he was being pushed down the steps. He tried to yell, but a hand clamped hard over his mouth so he could scarcely breathe, and he caught a glimpse of a face he'd never seen before. That added to his terror: a fierce face, all dark, with terrible eyes and a black beard, and he thought jeez, jeez, it's the devil—that's what it is, it's the devil old Mrs. Park used to talk about in church, and I'm being dragged down to hell, and I'll never see Matt again, ever . . . ever.

Washington.

Gormane put the cable back in his pocket, and studied his wife sitting opposite him at the small dining table. For once there were no guests, but she still liked it formal—candelabra in the center, the best dinnerware, the black dress she felt showed off her figure best. It was always the same. "Darling you never know when someone's going to drop by, you know the way it is," she said to him once. "And after all, you are the security advisor to the President of the United States."

He let it pass, she liked to do it, but it would be nice every now and then if he could just kick off his shoes, undo his tie, and have a club sandwich sprawled out on the couch. Maybe that was a more fitting way for an accessory to murder to behave. He might engage in doublespeak with colleagues, with the media, even sometimes with the President, who preferred unpleasant reality doused in soothing syrup, but it was ridiculous to use doublespeak to himself.

Corliss had found Leiman in Australia, and he was going to kill him. It was as simple as that, and he could rationalize all he liked that Leiman was only human scum, but even scum deserved a trial, that's what it was all about. Or at least that's what he thought he believed it was all about.

He knew he wasn't going to lift a finger to stop Corliss, he just couldn't bring himself to throw away his life like that.

"You're very quiet, dear," said his wife. "You don't care for the dinner?"

He dabbed quickly at his mouth. "No, the dinner's fine, Lorene, just fine."

"The wine?"

"The wine's excellent."

"Things on your mind then?"

He manufactured a martyred sigh. "You know that's the way it is sometimes. It's been a pretty tough six months."

She put down her fork, and chewed rhythmically until her mouth was clear. Then, "I think we should try and get away for a few days," she said.

He showed surprise. "That could be a little difficult right now."

"You talked about it yourself last week, you felt the President would probably agree."

He frowned, concentrating on the steak. He couldn't leave Washington now, there might be other cables from Corliss, if he left he'd be like a bear dancing on a hot plate.

"I don't think the world is going to explode if you're not around for a few days," she added.

"Maybe in a few weeks," he said with an encouraging smile. "We could go somewhere special; maybe down south, Rio de Janeiro, Buenos Aires, or even an island—perhaps Tahiti."

She sparkled. "Dick, that would be fantastic."

"I need somewhere like that to recharge myself," he said ponderously. "Get a fresh perspective."

She was all excitement. "Would you speak to the President about it now?"

"Why not? I'm seeing him a little later. I'm sure he'll agree."

She pushed her plate aside, the meal forgotten. "You'll have to give me time to do some shopping. I mean, I'll have to have new clothes."

He contained a spurt of annoyance. God, she was so predictable. It was nonsense; there were so many items in her wardrobe she needed to run an inventory to find out what she actually had.

"You'll have time," he replied brusquely. Then he raised a cautionary hand. "But not for a few weeks," he warned.

He doubted she heard him, her mind was already off and running. "I'll call Paula," she said. "She's found a new designer who makes absolutely fabulous clothes. I'll have him working around the clock, so he'll create something that'll make you proud of me, no matter when we go darling."

He gave a resigned shrug, and returned to his meal. It would all be over in a few weeks; Corliss would be back in Washington, and he'd be able to gauge if there was going to be any reaction from the Israelis. What could they say? They were always so goddamn secretive anyway, they'd probably just keep their mouths shut. If nothing went wrong. He paused, with the food halfway to his mouth, as a sudden spasm seemed to block his throat. He'd put his life in Chip's hands. If the colonel blew it, or ran afoul of the local authorities, there was no way he could totally disown him, not when he'd so avidly promoted him here in Washington. It would bring the media hawks sniffing around. Even the thought was sufficient to ruin the remainder of his meal.

Normanton.

Women called it intuition, men called it a sixth sense, Andre Reine called it his own special warning device, protruding from his head like an invisible antenna. And it had vibrated, ever so slightly, since he'd left London, but without any seeming cause. In the end he'd rationalized it had something to do with the fact that this was the last mission he would ever undertake for the Mossad. It wasn't a warning of danger, but of emotional disturbance, his dread of retirement. During the journey he'd made an effort to think positively about retirement, planning the good things he could do with his time. He had even tried to interest himself in the Gulf tour. This was his first visit to Australia, it was something new, entirely different from Europe, the people were so relaxed in manner. It had been a friendly tour. The Japanese had kept to themselves, but the Australians were quick to establish conversation on a first-name basis, and also the two Americans. He didn't care for the older American, a crude man, and they appeared a mismatched pair to be traveling together, but they seemed to take a great interest in everything on the tour.

But standing with the other tourists in front of this Burns Philp store in Normanton he found the voice of the tour guide describing the history of the building simply meaningless noise, scrambled by the agitated vibrations of his warning antenna.

He was mystified by Hegarty's fight with the aggressive hooligan outside the station, relieved that Hegarty had been the victor, but what in God's name did it mean? Would

Hegarty have formed such a vehement enemy in such a short time in Normanton? Did it in some way threaten the coming kidnapping of Leiman? The continued throbbing of his antenna was only confusing him. Why did the Americans stay with the injured man? Maybe he was being uncharitable, but they didn't seem the type to involve themselves in samaritan acts. He stared at the building, seeing and hearing nothing, trying to decide what to do. It had been his intention all along to just continue on with the tour, then return to Tel Aviv, but was there something here of which he was unaware that threatened the Leiman operation? Should he stay on in Normanton and attempt to contact Hegarty again? Or Jules?

He suddenly realized the voice of the tour guide was no longer addressing the group, and glanced over to see him in deep conversation with the Americans Corliss and Jaroff. He was surprised. The tour leader had alerted the hospital on the way to the town, but there was no sign of the bloodied hooligan. Corliss was smiling with that rather affected charm and making apologetic gestures. The tour leader gave a shrug of resignation, then the Americans turned away and walked toward the large hotel further along the street.

"Well, I'm afraid we've just lost two of our group," announced the tour leader, with an edge of annoyance.

"Is the man in the fight all right?" asked someone.

The tour leader shrugged again. "Well he wouldn't wait for anyone from the hospital, so I suppose he's all right. But Mr. Corliss and Jaroff have decided to leave us, and stay on in Normanton for a time. I think they're making a mistake, because they'll miss out on seeing Karumba. They've made up their minds they want to see a good deal more of the country than perhaps we can show them in a short time." He frowned. "I'm sure we all wish them well, but I just hope they don't get themselves lost out on the savanna. It can happen you know." He turned back to the building. "Now, as I was saying about the Burns Philp store, . . ." he began.

Reine shut him out, conscious only of a fearful tightening in his stomach. He was certain now there was something terribly wrong here. Hegarty's fight, the Americans' phony concern, and now they were staying on in Normanton. He placed a hand to his forehead, concentrating on a mental reprise of the fight. Everyone had been agog at the brawl, but what had he actually seen? He recalled Corliss was somewhere in the front of the group, and Jaroff . . . Jaroff had gone across and *picked up the bike and the newspaper with the Leiman file inside*. My God, he had! Could he have seen the Leiman file taped inside? Even have taken it out? And there was something else, just a glimpse, almost a subliminal flash: Jaroff with his hand at the rear wheel guard of Hegarty's bike, with something small and black in his fingers, but too quick to register at the time. A bug maybe? Was that possible? Had they bugged Hegarty's bike so he could lead them to Leiman? But why? Who were they? His breath quickened, and he rubbed at his bare arms, suddenly cold, even with the warmth of the sun. He didn't understand any of what he'd seen, but he was sure now there was danger here—danger to Hegarty, to the operation. He made a decision. He too would stay on in Normanton, keep those two under surveillance; he didn't give a damn if they realized it or not—what could they do?—and it might just stall any plans they had. Even if his suspicions were unjustified, he couldn't possibly risk just doing nothing. Was there the chance they had something to do with Eli Brandt's murder? It seemed so remote, but it was the only connection he could make. Favett suspected German Nazi sympathizers back in Europe. These men were Americans, and much too young for wartime memories; why on earth would they be trying to protect someone like Leiman? He shook his head forlornly. He would have liked to put it all down to paranoid imagination, but his instincts were too strong for that; he should have been listening more acutely to his antenna long ago.

"Now we'll all go along to the hotel for what I can promise you will be a delightful lunch," the tour leader concluded.

The group began to slowly wend its way to the hotel, and Reine straggled along in the rear. He would speak to the tour leader after lunch about staying on; doubtless he'd be annoyed, but that couldn't be helped, and didn't even matter.

He was disturbed by another mournful thought. If Corliss and Jaroff in some way posed a dangerous threat to the Leiman operation, there was only one way they could have got to Normanton, and that was by following him all the way from

London. Good God, how could they know so much? How? How? Had he inadvertently led them to Leiman? Andre Reine, the Mossad legend, used like a bumbling apprentice? It was a humiliating possibility. For the first time he wondered if Favett was right, his wife was right—the edge was gone, blunted by age, and he was indeed ready for retirement.

When Hegarty came close to the fork that branched off to the old house, he left the road and traveled by a circuitous route across the savanna, moving at a crawl to diminish the burbling sound of the motor. He was probably too far away for the sound to carry to Cathedral Rock, but he decided to play safe anyway. Bemused recollections of the fight had occupied his mind during the return journey. Maybe he'd never know who set him up with Orton, but did it matter? He was sure it was a personal thing over Anna, and had nothing to do with the operation. He wouldn't say anything about it to her, and only to Jules if it was absolutely necessary. It might only stir Jules's ire again about his involvement with the family; he didn't want to chance a rift with Jules, when cooperation between them was so essential.

He didn't leave the Kawasaki out in the open this time, but wheeled it around to the side of the house, laid it on the ground, and covered it with an old rusted piece of sheet iron. He didn't know how long it would take Jules to make the comparison test, but this was the first time he'd come to the place in daylight, so he needed to be more cautious. There were scuff marks on the gas tank where Orton's boot had kicked it, but no real damage, and he felt better after the ride, the soreness gone from his neck. Hopefully there'd be no bruises after all.

He went swiftly into the house, crossed to the trapdoor, lifted it, and peered warily into the cellar. It paid to be cautious of Jules's inclination to be quick with a gun.

"Jules," he whispered.

There was the grating sound of a chair moving out of his range of vision, then the bearded face of Jules came into view.

"Come on down, Matt," called Grubin. "I heard you ride up on the bike."

Hegarty reversed about, clambered down the steps, and

lowered the trapdoor after him. Grubin was instantly at his side, offering assistance with a hand at his elbow, all eager anticipation.

"You got them, Matt, you got them?" he asked urgently.

Hegarty paused at the bottom of the steps, took the newspaper from under his shirt, extracted the envelope, and with a grin handed it to Grubin. "It was a piece of cake," he lied.

"Christ, good man, good man," said Jules excitedly. He moved away to the table, avidly opening the envelope and laying out the contents beside the drinking glass with Kisek's fingerprints. He read Reine's note as Hegarty came up behind him.

"Great, Matt, great," he said. "The Berlin police verification is terrific." He glanced at Hegarty. "There were no problems? You didn't have to approach Reine?"

Hegarty dropped the newspaper on the floor. "Oh no, we saw each other okay, but there was only eye contact between us. He just left the newspaper on a station seat for me to pick up." He pointed to the note. "Poor old Eli Brandt really had something going for him this time. Reine doesn't say anything about his murder I see."

Grubin shrugged, settled himself down on the chair, then took a piece of black paper and inserted it inside Kisek's drinking glass. "Does it matter about Eli now?" he asked.

Hegarty figured it mattered to Eli, but he let it pass.

"How did Andre look?" asked Grubin.

Hegarty chuckled. "Like a tourist. I didn't recognize him at first. I've never seen him dressed any other way but looking like a conservative banker."

Grubin took out a soft brush, dipped into a small bottle of white powder, and began to apply it to the outside of the drinking glass. Almost immediately Kisek's prints began to stand out in sharp relief against the black paper. "We're going to miss the old guy when he retires," he remarked.

"Is this going to take long?" asked Hegarty.

"I'd say only a few minutes."

"What's the powder?"

"Laconide. See how it makes the prints stand out. They're a good set."

"You can tell from that?"

Grubin picked up a small magnifying glass, and hunched forward, alternately peering through it at the prints on the glass, then at the prints from Reine. "These prints from the Berlin police files are pretty old, so there's been some fading, but yes, I can tell," he said. "It's still possible to accurately compare the ridge characteristics—see if they're in the same relative position; the same coincident sequence."

He concentrated, refusing any further conversation, still moving the magnifying glass back and forth. The hissing sound of the lamp filled the room like escaping steam. Hegarty could feel the beat of his pulse in his ears as his feelings alternated between anticipation and anxiety. Was he really hoping for Anna's sake, for Pony's sake, that the prints didn't match? Not that it would make any difference, the kidnapping would still go ahead. There was a scratching from the corner where the crates were stacked, and Hegarty wondered if Jules had rats keeping him company. If Jules heard it he gave no sign, just sat back in the chair, put the magnifying glass aside, then looked around at Hegarty with a smug grin of satisfaction.

"That's it. Christ, that's it, Matt," he declared exultantly.

"They match?"

"Absolute identity. Absolute."

"You're certain?" Shit, didn't he want to believe?

Grubin nodded. "Like I said, absolute identity. God, we've got a foolproof case to take to court now, Matt, foolproof. This'll put the bastard at the end of a rope, where he should have been years ago. Favett'll be ecstatic." He abruptly stood to his feet, and slapped Hegarty exuberantly over the shoulders. "They'll give you a medal for this, my friend—you've done a fantastic job, absolutely fantastic." He vigorously shook Hegarty's hand. "You've got my congratulations first, but by God there'll be plenty of others lining up to do the same."

Hegarty tried to match Grubin's jubilation, but the expression on his face belied the feeling in his belly. They had the monster; Jesus, they had the sonofabitch, he should feel unrestrained elation, yet Anna and Pony were like a barrier across his mind.

"I only got Kisek's fingerprints," he said.

"Forget about calling him Kisek; he's Leiman, Horst

Leiman, the Whipmaster of Treblinka, and you've put a noose around the bastard's neck. All the other information you've gathered will be invaluable too, don't worry."

"Eli Brandt's the one we really owe, Jules. Christ, it cost Eli his life."

Grubin was momentarily subdued. "You're damn right, Matt; yes, Eli really wiped his slate clean with this one." He shook his head, then leaned across the transmitter and brought out a camera. "I'll take some shots of the fingerprints on the glass for the record, then we'll drink a toast to Eli."

"And to nailing his goddamn killers."

"Right, yes to that too."

The scratching came louder from behind the crates, but excitement made Grubin oblivious to it, crouched down with the camera aimed at the drinking glass. "Everything's going for us now, Matt, everything," he crowed. "Even our man in Australian Intelligence has dug out the name of the American OSS officer who engineered Leiman's escape from Germany, and he believes he's still alive. Jesus, are we going to blow his daydreams away. They're running it through the computer back at Tel Aviv right now." He turned his head from the camera and grinned at Hegarty. "I told you that story the daughter fed you about an executed brother was shit, Matt, all shit."

But did she know that, Hegarty wondered? "I think she believed it," he said.

"Maybe she did, and Leiman was just playing safe."

"We'll still take Leiman out tonight?"

"We've got to, Matt." He put a different lens on the camera and moved closer to the glass. "Why don't you pour a couple of drinks for Eli while I finish here?"

Hegarty didn't answer. He stood as if chiseled out of the flagstones underfoot, eyes wide in disbelief, staring at the small, white-faced figure emerging unsteadily from behind the crates.

"Matt, . . ." croaked Pony. "Matt, please I . . . Matt . . ."

"For Chrissake—Pony?" cried Hegarty in astonishment.

The boy swayed on his feet, one hand on the crates to steady himself, eyes flickering nervously from Hegarty to

Grubin. Then Grubin caught sight of Pony, and the camera spilled from his hand to clatter on the table.

"What the hell is Pony doing here?" demanded Hegarty.

"Grab the kid," snarled Grubin.

Pony pointed a trembling finger at Grubin. "That . . . that bugger grabbed me, Matt, pulled me down here, and did something to put me to sleep. Is . . . he a friend of yours, Matt?"

Grubin started to lunge toward the boy, but Hegarty seized him forcefully by the arm.

"Hold it, Jules, Christ just hold it. What the fuck's he doing here?" he aggressively demanded again.

Pony began to edge nervously along the wall. "Jeez, he's not a friend of yours, is he, Matt?" shakily asked the boy. "He's a mad bugger."

Grubin angrily shook Hegarty's grip free. "I said grab him," he cried furiously.

"Goddamn it, tell me what he's doing here!" persisted Hegarty.

Pony's eyes were glazed with confusion. "Aren't you going to help me get out of here, Matt?"

"For Chrissake, the kid stumbled in here," rasped Grubin. "What did you expect me to do, offer him a Coke?"

"Why the hell didn't you tell me as soon as I came in?"

Pony renewed his retreat along the wall, face clouded with a mix of fear and uncertainty. "I'm . . . I'm going back to Cathedral Rock, Matt," he declared, with sudden determination. He kept his eyes on Hegarty, ignoring Grubin. "Are you coming with me?"

"Why didn't you tell me, Jules?" repeated Hegarty angrily.

"Christ, how could I," said Grubin. "You were always sounding off like a bleeding heart about the Kisek family—this kid, his damn mother; I was getting the feeling you were more concerned about them than about getting Leiman."

"That's a goddamn stupid thing to say," claimed Hegarty hotly.

"Is it?"

"You fucking know it is. You gave the boy a shot, didn't you? Jesus! You were going to keep him hidden down here until we got Leiman out, and not say a goddamn word to me about it."

"What of it," admitted Grubin sullenly. "I just didn't expect the shot to wear off so quickly. All I want is Leiman at the end of a rope, and I'll stop anything that gets in the way."

"You asshole, Jules. I want that too."

"You were letting the kid get in the way, Matt, and his mother. Believe me, I could tell, even if you didn't realize it yourself."

Hegarty felt guilty that it was part true, he just hadn't wanted to admit it to himself. It only made his denial more adamant. "Bullshit, Jules, absolute bullshit," he raged.

"I'm not so sure."

"Are you aiming to kill the boy? Is that what you're figuring on? Favett wouldn't buy anything like that; or Reine. And goddamn it, neither would I. What if it came out at the trial?"

"Don't talk crazy," Grubin retorted. "I figured he could stay here until we had Leiman out, then he could find his way home."

Pony's eyes were darting from one man to the other, alertness returning to his face, along with color. "I'm going, Matt," he said in a stronger voice. Whatever Jules had injected into him was wearing off fast. "Schon's waiting outside; I'll ride him back."

Hegarty stared at him. He hadn't seen the horse anywhere. Maybe it had wandered off back to Cathedral Rock. "Just wait there, Pony," he ordered. "We'll see."

"Are you out of your mind?" snarled Grubin. "If the boy goes back now we risk blowing the whole operation." He gestured to the fingerprints, his voice changing to a persuasive tone, "For God's sake, Matt, it's all about to happen for us, we've got the proof, everything we need. I'll see the kid isn't hurt, but you have to understand it's impossible for him to go back to Cathedral Rock now. That'd be crazy."

Hegarty knew he was right. From the beginning he'd known it was inevitable that Pony and Anna would be hurt, so why should he be surprised? But Pony stumbling in here like this was the worst kind of luck. He tried to smile reassurance to the boy.

"Listen, Pony, I know you don't understand what this is
all about, but you're going to have to . . ."

"Aren't . . . aren't you my best friend any more, Matt?"
queried the boy.

"Of course I am. I can't explain this to you right now."

"You're not a fair dinkum friend if you're helping that
bugger," accused Pony.

"You don't understand," Hegarty soothed.

"I don't want to understand."

There was a break in the boy's voice that cut at Hegarty in
a way he once wouldn't have believed possible. "Some things
just have to be done, Pony," he said.

"I came to warn you Grandad was going to fire you, Matt,
when you got back from Normanton," said the boy. "I didn't
want you leaving like that."

"That was terrific of you, Pony; just terrific, but . . . ,"
Hegarty offered in futile gratitude.

"Break it up, for Chrissake," growled Grubin. "We've got
things to do."

"I'm going back to Cathedral Rock," cried the boy shrilly.

"Forget it, Pony," said Hegarty firmly. His expression
hardened. "That's impossible right now."

The boy crouched by the wall on the other side of the
crates, his head lowered as if accepting the decision, then
without warning he made a sudden dash for the steps.

"Christ, grab him!" shouted Grubin. He jumped to his
feet, sending his chair crashing backward into Hegarty's path.
Hegarty gave a startled leap over the chair, floundered into
Grubin, and they both rebounded to opposite sides of the
cellar, as if in a slapstick comedy routine. By then Pony was
lithely bounding up the steps and through the trapdoor.

"Get him, get him," screamed Grubin. "The little bastard!
Christ, you let him twist you around his finger."

Hegarty lunged across the cellar and swarmed up the
steps in pursuit. He shot a swift glance back and saw Grubin
had a pistol in his hand.

"Put that away, you don't need a damn gun," he shouted
back.

"I'll use anything I have to, to stop the little bastard,"
bellowed Grubin.

"You idiot, you'll have to shoot me first," Hegarty flung back at him, as he scrambled into the room.

Pony was already gone. Hegarty cursed as he sprinted for the front door, feeling the old floor boards threatening to give way under his weight. It was always going to be bad for Pony, but Christ, he hadn't wanted it this way. At least Schon had gone, so the boy couldn't get far on foot. He blundered through the doorway, nimbly dodging the rotting timber scattered around, and spotted Pony, strangely not running, but standing stock still off to the right of the old tree, just staring down at the ground, then as Matt drew close, slowly kneeling into the grass.

Hegarty curbed his pace to a walk, but the boy ignored him. It was Schon, sprawled in the grass, roan coat gleaming in the sun, but now like inanimate polished wood, a dribbling line of dried blood coming from a small hole in the center of its forehead. Pony crouched over the body, stroking at the mane, and Hegarty could see tears splashing down, spotting the horse's neck. He stopped, with a mournful sigh of sorrow, and felt the taste of vomit in his mouth.

"Jesus . . . Oh, Jesus," he barely got out. "I'm sorry, Pony, I'm so sorry." He'd never felt so helplessly inadequate. When Pony turned to look at him he could scarcely bear the expression of such desolate grief, the wash of so many tears.

"You bastard, Matt," the boy whispered viciously. "You're a bastard, y'hear. No friend, no mate, just a bloody bastard. Jeez, Schon never hurt anything in his whole life, not even a fly. He was just a . . . a beautiful thing that loved everyone, an' I loved *him*. You're just a bastard, Matt. Y'hear? A bloody bastard."

The words trailed off into sobs. Hegarty struggled to find words of consolation, when he knew there were none. He heard the stamp of running feet swishing through the grass, then Jules's heavy breathing at his side.

"Thank Christ you caught him," Grubin panted. "Thank Christ." He made a brief, swift survey of the surrounding countryside. "Lucky there's no one around. Let's get him back to the cellar."

"Bastards," sobbed Pony. "Just bastards, Schon boy."

"You shot the horse?" said Hegarty coldly to Grubin.

He rarely lost control, it was a matter of pride with him. Orton, Kisek, he could coolly estimate his chances with all of them and act accordingly. But he could feel an inexplicable fury coming fast to the boil inside him.

Grubin gave him a withering stare. "Of course I shot the damn horse," he rasped.

Hegarty hit him. It was crazy, illogical. Ever since he'd arrived in the Gulf nothing had been more important than establishing a close working relationship with Jules, it was essential to the operation. It was all swept aside by the sight of the dead Schon, the sound of Pony's sobs.

It was Grubin's superb reflexes that saved him, he instinctively rolled with the punch, so that the fist connected at the side of his face instead of flush on the jaw, or he might have been knocked out. But he went down, almost in slow motion, reeling, arms flailing, then toppling into the grass. Hegarty didn't wait for him to regain balance, but flung himself over him, both of them rolling over and over, while he rained punches that did little damage, some connecting, most missing, doing little more than expend his raging sense of contrition. He scarcely knew what he was doing, screaming obscenities, with Jules answering in kind, until he suddenly felt the muzzle of the gun jam up under his chin. The cold hardness of the weapon jerked him back to sanity.

"Get off . . . Jesus, get off, you meshuga asshole," gasped Grubin.

Hegarty rolled to one side, and stayed for a moment on his hands and knees, coughing, gasping for breath, heart thudding, then he lurched into a sitting position, arms straddled over his bent knees. He felt like a goddamn fool. He glanced to Pony, but the boy seemed oblivious to the fight, his face buried in the horse's mane. He wanted to somehow try and explain to the boy that it wasn't his fault, yet—maybe he hadn't fired the shot, but he was just as responsible.

"If there was bloody time, I'd ask Reine to send someone to take your fucking place," panted Grubin. "Jesus, I never thought there'd be a day I'd have to pull a gun on you. My God, you're Mossad, out here to bring a criminal monster to justice, for God's sake; not let a kid and his damn horse get up your nose so much you can't fucking function any more." He wiped at his mouth, dripping saliva, stared at the pistol, then thrust it disgustedly into his belt. There was an ugly red mark on his cheek, where the first blow had landed.

Hegarty shook his head. "Don't tell me I can't goddamn function. I got you the information from Cathedral Rock, I got you the fingerprints. Don't give me that shit."

"Dammit, I told you you didn't realize how much the kid and his mother had gotten under your skin," rasped Grubin. "I told you. Okay, I'll live with that, I've got no choice now, but for Chrissake—are you going to let a fucking horse get in the way of bringing scum like Leiman to trial?" He threw his hands in the air. "A horse, for God's sake, a horse."

Hegarty took a deep breath, waiting for the rapid beat of his pulse to subside. "The horse meant everything to the boy," he muttered.

"You carry on like he's your damn son," retorted Grubin.

I want that, thought Hegarty. I really want that, but it's impossible now. "We'll get Leiman all right," he said sullenly. "Don't get yourself in a knot about that, but we don't have to spread goddamn misery while we're doing it."

Grubin crouched up on his haunches, calmer now, sourly studying Hegarty. "What did you want me to do, Matt?" he soberly asked. "Just let the horse stand around, and risk someone seeing it? Or turn the horse loose, so it would go back to Cathedral Rock, and maybe set off a search for the kid; perhaps even Leiman himself coming looking? To do either was an unacceptable risk to the operation. God, you know that as well as I do."

Hegarty did know it. It was what he would have had to do himself, but could he help it if Pony and Anna had made him feel more like a human being than anyone had in a long time? He couldn't explain it to Jules, maybe not even to himself, but he wasn't the same man who'd left New York to come to Australia.

"Okay, okay. I'm sorry I blew my top, Jules," he muttered. He extended his hand. "I know you had no choice." He nodded to the grieving Pony. "He's like a beautiful flower growing up out of garbage, he might be Leiman's grandson, but he's a terrific kid, and I hate to see something like this happen to him."

Grubin took the offered hand. "I didn't enjoy it," he stated coldly. "Just let's concentrate on Leiman, okay?"

Hegarty nodded. Grubin's handshake was firm, but reserved, and Hegarty knew the friendship was finished. Oh, they'd work together like professionals during the hours it took to kidnap Leiman, but after the operation both would take care never to work together again.

"Let's get back down in the cellar," said Grubin.

Hegarty went across to Pony, and firmly but gently lifted him to his feet. "We've got to go back, Pony," he said.

The boy offered no resistance, but he didn't look at Hegarty. "I'll never forgive you for Schon, Matt, never, never," he whispered.

"Never's a long time, Pony."

"I don't know what you're doing with that . . . that other bastard, but I hate you. Jeez, I really do; and I was only wanting to warn you like I said. Mum and Ingrid had a terrible fight, and Grandad got me, and said he'd get rid of you as soon as you got back. And now Schon's dead, and I don't care if you ever come back. Jeez, I was stupid, I didn't tell anyone I was coming looking for you."

Hegarty couldn't have imagined such venom in the young voice, and it deepened his sense of remorse. "Sometimes things happen that are no one's fault," he tried to appease the boy. "You won't believe me Pony, but I love you, and your mother."

Grubin had impatiently paused at the doorway, waiting for them, his eyes anxiously to the countryside.

"Anybody who'd do something like that to Schon doesn't love anything in the whole world," said the boy dully. "And no one loves them. Whatever you and that bastard are doing, it has to be bad. Anybody who'd shoot Schon couldn't be doing anything good." Hegarty tried not to listen, steering the boy toward the house. "I don't know what you're trying to do, but you'd better not be hurting Mum, or Ingrid, or Grandad," Pony added, with spirit.

He didn't speak again, just went unprotestingly to the cellar, and sat morosely in a corner, nursing his grief, withdrawn from his surroundings.

Hegarty willed himself to ignore the boy. But what had

happened was an affirmation of his half-formed decision: once they had Leiman back in Israel, he'd hand in his resignation. Let someone else swill out the garbage. His father would be bewildered, but he'd had enough. Could he come back here? The look on Pony's face told him the thought was absurd.

"You realize shooting the horse only bought us time," he bluntly pointed out to Grubin. "Sooner or later the kid's going to be missed, and they're going to come looking for him."

"We'll keep him locked down here until we're gone," said Grubin defensively.

"There's got to be a chance they'll come searching here."

Grubin scratched anxiously at his beard. "Like I said, I had no damn option."

They both dropped into reflective silence, pondering a solution.

"Maybe there's a way we could make this work for us," said Hegarty, nodding to Pony.

"I was thinking the same thing, but I don't know how," said Grubin.

"We were trying to figure out a way to take Leiman from this house."

"Well you were," observed Grubin tartly. "We've still got to get him here."

Hegarty didn't want a flare-up over the family again. "He'd come for the boy," he said quietly. "He'd go anywhere for his grandson; he idolizes him."

Grubin shrugged acceptance. "Okay, you'd know about that. How do we work it?"

"The boy says no one knew he came here to wait for me."

"What's all this about you being fired, and him wanting to warn you?"

"I'm not sure. Seems like the daughters got into some sort of a fight, and it made Leiman decide to fire me as soon as I got back from Normanton."

"Maybe the girls reckoned they weren't getting an equal share of you," observed Grubin, with a sour grin. "But it's going to make it difficult when you go back."

"Not if I tell them I know where Pony is. I figure he's been gone from Cathedral Rock quite a time now. It'll be dusk soon, and they must be worrying by now where he is, if he went off without telling anyone where he was going."

"You're sure the boy isn't lying about that."

"Yes, I know Pony; he isn't lying."

"You'll tell them you've kidnapped the boy?" asked Grubin.

"No, no that'd only anger Leiman. It'd be better if I gave the impression I was trying to be helpful." He considered a moment. "I figure it'd be best to tell him the near truth; Pony ran away to be with me, and he says he's never coming back to Cathedral Rock if his grandfather fires me. The boy wants to go away with me." He shrugged aside the doubt in Grubin's face. "Don't worry, Leiman'll buy that, the boy threatened it once before."

"You must've really made quite a hit with the kid," Grubin sneered. He glanced toward the mourning Pony. "I'd say you can forget about that now."

Hegarty ignored the jibe. "I'll tell Leiman I know where the boy is, but he refuses to come back to Cathedral Rock. Leiman's going to have to come and see the boy, and try and persuade him, make him see reason." He gave a humorless grin. "Don't worry, I'll make it sound good. I'll make it plain there's no way I want the kid coming away with me."

Grubin rubbed his beard, still showing doubt. "The kid really thought that much of you?"

It was like the warming memory of a first love for Hegarty, a sudden kaleidoscope of images. Pony with him in the Bell, the crocodile, repairing the stockyards, the boy's unstinting admiration. Maybe that lavish polishing of his ego was part of it?

"Yes, I don't think I'm wrong about that," he murmured. He tried to put it aside. "I guess I was different from anyone he'd ever seen before. He's at a vulnerable age."

Grubin couldn't let it go. Perhaps he could still feel pain from where Hegarty's fist had landed. "The big hero helicopter pilot from the other side of the world," he jeered softly.

Again Hegarty ignored the sarcasm. Something a long time ago had turned Jules to stone inside, he'd never understand about Pony, Matt barely understood it himself.

"You're sure it'll work?" asked Grubin.

"Sure of it. The kid's the reason Leiman keeps going. He wants Cathedral Rock to belong to his grandson one day."

"It'd better work, Matt," Grubin scowled. "I'm warning you: if it fouls up, we go straight for Cathedral Rock, and the damn daughters'll have to take their chances."

"It'll work. I've gotten to know Leiman pretty well, the way he thinks, the way he'll react, especially where his grandson is concerned." He glanced at Pony, still crouched as if in shock, his head buried in his hands. "Make sure you keep him down here."

"I'll bolt the damn trapdoor. He won't get out again." He also looked at the boy. "And I'd say he's not going to give any trouble."

"Don't give him another shot."

"Only if he starts acting up."

Hegarty recalled Jules charging after Pony with the gun. "I don't want the kid harmed, Jules," he warned.

"For Chrissake, am I going to do anything to harm our precious bait?"

"You're responsible for him. I just want it understood," Hegarty warned.

Grubin glowered, as if considering another jeering rejoinder, but said nothing.

"You'll call the ship?" asked Hegarty.

"As soon as you've gone."

"We'd better agree on a timing."

"It'll need to be late; we'll want to play it safe."

"There'll be no one around here."

"We'd be crazy to take even the slightest risk. I plan on the helicopter touching down here around, say, midnight."

Hegarty frowned. "That'll mean a longer stall with the kid."

"It's your idea; make it work."

Hegarty rubbed reflectively at his chin. It was an added complication, but he could embroider the details to make it fit. "I'll make it work," he promised. He fell silent, pondering if anything had been overlooked. The acrimony between him and Jules was still simmering, and he knew another boil-over might just threaten the operation. But he was certain Leiman would rise to Pony as bait. At least he'd guaranteed Anna's safety. And even Ingrid. He didn't want to see her getting hurt, although the idea was growing in his mind that she had set him up with the ape in Normanton; even so, he wouldn't want her stopping a bullet. But there was no chance he could protect them from the fact their father was a wanted, sadistic monster, doomed to finish at the end of a rope.

He considered shaking hands with Jules to pledge success, but decided for a brief nod. "You've done a great job here, Jules," he offered, as a tentative peace gesture. He motioned about the cellar. "I know spending time in this hole hasn't been much joy for you."

Grubin nodded in curt acknowledgment. "You too, Matt. Reine sure picked the right guy. The trial's a foregone conclusion now that we know the fingerprints match. It'll be a nice retirement present for Andre." He paused uncertainly, studying Hegarty. "Perhaps you should pay a visit to the Yad VaShem when you're next in Jerusalem," he suggested gruffly, "the Museum of the Holocaust. Maybe you need reminding. Bastards like Leiman almost wiped my family out. I'm the only Grubin left."

Hegarty thought of his father, of the bedroom ritual. Reminding? How could he ever forget? "I once had a family too, Jules," he replied. "I don't need any reminding. Maybe vengeance has been letting me forget I'm a human being."

Grubin shook his head. "Only vengeance matters," he stated flatly.

That promised to be another area of conflict; Hegarty sidestepped it: "I'd better be getting back," he said quickly.

"How will I know if it's worked out using the kid as bait?"

"I'll come back here by ten-thirty. If Leiman hasn't accepted the story about Pony, and thrown me out of the place, then I'll go along with taking him from Cathedral Rock." He gave a firm shake of his head. "But believe me, Jules, Leiman will go for it. I know how he is about the boy."

Grubin seemed finally convinced. "Okay," he agreed. He placed a hand to the bruise on his cheek. "You throw a mean right cross, Matt." He smiled ruefully. "Just let's pretend it never happened."

Hegarty returned an embarrassed grin. Maybe Jules meant it, but more likely it was intended as a piece of temporary adhesive to hold them until Leiman was safely on the helicopter. That was okay with him. He nodded, and moved slowly to the steps. "I'll see you around ten-thirty, and we can set it up for Leiman's arrival."

"That I'll be looking forward to."

Hegarty paused in midstride as he passed Pony. He tried to think of something he could say, but how could he ever make him understand? Perhaps it'd be even worse if he saw his grandfather being dragged onto the helicopter at gunpoint.

"It'd be better if we kept him down in the cellar when Leiman arrives," he said, indicating Pony. "We don't want any complications."

Grubin seemed to have no objections. "Okay," he agreed.

"You'll be safe here, Pony," Hegarty promised awkwardly.

The boy sat against the wall as if turned to stone, arms wrapped about his drawn up knees, staring unseeingly at the floor. Then he slowly lifted his head, and looked at Hegarty as he would a stranger. He glanced across to Grubin, and there was no mistaking the fear in his eyes.

"You'll come back for me, Matt?" he whispered.

Hegarty was sure it wasn't forgiveness, but fear of Jules. "Yes, I'll come back for you," he tried to reassure the boy. "He won't hurt you."

He climbed the steps, went up through the opening, and paused for a final backward glance. Jules was already at the transmitter, and Pony had again buried his head in his arms. Like a recurring theme the image of the Tarantula Hawk came back to him. "People are like that," Pony had said. "Get right inside you without you knowing, and just eat you away." He shook his head, uttered a soft curse, and dropped the trapdoor back in place. The boy was young, and resilient; he'd get over it, he'd have to. And so would Matt.

Chapter 13

"I tell you the old guy's wise to us," muttered Jaroff. "There's no doubt about it, Colonel, the old sonofabitch is wise to us all right."

Corliss had just settled into the seat of the Toyota Land Cruiser beside Jaroff. They were packed and ready to go, suitcases and .30/30 Winchesters in the back, the receiver on the seat activated to pick up the signal from the bug on Hegarty's bike. Jaroff hunched forward over the wheel and pointed to the gaunt figure of Reine stepping out of the hotel. Corliss frowned, clasped his hands, and placed them thoughtfully to his mouth.

"He was in the bar," he mused aloud. "Some ancient geezer called Cutmore was giving me directions to Cathedral Rock, and telling me about Kisek. Seems like he met Hegarty on the train to Normanton and knew all about him going out to Kisek for a helicopter roundup job. He was telling me how Kisek lives like a goddamn hermit, with two daughters and a grandson." He nodded toward Reine. "Then he came in and ordered a drink and tried to listen in on what Cutmore was saying." He glanced irritably about the street. "What the hell's going on, Sam? I don't see the tourist bus anywhere."

"They've gone."

He turned back to Jaroff in startled surprise. "Reine stayed behind?"

"That's right. That's what I'm saying, Colonel; the old sonofabitch is wise to us. When I picked up our luggage the tour leader was sounding off about people not sticking by their agreements. He told me Reine had bailed out of the tour too, and was staying on in Normanton."

"If he is wise to us, then it's only happened since we hit Normanton," Corliss scowled. "There's no way he would have led us to here to Leiman, and made contact with Hegarty, if he'd spotted us before."

"Maybe so, maybe so," agreed Jaroff impatiently. "But what the hell do we do about the old bastard, Colonel?"

"You know what he's been doing?"

"Making enquiries about hiring a wagon same place as I got this one. And asking directions to Cathedral Rock, for Chrissake."

"Did he get a wagon?"

"Yeah."

They watched in morose silence as Reine waited at the side for a huge road train cattle transport to rumble past, then strolled casually across the street.

"The son-of-a-bitch wants us to see him, Colonel. Christ, does he think that's going to scare us off? Two guys who went through Nam together?" He shook his head. "We're going to have to do something about him, you know that."

Corliss nodded agreement. "You could be right, Sam." He wondered where they'd betrayed themselves. They'd played it very cool ever since leaving London, keeping out of Reine's way on both planes, and even then only making casual contact on the tour. It had to do with the fight. Maybe they'd been too obvious about involving themselves, but it would have been crazy to pass up such an opportunity. He suspected Reine might be fading with age, but he had one hell of a lot of experience behind him, and he must have seen something to make him suspicious enough to stay on in Normanton. He shrugged. If an error of judgment had been made, the only problem was how to correct it.

Jaroff read his mind. "You figure he could have seen something back at the fight? Maybe when I put the bug on Hegarty's motor bike?"

"It's possible."

"I played it smart, Colonel. You'd need quick eyes to see what I was doing."

"Reine's old, but he's been around, Sam."

"Maybe he's figuring to try and contact Hegarty again."

He beat his fist angrily on the steering wheel. "Christ, he might even figure we connect back to Brandt."

"Maybe a thousand things, Sam," said Corliss sharply. "Anything's possible, if you want to stretch it that far. But we're too close to Leiman to back away now. Reine staying around isn't going to stop us."

Jaroff gave a satisfied grunt. "I figured that's what you'd say, Colonel."

They silently watched the elderly Mossad agent step into a wagon similar to their own, start up, then leisurely drive into a side street out of sight.

"He sure isn't trying to keep under cover," observed Jaroff.

"He obviously wants it that way. I've a hunch he's only running on suspicion right now. He's not absolutely sure, otherwise he'd be headed straight out to try and warn Hegarty."

"You want me to tail him, Colonel?"

"Hell no, we'll make all the play, Sam."

"You think he'll come after us?"

"He has to. We move out toward Cathedral Rock, and it'll confirm everything for him."

"You figure he's armed?"

"I doubt it. He wouldn't have been able to get a gun onto the London plane. I'd guess he'd figure he wouldn't need one anyway," said Corliss.

"He could have bought one in Brisbane, same as us."

"Why? He's not figuring on any gunplay, he's only making a drop to this Hegarty." He paused, and peered into the sky. Already the sun was caressing the horizon, setting the town alight with a pink glow. A bridge of elongated shadows now linked both sides of the street. "We'll move out around dusk, Sam," he decided. "I want it to be dark by the time we make Cathedral Rock." He glanced again at the sky. "Last few nights on the tour the moon's been so bright you scarcely needed any lights. I'm hoping we get it the same, so we can do the run without any headlights."

"It's not going to be easy spotting the place at night, Colonel," warned Jaroff.

"Even if we had the time, we couldn't risk daylight. I

guess even out here there's a chance of being spotted." He grinned, and slapped Jaroff on the shoulder. "Anyway, we've got the bug you put on Hegarty's bike to guide us. That was quick smart thinking. Once we're in range, we'll have no problem about location with that to guide us."

Jaroff was still dubious. "I guess you're right," he conceded. "But what do we do about Reine?"

"We'll take care of that problem when we're well out of town. You're still the best sharpshooter I ever saw, Sam."

"If he follows us?"

"He's got to follow us. Believe me, I know how a guy like that thinks."

"We'll need an out, Colonel. We terminate Reine, and then Leiman, we won't want to be hanging around here. No sir."

Corliss half closed his eyes, considering the implication of Jaroff's point. A group of aborigines passed, regarding them with lingering, inquisitive glances. "It shouldn't take us long, Sam," he said, half to himself. "On the way out we'll pick our own time and place to take care of Reine. Then we hide his wagon somewhere off the road, and pick him up on the way back." He plucked at his mouth; he liked to plan a strategy, think ahead, it kept you alive.

"What do we do with him back here?" queried Jaroff.

"I figure the Norman river by the side of the town'll take care of that for us."

"The body could still be seen."

"This is crocodile country, Sam. They'll take care of Reine for us. He'll just vanish."

Jaroff gave a nod of appreciation. "Right; pretty neat, Colonel. What about Leiman?"

"We go straight for this Cathedral Rock, and terminate him, Sam. Fast as we can. There's no time for pussyfooting around. The way Reine's acting the Mossad must be right at the edge of taking him out, and we've got to beat them to it."

"You said there were daughters and a grandson."

Corliss grimaced. "That could be a problem." He hesitated, closely studying his companion. "I think you realize by now this is a big deal, Sam, a real big deal for our country's security."

"Sure, Colonel."

"We've got to be ruthless when the stakes are so big. Like Nam. We'd be crazy to let them identify us. It could lead right back to our government."

Jaroff made a quick gesture of comprehension. "I'm with you, Colonel, you know that. Whatever has to be done, I'm with you."

Corliss showed his teeth in a savage grin. "Good man. We're going to have to play it as it comes. It might mean torching the place to make it look like an accident. My information is no one goes near Cathedral Rock; this Kisek-Leiman character doesn't welcome visitors. Chances are no one is going to know about it for days. I figure on us taking the first flight out of here in the morning."

"The Mossad'll know about it," grinned Jaroff.

"Let 'em eat their heart out. They won't be able to do a thing about it, except keep their mouths shut. The Australian government wouldn't be too happy about them trying to pull a kidnap stunt." He thought it over for a while, then gave a grunt of satisfaction. There were unpredictable loose ends, which couldn't be helped, but he'd make it work. He gestured to the rear of the wagon. "Why don't you load the Winchesters, Sam, just so we're all ready. Then we'll get ourselves something to eat."

"Good idea, Colonel," said Jaroff.

Corliss leaned back in the seat, folded his arms, and closed his eyes, while Jaroff busied himself with the guns. It was tough about Leiman's family, and he hoped he'd find a way without involving them, but if it came to the crunch they'd have to go. He wondered how Gormane would face up to knowing about that; after reading his cable the security advisor was probably stuffing himself at some fancy dinner party, sure that he was safe. Gormane wasn't going to like it when he put in his account for the job, but he'd been around long enough to know that everyone has to pay in the end. Even if it was only in favors.

Dusk had settled the savanna into a mystical stillness, bedding the Gulf down for the night, when Hegarty rode into

Cathedral Rock. He saw Anna and Leiman standing together by the corral, staring apprehensively toward the horizon. He'd have to watch himself. He had a trap to set, and he couldn't afford the slightest slip. For one thing, that bastard called himself Kisek. Remember, Matt warned himself, Kisek.

He came to a stop, and turned off the motor, debating whether he'd go first to his room, then he saw them walking quickly toward him. He straddled the bike, waiting. It was a pity about Anna being here, he would have preferred Leiman on his own. After Pony's warning he knew what to expect from Leiman, but he'd decided to wait until the storm blew itself out before he came out with the story about his grandson. He wasn't too sure what to expect from Anna, but she was first to him, her face creased with anxiety.

"Matt, did you see Pony anywhere on your way back from Normanton?" she asked anxiously.

As he'd figured, the boy had already been missed. It was what he was hoping for. Her father brushed her aside before Hegarty had a chance to answer, bristling with aggression, a mirror image of Red Orton's ugly belligerence.

"Just you never be bothering Hegarty about Pony, Anna," he snapped. He glowered at Hegarty. "I'm not wanting to be asking you about anything that's going on at Cathedral Rock."

"For God's sake, Dad, Matt might have seen Pony," Anna protested, but he cut her off with a furious sweep of his arm. He was like a boiling kettle.

"You think I might be changing my mind," he roared at Anna. "Nothing's changed since I separated you and your sister behaving like spitting cats."

"Mr. Kisek, if you'll let me . . ." Hegarty began.

Leiman waved a threatening craggy fist in Hegarty's face. "I'm not allowing you to be doing anything, bastard. We'll be the ones to look out for Pony." His deep tan complexion took on a purplish hue. "I want you out of Cathedral Rock, Hegarty, you hear? Out now. I'm not caring if you're the best helicopter mustering pilot in the world, nothing but trouble there's been since you came here. I'm putting an end to it—being an alley cat with my daughters; making it so they hate each other, ja, hate each other, trying to tear each other to pieces. Ja, and for the likes of you, mein dummkopf daughters, that's the crazy part."

Hegarty had seen Leiman's rages, but never one like this, saliva spattering his beard, the words tumbling over each other in a frenzied torrent as they gushed from his mouth.

"Making trouble with Pony," he continued. "That I won't tolerate, trouble between me and mein grandson; never before trouble between us. Crazy I was to be listening to Pony, to hire you; after the photographing I should have fired you then, ja, but I was dummkopf like mein daughters. Just enough time I'm giving you to get your things from your room, then you get on that damn bike and ride out of here, and never come near this place again, or . . . or, mein Gott, I'm blasting your head off with a shotgun—ja, Hegarty, a shotgun." He pointed a quivering hand to the shed. "Right now you are leaving, right now, out of Cathedral Rock."

Hegarty refused to move. Even with Pony's warning, he was still taken aback by the depth of Leiman's vehemence. The fight between Anna and Ingrid must have been really something to set him off like this. A quick glance at Anna's anguished face, clenched hands at her mouth, told him nothing had changed about her feelings toward him. He only wished he could tell her he was trying to protect her.

"Move, Hegarty!" shouted Leiman. "Are you wanting I should go and get my shotgun now, eh? Don't think I wouldn't be using it, not on vermin." He paused, breathing hard, chest heaving as he gulped air, glaring fiercely at the unflinching Hegarty as if willing him to dissolve away.

"For God's sake, you will please just let me ask him about Pony?" pleaded Anna shrilly.

"We'll be forgetting Pony for now," shouted Leiman.

"I know where Pony is," said Hegarty.

"Using Pony won't be keeping your job this time," snarled Leiman.

"Please, Dad," implored Anna again. She turned to Hegarty. "Matt, he's been gone on Schon for hours; he went off without saying anything to anybody. He's never done anything like that. Tell me where you saw him."

"I don't want you talking to him," fumed Leiman, hands waving in the air. "Are you being surprised the boy is upset?

Seeing his mother and aunt tearing at each other like wild animals. More of your mischief it was, Hegarty." He took Anna by the arm and attempted to pull her away. "Pony's being able to look after himself, ja, he knows the savanna like he knows himself."

"Pony says he's not coming back to Cathedral Rock," declared Hegarty boldly. "He's saying he never wants to live here ever again."

It had the effect of momentarily silencing Leiman, disbelief abruptly terminating anger. Anna wrenched free of his grip, and he made no attempt to hold her.

"What lies are you trying to tell us, Hegarty?" he accused hoarsely. "Of course Pony is coming back. He's just being upset for now."

"You spoke to him, Matt?" anxiously inquired Anna.

"Yes. And like I said, he doesn't want to come back to Cathedral Rock. Ever."

"And I'm saying you're lying," rasped Leiman.

"Did he say why he doesn't want to come back?" asked Anna.

Hegarty focused intently on Leiman. "Because he's downright mad at his grandfather." He offered an apologetic tilt of his head. "I guess Pony's just taken to me, but he's mad enough about you intending to fire me to want to run away for good."

Again Leiman shook his fist under Hegarty's nose. "Turning the boy against his own blood, that's what you've been doing, Hegarty. Pony will come back when he gets hungry. And you get out of here."

"Okay, okay, I'll go," said Hegarty. "But I want Pony back at Cathedral Rock as much as you do, Kisek. You know what he's like; stubborn and determined when he's made up his mind." He shook his head. "He wants to come away with me."

"I'm warning you, Hegarty," said Leiman menacingly, "you'd better not try to take Pony away with you, it would be worth more than your life." He bobbed his shaggy head. "Ja, more than your life."

"Hell, I don't want the boy coming away with me," Hegarty declared harshly. "That'd be crazy. I don't want to be tied down with a kid trailing along with me, no way. He belongs here."

"Then tell us where he is?" pleaded Anna.

"He's hiding, Anna."

"*Where?*"

"You go looking for him, and he'll see you coming and just run away."

"You're playing tricks, bastard," accused Leiman. "Trying to keep your job."

"The hell I am," countered Hegarty, with a semblance of anger. "I can't take the kid with me, that's impossible." He paused, as if considering an option. "I'll tell you what I'm prepared to do. Leave Pony alone for the time being. He thinks I'm coming back to take him away with me. I'll go back to him later tonight." He rubbed thoughtfully at his chin, with the pretense of forming a plan. "How about I take him to your old house? You can be waiting there for him, talk to him, make him see reason." He shrugged. "Of course I guess you could drag him back, but I figure he'd only run away again. It'd be better if you explained you were sorry about what happened, and how much you want him back at Cathedral Rock." He stared challengingly at Leiman. "He'd listen. I know deep down he loves you."

Animosity still showed on Leiman's face, but at least the purplish hue had gone from his complexion. "Why would you do that?" he asked suspiciously.

"I'm doing it for him Kisek, not you. I happen to think he's a terrific kid, maybe better than you deserve."

"You're still fired," growled Leiman. "This won't be altering anything; I'm not wanting you at Cathedral Rock."

"Don't worry, I'll go. I won't come back here again after you've got Pony." There followed a tense silence. Hegarty didn't look at Anna; he suspected there could be a pleading expression that she come with him, and he didn't want to see it.

"What time?" asked Leiman.

"I told the boy late, so he wouldn't have to leave his hiding place."

"Wouldn't it be better if you just told us where he is?" asked Anna.

Hegarty gave a firm shake of his head. "I know the boy's state of mind, Anna. Believe me, he'd just take off if he saw you coming, and that wouldn't solve anything. For now I'm the only one he trusts."

"What time?" Leiman sullenly repeated.

"I'd say at the old house around twelve."

"That late?"

"I figure that's the way it should be."

Leiman tugged doubtfully at his beard, with no lessening of the hostility in his face.

"What in God's name are you waiting for?" exclaimed Anna in exasperation. "Don't you want Pony back?" She turned to Hegarty. "I'll come. God, I am his mother."

Hegarty suppressed an abrupt surge of alarm. That was the last thing he wanted. "No, no, he's mad at his grandfather, not you," he said quickly.

"He's running away from me too," she replied bitterly.

"I'm sorry, but I think it's important only your father comes. You'd stand a better chance with him that way, believe me."

"I'll come," muttered Leiman. "Ja, but I'm not thanking you Hegarty; this is being trouble of your own making."

"I'm not asking for thanks," said Hegarty.

"I'm coming too," insisted Anna.

Hegarty gave an irritable shake of his head. He hadn't counted on this, maybe he should have waited to get Leiman alone. Christ, he was trying to protect Anna, there was no point if she came. And maybe he didn't want to see the way her love turned to hatred. "I know the way the boy's thinking, Anna," he said sharply. "This is between him and his grandfather. That's the way it has to be."

"I am his mother," she emphasized stiffly.

"If this is being between Pony and me, then I go alone," said Leiman flatly.

Anna flushed with anger. "God, don't try and tell me how to handle my own son," she flared. "You've been trying to do that ever since he was born."

"Enough," growled Leiman. "I go alone. It's best for Pony."

"Damn you, I'll decide what's best for Pony," she said, her teeth clenched.

The unexpected confrontation with his daughter only served to rekindle the short fuse that always seemed to be smoldering in Leiman. Yet it was more than antagonism, it had that strange edge Hegarty had sensed between them before.

"Hegarty's been turning your head as much as Pony's," Leiman baited her. "You are being a fool of a woman, acting like this man's . . . whore."

"I'll act any way I damn well please," she retorted venomously. "You wouldn't know the bloody difference between loving and whoring anyway."

"Loving? Loving?" cried Leiman contemptuously. "Would you, eh? Would you? Only Pony I'm thinking about, and you're thinking only of yourself."

"God, the hell with your always trying to interfere with the boy, I'm sick of it, you hear? Sick to death of it," she shouted.

It pushed Leiman again into a barely controllable rage; he became like a man possessed, eyes slitted, mouth ugly, arms waving as if to inflict pain. Was he seeing the way it had been with him at Treblinka, Hegarty wondered?

"I've a right to think about Pony, care about him," Leiman barked. "I'm sick too, sick of playing grandfather, when I'm his rightful father! He's my son, my son as much as yours. That gives me every right, as much right as you, ja, dammit, as much right."

What followed was like the eerie silence after a thunderous explosion, as if the eardrums have been punctured, and there is only a sense of stunned shock. Leiman's mouth snapped shut, an expression of agonized remorse swept the anger from his face, he was a man suddenly floundering, looking neither at Anna or Hegarty. The tan in Anna's face appeared to pale, and she cast a stricken look at Hegarty, eyes wide and misting with tears. Hegarty could only stare in disbelief from father to daughter, yet it immediately explained so much of what had bewildered him about their relationship.

"I . . . I will be seeing you at the old house . . . around twelve, Hegarty," Leiman managed to say, his eyes still directed to the ground. Then he swiveled about and shuffled away with the gait of a man suddenly realizing that he is old. He left a vacuum between Hegarty and Anna.

She stared after her father, mouth tightly set, hands nervously fluttering. "You want me to go too?" she asked dully.

"You want to go?" he answered quietly.

"You think I owe you an explanation?"

"You owe me nothing."

"You said you loved me," she murmured.

"I do."

"After . . . after this?"

"You're still the same woman."

"Yet you're leaving."

He shrugged. "It won't work, Anna, not now, when I know the way it is with your father." He paused. "He is Pony's father?"

"Yes." She frowned. "Oh yes. He despises himself now for blurting it out in front of you, but it's the way he is, the way he's always been; when he gets in a rage he scarcely knows what he's saying. He could never control his temper."

"Pony doesn't know?"

"Of course not, nor Ingrid." She pushed at her hair, face expressionless, as if she couldn't dare show the hurt inside. "There was a casual worker here at the time, one of the very few. It was easy to claim he was the father after he'd gone." She stared at him with the cold appraising look so typical of her father. "I think you love Pony too."

It was all coming to an end, and he hesitated over giving her a straight answer. "I've never seen anyone I wish so much was my own son," he answered truthfully.

"You've had quite an effect on him."

"He's had quite an effect on me."

"I . . . I never thought he'd ever want to run away from me," she said huskily.

"Not you," he quickly consoled. "It's your father. He's just not thinking straight right now. Don't worry, he'll be back."

She stared at the ground, stirring the dirt with her foot, wiping at her tears. "It's not easy to explain about my father," she almost whispered.

"You want to?"

"Yes." She lifted her head. "We were always close.

Not . . . incestuous, or anything like that, just close." She shrugged. "When my mother died it was a bad time for both of us. I . . . well, I'd been through a bad love affair. We were alone in the house, consoling each other. . . ." She stopped, searching for the right words. "I don't even know how it happened; you know, it wasn't rape or anything like that. Maybe he doesn't know either—it just happened." She closed her eyes for a moment, and uttered a sigh. "Crazy," she said. "It was just that once, but Pony was the result." She gave a doleful laugh. "It was all unreal in a way; he never spoke of it again, neither of us did, like we were trying to pretend it never happened. When Pony was born he even assumed the grand-father role without question, even though we both knew it was his son." She shook her head. "I suppose I should have gone away, taken Pony with me. But I loved the Gulf Country, and I wanted my son to love it too. But it's always been difficult; conflict with him over raising Pony, jealousy from Ingrid. There've been times when I hated him, and he hated me, it was so complicated. It soured everything. I guess I hate him now; I mean real hatred." Her hands were clasped in front of her, voice low and mournful, her gaze directed past Hegarty to the savanna. "Sometimes it's like having a rejected jealous lover around, you know, which is ridiculous really, but I always have the feeling I have to watch myself with another man when he's around—like with you. That's why I couldn't ask you to dinner. I knew he'd see how I felt in my face, I wouldn't be able to hide it."

"I figured there might be something between you and your father," he admitted.

"I thought you might hate me now too," she said.

He was still in shock, but nothing had changed. "Like I said, you're still the same woman."

"It's easy to say that when you're leaving."

"Maybe I'll come back when this has all settled down," he lied.

He couldn't help himself, he just wanted to do something to soothe her hurt.

She searched his face, probing for truth. "You mean it, Matt?"

"Yes," he lied again. It would be easy to rationalize that he just wanted to keep her happy until they had her father on the helicopter, but he'd only be fooling himself. "But I have to go away for a time. Now that I know about Pony it'd be impossible with your father."

"It will always be impossible." Her gaze went to him, with a look of intense yearning. "I'll come to you, if you want me to?"

"Of course I do." Was it possible? Surely he was only entangling himself in a way that would make her eventual hurt deeper.

"Let's just concentrate on getting Pony back first," he said, backing off.

"I do love you, Matt," she said.

"And I love you."

"I don't know I deserve such understanding."

God, she made him feel like a sleazy son-of-a-bitch. "You've got Pony. That's the important thing."

"I will when he comes back."

"He will."

"You don't think I should come tonight?"

He shook his head. "I'm sure it's best for Pony if you don't."

She appeared too emotionally exhausted to offer further resistance. "All right," she agreed heavily. "I'll see you afterward?"

He contained a sigh of relief. "I'll make sure I see you before I go."

There was a poignant pause. He thought of kissing her, but if Leiman was watching it would be a stupid risk. He considered asking her about Red Orton, but what was the point, this was the last time he'd ever see her. What could he say, what was there to say? He loved her, but when the truth came out of why he was at Cathedral Rock, doubtless she'd think it was just part of the charade.

"I'd better go and pack my things," he said.

She nodded. "I'll see you later then." She hesitated. "I meant it, Matt; I will come to you, if you want me to."

His hands quivered with the desire to touch her. "We'll work something out after you've got Pony back," he lied again.

He couldn't stand and just look at her any longer. He forced a reassuring smile, lifted his hand in a brief gesture of farewell, then turned away toward his room. He refused to allow himself to look back until he reached the door, and she was still standing there, watching him, blended with the savanna so she seemed part of it. He tried to lock it into his memory for all time.

Jaroff crouched down in the grass, rested the Winchester on the mound of earth, and squinted through the sights. He had terrific coverage of the road. Off to the west, the spume of dust marking Corliss's trail was like a gossamer veil in the moonlight.

"I figure he's only twenty minutes behind us at the most," the Colonel had estimated. "So I'll drive on for about thirty minutes, Sam, then come back for you. I know I can rely on you. Like the old times, with you covering my rear." Then with that slap of confidence across the shoulders Jaroff remembered so well from the Vietnam days, the Colonel had driven off.

He glanced around at the darkness. Well it wasn't exactly like Nam, no palm trees, no rice paddies, no tangled foliage spitting out bullets zip, zip, from unseen guns. Just stillness, and emptiness, like he was the last hunter left alive in the world. It made him feel a little like Crocodile Dundee, except he hadn't seen a sign of a crocodile since landing in Australia. He grinned in the darkness.

He heard the gathering drone of a motor to the east, and then saw the headlights. The moon was throwing out all the light he needed. He shifted position to make himself more comfortable, and snugged the rifle butt to his shoulder. Christ, he could remember setting himself up on a night like this long ago, when they'd spotted the entrance to one of Charlie's underground tunnels. He'd got five as they came out, before they knew what was happening. He peered along the sights, as the headlights rapidly grew larger. Reine wouldn't know what happened either.

Reine considered the possibility that he might be slightly mad. What in God's name was he doing out in this wilderness at his age, trying desperately to keep in touch with the Americans? His eyesight wasn't the best anymore at night, and several times he'd almost run off the road, such as it was. Always he liked to work to a carefully structured plan, meticulously put together with foresight, and expert intelligence data. But he had no intelligence reports to guide him here. He was now certain the Americans were up to something that connected to Leiman, and Hegarty, and Grubin. For all he knew the Americans were Brandt's killers, but he couldn't even begin to hazard a guess at their motive. Perhaps it was ludicrous rushing through the night like this, when he didn't have any set plan of what he was going to do when he reached Cathedral Rock, except that he had to somehow warn Hegarty and Grubin of danger. What alternative did he have, when he'd seen Corliss and Jaroff leaving Normanton, heading in the direction he'd been given for Cathedral Rock? God, he just couldn't allow anything to endanger the Leiman kidnapping now. As much as anything else, to see Leiman at the end of a rope would be his grand exit from the Mossad, he would go into retirement on a triumphant note.

He pushed hard on the gas pedal, failing to see a gaping hole in the road, and in an instant found himself frantically struggling for control, clinging to the wheel as his head slammed against the roof, the wagon bucking under him like an unbroken horse. He didn't hear a shot, not even the splintering of glass, just a fractured hole suddenly appearing in the windshield, and fragments spraying his hands. But instinctively he knew he was under fire. He felt no fear, all his time with the Mossad there had been people trying to kill him, and he'd outlived them all. He couldn't believe this was anything more than another near miss, that he'd survive as before, even while he cursed for blundering so stupidly into an ambush. So much for being pushed into defensive action without a plan. Crazy. Crazy. But he hadn't yet grasped how his reflexes lacked the sharpness of earlier encounters, he swung the wheel hard left to take evasive action, yet too late. His head seemed to explode in a violent cataclysm of pain, then he knew no more. Andre had retired—forever.

* * *

Carl hunched in the study chair and glowered across the desk with that foreboding scowl that always indicated trouble.

"Dorf, it has the smell of a rotting carcass," he said accusingly.

A hiss of exasperation escaped Leiman's mouth. He had to keep reminding himself that although Carl was aged, his eyes still had the sharpness of an eagle's. He'd seen the confrontation with Hegarty, insisted on being told what it was all about, but Leiman was determined not to get involved in another security harangue.

He sat back from the desk and returned Carl's scowl in kind. He'd be relieved in a way when death severed the partnership.

"Always you are looking under rocks for demons that aren't there," he said patronizingly.

"Then tell me why Hegarty would be helping you with Pony, when you are throwing him off the place?"

"He's not helping me, he's doing it for Pony. The man has a special feeling for the boy. You find that so hard to grasp?"

Carl scratched reflectively at the scar tissue on his face. "Ja, a special feeling—you mean like the boy had for you?"

"And still has," said Leiman curtly. "It'll be as it was when Hegarty's gone."

Carl's head shook in disagreement. "I was right about Hegarty," he pointed out. "Trouble I said it would be, and trouble it's been; with your daughters, with your grandson. You should never have hired him."

"All right, all right," said Leiman irritably. "It was a mistake, and I'm correcting it. But it's been family trouble, not the sort of trouble you were whining about." He uttered a derisive laugh. "An avenging angel you thought had come, after more than forty years of safety; materializing out of nowhere."

Carl refused to be baited. He tapped a long, bony finger against his nose. "It has a smell," he repeated. "This business with Pony has the smell of a rotting carcass."

Leiman folded his arms as if forming a bulwark, and glared across the desk. No matter what, he wouldn't lose his temper again. He was still cringing inside over betraying Anna with the revelation that he was Pony's father. And God, how could he do it to her with Hegarty there, those terrible words tumbling out in the heat of the moment. Would he never learn to control his temper? At least he could be sure it had destroyed anything that might have been growing between Hegarty and Anna; no man would go with a woman guilty of incest. But it did little to ease his remorse, and it left him in no mood to listen to his partner's senile ramblings.

"I'm thinking the rot is in your head," he muttered.

Carl merely returned a cadaverous smile. "Rot there may be in mein body, but not in mein head. I'm warning you not to go to this nighttime meeting with Hegarty at the old house. It's being foolhardly, Dorf."

"Ah, you think I want this trouble with Pony going on?" said Leiman impatiently. "I want it settled; it has to be settled. I must go. Tomorrow Pony will be back, and Hegarty will be gone, and you will see all of your fears were like shadows."

"Don't go," insisted Carl.

"I'm going, I have to go."

"The boy fogs your brain, you love him too much," grated Carl.

"The fog is in your head, not mine."

"Then at least be going armed."

"You think Pony's so mad at me he's going to shoot me?" jeered Leiman.

"Hegarty's the dangerous one."

"Only in your fearful mind."

"Why won't you listen to me?" asked Carl in exasperation.

"We've been over this, Carl, over and over it. The Gulf Country is our haven, always has been, always will be. Sick I am of fearing every strange face, too long it's been going on, and now we're safe. The name Leiman is dead."

"But not crossed off the records. That I'm being sure; the Jews would never cross the name off." He paused, then gave a resigned shrug. "Then take Anna with you," he suggested.

"Pony only wants to see me. That is agreed with Hegarty. The boy's problem is with me, not his mother."

"Then for my sake take Anna with you."

"You think I need my daughter's protection?" scoffed Leiman.

"No, but if Hegarty feels something for Anna, then he would be less likely to make trouble with her there."

"What sort of trouble?"

Again Carl placed a finger to his nose. "You know I have a nose for the Jews. It has the smell of . . ."

Leiman slammed his hand down on the desk. "Don't! For God's sake, don't be saying that again." He stood to his feet, a brusque move of termination. This constant conflict because of Hegarty was driving him mad. He could scarcely wait to get to the old house, heal the wounds with his son, and be rid of the troublemaking American. He took a deep breath, and kept the lid down firmly on his antagonism. "Believe me, Carl, the American is not going to be waving a magic wand and whisk us all away to Israel," he said, with unknowing irony.

Carl called to him once more before he passed through the door. "Take Anna," he pleaded. "At least for me, for all the years, for what we had back in the fatherland, for what we've been through here."

Leiman refused an answer, merely closed the door with slow deliberation.

Carl did not move from the chair, his bony shoulders hunched into sullen contemplation. Perhaps it was difficult, if not impossible, to argue against a safety that had endured unchallenged for more than half a lifetime, with not even a hint of exposure, but he was sure only the grave would guarantee safety.

He was a great believer in instinct. Let the mealy-mouthed intellectuals ponder, deliberate, and thresh themselves into impotence, for him it had always been instinct that rarely failed him. Right from the beginning he had an instinctive doubt about the American, but how do you convince others of a feeling not based on logic? There had been other instinctive fears, which hadn't materialized; perhaps that was why Dorf was so impatient with him now.

But Dorf should have paid heed to his keen nose for Jews, remembered how he'd used it so skillfully in the old days; at Treblinka it would have been absurd to put themselves at risk for some insignificant boy. Maybe he was old, but he still craved to die a free man.

He came to a decision, pried himself out of the chair, and

stood for a moment checking his balance. There were times he
needed to be wary of a trembling in his legs, when they took
the full weight of his body, but by God it was still possible for
him to walk. If he left now, and took his time, he could be at
the old house in a little over an hour.

Carl crossed slowly to the large cabinet by the window,
opened the door, and took out the Lee Enfield with the telescopic sight. The rifle was a prized possession of many years,
and once he'd prided himself on the accuracy of his shooting.
He could still do it, if he steadied the rifle against something
solid; his eyesight was still sharp enough to hit a target. If Dorf
stubbornly refused to heed any warnings about Hegarty, to
even consider Anna as a safety precaution, then he had to act
himself. He knew the area around the old house thoroughly,
he'd lived there long enough; there were many places where
he could hide and have a clear view of the place. He would find
somewhere, and settle there out of sight until Dorf arrived. It
was going to be difficult, but he had to force himself, make his
aged bones respond to his wishes. If all his instincts proved
right, that in some way he failed as yet to understand it was a
trap, then he would put a bullet through the American's brain.
The bright Gulf moon would give him all the light he needed.
Dorf would thank him, be forced to admit there were times he
needed to be protected. And if he was proved wrong, then he
would creep back here and say nothing.

It took Hegarty only a short time to put his few things into
the backpack. He checked the Colt to make sure it was fully
loaded, then put it on the bed beside the pack. He wasn't
expecting trouble, but he wanted to be ready, just in case. He
figured Leiman was going to be taken so much by surprise that
they'd have him bundled onto the helicopter before he realized what the hell was happening.

He stretched out on the bed, lit a cigar, and thoughtfully
expelled smoke toward the ceiling. Everything was set; he
couldn't see a flaw at the moment. It had worked just as he
wanted, in spite of Jules—protection for Anna, a carefully set
trap for Leiman. Christ, he wished he could feel self-satisfied
triumph, instead of the sour taste curdling his mouth. The

Mossad wouldn't understand his resignation, and he wouldn't give reasons; they'd just have to accept it.

He plotted his movements. He'd go back to the old house around ten o'clock, earlier than he'd told Jules, but they'd need to talk about how to handle Leiman when he arrived. Keeping Pony down in the cellar meant the boy wouldn't be exposed to any danger, and that way he wouldn't have to see him again, not face that expression of hatred. He guessed it was chickenhearted. Christ, only a short time ago he wouldn't have given a shit what a kid like that thought about him.

He wondered what Anna was doing. Jesus, there was a temptation to go and see her, make love to her just once more, but that'd be crazy, for him as well as her.

There was a tentative knock on the door, and he sat up on the bed and swung his legs to the floor. He knew it had to be Anna. Logic told him to send her away, but he knew he wasn't going to do it.

It was Ingrid, but almost unrecognizable from the hip-wriggling, in-heat girl he'd first met in the living room of the house. Features drawn, white-faced, deep shadows under her eyes, long hair straggling about her face. She took him so much by surprise that she was past him and into the room before he could shut the door. The last thing he wanted at this stage was trouble with Anna, or Leiman, so he quickly closed the door and warily studied her.

"Were you figuring on throwing any more bottles?" he asked with attempted humor.

She didn't immediately answer. He could tell by the way she moved she was uptight as hell, brushing repeatedly at her hair, casting quick nervous glances about the room. She had on jeans and a blue jacket with leather inserts.

"You're going away," she muttered. "I heard you were going away."

He didn't move from the door. "I think it's better, and I figured you'd welcome it," he said. "I've made a lot of trouble for all of you."

She stared at him. Christ, she looked terrible, as if she hadn't slept in a long time. Her mouth was trembling.

"I don't know what to do about you, Hegarty," she

moaned. "When I want something bad enough, I usually don't give up until I get it, and I usually do."

He spread his hands regretfully, wanting her out of here. "Life's not like that," he said softly. "I'm surprised you haven't found out before this."

She gave a shrill laugh, and tugged at the fronds of her hair. "God, how I hate myself for being here," she rasped. "Demeaning myself by saying shit things like that. I wished you to bloody hell after that last time, swore I wouldn't even look at you again."

"I'm not worth it, Ingrid."

She tossed her head. "Oh Christ, I know that, Hegarty, how I know it, but it doesn't help."

She looked a little crazy, He hadn't meant to do this to her, hadn't realized her brazen front was only a fragile shell. He tried to shock her into retreat.

"I saw your friend, Red Orton, in Normanton," he said.

She merely answered with an ugly laugh, with no attempt at denial. "Ha, I got a call about that. You're a tougher nut than I reckoned on, Hegarty. I couldn't believe it when you turned up back here without a damn scratch. I didn't think there was anyone who could make pulp of Red."

"You wanted to hurt me that much?"

She performed an unstable pirouette about the room, and nearly lost her balance. He figured she was close to hysteria, and was anxious not to push her over the edge.

"I don't know what I wanted to do, Hegarty. Maybe I'm a little crazy when someone hurts me really bad."

"I didn't want to hurt you."

"Then take me away with you, Hegarty."

"You love the Gulf Country."

"I don't fit in here any more. Maybe I never did. Take me away from Anna, away from my idiot of a father; the hell with the lot of them," she said bitterly.

"It wouldn't work, Ingrid, and you know it wouldn't work," he said heavily. "I'd only make you unhappy."

"Christ, who's talking about happiness," she said wildly. "Beat me, fuck the hell out of me if you want. Jesus, you . . . you shit, maybe it'll cure me." She scrabbled in her jacket, and threw two passports down on the bed. "Look, I got

them for you, Hegarty, damn you; what more do you want?"
She gave a crazed laugh. "It's a good price, the best offer
you've had around here, I'll bet, even from that bitch Anna."

He stared down at the passports. They'd certainly be
useful at the trial, but they weren't that important now that
the fingerprints matched. He walked cautiously past her to the
bed, and picked them up.

"I brought Carl's as well, seeing you're so all-fired interested in ancient photographs," she added breathlessly. "I dug
it out of an old file in the study. God, even Carl must have
forgotten it was there."

She couldn't stand still, swinging her arms and body
about, her hair swirling. He had to get her out of here, tell her
anything, before she disintegrated. He made a gesture of
gratitude to the passports. "I think it was terrific of you to bring
them, Ingrid, I really appreciate it. But I have to go—you've
heard about Pony running away."

"Fuck Pony. The little bastard could always look after
himself. I don't believe that shit about him running off anyway.
Little creep's trying to manipulate you."

"I can't be sure of that. I've got to go. Please Ingrid, just
let's talk about this when I get back. You'll be calmer then,
and . . ."

She cut him off with a furious gesture at the passports.
"You think I'm an idiot? I know you're not coming back. God,
I brought you the passports, what more do you want? You want
me down on my hands and knees? Aren't you even going to
look at the damn things?"

He was desperate to do anything to placate her, and he
opened them in an attempt to calm her. "Okay, okay," he said.
"Goddamn it, take it easy."

"I'm going with you, Hegarty," she declared, with sullen
determination.

He glanced rapidly at the two passports, his mind more
preoccupied with ways to extricate himself without another
temperamental explosion. Christ, she'd certainly inherited her
father's volatile nature.

He glanced at Carl Beaunig's passport photograph, absently wondering why it looked so familiar. Then it hit him,
like a jarring punch from Red Orton, leaving him momentarily

dazed, and open-mouthed. He pushed Ingrid hastily aside, scrimmaged in his backpack until he found the envelope containing the old photograph of Horst Leiman as a young man, then placed it alongside Beaunig's passport picture. The identification was unmistakable. Christ almighty, *it was Horst Leiman! Carl Beaunig, not Kisek, was Horst Leiman!* He turned in a blind circle, trying to grapple with the revelation. How could the fingerprints possibly be wrong?

"What shit are you trying to pull on me now, Hegarty?" demanded Ingrid stridently.

He scarcely heard her, making a convulsive effort to adjust to what he was seeing. Then who the hell was Kisek? The photograph in Kisek's passport told him nothing. How could Kisek's fingerprints match with the ones Eli Brandt found in Berlin if he wasn't Horst Leiman? Reine had *verified* those Berlin fingerprints as belonging to Horst Leiman. All along they'd figured there was a strong possibility Carl Beaunig was the man Stauffer, who'd been Leiman's aide in Treblinka, but were the roles actually reversed? Was Kisek Stauffer? Yet Kisek's photograph looked nothing like the picture of Stauffer Jules had shown him, and would Horst Leiman allow his aide to be the dominant figure at Cathedral Rock, as Kisek obviously was?

He kept coming back to the fingerprints, which had seemed the ultimate conclusive proof, and it only added to his bewilderment. Somewhere Brandt got it wrong. And Reine. And the Wiesenthal organization. Whomever the fingerprints that Eli Brandt had found in Berlin belonged to, it certainly wasn't Horst Leiman. He checked the photographs again, to make sure his eyes weren't lying to him, but there was absolutely no mistake. He glanced at his watch. It was nine-thirty. He was going to have to get to Jules fast and straighten this out before they pulled a blunder that made them all look ridiculous. Resignation or not, Favett would have their balls if they took the wrong man back to Israel. He placed the passports in his hip pocket and tucked the envelope back in the backpack. It might be a good idea to check out where Carl was, before he went to Jules.

"I'm late, I must go, Ingird," he said over his shoulder.

"Not without me," she retorted.

He tightened the pull string on the backpack, debating with himself how blunt he should be. "Without you," he stated firmly.

"You two-faced lying bastard, you're going away with Anna, aren't you?"

Hegarty turned angrily. "For Chrissake, Ingrid, will you . . ." He stopped short when he saw she'd picked up the Colt and was aiming it at him. She knew enough to have flicked off the safety catch. He attempted a disarming smile, and held out his hand. "You'd better give that to me before someone gets hurt," he said carefully. There was a glazed look in her eyes that warned him she was over the edge, capable of anything. She backed unsteadily to the small chair by the door, the gun never deviating, and sat down.

"This is goddamn stupid, Ingrid," he said.

Her face was an emotionless mask. "All my life I've been taking shit," she muttered. "Shit from my father, from my mother, from Anna, and now shit from you. Sit down on the bed, Hegarty."

He eased himself carefully onto the bed. "You don't really think you can use that on me, do you, Ingrid?"

"Maybe."

"You won't be able to go away with me then."

She uttered a manic giggle. "Perhaps I'll shoot us both."

"That's crazy talk." He started to stand up, but she gestured menacingly with the Colt. "Don't tempt me, you bastard."

He relaxed back on the bed. "I'm not going away with Anna, that's ridiculous," he said.

"Don't lie. I saw you talking to her before, like you could hardly keep your damn hands off her. Pony hasn't run away; he's waiting for you and Anna over at the old house, and you're all going away together."

He managed a scoffing laugh. "Christ, that's crazy."

"Is it? Is it? What is it with you, Hegarty? Where'd you learn the knack? I've never seen anyone lie so easily."

"If it was true I was going away with Anna, I'd be doing you a favor."

"How do you work that out?"

"Cathedral Rock would be all yours."

"It wouldn't mean a bloody thing out here on my own."

He leaned forward and rested his elbows on his knees, trying to appear unconcerned. "You've got it all wrong, Ingrid," he said persuasively. "I promise you I'm not going anywhere with Anna, or Pony."

"Liar. Liar."

He shrugged, as if bemused by the accusation. "How can I convince you?"

"You can't."

"Are we just going to sit here like this all night?"

"Maybe. Anna and Pony can wait over at the old house forever as far as I'm concerned. You won't be going to meet them. I don't give a damn what you do, but you're not going away with that bitch."

"I can't just sit here. You're father's ordered me off Cathedral Rock."

"The hell with my father," she said stubbornly. "I'll tell you when you can go." She gave a crazy little smile. "It's getting to you, isn't it, Hegarty, having to take shit for once in your life."

"You don't love me, Ingrid."

"I hate your guts."

"Then why don't you just let me walk out of your life?"

"God, I wish it was that easy."

"Go and ask Anna, if you don't believe me," he offered.

She uttered a scornful laugh. "Do you think I'd believe anything she said? God, she lies like you."

He judged the distance between them. If he was fast, and took her by surprise he might just make it. The way she was he couldn't discount the possibility she might shoot.

She read his intent. "You try coming at me, and I'll kill you, Hegarty, so help me I will."

He realized she was unhinged enough to mean it. "You're really aiming for us to sit here all night? Is that what you want?"

"If that's what it takes."

"You think I'll take you away with me then?"

She didn't answer. He figured she wasn't thinking that far ahead, hatred had jammed shut all the exit doors.

She reached up to the switch behind her, and turned

off the light. In the shaft of moonlight through the window
she resembled a frosted figurine, except where a reflection
gleamed on the barrel of the Colt.

"You're not going away with Anna," she muttered fiercely.
"I don't give a damn what happens, but you're not going away
with that bitch. If she doesn't see a light in here she'll reckon
you've gone anyway."

He felt a sense of desperation. He couldn't believe this
was happening. Even if he made a lunge for her in the darkness, there had to be a good chance he'd stop a bullet. Christ,
they'd be readying the helicopter on the ship, he couldn't just
sit here and let Jules kidnap the wrong man. Ingrid was
sustaining her crazy anger on a bitter mix of love and loathing,
and there had to be a chance such an intense fire would burn
itself out.

"This won't change a goddamn thing, Ingrid," he said
curtly.

She didn't answer, there was just a tiny shaft of light
dancing on the Colt as she moved it in a threatening arc. How
long could he wait? Time was the last thing he could afford, yet
he realized there was no way he was going to convince her with
words.

But the virulence feeding her didn't abate. She continued
to sit in mute concentration, knees primly together in unconscious reproach of her former sexual aggressiveness. Several
times he considered calling her bluff, challenging her to shoot,
standing to his feet, picking up his backpack, and walking out
the door. But to merely shift position brought a menacing
jiggle of the gun, and he knew nothing had changed. Once or
twice he tried to repeat his denial that Anna was going away
with him, but he might as well have been talking to someone
totally deaf. By ten-thirty he was desperate enough to try
anything. And he had an idea.

"You won't go to the house and ask Anna?" he said.

At least he got an answer this time. "I told you it'd be a
waste of time. She'd lie, like you. She's probably waiting for
you at the old place by now anyway."

"I can prove you wrong," he said.

"Liar," she responded.

"Then come with me."

She awkwardly shifted position, as an indication of interest. "What do you mean, come with you?" she asked suspiciously.

"Come with me to the old house, see for yourself. If Anna's waiting there for me, you can goddamn shoot me. That's how sure I am you're wrong."

"You're trying to bullshit me, Hegarty, and it won't work," she hotly declared.

"What's the matter, can't you stand the thought of being proved wrong?" he taunted. "Are you so goddamn scared of being made to realize you're acting like a fool?"

She took time to think about it, the gun wavering indecisively enough to give him hope. Maybe the fire was dying, reason gradually beginning to reassert itself.

"I'm not falling for that," she sneered. "You know I won't come. You're still working your devious little bloody mind for a way to get the gun off me."

"I'm not aiming to get myself shot. You're so screwed up about your sister I figure you couldn't bear the thought of being proved wrong. That you're acting like a stupid asshole," he said scornfully.

She stood up so quickly it surprised him. He must have hit an exposed nerve that gave off an immediate reaction.

"I'll call your damn bluff, Hegarty," she said. "It'll be worth it just to see you proved a bloody liar."

"We'll see who's the liar," he said.

He stood up, ever so slowly, the muzzle of the Colt following him to an upright position. Maybe deep down she was hoping she was wrong. But she was knotted so tight he was sure if he made any sudden movement her finger would involuntarily jerk on the trigger. He was just relieved to have gotten a response from her.

She opened the door, and motioned with the Colt. "You first—and my God, I'm warning you Hegarty, don't try anything smart."

He had no intention of trying anything. He went out the door and glanced quickly to the house. Light showed in ʋeral windows, but there was no sign of anyone. The air was ˙rp, and he turned up his collar. He didn't look around, bu╵

heard Ingrid close the door, and he began to walk slowly to where he'd parked the Kawasaki.

"Wait," she hissed. "Where do you think you're going?"

"To my cycle."

"We'll go in the jeep."

"No, we go on the cycle," he insisted. "That's what Pony's expecting. We go in the jeep, Pony'll think it's someone else, and run away."

"You're still sticking to that story."

"It's the truth. Anna's not there, only Pony."

She stopped, but he kept walking, and after a moment he heard the sharp rap of her footsteps catching up.

"I don't trust you, you devious bastard," she breathed.

"You'll find out you're only making a fool of yourself," he retorted.

"We'll see who's the damn fool."

He straddled the bike, kick-started the motor, then felt the cold muzzle of the pistol hard into his back, as she settled on the pillion seat behind. He still couldn't be sure she wouldn't suddenly snap and kill both of them, as she had threatened. One arm encircled his waist, while the pressure of the muzzle slid across his back, and lodged against his ribs.

"Don't think I wouldn't do it, Hegarty," she muttered into his ear.

"I know," he said.

He knew he was going to have to do this well, take her completely by surprise, or a bullet would smash into his ribs. He revved the motor hard, threw the clutch with abrupt sharpness, and forcefully hauled back on the handlebars. The rear wheel spun with a shriek of rubber on dirt, the front wheel lifted like a rearing horse, and he grimaced with the feared anticipation of a bullet slamming into his ribs. But it worked. He felt her fall away with a sudden cry of surprise, and he cut back the gas until the front wheel dropped back to earth. He came around in a tight circle and saw her lying huddled on the ground, not moving. He rode up alongside, turned off the motor, propped up the bike, and went to her. The fall had knocked her cold, and there was a nasty scrape on her forehead, but she was breathing evenly. The Colt lay a few feet from her outstretched hand, and he picked it up and

thrust it into his belt. It could have been that he'd just taken
her by surprise, but he wondered if at the last minute she
hadn't been able to pull the trigger. He wasn't going to wait
around to ask her. He glanced indecisively about the yard,
then across to the house. He couldn't possibly take her in
there, and he couldn't leave her lying where she was. He
knelt, picked her up in his arms, swiftly carried her back to his
room, and laid her on the bed. She moaned, and a sobbing sigh
oozed from her mouth, but her eyes remained closed. Christ,
he wouldn't have gone near her if he'd known he was going to
set off a psychotic time bomb. He hastily pulled a blanket over
her, picked up his backpack, went back to the door, then
paused for a final check of the figure on the bed. He felt a
twinge, as when he'd left Pony: she was another unintended
victim; he hadn't wanted to do this to her, and it was a sobering
irony that her father wasn't even Horst Leiman after all. He
couldn't think about that now. He went outside and locked the
door behind him, then put the key in his pocket. It would
be all over by the time she came to and got out of there.

He hesitated, again caught with indecision. If Carl
Beaunig was Horst Leiman, should he make an attempt to grab
him now, and forcibly take him to the old house? He squinted
at his watch. It was ten forty-five. Leiman would probably be
getting himself ready to go to the old house. He shook his
head. Christ, he was going to have to think of him as Kisek
again, not Leiman. But could he chance prowling through the
house tying to locate Carl, without alerting Kisek and Anna?
Maybe it would be best if he went directly to Jules, and made
some change in the kidnap plan to fit in with the new situation;
reroute the helicopter to Cathedral Rock, and carry out the
kidnapping from here, as Jules had wanted to do in the first
place. Anna would be safe, and the old man wouldn't offer any
resistance. But would Kisek?

Only God knew who Kisek actually was, but Kisek had to
know that Carl was Horst Leiman, had obviously protected
him all these years, and quite possibly might use force to
protect him again. He decided for Jules and the old house.
Whatever changes had to be made, Jules was the only one in
  ch with the helicopter. And what about Pony? Using the
    as bait was no longer relevant. He went swiftly to the

Kawasaki, kick-started it into life, and switched on the head-light. It didn't matter a damn about his being seen now. There had to be an explanation for the fingerprint mistake, but Jules was in for one hell of a shock when he saw the passport photograph. But even as he rode, there was still a place in his thoughts for Anna. She'd made it obvious enough she cared nothing for Carl, and now that her father was in the clear, maybe there was a chance for them.

Chapter 14

Jaroff ran the rented ranch wagon into the shelter of a small clump of scraggly trees, and switched off the engine. Both men sat quietly for a moment, warily listening. The savanna glistened with a silver mantle of moonlight, the beep, beep of the receiver in Jaroff's hand in contrast to the soft rustle of the surrounding trees. They could see the craggy silhouettes of the ant hills, like snow-capped sentinels forming a path to the Cathedral Rock homestead. Two windows of yellow light set the house apart from the dominating black mass of the Rock itself.

"Just like the old guy Cutmore described," muttered Corliss.

Jaroff lifted the receiver, and pointed it toward the house. "Well, the sonofabitch Hegarty's there all right, Colonel. The bug's working like a charm."

Corliss gave a silent nod of satisfaction. One of the house lights flicked off, then after a few moments back on again.

"Wherever we find Hegarty, that's where we'll find Leiman," said Corliss. "That's the way it has to be."

Jaroff made a cautious inspection of the countryside. "Maybe the Mossad are somewhere around here, watching just like we are, Colonel."

Corliss shrugged. "If we hear the helicopter, then that's when we can start worrying, because that's how the Mossad are planning to take Leiman out. Don't worry, we'll still beat 'em to it, Sam."

"How do you want to handle it, Colonel?"

"Let's give it a while for the lights to go out, and for them

to get bedded down. And we keep listening for the first sounds
of a chopper. We hear that, then we move in fast."

"And the family?"

"Just let's see how it develops," said Corliss noncommit-
tally. "All I want is to do a professional job."

"The Mossad aren't likely to go running to the cops?"

"No way. Those guys are out to pull an illegal kidnapping,
so when we beat 'em to the punch they're not going to run
screaming to anyone."

"I'll back you however it runs, Colonel. We gotta waste
the family, then we gotta do whatever's best for our country.
That's the way I see it."

Corliss offered a grunt of approval. "I'm lucky to have
someone like you backing me up, Sam."

"I believe in paying my dues, Colonel. You know that."
He nodded to the house. "Who's to say it wasn't the Mossad
guys who killed Leiman anyhow?"

"I'm hoping that's the way the cards fall. It would put us
beautifully in the clear."

They were interrupted by the staccato burble of a small
engine revving hard, from the direction of the house, then the
sound tailed off, and stopped as suddenly as it had begun. The
two men peered anxiously toward the homestead.

"Sure as hell sounded like a goddamn motorcycle," said
Jaroff.

"Then it has to be Hegarty."

"I guess so."

"What's the sonofabitch up to?" He glanced at the receiver in Jaroff's hand. The beep, beep, still piped out its
detecting message in clear, even tones. "He's not moving
anyway."

"Maybe he was going somewhere, and changed his
mind."

"Maybe," said Corliss, scowling. He shrugged down in
the seat. A fluid situation like this was always a challenge, a
test of adapting rapidly to changing conditions, yet there were
so many imponderables here. As long as Hegarty stayed put
they had a guideline to follow. Where Hegarty was, Leiman
was. As long as he kept that firmly in mind he wouldn't go
wrong.

"I don't see a damn thing," growled Jaroff, squinting toward the house, "except those lights are still on."

"Patience, Sam," murmured Corliss.

They sat waiting in silence, ears straining for the slightest indication of an approaching helicopter. The breeze faded, and the trees stilled, as if with a sense of anticipation. Occasionally a bird called, to challenge the primacy of the receiver's repetitive beep, while Corliss brooded on the wisdom of waiting. He guessed he was hoping there was some way they could waste Leiman without involving the family, but to hold off was dangerous. It was only a hunch, but he had the feeling they had a time edge over the Mossad, and just sitting here could be throwing away the advantage. Did it matter a damn if the lights were on or not?

"I wonder if this Leiman has nightmares about those concentration camp days," said Jaroff after a moment.

"Guys like that don't have nightmares about what they did; only about getting caught, and hung," Corliss replied.

"I had my nightmares over Nam."

"You weren't working in a slaughter house. Just stopping the commies for your country."

"I still remember the first guy I wasted. That kept me awake at the time."

"The first is always the worst. It's the same for all of us."

"Yeah, you're right about that. After a while I didn't think about it any more."

Corliss gestured toward the house. "Maybe it was the same for him. Like slaughtering goddamn cattle." He straightened, and irritably glanced around. "I don't think we should wait any longer, Sam. I'm getting nervous just sitting here."

"You want we should drive over there?"

"No; we walk. I don't want them to hear us coming."

Almost immediately the burble of the motorcycle started again.

"There's the bike again," said Jaroff. "You think the Mossad might be starting to make their move?"

"Maybe. I guess it's a possibility."

Jaroff raised the receiver as the beeping signal began to

ose strength. "The sonofabitch is starting to move away from
us, Colonel," he warned urgently.

Corliss cursed and leaned forward, peering intently toward the house. "Can you see anything?"

"There—across to the right," said Jaroff, pointing. "See
he headlight?"

"Goddammit," muttered Corliss. "Switch off the receiver
a moment."

Jaroff flicked off the switch, and Corliss tilted his head,
istening.

"I don't hear any fucking chopper," grunted Jaroff. "Only
he bike."

"Neither do I. Switch it on again, Sam." The beeping
signal resumed, while Corliss pawed indecisively at his chin.
Already the sound of the bike was fading.

"He'll be gone soon, Colonel," said Jaroff nervously. He
motioned with the receiver. "And he'll be out of our range."

"Where Hegarty is, that's where we'll find Leiman,"
muttered Corliss, like a priest reaffirming his faith.

"Maybe the Mossad have got it figured not to take Leiman
from the house," suggested Jaroff.

"That could be the way they've planned it. Maybe they've
got the same worries about the family we have."

"I guess it has to be Hegarty on the bike?"

"It's got to be," said Corliss firmly.

"If we're going to follow him we'd better make up our
minds quick, Colonel," urged Jaroff.

Corliss anxiously tapped his clenched hands against his
mouth. What if they moved on the house now to terminate
Leiman and he wasn't even there? They'd only alert the
family, maybe needlessly be forced to kill them. Perhaps the
kidnap had already taken place, and Hegarty was holding
Leiman prisoner in another location, waiting for the helicopter. It made sense, there was nothing surer than that the
Mossad would want to stay clear of involving the family; they
wouldn't risk anything that could make them look bad, not if
they were figuring on a showpiece trial in front of the world for
Leiman.

"Go with him, Sam," he ordered suddenly. "No headlights. Reine led us to Hegarty, and Hegarty will lead us to Leiman. I've got to stick with that."

Jaroff reached for the ignition. "You figure they might have Leiman already stashed away somewhere, Colonel?"

The engine turned over with a throaty burr. Jaroff thrust into reverse, and backed cautiously out of the trees.

"It makes sense, Sam, Christ, it makes sense. We can't risk not checking it out."

Jaroff braked at the edge of the road, and handed the receiver to Corliss. "See if you can get a bead on the goddam bike, Colonel—give me a direction."

Corliss nodded, pointed the receiver to the windshield and swung it slowly back and forth in an arc. "Straight ahead Sam," he commanded.

Jaroff slipped quickly into first gear and tentatively eased forward, tires rippling over the gravel, stones pinging against the underside of the wagon.

"Keep your eye on the range indicator, Colonel," he warned. "We'll want to know when Hegarty comes to a stop, so we don't get too close and risk him hearing or seeing us. When we want to get up close to him it'll be safer on foot."

Corliss nodded agreement, letting the signal guide him, ordering adjustments to their direction as they headed west. He didn't let it show, but he still had doubts. He never believed in going back on a command decision once it was made; that was a sure way to confuse the men in the field. But God, here he was running blind; he just hoped trailing Hegarty was the right way to go. He tried to be philosophical about it. What was there to lose anyway? If they washed out on this option, they still had time to get back to the house and take care of Leiman. But Sam had put his finger on a delicious contingency. If they could make it look like the Mossad were responsible for the killing, then they were off the hook in every direction. That'd be one hell of an irony for Gormane to muse over in retirement.

Beaunig lowered himself awkwardly into the small depression, warily leaned back until his spine rested on the small mound of grass, cradled the Lee Enfield in his arms, then slowly let his head tilt back until his eyes were directed at the

tar-crammed sky. He let his mouth hang open, tongue lolling,
o he could suck as much of the crisp night air into his lungs as
ossible.

There had been moments when it had seemed like the
ourney was beyond him, aching legs at times giving way
nder him, heart hammering with an unsteady beat, sweat
luing his clothes to his skin. At such times it would have been
o easy to convince himself his suspicions were only the para-
oid meanderings of an aged mind, to give it up, go back to
Cathedral Rock and restful sleep. He had steeled himself to
eject such temptations, that was the easy way; besides, he was
ertain he was right, the unmistakable scent of Jew was too
trong to be ignored, and had been ever since Hegarty had
rrived.

He sat immobile until his heart resumed a normal pace,
hen he gently brought his head forward, and stared at the
ouse. He positioned the Lee Enfield on the rock in front of
im so that the muzzle pointed at the front door of the old
ouse, then laboriously crouched forward, squinted through
he telescopic sight, and moved the rifle in a slow arc to test his
eld of fire. Yes, it was ideal, perhaps only sixty meters from
he house, and if he steadied the rifle in the cleft of the rock,
e was reasonably confident of cutting anyone down. Espe-
ially the Jew.

Then he relaxed, eased himself back, and morosely
tudied the old building. Dorf had never understood his
atred of the Gulf Country, why he had never ceased to long
or the soft green of Wismar, but he had been at his happiest
iving here at the old place, before Dorf got his illusions of
randeur. Now he and the decaying building shared a common
roblem, both quickly succumbing to the onset of time. The
ears had passed so rapidly, but memory remained, with the
harpness of instant recall, his adulation of the Fuhrer just as
trong as if it were yesterday. He regretted nothing. The
leansing of Europe of the Jews was still the most worthwhile
hing he'd done with his life. But if he lived a hundred years,
e wasn't going to hang for it. He had no doubts history would
ventually see the Third Reich as a valiant attempt to save
vestern civilization.

Washington.

Richard Gormane had no idea how many times he'd bee
in the Oval Office, sitting opposite the president with meti
ulously written briefs in his hand, persuasively arguing
course of action.

But this meeting was quite different, a sudden, out-o
the-blue summons for an immediate meeting with the pres
dent, requiring no well-researched brief, simply his presenc
He could only surmise that some explosive situation ha
abruptly surfaced in the Middle East, and urgent consultatio
was necessary.

But if it was urgent, the president seemed in no hurr
offering an apologetic smile while he signed some papers. Th
consummate politician seemed as unruffled as ever, the car
fully combed gray hair with not a strand out of place, th
benign, wrinkled, fatherly features, the immaculate suit.

He finally pushed the papers aside and beamed his mos
effusive smile. "Sorry about that, Dick," he said.

"That's all right, Mr. President."

He waited again, mystified, while the president absentl
shuffled through some notes.

"I want to thank you for coming so promptly, Dick," th
president began again.

"I'm always at your disposal, Mr. President."

"Yes, I know, I know." The president paused. "I've ha
some information passed through to me which I'd like you t
comment on."

"Of course."

"As you know, our intelligence organizations monito
all sources of activity around the world." He smiled, an
shrugged. "Just so we know what's going on. Even our friend
don't always tell us."

Gormane returned a vague smile. Of course he knew tha
what was the man getting at?

"Well, they've picked up this thing coming out of Israe
Intelligence," the president continued. "Seems that one c
their agents down in Australia has ferreted something out fron
the files of Australian Intelligence that supposedly—I stres

supposedly—implicates an American OSS officer in organizing the escape from justice of a leading Nazi war criminal from Germany, back in 1945."

It was as if Gormane's intestines had abruptly turned to ice, as if circulation had ceased, but he disciplined himself to betray nothing in his face. What had happened to his control system, for God's sake? That information should have come direct to him before reaching the president, and he could have put it under wraps, like the Leiman thing. It was a painful reminder that he had enemies in Washington.

"That's a long time ago, Mr. President," he managed to say offhandedly.

"You're right, Dick, yes, a long time ago."

"Then how does it concern me?"

The president hesitated once more, and shuffled his notes about. "Well, Dick, it appears the Israelis have at last located this Nazi war criminal."

"That's good, I'm glad to hear it."

"There'll probably be a big trial, you know, a showpiece."

"If he's that valuable, then I'd imagine so."

The president coughed. "They also believe they've located the OSS officer."

Gormane crossed his legs with difficulty, it felt as if each limb were encased in lead, but it seemed essential to contrive an appearance of indifference. There was an uncomfortable tremor in his larynx, and he forcefully cleared his throat to prevent it showing in his voice.

"He's still alive then?" he asked.

"So they claim. Um . . . name of Gormane, Dick."

With supreme effort Gormane forced a laugh. "What d'you know. Well, I guess there's more than one Gormane in the world."

"You were in the OSS during the war, Dick."

Gormane managed a laugh with a hint of annoyance. He was trying to force his mind to outrace the president, to be one step ahead with an answer, but his brain seemed to have gone into a stall. "Yes, I was, Mr. President, but I think it's ridiculous if they're suggesting that I was the one who helped this . . . this Nazi war criminal escape justice."

"Yes, I think it's ridiculous too, Dick," said the president hastily. "Absolutely ridiculous, and I hope we can pressure them not to push this . . . this nonsense any further." He paused, frowning. "It would be a grave political embarrassment to have someone as valued in the administration as you are, put in the position of being . . . pilloried in such a trial." He nodded somberly. "A grave political embarrassment indeed. Long time ago or not, that's what they'd do to this former OSS officer."

For a fleeting instant Gormane had the impulse to blurt it all out, to admit he was the man, throw himself on the president's mercy; surely he'd understand how different the circumstances were then—God, it was another world. He held back. He knew the president was first and foremost a political animal who would string up his grandmother if she was a political embarrassment. What did he really have to worry about anyway? Chip would get rid of Leiman, there would be no trial, and he'd be in the clear. The Israelis could think what they damn well liked; without Leiman they couldn't prove a thing.

"I absolutely deny it," he said.

"Of course, Dick. So you should." The president linked his hands, and laid his forearms on the desk, like a judge delivering sentence. "All I want is your complete assurance that the Israelis have got it wrong. You give me that, and I'll stand by you. Absolutely."

Gormane didn't believe it for a moment. If he caused the slightest tremor to the president's political power base, he'd be dumped overboard like contraband cargo.

"You have it, Mr. President," he stated firmly.

The president stood up, and extended his hand. "Then that's all I need, Dick," he said warmly.

Gormane returned home to an empty house. There was a note from his wife to say she was out shopping for their planned vacation, and he was glad to be alone. If he'd had any stirrings of conscience about sending Chip on the assassination assignment, they were completely gone. Now that the Mossad had somehow uncovered his role, he only felt an enormous sense of relief that he'd acted when he did. God, the president was right, put in the spotlight of an international trial he would have been utterly destroyed. He had to survive this, he had to.

He sat down, and put his head in his hands. Please let Chip succeed, he pleaded, as if in prayer, and for God's sake don't let him come to harm. That was one scenario he couldn't control. Corliss was a good soldier, the best, but if by some freak mischance he got himself killed, it could set off a chain of inquiries that would lead directly to him. The thought was too horrendous to even contemplate, and he felt the urgent need of a drink.

"I want you to be believing that I'm . . . I'm truly sorry," said Kisek huskily. "Truly sorry. You know how mein temper sometimes gets the better of me, I would sooner be cutting my tongue out, than blurting out about Pony to . . . to a man like Hegarty."

Anna refused to answer, would not even look at her father. She was curled like a cat in the large chair, morosely staring through the window at the darkness.

"Truly sorry," Kisek continued penitently. "For everything. For that crazy night so long ago, which we're not understanding; for being so . . . difficult."

He fell silent. They were in the small sitting room off the study, where she liked to be, the furniture well-worn and comforting as an old friend. The room had been Kisek's only concession not to furnish in the grand manner.

"It's done," she said with quiet resignation.

"All I wanted to do was warn you against Hegarty."

She turned a stony expression to him. "I don't need any warning; I don't need it, I'll make my own decision about Hegarty. I'm an adult; a mother."

He was standing in the center of the room, like a recalcitrant servant, begging forgiveness. "There are things about the past you're not understanding," he said. "Things I could never talk to you about."

"I don't want to know; not now."

"I don't want you hurt."

"You should have thought of that earlier."

"I'm not wanting Pony hurt either."

"You drove him away," she accused hotly. "The fact is Pony worships Hegarty, and you were just damn jealous."

"I don't want him worshipping a man like that."

She irritably ruffled her hair. "The trouble is you just don't understand a man like Hegarty. My God, you should have heard how understanding he was after what you blurted out about Pony. Some men would have—despised me."

"He's wanting something from you to be like that."

"He wants me," she said, with sudden anger, slapping her hand to her chest. "And I want him. Can't you understand that?"

Kisek did not reply, hands thrust into his pockets, expression brooding and uncertain.

"I'm maybe having to accept that," he muttered reluctantly.

"I'm not too sure I believe you. God, how can I believe you?"

"Would you believe me if I said I want you to come with me tonight?"

She stared at him. "I thought that was the last thing you wanted. I know how much Hegarty is against my going."

"I think I was wrong," he said apologetically. "And Hegarty. You're right, you are Pony's mother, and it's unfair, not right that you aren't coming. I want you to come now, I think it's for the best."

"Hegarty won't like it."

"Maybe not at first, but he'll accept it, if he's an understanding man like you are claiming. He must be seeing it's just the concern you have for your son."

She was thoughtfully silent for a time. Then, "I always thought it was my right to come," she said.

"I'm agreeing with you now," Kisek encouraged.

"Then maybe I will," she said defiantly.

"Good, good. It'll be proving I want things to be different between us from now on."

"Hegarty'll understand."

"For sure he will. He knows of your love for Pony; he'll recognize your need to be part of bringing the boy back to Cathedral Rock."

She merely nodded. She'd given her word to Matt, but surely he had to see how important it was for her to be with her son. Besides, she couldn't honestly understand why Matt was so adamantly opposed to her going; for God's sake, she had a right. But the old ambivalence toward her father was still here, veering wildly between hatred and love, and she just couldn't quite trust him. Maybe his motive for asking her was to make amends, but he could be so devious. Maybe she should just accept it at face value.

"All right," she softly agreed. "I'll come."

Grubin was waiting anxiously in the shadows of the decrepit doorway when Hegarty rode up. There was no sign of Pony. It was eleven-thirty. When Grubin stepped out of the shadows Hegarty saw he held a Uzi submachine gun loosely in his hand. Jules wasn't taking any chances.

"I've been wondering where the hell you were," growled Grubin. "It's gotten so late now I just hope to Christ Leiman bought the story about the boy running away, because it's all set for the helicopter to rendezvous here around midnight."

"There were problems. Big problems."

Grubin scowled. "What do you mean, problems?"

"Where's the boy?"

Grubin motioned to the house with the Uzi. "Don't worry, he's safe in the cellar. Forget him, what sort of problems?"

"Kisek isn't Horst Leiman."

Grubin stared at him as if he'd just been certified as insane. "What sort of shit lunatic statement is that?" he rasped.

"Don't ask me how, but Eli Brandt got it wrong."

Grubin shook his head in disbelief. "And Reine, and the Wiesenthal Organization, and the Berlin police," he mocked. "I can't believe this crazy last minute bullshit. God, Matt, the fingerprints matched perfectly."

"They can't be Horst Leiman's fingerprints from Berlin."

"I see. You're telling me Reine brought us fingerprints from the other side of the world that don't really belong to Horst Leiman. I can't believe this. Where's your proof? Reine verified those fingerprints in Berlin."

"They're wrong."

"You're out of your mind."

Hegarty took him urgently by the arm, and drew him back toward the house. "Let's go down in the cellar, and I'll show you what I mean."

Grubin angrily shook his arm free. "What the hell are yo
up to, Hegarty?" he demanded suspiciously.

"I just want to make sure we take the right son-of-a-bitc|
back to Israel, that's all."

"We've got the right son-of-a-bitch. Kisek's Horst Lei
man. The helicopter's on its way, and we'll be out of her
inside an hour. That's it as far as I'm concerned. And Reine
And Favett."

Hegarty impatiently moved past him into the doorway
"I'm telling you if we take Kisek back to Israel, we're going t
look goddamn idiots. We can still use the helicopter to take ou
the right man."

"We've got the right man," stated Grubin furiously.

"For Chrissake, will you just take a look at what I've got?
asked Hegarty. "Is that too much to ask?"

Grubin hesitated, then sullenly relented, and they wen
silently down into the cellar. Pony was lying down on the bed
but he sat up when he saw Hegarty. The brief flash of relie
that crossed his face was immediately replaced by bitter hos
tility. Schon would rankle for a long time, and Hegarty won
dered if he could ever overcome the resentment. How do yo
explain the death of something beautiful in the pursuit o
something evil?

"Hi, Pony," he muttered.

The boy didn't reply, just lay back on the bed and turnec
his face to the wall.

Grubin stood to one side of the hissing lamp, and irritably
gestured with the machine gun. "Okay, let's see this grea
revelation about Kisek," he said with a sneer. "We haven't go
much time."

Hegarty dropped his backpack on the floor, took the
passports from his pocket, and laid them out on the smal
table, together with the original photograph of Horst Leiman
"I got hold of the passport I told you about."

"How did you manage that?"

"That doesn't matter for now; take a look at the photo
graphs."

"You've got two passports."

"One belongs to Kisek, the other to Carl Beaunig."

"I told you Beaunig's irrelevant," said Grubin scornfully. "Only Leiman matters."

"Take a look at the goddamn photographs; a close look," Hegarty persisted. He placed the original photograph of Horst Leiman alongside the picture in Carl Beaunig's passport, and pointed his finger repetitively from one to the other. "See it, Jules? Christ, see it? The resemblance is unmistakable."

Grubin placed the Uzi on the chair and crouched down to peer intently at the photographs.

"Beaunig is Horst Leiman, not Kisek," said Hegarty. "We had the location right, but we pinpointed the wrong man. We nearly made one hell of a foul-up, Jules. Favett would've had our balls if we'd taken the wrong man back."

Grubin ignored him, still poring over the matching photographs, as if willing himself to disbelieve his own eyes. Then he finally straightened, and snapped the passports shut.

"It makes no sense," he said tersely.

"It makes no goddamn sense if we take back the wrong man."

"Then who's Kisek?" Grubin demanded.

"I don't have the foggiest idea. Does it matter?"

"Kisek matched the fingerprints."

"Eli got it wrong," stated Hegarty. "Christ knows how, but the Berlin fingerprints obviously don't belong to Horst Leiman."

"Reine verified them," said Grubin stubbornly. "Andre wouldn't make such a mistake. Not a man with his experience."

"It happened, Christ, it happened," fumed Hegarty.

Grubin scowled down at the passports. "Passports can be doctored."

"Not these. They were put away a long time ago, and not looked at again. This is still their original condition, and they've been kept under lock and key." He shook his head. "Beaunig is Horst Leiman all right, Jules."

"The daughter gave them to you—the boy's mother?"

"No, the younger daughter. It doesn't matter a damn how I got them."

"I warned you about getting yourself involved in the family."

Hegarty glowered at him. "What the fuck's that got to do with the fact the passports prove Beaunig is Horst Leiman?"

"They've sucked you in, Matt," declared Grubin contemptuously. "Right in. I've watched you, listened to you." He gestured to Pony, who had turned from the wall at the sound of angry voices. "I think you were more concerned over the kid and his damn horse than with bringing a murdering monster to justice."

"We've been through that. It's a goddamn stupid thing to say. I just don't want to risk innocent people getting hurt."

Grubin gave a disdainful shrug, and picked up the Uzi again. "Well, I'll tell you the way I see it; the daughters know all about their father being Horst Leiman. Always have." He nodded to the passports. "Those passports are shit, and the photographs in them. The daughters played you for a sucker, fed you those shit passports to save their father's damn neck. Just like that other garbage about Leiman being executed by the Russians after the war." He gave a ferocious scowl, and shook the machine gun aggressively in the air. "Well, it isn't going to work," he grated. "Not with me it isn't."

"I know the daughters, and I'm telling you that's bullshit," declared Hegarty angrily. "Absolute bullshit." He jabbed his finger at the passports. "Carl Beaunig is Horst Leiman, for Chrissake, how can you possibly deny the identification?"

"I don't have to. I say it's a fake. If I've got to make a judgment between that photograph in the passport, and the fingerprints Reine brought us, then I'll come down on Reine's side every time. Andre just wouldn't make a mistake like that."

"You think they're trying to railroad Carl to save their father's neck," challenged Hegarty. "That's crazy."

"Like a fox. They've got it worked out we take Beaunig back to Israel, and by the time we find out we've got the wrong man, they'll have vanished. Forever."

Hegarty could barely contain his anger. It wasn't Anna, it wasn't that he wanted her father to be in the clear, he just knew the passport was telling the truth. He furiously slammed his hand down on the passports. "Jesus, don't you believe your own goddamn eyes?" he vehemently protested.

"I know what I believe," muttered Grubin. "I believe in Andre Reine, one of the best Mossad agents of all time." He studied Hegarty with eyes as hard as cut diamond. "I'm disappointed in you, Matt. I never thought a man with your experience would let the family get to him, not after all the things I'd heard about you. Kisek is Horst Leiman, the Whipmaster of Treblinka. This changes nothing for me." He made a casual motion of the Uzi muzzle toward Hegarty, but the implication was menacingly obvious. "He's the one we're taking out. He is coming for the kid, isn't he?"

"He's coming, but I'm telling you he's the wrong man," persisted Hegarty. He was certain he wasn't being influenced by Anna, every instinct told him he was right about the passport, but how would he ever convince Jules?

"Kisek goes," stated Grubin flatly.

"Then my God, we're going to finish up looking like fucking prince assholes," said Hegarty hotly. He seized the passport, and thrust it toward Grubin. "What the hell do you think Favett's going to say when he sees this?"

The words fell without any impression on Grubin's granite expression. "He'll say the same as I do when he finds out how the daughters set you up; how you've been bleeding all over the place for the kid, and his mother, ever since you got between her legs. That's the truth."

Hegarty gave a despairing shake of his head. Getting Leiman had always been his first priority, no matter what he felt about Anna and Pony. He was positive Ingrid's bringing him the passports was nothing more than a final desperate ploy to ingratiate herself.

"We'd better get outside, if you're leveling that Kisek's coming," said Grubin, glancing to the cellar ceiling.

Hegarty scowled at the implied lack of trust. "Don't worry, he'll be here, but it'll be a goddamn waste of time."

"You're wrong, Matt. Dead wrong." He started to move, and Hegarty gripped his arm.

"Listen, for Chrissake, just listen, Jules," he said desperately. "Let me explain how it was with Ingrid, then you'll understand why she gave me the passports. It wasn't anything to do with protecting her father."

"We're running out of time," said Grubin coldly.

"Ingrid isn't protecting her father; that's not the way it is," insisted Hegarty.

Grubin hesitated, glanced again to the ceiling, then to Hegarty, with the expression of humoring a spoiled child. "Prove it," he said bluntly. "But fast."

Hegarty went through it as quickly as he could—Ingrid's hatred of her sister Anna, her psychotic reaction to being rejected by him, how she'd set up the fight with Red Orton in Normanton, and her final desperate ploy in bringing him the passports. "Giving me the passports wasn't some goddamn set-up to protect her father," he concluded. "She doesn't give a shit about her father. She just wants out of Cathedral Rock, she wanted to come with me." He paused and spread his hands. "That's the way it was, Jules." He searched the man's face for acceptance, but the answering look of inflexible disbelief told him he'd just been wasting his breath.

"You've been a busy boy over there," mocked Grubin. "Stirring up a real hornet's nest. You should have told me what was going on."

"My job was to get the fingerprints," said Hegarty. "And any other evidence about Leiman. How I went about it is my business. I didn't have to fill you in on the details."

Grubin read him like an open book. "You didn't tell me because you didn't want me to know how much you were getting involved in the family," he scathingly accused. "That's the way it was, Matt. What you've told me about Ingrid only strengthens my point."

Hegarty didn't challenge the assertion about the family. It was true enough. Jules was a shrewd sonofabitch. "How do you figure that?" he said.

"I'd say if she hated you that much, then she'd get a lot of pleasure from making you look a damn fool, and getting her father off the hook at the same time."

"Then for Chrissake, she'd tell him not to come here," pointed out Hegarty in exasperation. "You stupid jerk, I just can't get through to you."

Grubin determinedly shook his head. "You're not thinking straight. You can't see how you're being used. I'm backing Reine's fingerprints, and that's it."

"Fuck you Jules; what the hell can I say to convince you?" said Hegarty in frustration.

"Forget it," Grubin threw at him. He turned abruptly

away to the bed, seized Pony by the arm, and pulled him to his feet. "Come on, kid, we're going outside."

"The idea was to leave the boy down here," Hegarty sharply interceded.

"I figure it's important that Leiman see the kid when he drives up to the house. Without that he could get suspicious and run for it at the last minute."

Hegarty couldn't argue with the tactic, except that it was for the wrong man. Pony was breathing rapidly, eyes apprehensive, staring at Hegarty for some form of reassurance.

"It's okay, Pony," Hegarty said soothingly. "It's okay. No one's going to hurt you."

"Can't I just go back to Cathedral Rock?" pleaded the boy.

"You will, but not right now."

"Why . . . why are you doing this to me, Matt?"

Grubin didn't give Hegarty the chance to answer. There was the muffled drone of an engine from far off as Grubin urged the boy toward the steps.

"That sounds like it could be Leiman now," he snapped. "Come on, we'd better get out there."

They went up the steps and through the trapdoor, while Hegarty morosely put the passports into his backpack. They were for Favett's eyes now. He couldn't see what else he could do here, it was clear Jules refused to be convinced. If it came to a conflict about who was right, and who was wrong, would Jules back his conviction with the Uzi? With what he knew about Jules, it had to be a possibility. He gave a frustrated shake of his head, and moved slowly to the steps. They'd take Kisek to Israel, and be castigated by Favett when the Mossad found out they had the wrong man. Maybe his resignation would be forced, rather than voluntary.

When he reached the front room Jules and Pony were standing in the shadows of the door, looking out to the savanna. He went up behind them, and saw the headlights slowly approaching up the road, the drone of the engine gathering volume. What would Jules do if he stuck the Colt into his back? Laugh probably, with the certainty he wouldn't shoot. No, that wasn't the way to do it, it was crazy—this was going to have to be resolved back in Tel Aviv. But he wasn't going to give up on trying to change Jules's mind.

Grubin pushed Pony toward Hegarty, and stepped away from the doorway. "You take the kid," he muttered. "Just so Leiman can see everything's on the level. I want him out of the vehicle before I move." He poked Pony in the back with the Uzi. "You say one word to your grandfather, boy, and I'll kill him. And you too," he threatened. "You understand?"

Pony glanced beseechingly at Hegarty, and gave a mute nod.

"Jesus, you're making a God-awful mistake, Jules," said Hegarty.

Again Grubin made a menacing gesture with the machine gun, and it confirmed for Hegarty that Jules would use the Uzi if he made any forcible attempt to try and stop him taking Kisek. How could the bastard be so goddamn sure he was right, sure enough to kill a fellow agent if he thought it necessary?

"Just do it, Matt," Grubin muttered.

"What about the helicopter?"

"Don't worry, it'll be here. Those guys know what they're doing."

Hegarty hesitated, thought of arguing further with Jules, then gave a resigned shrug, took Pony by the arm, and walked him slowly out into the yard as the vehicle swung off the road with a swish of tires. He could feel Pony trembling under his fingers.

"Is he going to kill me?" whispered the boy fearfully.

"No. I won't let him, Pony."

"He's got a machine gun, Matt."

"It doesn't matter; I'll make sure he doesn't harm you," promised Hegarty.

"He's not going to kill Grandad, is he?"

"He's not going to kill anyone."

The ranch wagon braked to a halt facing the house, the headlights framing them, and Hegarty raised his hand against the glare. The motor died, but the headlights remained on. There was the click of opening doors, sharp on the night air, then their slamming, like gunshots. Two dark figures materialized, one on each side of the wagon, and Hegarty experienced a spurt of alarm. Kisek had promised to come alone, unless he'd brought Beaunig; Christ that could be a break, maybe he could persuade Jules to take them both, and they'd sort it out in Tel Aviv.

"Pony?" came Kisek's guttural voice.

The boy looked uncertainly at Hegarty, but didn't answer.

"Pony?" called Anna.

Hegarty cursed in consternation. Dammit, after he'd set this all up for her protection, she'd gone back on her word not to come. He glanced quickly back to the house, conscious that the Uzi was probably pointed at him. Spotlighted in the headlights he made an easy target. "Get back in the wagon, Anna," he demanded angrily.

"I'm sorry, Matt," she apologized. "But I had to come; I just had to. Pony's my son, I need to be here, I really do."

"Get back in the goddamn wagon," he repeated furiously.

The compelling urgency in his voice brought her to a halt, but Kisek kept coming until he was standing by the headlights. Then he also stopped.

"I'm wanting to talk to you, Pony," he called, in a strained voice.

"Stay where you are, Leiman," ordered Grubin from the doorway. "Don't move, or I'll kill you."

There was only a shocked silence from Kisek. Then he slowly lifted his hand to shade his eyes, and peered into the darkness.

"Who is there? Who is calling me Leiman?" he queried unsteadily. "What trick is this, Hegarty?"

"This is the Mossad, Leiman," said Grubin. "Israel Intelligence. I arrest you, Horst Leiman, Whipmaster of Treblinka, and bloody murderer, for monstrous crimes against humanity, and the Jewish race, in the Treblinka concentration camp."

In a way Hegarty was relieved darkness concealed Anna's expression. He could tell by the way she suddenly gripped at the car it had hit her with as much force as her father. Jesus, how much did she really know?

Kisek slumped to the wagon as if in need of support to remain upright, head bowed into his shoulders. "What . . . what nonsense is this, what nonsense are you saying?" he protested. "Who is calling me Leiman? Who is threatening to shoot me? What lies have you been spreading, Hegarty? Ja, lies."

"God, don't hurt Pony," came Anna's voice, thready with fear.

Somewhere to the north Hegarty heard a faint, beating throb that had to be the helicopter.

"Pony's safe, Anna," he reassured her.

"Please let me go to Mum," urged Pony.

Hegarty shook his head, and kept a tight grip on the boy's arm. If there was any shooting he wanted Pony out of the line of fire. And Anna too, if she'd just get back in the vehicle.

"You're going to Israel to stand trial, Leiman," declared Grubin. "For all the misery and butchery you caused at Treblinka."

Kisek relinquished his grip on the car, steadying himself, still staring toward the darkness of the doorway, in an attempt to distinguish Grubin. "You are making a big mistake," he faltered. "I am Dorf Kisek, not anyone called Leiman."

"Oh my God, tell me it isn't true, Matt," pleaded Anna. "You're not Israel Intelligence too—you can't be?"

Hegarty shut his ears to the agony in her question. "Do what I tell you," he ordered fiercely.

"How could you do this to me?" she moaned.

"For Chrissake, Pony's going to get hurt if you don't get back in the wagon," he shouted at her.

There was a brief silence, then, "God, oh my God, you bastard," she muttered savagely.

Hegarty just managed to hear the bitter denunciation, delivered in a voice low, and trembling with anguish. He wanted to go to her, try to somehow explain, but Jules would only see it as an attempt to frustrate his taking out Kisek, and if he opened up with the Uzi she was certain to be hit.

"You bastard, Hegarty," she said, but louder, and with a cutting edge. "God, Israel Intelligence. How could I have been so stupid, so unbelievably stupid?" She dolefully shook her head, and extended a hand across the car toward her father. "Tell them the truth, Dad, tell them."

"Keep your mouth shut, Anna," commanded Kisek angrily.

"We know the truth, Leiman," called Grubin. "Monster, murderer, human scum. We have all the proof we need."

"Then you're wrong," cried Anna passionately. She made

pleading gesture to Kisek. "Tell them Horst Leiman was your
rother, Dad, that you disowned him for what he did; that he
was shot by the Russians at the end of the war. Tell them
they're wrong." She switched back to Hegarty, leaning forward
o the headlight revealed the scorn in her face. "Tell them they
asted their time sending an agent to Cathedral Rock to tear
ur family apart."

"It wasn't like that, Anna," Hegarty hoarsely tried to
ounter. But he was stunned by her revelation. If Kisek was
Horst Leiman's brother, and Carl Beaunig was the real Whipmaster of Treblinka, then the two men had to be brothers.
They were both Leimans. Was that how the mistake had been
made about the fingerprints? They belonged to the wrong
rother? Yet Anna couldn't know about Carl's identity, or
he'd use it to clear her father; she obviously believed the
hony story about the Russian execution. He glanced anx-
ously to the sky. He seemed to be the only one aware of the
rowing sound of the helicopter.

"That's . . . that's the truth," admitted Kisek, in a
tronger voice. "Ja, all right, my real name is being Dorf
Leiman, not Horst. That was my brother, dead years ago, shot
y the Russians at the end of the war. I was not wanting to use
my real name, because of the way Horst was running the
oncentration camp, ja, I wanted to be forgetting he was my
rother." He attempted a mocking laugh. "You're being forty
ears too late; you too Hegarty, worming your way into mein
ome, making trouble for us all, and for nothing, ja nothing."

Hegarty knew he was lying. Christ, the bond between the
rothers must be strong; even now he was going to try and
luff it out to protect Horst.

"I've heard that shit story about your supposed executed
rother," jeered Grubin. "It won't work, Leiman. Maybe
ou've managed to hide here in the Gulf Country for over forty
ears, but it's over now scum. Kaput." He paused, with the
ound of the helicopter now intrusively obvious. "Hear the
elicopter coming, Leiman? It's your exit to Israel."

"Please, please, you're so wrong," cried Anna. She moved
cross the headlights until she was in front of Kisek, pleading
ands extended toward Hegarty. "Maybe you did make fools of
s all, Matt, but you've got to believe my father isn't Horst

Leiman. If you take him back to Israel, you're the ones who'll look the fools."

"Get away from him," ordered Grubin sharply.

Hegarty turned cautiously to Grubin. Now that he knew Kisek and Carl were really the Leiman brothers, surely there had to be a way he could persuade Jules to at least consider the possibility he was wrong. "There's something new here, Jules," he called. "For Chrissake, let's talk about it." He gestured to Kisek. "If he and Carl are brothers, don't you see that's how the mistake could have happened with the finger-prints?"

"Give it up, Hegarty," rasped Grubin stubbornly. "You're not going to betray the Mossad."

"You asshole, you're the one betraying the Mossad," cried Hegarty furiously. "Can't you at least concede the possibility you've got the wrong fucking brother?"

Grubin didn't answer, but suddenly began walking slowly toward Hegarty, with the Uzi no longer in his hands. Hegarty gave a sigh of relief, he'd finally got through, and at least Jules was prepared to talk about it. Then he suddenly realized the machine gun was in the hands of another dark figure, walking closely behind Jules. He quickly pushed Pony aside, and reached for the Colt stuck in his belt.

"Do that and I'll kill you," threatened the figure.

Hegarty froze his hand in mid action, then carefully lowered it to his side. He recognized that American accent but from where? It wasn't until they stepped into the car headlights that he saw there were two men behind Jules; then as the light caught their faces came the stunning realization that they were the two Americans from Reine's tour group who had spoken to him after the fight with Red Orton. They must have come through the house to get behind Jules. He was dumbfounded. He hadn't given them a thought in Normanton. How in God's name did they connect to Horst Leiman? Who were they? But just the fact they were here, and menacingly holding the Uzi, made him fear for Reine. And for all of them.

"What the hell is this?" he demanded harshly. "What do you think you're trying to pull?"

Grubin's expression was deceptively passive. "You know these two?"

"They were on Reine's tour. I saw them in Normanton after the fight with Orton," said Hegarty.

"Shut your mouths," said the tall one. "I'd just as soon waste both of you." He shoved Grubin roughly toward Hegarty. As well as the Uzi they'd taken from Grubin, both men carried rifles. The smaller, broad shouldered man came up behind Hegarty, plucked the Colt from his belt, and hurled it into the darkness.

Corliss pointed to Kisek. "You're Horst Leiman, alias Dorf Kisek, wanted Nazi war criminal?" he asked curtly.

Kisek seemed stunned into silence.

"No, no, you're wrong, he isn't," Anna answered for him.

"It's none of your goddamn business," protested Hegarty. "He's not the . . ."

Corliss cut him off, swinging the Uzi around to aim it at Grubin's midsection. "You! Quick, you son-of-a-bitch, before I cut you in half," he ordered harshly. "He is Horst Leiman, isn't he?"

Grubin scowled at Hegarty. "This is something to do with you, isn't it, Hegarty? My God, I didn't believe you'd go this far to stop me taking out Kisek."

"Are you out of your goddamn mind?" snarled Hegarty. "These bastards are nothing to do with me."

Corliss prodded Grubin viciously with the Uzi. "You've got three seconds. Is he Horst Leiman, the Nazi war criminal?"

Grubin gave a grudging nod. "Yes. Who the hell are you?"

"You'll never know, bud," grunted Corliss.

The helicopter was close now, hovering with baleful yellow eyes like a huge black bird of prey about to make a kill, filling the air with a throbbing roar. Turbulence beat down on them like a strong wind, flaying the grass, vibrating the trees, sending the loose iron on the roof of the house flapping, as if applauding the drama. Corliss waited as the landing lights suddenly flicked on, the beam guiding the chopper like a seeing eye, the roar gradually subsiding as it passed over the house, and began to descend out on the savanna.

Then Corliss again pointed to Kisek. "Kill the son-of-a-bitch, Sam," he ordered.

Jaroff stepped forward, lifted the Winchester to his shoulder, and aimed at Kisek.

"Wait, wait, Jesus, you don't have to do that," screamed Grubin in frustration. "We're going to hang the bastard anyway."

Corliss gave an ugly grin. "Think of the expense we're saving you," he jeered. "Kill him, Sam."

Pony broke away from Hegarty, and frantically slithered on all fours to Anna's side. She was backed protectively against her father, her face stark white against the night, eyes wide with terror, arms spread in a plaintive plea for mercy. "No, no, please believe me, he isn't Horst Leiman," she cried.

"You stupid bitch, get out of the way or I'll waste you too," snarled Jaroff.

Hegarty had no idea why these creeps wanted Horst Leiman dead, but he was horrified at the thought of Anna being gunned down. She claimed a love-hate relationship with her father, but when it came to the crunch she was still his blood. "For Chrissake, get out of the way, Anna," he yelled. "You can't do anything, you'll only get yourself killed."

Then he instinctively flinched from the sudden sharp crack of a gunshot, and just briefly glimpsed the flash, out in the grass to the right of the house.

The rifle spilled from Jaroff's hands, blood blossomed from his chest, he turned a baffled expression to Corliss, his mouth gaping as if attempting words, then he toppled to the ground and didn't move. Corliss cursed, and quickly swung the Uzi in a fast arc in the direction of the flash, spraying the area with furious bursts of fire. Bullets whined and ricocheted into the darkness, spanging off rocks, slicing branches. For a moment Hegarty floundered, bewildered by the bizzare turn of events beyond his understanding. Who the fuck was the sniper somewhere out in the grass? Who were these men? Jules had hit the dirt, but Hegarty had a hunch this son-of-a-bitch with the Uzi was out to snuff them all. The man was distracted, his face contorted with anger, Leiman temporarily forgotten, for now intent only on protecting himself from the hidden killer, and Hegarty figured it was probably the only chance he'd get. He hurled himself at the man's legs, hitting with his shoulders, arms lashed out about his thighs. The Uzi was abruptly silenced, jerked from Corliss's hand by the impact, and they both crashed to the ground, hammering at each other with desperate ferocity, knowing there could only be one survivor, using anything, fists, knees, boots, teeth. It took only a moment for Hegarty to grasp this was no over-weight Red Orton he was tackling, but a muscled, trained fighter. He reeled back as a karate chop thudded against his head, then a boot crashed into his ribs, sending him sprawling. He twisted out of range, scrabbling frantically at where he thought the Uzi had fallen. Where the fuck was Jules? Had the bastard abandoned him? The American had picked up one of the Winchesters, and Hegarty knew he was going to die unless luck turned another card for him. He desperately rolled in the opposite direction, and felt the angular sharpness of the Uzi under his back. In one swift motion he came to his knees with the machine gun in his hands, then was forced to duck as Corliss fired. It screwed him sideways off balance, and he felt the heat of the bullet scorch past his face. The man was fast on his feet, already making a crouching dash for the far side of the house, then the Uzi was juddering in Hegarty's hands, reaching for the man, bullets slamming along the old walls, splinters flying. He was gone before Hegarty could nail him, vanished into the darkness. Hegarty warily stayed low to the ground. Maybe the sniper had survived the fusillade directed at him, and he didn't want to be the next target. He took a deep breath to control the thudding of his heart, and glanced around. The dead man lay where he'd fallen, God knows who'd killed him. Jesus, what a foul-up, what a goddamn fucking foul-up! The wrong Leiman. Killers coming from Christ knows where, and for Christ knows what reason. A hidden goddamn sniper. Pony and Anna were crouched by the side of the wagon, her arm protectively about her son. Her father was gone. Several hundred yards out from the house the helicopter was on the ground, silhouetted against the frosted sheen of the savanna, the rotor blades already slowed to an idling thrum. The figure of a man stood waiting in the muted light of an open door.

Then Hegarty spotted two other figures, maybe fifty yards away, stumbling toward the helicopter; there was no mistaking Jules, and the bulky form of Kisek. Or Dorf Leiman, as he now knew him to be. Fucking Jules didn't give a damn if he survived or not, he'd abandoned him, used the fight as a cover to get Leiman to the helicopter.

"Stay where you are, Anna," he bellowed. "For Chrissake, just stay there—and kill the headlights. Then get under the goddamn car. There's a sniper out there somewhere, and Christ knows who he might shoot next."

Neither mother nor son answered, too shocked for words, but they obeyed, Anna switching off the headlights, then dragging Pony back toward the rear wheels.

Hegarty ran quickly to the side of the house where the American had disappeared, but there was no sign of him. There had to be a chance he was hit, and had gone to ground somewhere. He'd have to wait, for now the main urgency was to stop Jules taking the wrong man. Matt had the Uzi now, and he'd force the stubborn sonofabitch to see reason. He began to run at an intercepting path, to cut them off before they reached the helicopter. Even now, through all the death and confusion, he knew it was more than preventing the wrong man being kidnapped, it was for Anna. For Pony.

"Jules, wait, wait—for Chrissake, wait," he yelled.

The two weren't to the midway point yet, but if Jules heard he ignored it, pushing Leiman on ahead of him. Then Hegarty spotted a moving shape over to his right, running at a crouch on almost a parallel path. Christ, it had to be the man he'd just fought, but he gave no sign of being wounded. The goddamn son-of-a-bitch was determined, Hegarty had been sure he'd stay under cover after nearly being killed. He wouldn't miss this time. He jolted to a breathless halt, steadied to take aim with the Uzi, but was forestalled by the sharp crack, crack, of the Winchester. Then Jules was only standing alone, with the dark form of Leiman huddled at his feet, and the killer had turned about, ducking and weaving with tremendous agility as he scuttled back toward the house. Fury almost ruined Hegarty's aim. He kept his finger tight to the trigger, tracking the man with rapid bursts of fire, decapitated grass marking a path until the fusillade caught the assassin as he reached the sagging corner of the house and knocked him into a tangle of old fencing wire. Hegarty knew he was dead; the man had taken a gamble, and lost, no one survived a full burst from a Uzi. He shook his head in frustrated confusion, and went slowly to where Jules was kneeling beside Leiman.

Dammit, he wasn't going back on the helicopter, wasn't going to leave the Gulf. He guessed deep down he'd known that for a long time now. He had no comprehension of who the man was he'd just shot down, was bewildered by his fanatical determination to kill Horst Leiman, even though there was grim irony that he'd killed the wrong brother. But there was no way he could leave this gory shambles to Anna. Maybe it would be impossible to convince her and Pony he loved them, but there seemed nothing more important in his life than to try. And he had to do something about the real Horst Leiman. He owed that much to his father. To Reine. To the Wiesenthal people. There was still the sniper, if he was alive. He glanced anxiously back at the house. Anna and Pony were safe under cover, and he was already speculating there was only one possible man who could be the sniper, and he'd have no reason to harm them.

Jules was livid. In the moonlight, his expression of fury was macabre. He was standing over Leiman's body, making aimless gestures with a Beretta automatic in his hand, as if trying to will the corpse back to life.

He shook the Beretta at Hegarty. "He's dead, Hegarty," he raged. "Dead, damn you. God, fucking dead; no trial, nothing. Favett will destroy me over this." The words were choked with saliva, forcing him to pause, breathing heavily. He stabbed a finger repeatedly at Hegarty, as if it were a dagger. "This is what you wanted, isn't it, Hegarty? You played me for a fool, set it all up with those other bastards. I don't know what the hell you're up to, but by God, I'm going to find out. You betrayed the Mossad, Israel, your father, yourself, me, damn you. You're going to stand trial for treason over this." He was close to being incoherent with rage, words tumbling out in a torrent, without thought, without reason. "Treason," he screamed, "you hear me, you bastard? Treason!"

Hegarty stared at him in disbelief. He'd expected Jules to be upset, but didn't anticipate this hysterical onslaught.

"You're crazy, Jules," he roared back. "Out of your mind. I didn't know those two guys. I haven't got the faintest goddamn idea why they wanted to kill Horst Leiman. Goddamn it, they're dead too."

"That's the way you wanted it, to shut their mouths."

"For Chrissake, you're not making any sense," declared Hegarty angrily. "No goddamn sense at all. What the fuck about the sniper?"

"You set that up too. God, it had to be you, no one else knew." He waved the pistol toward the house. "You did it for that bitch, didn't you; she sucked you in, turned your blood to piss," Jules ranted.

The man at the door of the helicopter waved urgently, but neither man took any notice, snarling at each other across the body like it was disputed carrion.

Hegarty made a furious sweep of his hand to the dead Leiman. "You're insane, dammit; absolutely insane. Why the hell would I want him killed? I tried to save him, tried to tell you, goddamn it, I tried. The wrong man's been killed, the wrong Leiman."

There was something maniacal in the way Jules brandished the Beretta in his face; clearly he saw Hegarty as having destroyed his career. Hegarty gripped the Uzi, and stepped back a pace. He didn't intend to just stand there and let Jules carry out a paranoid execution. The man in the helicopter was shouting something now, but the words were drowned by the chutter of the rotor blades.

"You treacherous bastard, get on board the helicopter," Grubin shouted.

Hegarty spread his feet in a stance of defiance. He could see it was useless trying to talk, Jules was past rational discussion, only obsessed with lunatic accusations.

"Go to hell, Jules," he said harshly.

"What's that supposed to mean?"

"I'm staying here."

Grubin glared savagely at him. "With her, that's what you mean isn't it, with that bitch. God, I should have known.

Christ, she really got to you, her and her son, right under your damn skin. Turned you into a traitor."

"I'm no traitor. You're all wrong, Jules, as wrong as you'll ever be. I could never make you understand."

"Get on the helicopter," screamed Grubin. "My God, you're going to stand trial."

"Give my regards to Favett, and Reine," Hegarty retorted. "Tell them I think you're an asshole."

"Get on the fucking helicopter," Grubin screamed again.

Hegarty raised the Uzi just enough to be threatening. "Are you going to shoot me if I don't, Jules?"

"They'll lock you up here when they find the bodies, charge you with murder," Grubin blustered.

"They'll understand when I capture the real Horst Leiman."

Grubin made a vicious gesture to the corpse. "God, you're all sorts of a fool, Hegarty; there's the real Horst Leiman. She blinded you, hypnotized you. You don't deserve to be a Jew."

"I'm the best kind of Jew, one with compassion. That's what she taught me, Jules."

"You traitorous moron," Grubin jeered. "We show compassion and the world won't let us live. Who the hell ever showed it to us?"

"The world won't let us live if we don't," Hegarty flung back at him.

The helicopter pilot impatiently opened the throttle, and turbulence swept them as the rotor blades began to whirr faster, blanketing them with throbbing sound. The man at the door was clearly agitated now, frantically waving his arms. Grubin looked quite mad as he began to back away, his hair swirling, face rabidly contorted with hatred.

"Traitor," he screamed at Hegarty. "Traitor. You can't hide from the Mossad, even out here, Hegarty. This isn't the end of it."

"It'll be the end of it for you, Jules, when the truth comes out," Hegarty hurled back at him.

Grubin turned abruptly away, ran to the helicopter, jumped in the doorway and made an angry gesture to the man, then turned to face Hegarty, his legs dangling over the side.

The pitch of the engine swelled to a thundering roar, the rotor blades blurred, sweeping the ground like a fierce gale, and the helicopter began to lift. Grubin sat staring at him, hunched forward with brooding animosity, then he went up, and up, until he was merely a vague speck. Then nothing.

Chapter 15

Hegarty utilized all the cover he could find on his way back toward the old house. There'd been nothing more from the sniper, but he intended to play safe.

Anna and Pony were still crouched by the ranch wagon, their faces a mutual luminous white.

"Are you both okay?" Hegarty queried.

They both offered mute nods, their expressions still glazed with shock.

"What are you doing here?" asked Anna in a hostile whisper. "I thought you'd be gone on the helicopter."

He hesitated, not sure this was the time. "I stayed for you, and Pony," he said.

She made a hoarse, derisive sound deep in her throat, like a whimper of pain. "God, oh my God, you really expect me to believe that? You're lying."

"It's true," he said.

She shook her head. "I can't believe that. You're thinking there's another way you can manipulate us."

"No. It's the truth." Even in the semidarkness he could see the hurt in her eyes. Pony didn't look at him, his face directed to the ground. Anna turned and looked out to the darkness of the savanna. "Where's Dad?" she asked.

He gestured where the helicopter had been. "Over there," he said.

"He's dead, isn't he?"

There was no way to soften it. "Yes. The man I fought with killed him—then I killed him." He said it as if it made amends, but knew it was a stupid attempt at contrition.

"They thought Dad was Horst Leiman, and so did you," she accused.

"For a time. I only found out I was wrong a few hours ago."

For the first time her voice broke with anguish. "God, then why didn't you stop all this, damn you, Matt, why didn't you stop it?"

"I tried," he said, "believe me, I tried."

"But . . . but he died for nothing," she choked. "Christ, for nothing."

Hegarty didn't believe it was that simple; brotherly love or not, her father had protected the real monster all these years.

"We can't talk about this now, Anna," he said, motioning to the ground outside the house. "There's a sniper out there somewhere who killed the first man. He could be dead, or he could be gone, but I've got to go and find out."

"You know who it is?"

Hegarty was sure it had to be Carl Beaunig, the real Horst Leiman. There was no one else it could be. It would have been a struggle for the old man to get here, but if he'd gotten wise to what was going on, desperation would have found its own strength. He wouldn't tell Anna Carl was Horst Leiman, that was for later, she'd had enough shocks for one night.

"I don't know," he lied.

She didn't say anything, but he could tell she figured he was lying. Christ, he wanted so much for Horst Leiman to be alive; for his father, for himself. There could still be a trial if he was.

"Is there a flashlight in the car?" he asked.

Anna still kept her eyes averted. "In the glove box," she muttered.

Maybe he was just fooling himself. It was going to be impossible for him with her, the hostility in her voice was unrelenting. He quietly opened the car door, groped in the glove box, and located the flashlight. Perhaps he wouldn't need it, but it might pay to take it along.

"Stay by the car," he warned. "I won't be long."

Neither said anything. It was impossible to tell with Pony,

but maybe his silence said it all. Anna just sat holding Pony, her face in his hair.

Hegarty was guided by an intermittent, rasping cough to a dark shape lying in a hollow of grass, and he felt elation that the sniper was still alive. He stopped by the cover of a tree for a moment, watching the shape quiver in concert with the cough, then he cocked the Uzi, and crept cautiously to the brink of the hollow. If the man heard his approach, he gave no outward sign.

His hunch was right. He could see it was Beaunig, or rather Horst Leiman, stretched out as if reclining on a couch, hands folded over his stomach; a rifle lay at his side.

"Move, and I'll kill you," he coldly threatened.

The man merely coughed again.

Hegarty flicked on the flashlight, and focused the beam on Leiman's face. The scarred features seemed devoid of life, but the eyes were wide, glittering with malevolence. He watched as Hegarty warily skirted the hollow to pick up the rifle and throw it out of reach, then he laughed, an ugly, crackling sound.

"I was thinking you would be gone on the helicopter, Hegarty." He snorted. "You stayed for her. Ja, never underestimate the power of what a woman is having between her legs, ja, even for a Jew."

"I'm an agent of the Mossad," stated Hegarty curtly. Was he still? "And I arrest you, Horst Leiman, known as the Whipmaster of Treblinka, for monstrous crimes against humanity in the Treblinka concentration camp."

Leiman gave a resigned sigh. "Ah, the Mossad, of course. I should have known. If it wasn't for my old bones I would have been gone by now." He cocked his head to the side. "You know about me, ja, Hegarty?"

"I know."

"How are you knowing?"

"It doesn't matter for now, but I can prove it."

Leiman coughed again, and shook his head. "Ah, Dorf should have been listening to me. I tried to tell him. Being safe for so long blunted Dorf's caution, ja. I was telling him I could always smell out a Jew, and I could smell you, Hegarty, ja, easily." He stirred awkwardly, and there was the soft cracking of ancient joints. "You tried to take my brother; you thought he was me, ja?"

"That was someone else's mistake, not mine."

"How could they be making such a mistake?"

"There were fingerprints from a Berlin police file, from before the war."

Leiman closed his eyes in thought a moment, then the cackling laugh came again. "Ja, ja, I'm remembering; the 1932 riot. Dorf was giving my name to the police when he was arrested, so I could be having an alibi for . . . for other things I was doing." His mouth twisted into an evil grin. "Killing Jews, I'm remembering."

A voice pierced Hegarty's brain like a searing laser beam: *"Kill him, kill him, kill him," screamed his father. "Monster, murderer, animal! Don't leave him to silver-tongued lawyers."*

Hegarty blocked out his father's voice. "Get up, Leiman," he snarled.

Leiman shrugged. "You're giving me a few moments, Hegarty. I'm exhausted." His words bubbled with phlegm. "Unless you're wanting to carry me?" He closed his eyes against the flashlight, and sighed. "Sometimes we fought, but Dorf was a brother who was understanding the meaning of real love," he muttered. "Ja, close we were from childhood, especially when the stupid Americans were getting us out after the war. Dorf was SS too; not in my special division, but he was knowing what was going on all right with the Jews." He opened his eyes and glanced about. "Dorf was getting too ambitious out here; never were we needing all this." He shrugged, and stared up at Hegarty. "He's dead, ja?"

"Yes," answered Hegarty tersely.

Leiman's scarred face settled into resigned repose. "Nothing matters now he's dead," he whispered huskily. "Nothing." His head fell back. "Your helicopter's gone, Hegarty."

"I'm going to hand you over to the Australian authorities."

Leiman's eyes sparkled with virulent mockery. "You are thinking they will be hanging me, Hegarty?"

"Someone will."

"I beat you, Jew, aren't you understanding that?" Leiman

id, with sudden venom. "Beat all of you. God, I'm being
ghty years old." He laughed. "What are you going to do, Jew,
ke away the last forty years of my life?" He squinted into the
ashlight, as a jeering cackle burst from his misshapen mouth.
You're too late, too late, life is being over for me now. Too
te, too late. I'll never hang, Jew, never."

*Hegarty's father tapped each photograph in turn.
Repeat the names after me: Mathew, Aunt Tatania, Aunt
ella, Uncle Efram, Uncle Januse, all butchered. When you
unt out the monsters responsible, exterminate them without
ercy.*

The memorized names beat in Hegarty's mind like a cry
r vengeance.

"You'll hang," he snarled. "You've had to live with the
ousands you murdered, scum."

"Are you talking conscience, Jew?" Leiman retorted
ontemptuously. He spat forcefully at Hegarty's feet. "Not for
moment was it keeping me awake. Not for a second.
leansing the world of vermin we were, you are hearing?
leansing it. And you made it easy for us, Jew, ja, easy.
urning you against each other we were at Treblinka, using
e Kapos, making you collaborate in your own doom."

Rage swept Hegarty with a surge of heat; he felt the
urning hatred his father had tried to pass on. The Uzi
embled in his hands, his sweat-greased finger slipped tempt-
gly over the trigger. The whole world seemed drenched in
ed, as if spouting from multiple punctures in Horst Leiman's
ead, and for an instant he thought he'd actually pulled the
rigger. No! The monster has to hang, he swore to himself,
eiman has to hang.

"Our time will come again," predicted Leiman. He lifted
is left hand into the flashlight's beam and Hegarty was
urprised to see that it dripped blood. He had been hit. "All of
ou I would have shot but for this," Leiman boasted. "All of
ou, not only the fool who tried to shoot Dorf. Right from the
eginning I'm knowing the plan with Pony is being a trap, but
Dorf is not listening to my warning, so I'm coming here to
rotect him. Those other fools got in the way, whoever they
vere. That first bullet should have been for your brain,
Iegarty; ja, that I'm regretting."

"You are betraying me, betraying all of us," cried Hegarty's enraged father. *"Why are you just standing there? Put the Uzi to the back of his head, and pull the trigger until the clip is empty."*

Again Hegarty resisted the clamor of his father's voice. "Goddamn you, no more of this, Leiman," he rasped. He gestured irritably with the flashlight. "It's time to go. Get up on your feet. I don't give a damn if they have to take you to the scaffold in a wheelchair, you're going to hang."

Leiman fixed him with a long, concentrated stare, then shrugged, and gingerly pushed himself into a sitting position. Then he stopped, his eyes still on Hegarty, and slowly raised a hand to his mouth.

"Wrong, Hegarty, you are being so wrong," he muttered. He gave a slight, nervous snicker. "They're telling me a sealed cyanide capsule is staying potent for a lifetime, and I've been keeping it a long, long time for a moment such as this."

Cyanide? In an instant Hegarty remembered that a cyanide capsule had been a favorite Nazi method of suicide after the war, then he was galvanized into action. He flung the Uzi and flashlight aside and threw himself at Leiman's raised arm, but the man's hand was already at his mouth. Hegarty cursed, grappling frantically at Leiman's tightly clamped mouth, feeling saliva bubbling over his fingers as he tried to force it open. Christ, he couldn't be cheated, not now, not now. He heard a sharp cry of agony as Leiman stiffened under him, then his body buckled with convulsions until it finally went limp.

Hegarty felt a maddening sense of frustration, his fingers still tight on Leiman's mouth, then he slowly released his grip and disgustedly let the body fall away. He sat back wearily on his haunches, his mind a ferment of self-recrimination. Christ should he have been watching for something like a cyanide capsule? He shook his head, and wiped the saliva from his fingers. How could he have even guessed Leiman would have kept the capsule with him all these years? He rose unsteadily to his feet, retrieved the Uzi and flashlight, and cast the beam into Leiman's face. He'd been ugly in life, but hideous in death, eyes wide, face twisted like a gargoyle. Yet death had come for him so fast. Was that all of it? That brief moment of

d taken for Leiman to kill himself seemed somehow trivial
engeance for the slaughtered millions. The chance of a trial
d been snatched away again. Had he failed his father? Failed
e Mossad? Was there any way he could balance it out? The
hipmaster of Treblinka was dead, yet so was his brother, and
e other two, whoever the hell they were. Maybe even
eine. And there was the pain inflicted on Anna, on Pony, on
grid. He didn't have an answer, knew he never would, and
only made him more certain that Anna and Pony were the
ly things that really mattered in his life now. He felt an
tense yearning to become part of this vast, purifying sa-
nna.

He turned away from the corpse, and tramped morosely
ck to the old house. The ranch wagon was gone. He'd
either heard nor seen anything, he must have been too
volved with Leiman to notice it had driven away. Perhaps it
as Anna's way of saying she never wanted to see him again.
e would have to anyway, he was going to need to call the
lice from Cathedral Rock.

The man Leiman had shot lay as if already part of the
rrounding decay. Hegarty rolled him over and swept the
ashlight along the body. He must have died quickly,
eiman's bullet had hit him plumb in the center of the chest.
he old man had retained the knack of killing. He searched
rough the dead man's pockets, but there was nothing, so he
ent looking for the man he'd gunned down.

He found him where he'd seen him fall, spread-eagled
ntidily amid the tangled wire fencing, blank eyes staring at
e moon. There was a slim wallet in the inside pocket of his
cket, and Hegarty exposed the contents to the flashlight. A
Washington driver's license in the name of Corliss. An iden-
fication pass to the State Department, made out in the name
Colonel Charles Corliss. A receipt for two Winchester rifles
om a Brisbane gun shop. A photograph of a pretty woman,
sed with two good-looking teenage boys. He guessed they
ere about to become innocent casualties too. He replaced the
ems, and put the wallet in his own pocket. The name Corliss
eant nothing to him, but it was going to be easy to trace the
an. He was puzzled by the fact the dead man had obviously
orked for the American Government. His mind went back to

the American OSS officer responsible for Leiman's escape from Germany. Was that the connection? Was that the reason Eli Brandt was murdered? It was a long shot, but Christ, if it was true what a fucking crazy irony, with all of them targeting the wrong man. He stood back from the body and glanced across to where he knew Dorf Leiman lay, cloaked in darkness, and he felt his stomach squirm. There was nothing to be gained from going over there. For now he just wanted to be away from the old house; it was as if the crumbling building had cast a vicious spell of destroyed hopes and sudden death.

Jules would be broken by Favett for failing to capture Horst Leiman, and his own hopes for Anna and Pony seemed shattered. No, the hell with it, he wasn't going to accept that, and he set his mouth with determination as he walked to the Kawasaki. First he had to call the police, then whatever was needed, no matter how long it took, he was going to convince Anna and Pony that he loved them. Maybe in time they'd come to love him again. And somehow he was going to have to make peace with Ingrid.

When he got back to Cathedral Rock he found the door to his room open, but no sign of Ingrid. He left the Uzi on the bed and walked slowly across to the homestead, feeling some trepidation as to where she might be. A single light burned in the front window, and for a time he stood hesitantly watching for any sign of life, then he knocked on the door.

No one answered at first, then Pony finally came to the door, his small face still mirroring the terror of the night. He poised there, solemnly studying Hegarty.

"I have to call the police, Pony," said Hegarty.

Pony gave no indication he'd heard.

"They'll have to be told what's happened out here," persisted Hegarty.

The boy still said nothing, rigidly barring his way, and Hegarty hesitated to push him aside. "I'll make it up to you, Pony," he offered, "somehow."

"I don't understand any of it," said the boy dolefully. "And Mum won't tell me, not yet anyway. I don't understand why Grandad's dead, I don't understand you, those men, th helicopter, any of it." He shook his head, his face wrinkled with confusion.

"I'll try and explain it to you, Pony, but later," said Hegarty.

The boy stared silently at him for a time. "Did you really stay for us, Matt?" he asked softly, so softly Hegarty scarcely heard.

"Yes," said Hegarty. "Yes, you're the reason I stayed. That's the truth."

The boy gave no indication whether he believed or not. He was clearly still in shock. Then he turned abruptly away and closed the door.

It left Hegarty undecided whether he should wait, knock again, or just walk in, he was sure the door would be unlocked. It was resolved by Anna suddenly opening the door. Like her son, she bore all the hallmarks of the night, her expression harrowed, hair awry, deep shadows under her eyes, tear stains on her cheeks. She leaned against the side of the doorway as if exhausted. He would have given anything just to take her in his arms, try and console her.

"I have to call the police, Anna," he said flatly.

She stared dully at him. He wondered if Ingrid was inside, formenting trouble.

"Is Ingrid with you?" he asked.

"Ingrid's gone," she said.

"Gone?"

"Yes; packed and gone."

"Is she coming back?"

"I don't know. Maybe. She left a note, but it didn't say."

He uneasily cleared his throat. "Is Pony all right?"

She shrugged. "He's in shock. What did you expect?"

Hegarty shook his head. He was going to have to do better than this. "I'll make it up to you, Anna," he said, as he had to Pony.

"Will you?" she asked sullenly.

"Yes. If you give me the chance."

She gave a short, bitter laugh. "God, how could I ever trust you?" she whispered. "You lied to all of us; came through Cathedral Rock like some damn plague. Nothing will ever be the same again. Ingrid's gone. Dad's dead. Those other men."

She made a listless movement of her hand. "Who were those men?"

"I don't know. I know they came here to kill Horst Leiman, but I don't know why."

A sour, cynical laugh escaped her mouth. "You're lying again," she accused.

"No. But I'll find out about them." He spread his hands imploringly. "I meant everything I ever said about loving you. You have to believe me when I say you're why I stayed. I don't belong to the Mossad any more; that's all over."

She put a hand to her face, and Hegarty could see her trembling.

"Why couldn't you just let us be?" she moaned.

"You were lucky this didn't happen a long time ago."

"But Dad wasn't Horst Leiman," she burst out passionately. "Don't you see, that's what's so terrible. He died for nothing."

"It wasn't quite like that," Hegarty said.

"What do you mean?"

He took a deep breath. It was time. "Carl was Horst Leiman," he said. "Carl was the one we were after. I can prove it."

It jolted her from bitterness to incredulity. "Carl? My God, Carl? Do you really expect me to take you seriously?" she asked with scorn. "You're lying, lying. It's ridiculous." She made a contemptuous gesture to the interior of the house. "I'll go and get him, and make you accuse him to his face. God, he'll think you're mad."

"He's dead," stated Hegarty bluntly.

He used it as a shock tactic, to try and prepare her for the reality of Cathedral Rock, and she was stunned. "Carl? Carl's dead too?" she whispered faintly.

"Yes. I found him just off from the old house. He was the one who shot the other man. He'd gone there to protect your father; and to kill me, because he suspected who I was."

"He couldn't have made it to the old house. He was too old."

"He got there all right. Desperation gave him the strength."

He anxiously watched her. She brushed aimlessly at her

hair, and there was the pallor of fatigue in her face. "You killed him?" she asked.

Hegarty shook his head. "No, he killed himself." He scowled at the memory. "He knew it was over for him. I wanted to see him put on trial." He gave a morose shrug. "I guess in a way he beat us anyway, living out his life here in the safety of the Gulf Country."

"You have to be lying," she declared with sudden fire. "You have to be. God, I've lived here all my life, I would have known."

"No. All the years they kept it from you. They had to. I can show you the proof, Anna, and he admitted he was Horst Leiman to me before he died. He was one of the most wanted Nazi war criminals in the world." He paused. "Carl and your father were brothers. That story of the executed brother was a lie. Your father protected him ever since they arrived from Germany. That's why he lived the way he did, trusting no one, suspicious of everyone."

She bowed her head. Hegarty knew he was coming at her hard, hitting her with savage, repeated blows on top of what she'd already been through tonight, but it was the only way. For her, and for himself.

"Brothers," she muttered dully. "God, brothers." She numbly lifted her eyes to Hegarty. "Are you trying to tell me Dad was guilty too?" she whispered.

He wasn't going to try and soften it, maybe he needed the accusation to justify himself. If her father had also been SS, Hegarty had a feeling he'd been protecting himself as much as his brother.

"He was guilty of protecting a monster," he said firmly.

"You have proof?" she asked.

"Yes, I have proof."

She fell silent, her head resting listlessly against the door as she groped for words. "Dad must have loved him very much to protect him like that, for so long," she faltered. "But I didn't know, it's not my fault; nor Ingrid's, nor Pony's."

"I know that," he said. "I can make it up to you, Anna. Loving you is why I stayed." He let it hang for a moment, gravely studying her tormented face, then made a weary gesture for understanding. "Okay, I'm sorry about what happened to your father," he said, "but do you have any idea how many thousands died terrible deaths because of Horst Leiman?"

She didn't answer, didn't look at him, her eyes directed intently to the floor. The silence of the savanna seemed to embrace them, timeless, renewable, healing.

"I have to call the police," he said again. "There's going to be one hell of an uproar when they find out about the kidnapping attempt, but there isn't any other way."

She nodded, then shuffled aside, holding the door open, lifting her face clouded with uncertainty to him. He caught her marvelous fragrance as he passed, the sudden flush of warmth, the fluttering of her breath, yet he didn't dare touch her. But he walked toward the study with a lighter tread. God, there was a chance for him with her; there had to be a chance.

ABOUT THE AUTHOR

ARTHUR MATHER, who lives in Melbourne, Australia, spent many years in the advertising profession as a copywriter before becoming a novelist. Since then he has become a prolific adventure thriller writer. His books are now being published around the world. Among the most recent have been: *The Raid*, *Deep Gold*, and *The Los Alamos Contract*. *The Tarantula Hawk* is his latest.

THRILLERS

Gripping suspense...explosive action...dynamic charac-
ters...international settings...these are the elements that
make for great thrillers. Books guaranteed to keep you
riveted to your seat.

Robert Ludlum:

☐	26256	THE AQUITAINE PROGRESSION	$5.95
☐	26011	THE BOURNE IDENTITY	$5.95
☐	26322	THE BOURNE SUPREMACY	$5.95
☐	26094	THE CHANCELLOR MANUSCRIPT	$5.95
☐	28209	THE GEMINI CONTENDERS	$5.95
☐	26019	THE HOLCROFT COVENANT	$5.95
☐	27800	THE ICARUS AGENDA	$5.95
☐	25899	THE MATERESE CIRCLE	$5.95
☐	27960	THE MATLOCK PAPER	$5.95
☐	26430	THE OSTERMAN WEEKEND	$5.95
☐	25270	THE PARSIFAL MOSAIC	$5.95
☐	28063	THE RHINEMANN EXCHANGE	$5.95
☐	27109	THE ROAD TO GANDOLOFO	$5.95
☐	27146	THE SCARLATTI INHERITANCE	$5.95
☐	28179	TREVAYNE	$5.95

Frederick Forsyth:

☐	05361	THE NEGOTIATOR (Hardcover)	$19.95
☐	26630	DAY OF THE JACKAL	$4.95
☐	26490	THE DEVIL'S ALTERNATIE	$4.95
☐	26846	THE DOGS OF WAR	$4.95
☐	25113	THE FOURTH PROTOCOL	$4.95
☐	27673	NO COMEBACKS	$4.95
☐	27198	THE ODESSA FILE	$4.95

Buy them at your local bookstore or use this page to order.

Bantam Books, Dept. TH, 414 East Golf Road, Des Plaines, IL 60016

Please send me the items I have checked above. I am enclosing $_____
(please add $2.00 to cover postage and handling). Send check or money
order, no cash or C.O.D.s please.

Mr/Ms _____

Address _____

City/State _____ Zip _____

TH–11/89

Please allow four to six weeks for delivery.
Prices and availability subject to change without notice.